THE KILLER

Jake Farrow has spent his _____ ... he's one of the best. Still, he is a bit surprised when his old friend Walter Stennis has him brought over from Africa for a special hunt. Stennis wants him to track down and kill the armed robber responsible for the death of his son. Farrow reluctantly agrees, but is soon thrown into a mission more deadly than he bargained for when he meets the bank robber's Southern wife, Marget, intent on protecting her man. Then there's Sam Augustine, who's working on a manhunt of his own. And Terese, the alluring key to the killer's hideout. Farrow will need all of his skills, because it soon becomes obvious that in this deadly game, there is small distinction between the hunter—and the hunted.

DEVIL ON TWO STICKS

Steve Beck works for Pat Garland, the crime boss of San Diego. Garland suspects a traitor in the organization, and sets Beck to ferret him out. Beck has five suspects—Sid Dominic, Eddie Cortes, Hervey Isham, Paul Moon and J. J. Everett. Each one holds a position of power, but only one is working for the Attorney General's office. Beck suspects Everett, Garland's lawyer. But Beck is also falling in love with Everett's 20-year-old daughter, Marcy, while at the same time trying to fend off the advances of Garland's wife, Lena. Torn between his allegiance and his heart, Beck finds he isn't as tough as he thinks he is—because whoever the informer turns out to be, it's still his job to kill him. And the weakest link in the organization is turning out to be Beck.

WADE MILLER BIBLIOGRAPHY

(Robert Wade and Bill Miller)

Deadly Weapon (1946)

Guilty Bystander (1947)*

Pop Goes the Queen (1947;
  in pb as Murder—Queen High)

Fatal Step (1948)*

Uneasy Street (1948)*

Devil on Two Sticks (1949;
  in pb as Killer's Choice)

Calamity Fair (1950)*

Murder Charge (1950)*

Devil May Care (1950)

Stolen Woman (1950)

The Killer (1951)

The Tiger's Wife (1951)

Shoot to Kill (1951)*

Branded Woman (1953)

The Big Guy (1953)

South of the Sun (1953)

Mad Baxter (1955)

Kiss Her Goodbye (1956)

Kitten With a Whip (1959)

Sinner Take All (1960)

Nightmare Cruise (1961; in the UK
  as The Sargasso People)

The Girl from Midnight (1962)

*Max Thursday series

As by Will Daemer

The Case of the Lonely Lovers (1951)

As by Dale Wilmer

Memo for Murder (1951)

Dead Fall (1954)

Jungle Heat (1954; reprinted as by
  Wade Miller)

As by Whit Masterson

All Through the Night (1955; in pb
  as A Cry in the Night, 1956)

Dead, She Was Beautiful (1955)

Badge of Evil (1956; in pb as A
  Touch of Evil)

A Shadow in the Wild (1957)

The Dark Fantastic (1959)

A Hammer in His Hand (1960)

Evil Come, Evil Go (1961)

[Note: all further Masterson
books are the solo works of
Robert Wade]

The Man on a Nylon String (1963)

711—Officer Needs Help (1965;
  in pb as Warning Shot)

Play Like You're Dead (1967)

The Last One Kills (1969)

The Death of Me Yet (1970)

The Gravy Train (1971; in pb as The
  Great Train Robbery)

Why She Cries, I Do Not Know
  (1972)

The Undertaker Wind (1973)

The Man With Two Clocks (1974)

Hunter of the Blood (1977)

The Slow Gallows (1979)

As by Robert Wade

The Stroke of Seven (1965)

Knave of Eagles (1969)

THE KILLER

DEVIL ON TWO STICKS

Two Mysteries by
Wade Miller

STARK
HOUSE

Stark House Press • Eureka California

THE KILLER / DEVIL ON TWO STICKS

Published by Stark House Press
1315 H Street
Eureka, CA 95501
griffinskye3@sbcglobal.net
www.starkhousepress.com

ISBN: 1-933586-23-0
ISBN-13: 978-1-933586-23-6

Cover design and layout by Mark Shepard, SHEPGRAPHICS.COM
Proofreading by Rick Ollerman and David Wilson

*The publisher wishes to thank Bob Wade and David Wilson
for all their help on this project.*

REPRINT EDITION

Contents

Introduction

by Bob Wade

I was naturally delighted with Greg Shepard's plan to republish two of the early Wade Miller thrillers and further gratified by the two titles he selected to represent the Wade Miller oeuvre since both Bill Miller and I ranked them among our best work. Be surprised, however, that the two differ greatly in story, style and scope.

Devil on Two Sticks is a dark and brooding melodrama in which the Southern California mob discovers it has been infiltrated by a government agent. The story is told from the point of view of the enforcer assigned to hunt down and dispose of the agent, a reversal of the usual hero/villain roles. As the chase heats up, the mobster, a sophisticated man who prides himself on his lack of feeling, is finally forced to confront his long-buried humanity. The title, incidentally, springs from *Diablo*, the classic juggling exercise, wherein an hourglass-shaped shuttle swings precariously on a string between two poles.

The Killer, on the other hand, is a modern western adventure starring an African big game hunter. The down-on-his-luck hunter is hired to track down and kill a dangerous criminal. Using his jungle-honed skills, he pursues the outlaw across the United States, only to discover that he has been duped—and that the human animal is, indeed, the most dangerous game of all.

Therefore, gentle reader, kindly approach these two samples from the Wade Miller inventory with great expectations that they will both entertain you royally, each in its own fashion.

San Diego
December 2007

Bob Wade and Bill Miller: The Deadly Collaboration

by David Laurence Wilson

"You can strip a gun down to its basic parts and it's lost its power. You can reduce man to his chemical elements but you've always got the spirit, or whatever you call it, left. And that spirit will find some damned way to do evil."
...from Deadly Weapon, by Wade Miller, 1946

A collaboration, a second or third pair of eyes and hands, is a good way to take some of the isolation out of the act of creation. It seems natural for songwriters or cartoonists to gather into teams of lyricists and composers, gag writers and draftsmen. And then there are all those collaborations that go along with the making of a film.

But pulp and crime writing seems to be a different matter, the product of hurried but singular points of view, plotting and quirkiness or peculiarity of style being what make the writers distinct. An assembly line perhaps, but still a cottage industry with a single employee.

"Wade Miller," one of the most ubiquitous of paperback crime novelists, was an exception. Wade Miller was a team of two San Diego boys who grew up writing for the stage and a local radio station. They had no plans to go into print. Novels weren't part of the game plan.

When Bill Miller died in 1961, at the age of 41, it was the end of a friendship and writing team that ultimately produced thirty-three private eye and suspense novels between 1946 and 1962, twenty-one with the Wade Miller name. Today the partners are best known for their novels featuring private eye Max Thursday.

Though well received, the Thursday novels were just a small part of the two writers' production, including a second pseudonym, Whit Masterson. The majority of their novels, the non-series titles, were neglected for decades.

Though this volume focuses on the "Wade Miller" novels, Wade continued writing the Masterson stories after Miller's death. Altogether there were eighteen hardback, non-series Masterson novels written between 1955 and 1979, seven of them co-authored with Bill Miller. Wade would ultimately publish two of his favorite, most heavily researched novels, *The Stroke of Seven* (1965) and *Knave of Eagles* (1969), under his own name.

Neither Wade nor Miller had ever expressed a desire to end their partnership and go off on their own. If Miller had survived they would have probably still been writing together decades later.

"The secret of our collaboration, and what made it work—without a flaw or
a hitch—was the fact that we thought alike," Wade explained in 1984. "We just
absolutely meshed. The one rule we had in our collaboration was that we each
had an absolute veto. If one person didn't like it, that was it. There wasn't
any argument about it.

"Looking back at some of the old books, I've tried to think, Who did this?
Was it Bill or was it me? Who was responsible for this? And I have no idea.
I really can't tell. It didn't matter who wrote the first draft, or who did the
revisions. We had a consistency in our point of view.

"The worst part about Bill's death, as a collaborator, was not being able to
talk to him, to bounce our ideas back and forth and get the feedback."

As P. I. writers, the Wade Miller team is ranked with Howard Browne
(John Evans), William Campbell Gault, Dennis Lynds, and Roy Huggins as
one of the most successful disciples of Dashiell Hammett and Raymond
Chandler. They were transitional writers, a station on the trail from untar-
nished heroes to likeable villains and psychopathic leading men. They wrote
in the third person. It gave the stories an ambiguity and a sympathetic point
of view for almost all their characters.

If you look at hard-boiled as a time and place, as a matter of biography and
generation as well as style, then Wade Miller is the last of the hard-boiled writers.

A Wade Miller book was terse, but it also contained humor and an honest
depiction of human experience. "We wanted to give our protagonist some
problems," Wade said. "We wanted something to set him apart, to make him
interesting. So he was an alcoholic. That was the original problem. Then we
went from that to the situation where he considered himself trigger happy.
In *Guilty Bystander* (1947) we introduced Max Thursday in an alcoholic stu-
por in a flophouse on Market Street. In *Shoot To Kill* (1951) we left him with
a broken arm in a garbage dump in National City. That was the progression."

In 1988, at the Bouchercon convention in San Diego, Wade received a
Shamus Award from the Private Eye Writers of America for Lifetime
Achievement. Wade shared the evening with Dennis Lynds, who was honored with his own Lifetime Achievement Award. It was particularly appropriate that Wade received the award in San Diego, his birthplace and the
setting for the six Max Thursday novels written between 1947 and 1951.

For decades readers had been asking Wade for another Max Thursday novel.
Wade had decided it was time to resurrect the long-dormant private eye and
the *nom de plume* Wade Miller. Thursday was going to come back as a 55 year
old P. I.

"It's been a long time since I've written this kind of thing," Wade said. "I'm not sure whether I'm going to be able to go back to it or whether I even want to go back to it. I don't know what I'm going to come up with. I'm curious, really."

Ultimately, it was a book that was never written. Wade seemed to have the idea of enthusiasm, when it came to Thursday, but he never had the enthusiasm itself. He remained close to the genre, however, and contributed to crime fiction–and his city–in many ways. He wrote for *San Diego* magazine and the publications department of the San Diego Zoo. He began reviewing mysteries for the *San Diego Union* in 1977 and was still doing it more than thirty years later. A blurb from Robert Wade was a prize.

On Margaret Millar's *Spider Webs* (1986): "*Millar, she of the deft style and delicious wit, has long been recognized as tops in her field. The good news here is not that, after more than four decades, she is as good as she ever was. The good news is that she's even better.*"

On Lawrence Block's *When the Sacred Ginmill Closes* (1986): "*Lawrence Block is to be complimented on his attempt to break away from the strictures of the private-eye formula, than which there are no stricter.*"

On Ed Lynskey's *Blue Cheer* (2007): *Back in the 1950s, Fawcett Publications created a virtual revolution in the mystery field by inaugurating a line of original paperback novels known as Gold Medal Books. ... What emerged was a new style of thriller, unsentimental in its viewpoint, crammed with action and rich in character. ... Gold Medal books are long gone, but a comeback may be under way. A new wave of young writers is experimenting with the old-style thriller, often described these days as "noir."*

Wade also had his complaints. With as many as sixty new crime novels published each month, few of them were as taut and streamlined as the "Wade Miller" novels from the fifties... there were too many mysteries and way too many pages.

Postwar San Diego was a city on the go, one of the fastest growing regions of North America, ground zero for the Baby Boom. It was adobe and navy blue, with a Spanish Mission and a Mexican Presidio, a border town whose television sets picked up soap operas and bullfights from Tijuana.

World War II had increased San Diego's population and its economy. The city was paving streets, building schools and beginning a beautification program that never seemed to stop. It was sprucing up its landmarks.

Its literary achievements were meager, however. Like most of seaside California, it claimed a portion of Richard Henry Dana's career. Helen Hunt Jackson's *Ramona* (1884) seemed to have a place in every nascent feminist and civil rights bookshelf. Zane Grey... Erle Stanley Gardner... there were writers whose names were familiar but they didn't have the address.

With the Baby Boom came children's books. L. Frank Baum, creator of the Oz books, had wintered on nearby Coronado Island. It was a tough pedigree to beat but in 1948 Ted Geisel, better known as Dr. Seuss, moved to La Jolla's Mount Soledad, a vague destination that was not unknown to the city's children. Folk singer Sam Hinton moved to San Diego and began writing songs for children. Deeper in the county, Scott O'Dell hit big and elegantly with *Island of the Blue Dolphins* (1960).

There was also another side of the San Diego writing life. Alcoholism, domestic violence, gangs and murder–these social ills were not confined to the old industrial cities. They could thrive in the sun, too. This darker side expressed itself in journalism. The city's most popular writers were the columnists–Max Miller, Neil Morgan, Jim Murray–city-side and sports.

Max Miller became a best-selling author with *I Cover the Waterfront* (1932), a collection of stories about the San Diego docks. Sam Fuller, later the writer and director of *Underworld U.S.A.* (1961), worked for the *San Diego Sun*. The veteran Private Eye writers Raymond Chandler and Jonathan Latimer moved to La Jolla. As the suburbs pushed past the mesas and the canyons, Corinth Publications, publisher of the sexually provocative Nightstand Books and Midnight Readers, moved to Mission Gorge Road.

It was Wade Miller who put San Diego on the mystery map. Today there is even a site on the internet that features Max Thursday's haunts. The stories were blessed with a wonderful sense of place. The reader was introduced to the city's landmarks... the El Cortez Hotel, the Cabrillo Bridge, the Jessop's Jewelry Store Clock, tattoo parlors, "Joyland" on Broadway, and Marston's Department Store, a place so familiar to the two young writers that they simply called it "Marston's," in *Devil On Two Sticks* (1949).

In *Deadly Weapon* they gave directions: "... *A big black and white sign pointed left to San Diego State College. About a mile over Walter James could see the college tower, thin and square and brilliantly white, probing the hot sky.*" Also noted is the wooden roller coaster at Mission Beach, an impressive monument day or night, built in 1921, one year after the writers' birth.

These landmarks were featured in wonderfully entertaining plots, stories with so many twists and surprises that neither the reader nor the characters could trust anything until the last page.

Wade and Miller could go toe-to-toe with the toughest of stylists: "*Do you know what happened to me?*" a character asks, in *Stolen Woman* (1950). "*Not the beating. But while I was lying there afterward, a rat came and bit me... It's not the beating I'll remember, so much, but lying there and being bitten by a rat. Like carrion.*"

Rival gangsters were simply dropped from airplanes.

In 1984 Wade was asked to define the hard-boiled style: "I think it is the mindset of the author that makes it hard-boiled," he said. "We had read Hammett, and Chandler, and of course, you write what you like. We weren't trying consciously to imitate them, but I think it comes out that way, to a certain extent. I think I started out as a hard-boiled writer, and I consider

Thursday a hard-boiled detective. Some writers become hard-boiled, some drift away from it. I've drifted away from it over the past twenty years."

Twenty-four years later, as he prepared for this volume, Wade was asked if those decades of crime fiction made him want to revise his definition. "No, not really," he said. "I couldn't have said it better myself. Ha!"

The collaboration began in 1932, when the boys were twelve years old. The occasion was a violin lesson, with borrowed violins.

"I liked the piano but I had absolutely no talent, interest or liking for the violin," Wade recalled. "As far as I was concerned it was just absolute drudgery. But there was a guy sitting next to me who had the same feeling. That turned out to be Bill Miller." They were also going to be in the same freshman class at Hoover High School, where they would share an English class.

In many ways they had similar tastes. They read pulps and enjoyed Alfred Hitchcock and the Marx Brothers. Their English teacher suggested they attempt to write something together. The result was a one-act play, a mystery.

As high school seniors they edited the Hoover newspaper and published an item in the gossip column that angered the administration. After their graduation they were threatened with arrest if they returned to the campus. Their principal warned his friend, the president of San Diego State, that two dangerous agitators would soon be enrolling at his campus.

At State, Wade and Miller were allowed to skip their freshman English classes if they returned with a project at the end of the semester. They wrote a three act play, rented theaters, and staged it around town. They followed that up with a second three act play.

The pair continued writing together. In 1936 they produced a variety show. In 1937 they wrote *Knight in Arms*, an elaborate satirical musical about South American politics. "It was terrible, just awful, a ghastly performance from beginning to end," Wade said.

Later, a fraternity brother mentioned to them that the sets for Paramount Picture's *Beau Geste* (1939) were still standing in the Yuma desert, including the fort and the oasis. Within twenty-four hours Wade and Miller had written a screenplay, rented a camera, pieced together costumes and were en route to the desert.

When they arrived at the abandoned sets the interiors of the fort had been gutted, with just the walls and stairways remaining. Before they began filming they rebuilt rooms and made repairs. They spent six months and many trips to the desert making a silent comedy feature, a burlesque that they called, unfortunately, *Beau Geste*.

They took on part-time jobs at a Safeway grocery store to pay for gas and film. When they finally finished the film they planned to show it at San Diego State but the president of the school insisted they get an OK from Paramount.

Not only had they used the Paramount sets, but they'd used the same title. Paramount suggested, through their legal department, that the teenagers burn the completed film.

Later Paramount compromised enough to allow a single screening of the film at the college. Despite the concession the filmmakers still fell far short of breaking even.

They were taking a course in writing for radio when they were recruited by the local radio station KGB. The state department had requested a series of fifteen minute radio shows on the culture and history of Latin America. They would be written and taped at KGB, then broadcast in the U.S. and South America. They were supposed to cover every country in South America and Latin America.

"We turned it into a series of melodramas," Wade said. "If it had anything to do with the culture it was strictly by accident. We went in and we would find some interesting story regarding the history of a particular country. They were all based on fact. Then the imagination took over."

Wade and Miller edited *The Aztec*, the college's twice-weekly newspaper. They also took over the *East San Diego Press*, an orphaned advertiser that ran eight, sometimes twelve pages each week.

Their second silent feature, *King Congo*, was a satire of jungle films. This one was filmed in color in San Diego's Mission Valley. This time they rented a downtown theater for a week where they showed the film. Then Pearl Harbor was bombed. Everything changed, in San Diego and in the writers' lives.

The two young men finished their last semester and enlisted after graduation. Miller remained stateside, in Santa Ana, before being sent to Manila. Wade traveled to England aboard the Queen Mary. He survived German bombs in London and the invasion of Roan. He fought the Foreign Legion through Algeria and was involved in counterespionage missions in North Africa. Following that he was transferred to Air Force public relations, and he became an Air Force combat correspondent.

"There were a lot of life-threatening situations," Wade said. "I kept thinking, is this really happening? If I just get out of this alive, it's going to be great. And I was lucky. I got out of it alive."

During the three and a half years that Wade and Miller were in the military they stayed in touch by mail. Among their prewar projects had been an outline for a suspense story they planned to write as a play. Another was a satirical radio play about a talking hippopotamus who becomes vice president of the U.S.

Miller had the notes for the stories and a lot of down time while he served in the Philippines. He wrote Wade and said that he was going to try and turn the notes for the suspense story into a book. Wade had his own favorite among their works-in-progress. He wanted to stress the hippo story.

Miller wrote a 40,000 word mystery and sent the manuscript to Wade, who lengthened it to 60,000 words by adding two subplots. Wade had returned to San Diego and KGB and was writing a radio series, *San Diego Sketchbook*, which sold to the two biggest advertisers in the city, Marston's and San Diego Electric.

By chance, Wade encountered Sid Fleischman, a friend from San Diego State and the *Aztec* staff. They compared notes and Wade learned that Fleischman had sold a how-to book on magic tricks and was working on a private eye novel. Wade quizzed him and later sent the "Wade Miller" manuscript, now titled *Deadly Weapon*, to Fleischman's agent. Two days later he had a sale to a new publisher, Farrar Straus. The novel was sexually and racially charged but the publisher insisted they remove just one line: "Her body was a soft pillar of flame."

Miller soon returned to the U.S. and the veterans resumed their partnership. Their goals still included careers in radio and theater. A friend asked for their signatures in his copy of the new book. "No masterpiece–" they wrote, "but at least it's better than 'Knight in Arms'!"

Deadly Weapon was more successful than either of its authors might have expected. One of their new acquaintances, Max Miller, knew Roger Straus and urged him to give their new book the best promotion possible. Straus flew out to California and asked for another novel as soon as possible.

The partners rented a downtown office and began writing together from nine to five. Usually they'd try to work on two books at a time. Wade tried to produce 1,000 words a day. Miller was a slower writer, a perfectionist, so often Wade would type while they talked over their stories. "I need to be able to see what I am writing," he said. "I need to see the words on a page. Bill could dictate. I can't. I have to be able to see what the words look like on the page, the set up and the rhythm and the flow of them. When I can't see it I can't do it."

"Our method of collaboration was to settle on a plot idea. Usually one of us would come in with a 'Hey–what do you think about this?' Then, if the sparks struck, we'd talk about it. We'd talk and talk and talk about what we could do. Where would it go? Who would be the characters, and so forth. Finally we'd start putting things down on 3 by 5 cards.

"We always maintained an idea file. When something would occur to us we'd just jot it down on a piece of paper or a card or something and throw it in the file and then later, when we were trying to construct a new story, we'd always look through the file, to see if there was anything in there that we needed or wanted to use. Scenes, characters, incidents, everything like that, until we had a fairly thick deck. Then we'd start laying them out, and trying to get the order right. When we got to that point, then we would do a chapter outline. For a 70,000 word book they would probably run ten thousand words.

"One of us would take the chapter outlines and start the first draft. The other would follow at whatever pace, depending upon what else was going on. As soon as one finished a chapter the other would take it over. Usually we tried to work on two books at a time. In some cases most of the book would be written before the other writer would begin the rewrite."

They were writing finished copy: "We always felt that any draft, whatever we did, should be able to stand on its own. I don't think we got sloppy because there was someone coming up behind. We looked at the other person as somebody who would improve it, not save it."

Their second novel was *Guilty Bystander* (1947), the first of the Max Thursday novels. Neither of its writers wanted to author a long-running detective series so they wrote each of the books as if it were the last.

Farrar Straus was completely happy with the Max Thursday novels but the writers were ready for a change of pace. *Pop Goes The Queen* (1947) was an attempt to break out of their niche with a screwball comedy featuring a husband and wife detective team. This was another story that had originally been conceived as a radio drama for the *San Diego Sketchbook*. It was based on the legend of a lost Spanish treasure ship that sails up the Gulf of California into the interior of California and becomes trapped when floodwaters recede.

Devil On Two Sticks had connections with the novel *Deadly Weapon*, but it also introduced a variety of new characters, as well as a crime syndicate controlling San Diego county. Curiously, the dust jacket for *Devil On Two Sticks* advertised *Murder City* (1949), the first novel by Oakley Hall, another college classmate. That added up to four young writers, friends, acquaintances and San Diego State graduates who created fictional San Diego private investigators between 1946 and 1948.

The new market for original paperbacks came at a particularly opportune moment for the two young writers, who were feeling trapped by their Thursday character. They reasoned that if they weren't enthusiastic about the stories, their readers wouldn't be either. Farrar Straus had only reluctantly accepted *Pop Goes the Queen* and *Devil On Two Sticks* but Wade and Miller preferred the single, self-contained adventure novels. They wanted to write about a variety of locales and characters, adventurers and soldiers of fortune with a past who were maybe on their last adventure. They were determined not to write the same book twice. In their first year with Fawcett's Gold Medal series the team published four novels, including a Thursday novel for Farrar Straus. Wade and Miller would ultimately write eleven novels for Fawcett.

"Our hardback sales were around five or six thousand," Wade recalled. "Then the first Gold Medals–those books went absolutely through the roof. They sold in the millions. They were at the airports, in the drugstores and supermarkets. I took a trip across the country and everywhere I went I was running into copies of the books. It was a great feeling! We got a lot of recognition from people who had never read our hardbacks."

The first two, *Stolen Woman* and *Devil May Care* (1950), were both set in Mexico, the latter originally intended as a screenplay for James Cagney. Like Sid Fleischman, who wrote suspense set in the Far East (*Shanghai Flame* 1951; *Danger In Paradise*, 1953; *Malay Woman*, 1954), the Wade Miller novels filled a niche for the publisher.

They followed with stories set in Ensenada, Mexicali, Mazatlan, Aca-pulco and Tijuana. Though neither of the authors were particularly conscious of the books as Mexican novels, they were able to capture the otherness, that unexpected foreign-ness on the other side of the border as well as B. Traven (*Treasure of Sierra Madre*, 1927) or Dorothy Hughes, in *Ride the Pink Horse* (1946). Their milieu is the border town, criminals, expatriates and heroes who live on both sides of the border.

Several of these novels were set in the world of the crime boss Silver Magol-nick, a behind the scenes puppeteer who dominates Southern California crime and smuggling. He's referred to, we learn something of his history, but he never appears within these pages. The main characters within these nov-els resolve their immediate conflicts and that is the end of their existence. Magolnick remains.

Sinner Take All (1960) adapted from a screenplay attempt, was about an as-sassination in Tijuana. This is the setting for the team's stories in Mexico: "*Among them prowled the natives–shills for the bars, taxi drivers offering rides to the jai alai, children with trays of chewing gum and cheap jewelry... sur-veying each passerby with eyes of shrewd opportunism hardened to refusal and impossible to discourage, quick to note the hesitation that might mean a cus-tomer. Sound ran rampant — brassy music pouring out of open night club doors, taco venders hawking their wares, automobile horns blaring, mariachis strum-ming their guitars, all mingling together in a frenetic cacophony, both weird and compelling. Glare and noise were the twin components of Avenida Revolucion, and the dollar was King. It was neither Mexican nor American. It was, sim-ply, the border.*"

In 2008, on the occasion of this Stark House volume, Bob Wade reflected upon his career: "I never thought of them as Mexican books. They were books that happened to be in Mexico, but I never categorized them as Mexican." In truth, Wade and his partner had never stopped writing about Mexico and their own border town. Even when the city was unnamed in their books it was still San Diego.

They wrote a quick novel, *Memo for Murder* (1951), intended for Graphic Books, with an anagram for a name, Dale Wilmer. A second effort, *With A Vengeance*, was turned down by Graphic but printed in digest form as *The Case of the Lonely Lover* (1951), by the new publisher, Farrell. The author for that one was Will Daemer, yet another combination of the Wade Miller names. It was the publisher's first and last book. Later, it was rewritten as *The Girl From Midnight* (1962), the last of the Wade Miller novels. This is the one where the hero is a veterinarian and a trained cheetah takes out one of the hoods. The writers had studied the Cheetah for one of their South American radio stories. The stats on the cat must have been somewhere among their three by five cards. The team had a chameleon like ability to take on genres and categories: crime, international intrigue, war and private eye. *Nightmare Cruise* (1961) was set on a drifting yacht in the Sargasso Sea. *Kiss Her Goodbye* (1956) was filmed with enough changes and rewriting to make Wade disown it. *Mad Baxter* (1955) is a little known comic action gem suggested by Wade's yearlong wartime stay in Sardinia. It was optioned more times than any of the other Wade Miller novels. Wade's familiarity with the land and its near-feudal villages is particularly impressive.

Wade Miller was a big seller and Fawcett had the blurbs to back them up. Unlike their other publishers—Farrar Straus, Signet, Ace and Pyramid, Fawcett described them as a single writer instead of a team. It was there on the cover of *The Big Guy* (1953): "Wade Miller – The Hemingway of Suspense," almost as big as the title.

The novels in this collection highlight two characteristics of the Wade Miller stories: evocative character studies and intricate, sometimes deceptive plotting. *The Killer* (1951) moves so far and so quickly that the writers plotted their character's itinerary out on graph paper, with notes on what was interesting about each locale. It doesn't stop: from Kenya to Albany, New York, to the Okefenokee Swamp in Georgia... to Chicago, Yellowstone and the Mojave Desert. There seems to be several stories turning... a Great White Hunter in a variation of "The Most Dangerous Game"... a coincidental love story—like *It Happened One Night*—with guns. What seems to be an adventure novel turns melancholy, with the lingering aftertaste of noir. The most haunted character is in the background, one more example of the writers' ability to create full-color supporting players.

Devil on Two Sticks is the classic in this volume, a surprisingly mature effort that would not be uncomfortable on a list of the fifty greatest American crime novels. It is heavy on character, like *South of the Sun* (1953) and *The Big Guy*. In *The Big Guy* lifestyle is used as a weapon. In *Devil On Two Sticks* it is a subtle clue. "*The Devil On Two Sticks*—that's our *Glass Key*," Wade said. "That's what it is, really. I didn't even know it at the time, but that's what it actually is."

There are times in *Devil On Two Sticks* where the reader is sucked into a description of a character who is, basically, killing time: "*The second feature was half over but what had gone before was obvious. It was about a dog. ... The main feature was a musical in gay colors concerning a singing dancing loving tropical paradise where no one worked. Beck idly watched the magnificent doll faces, so clean, go through their paces and guessed ahead that it would all turn out to be a dream. It didn't, but he enjoyed it anyway. He also sat through a brutal cartoon and a stagnant newsreel.*"

Steve Beck, Max Thursday and P. I. Walter James all share the same San Diego settings and characters. Beck is a capable, even honorable man whose energies are set to less than noble purposes. He works for Pat Garland, a gangster with an interest in the Grand Theater, the same burlesque joint where a murder sets the plot in motion in *Deadly Weapon*. Larson and Ulaine Tarrant are a couple who are part of the criminal "ring" in *Devil On Two Sticks*, and Thursday's adversaries in *The Fatal Step* (1948). It's all witnessed by the roller coaster, a low-slung, shining ribbon, glowing like forgotten promises at the end of Jay Gatsby's pier.

"We wanted to create a world," Wade said.

A world with uneasy coincidences and lots of entertaining, 180 degree surprises.

"When you come right down to it, fiction itself is not realistic," Wade said. "Life isn't like a book. There's no beginning, middle and end to it. There's no conclusion in which things are wrapped up. Things just go along, they fade away or they come to improbable mini-climaxes, then they disappear. Any time you pick up fiction you're beginning with the given that this is not real, that you're suspending disbelief to some extent.

"It was on the job education, that's what it amounted to. We fell into the book business by accident, so we had to learn as we went along.

"The thing about books, particularly books that keep being reprinted–is you can never bury your mistakes. They continue to come back and remind you about themselves."

Boys, leave the shovels at home. No need to bury this pair.

Downieville, CA
May 2008

The Killer

By Wade Miller

Chapter One

THURSDAY, APRIL 26, 1:00 P.M.

The rifle in his lap was a .475 Jeffries. He had won it in a lion shoot in the Masai game preserve just twenty years ago and it had his name and the date engraved on the heavy barrel. "Jacob Farrow, Kenya Colony, 1938." It had been worth more than two hundred pounds then, and some men would have kept it under glass or mounted on the wall as a trophy. But he wasn't sentimental, a gun was for use, and he'd never found a rifle that suited him as well.

He tossed aside the rag, finished with the daily cleaning. His big hand stroked along the butt, absently and sensuously. He thought fleetingly, Perhaps a woman is what I need, and then he shrugged. The Jeffries hadn't been fire since January, the longest rest the gun had ever had. The only one of his many rifles that had been fired in the last three months was the Mauser, and that only to frighten the hyenas, the "dustbin patrol," skulking past the airport fence to raid the chicken yards and garbage heaps on the outskirts of Nairobi.

When he'd lovingly racked the Jeffries, he had nothing else he wanted to do and he was bored. He muttered, "Damn them," about the men who had taken his license away. He poured another gin and carried it with him as he prowled the three Spartan rooms of his brick cottage. Then he stalked out on the shaded veranda and faced the gray African vista and drank his gin.

"Perhaps a woman..." he said aloud. Perhaps he could lose himself in some stray wife around the Muthaiga Club, some thin-frocked, white-legged lady who'd become expert at deceiving her husband. There were several with moist dissatisfied mouths. Or—he hadn't remembered her for a year—in the Arab bazaar was a shop-girl, not even half Arab and surprisingly clean. She had regal breasts like sun-tipped dunes and plump thighs and a fiery talent of consummation. "Perhaps...." Then he damned his own stupidity, grinning angrily. A woman wasn't what he needed; he needed an excitement more lasting.

Farrow was a man of controlled violence. That was his trade, and he couldn't get used to having nothing to do. He was tall with big bones, and his flesh was drawn tightly over them. His hair grew back from a straight line above his forehead, giving his craggy face the appearance of a block of dark grainy wood. His hair and his ragged mustache were brown. His body, clad only in khaki shorts and unlaced safari boots, was also brown, partly from weather and partly from malaria.

But his eyes were gray, pale and flat and startling in their contrast to his general brownness. Today they sparkled restlessly because he was a little drunk. It showed only in his eyes and the taut grin. Normally his face was masklike, thus escaping ugliness or fierceness.

He got the .475 Jeffries from its rack again and stood on the veranda, sighting it at emptiness. The rain had stopped for a while and the air was brisk on his bare skin. Through the open sights of the rifle he picked out individual white blossoms in the coffee fields across the road. Beyond that, to the west, he could see the Athi slope rising gradually toward the Mua forests and the blue mountain of Donyo Sabouk. Elephant country. He swung the gun barrel south, toward the hundred-mile width of the Masai plains, flatness broken only by the four-peaked Ngong Hills. Lion country. And to the north, the modern buildings of Nairobi, its skyline lorded over by the twin minarets and dome of the central mosque.

The magnificently peaceful view didn't stir Farrow. But, as he gazed at the city, another vagrant idea did. He murmured to the rifle, "What if we didn't pay any attention to them? What if we simply left, had ourselves a good hunt?"

The outlaw notion hung fire as he spotted a moving target. It was a car sloshing at high speed along the road, disappearing now and then behind the clumps of stately eucalyptus. He got the car in the sights, kept it there, pretending the front door handle would be a heart shot. These outlying roads were unpaved, and the winter rains made them treacherous bogs, but the car's driver knew his business.

Farrow lowered the gun, apathetically curious as the automobile came nearer his cottage. He recognized the car as one rentable at the agency in Nairobi, which meant the driver was a European, the generic term in the colony for any white. He guessed further that the driver had been looking for the Somali village and had taken the wrong turn. He waited.

The car wheeled off onto his land and slithered up to the veranda steps. The driver's head poked out. Within the hood of a rain cape was a round white face with an embalmed look. Rimless spectacles glinted up at the veranda. The man's voice was crisp, faintly nasal. "Farrow? Jacob Farrow?"

"Yes. Come in." Farrow decided the visitor was American. His own voice was clipped and precise despite the gin, distinctly British. He went into the sitting room and was racking the Jeffries when the stranger halted inside the door to remove galoshes and rain cape.

"Osher's my name. Paul Osher." He wasn't very tall but he was erect, shoulders back and his large belly coming out to a point. His pale smooth skin appeared soft, but his handshake wasn't. Despite his fuzz of white hair he seemed ageless; despite his girth he didn't wheeze from climbing the veranda steps. He wore a black suit and tie as if in mourning. The starched collar constricted the roll of hard-looking fat that served as his neck, and his chin was little more than a dimple and his mouth was a small fish mouth. He inspected the sitting room.

Farrow shoved forward a chair. "I have gin. Care for it watered?"

"Don't bother, please." Osher sat down. His rimless glasses and his steel-blue eyes briskly surveyed Farrow. He had the air of a cattle buyer, his mind totting up the hairy muscularity of Farrow's legs, the three parallel scars on his left bicep, claw marks.

Osher said, "I'll state my business. You're a professional guide, what they call a white hunter. I'm told that you're the best there is."

"That was nice of somebody." He poured a straight gin for himself.

"The same source told me it wasn't wise to drink until sundown—and then go slow."

Farrow looked at him. The stranger was using Farrow's own words, a favorite aphorism. "You seem to have been told a good bit about me."

"We must have the best, no mistake about it. Do you smoke?" His hand darted forth with a case of cigarettes. Farrow said no and Osher screwed one into a holder. The holder filled up much of his mouth, but he spoke around it efficiently. "Mr. Farrow, are you available for a hunt?"

He felt an instant's thrill before he remembered. "No," Farrow muttered, "I'm not."

Osher ignored it. He droned, "The price will be five thousand dollars for you, plus expenses. Ten thousand if you make the kill. In pounds, that's—"

"Yes, I know what it is in pounds." Farrow leaned a bare shoulder against the brick fireplace. He felt a bit stunned. "Mr. Osher, at the risk of appearing to be a damned fool at business, let me tell you this: The most expensive safari I ever heard of cost only twenty-five hundred American dollars, including guide. It's still talked about in town. It was a high-water mark."

"Nevertheless, I've stated our price correctly."

"No hunter's worth it."

"You may be. If you're interested, Mr. Farrow."

"Certainly I'm interested. I'm—" He stopped suddenly, then grimaced. His face was a mask again as he poured himself another drink. "Gin is good for disappointment. I'm not doing any hunting, not presently."

"Not on British territory, not till December," said Osher. "They've suspended your license for poaching."

"You're thorough," Farrow said dryly. "If you've talked to the game office, why did you waste a trip out here?"

"I don't make waste."

"Did the office gentleman tell you how it came about? I was out for a long time with a youngster who wanted a lion very badly. He had promised his family, I believe. But his luck was no better than his shooting, so I took him onto the Masai preserve."

"And got caught."

"And got caught," Farrow agreed. "So I'm sorry we can't do business, Mr.

Osher."

Osher's steel-bead eyes studied him. "Something was said about a woman involved."

Farrow snorted. "There've probably been wilder rumors. No, there was no woman concerned or even within two hundred miles. I very seldom consent to take women as members of a party, and I certainly wouldn't poach for one."

Osher looked at his watch. "We're losing time. This hunt will not be any-where in British East Africa."

Farrow's heart turned over. He put down his glass and put the stopper in the gin decanter. He controlled his voice. "Where will it be, then?"

"I'm not at liberty to tell you."

"How big a party? What kind of game?"

Osher shook his head slightly. "I can assure you the party will be small. And the pay is large—which should atone for a temporary lack of details."

Farrow said nothing, staring at him. His visitor's words were as good as a warning. Something was wrong with this hunt. A hunt was a matter between man and beast, and there should be no need for secrecy between men about it. Osher said, "Leaving Africa wouldn't bother you. You've done it before, on those trips to India and Malaya."

Farrow's eyes narrowed. He said softly. "You know all about me but I know nothing about you."

"I don't matter," said Osher. "I merely represent another person."

"No use asking whom?"

"No."

"Well, you've talked about a lot of money, Mr. Osher. But since I don't know the client...."

Osher said quickly, "I'm authorized to pay you a sizable advance." The checkbook was already in his soft steady hand.

Farrow shook his head. "I'd like something more certain than money. I'd like a reference."

It was supplied immediately. "Walter Stennis."

"Walt Stennis," Farrow repeated thoughtfully. He guided the Stennis party regularly every two years. He always got along fine with Stennis, liked him as a friend, even respected him as a hunter.

The name made a difference and Osher could sense it. He held out the check. It was for a thousand dollars and already made out to Jacob Farrow. Osher was terrifyingly sure of himself. "May I consider it settled?" he asked softly.

Farrow still didn't like it. He hesitated, wanting to say no. But, hesitating, he was swept by a faint panicky feeling. If he didn't take this offer, he might sit around Nairobi and rot for the rest of the year. He thought angrily, Good God, he's only hiring me; he's not asking me to sell my soul.

He said, "All right, I'll work for you," and took the check.

Osher smiled for the first time, a crippled half-smile around the cigarette holder. He handed over a long white envelope. "We're booked out of here at dusk. I'm sure you'll be ready."

Farrow examined the string of airline tickets in the envelope. BOAC through Khartoum, Tripoli, London, arriving New York on April 29. Sunday, three days away. He said, "I've never hunted any big game in North America."

"This will be a new experience for you, Mr. Farrow." Osher's round body had relaxed noticeably, like a slug after a satisfactory meal. "I could have flown you myself in our own ship, but I've found British Overseas Airways most efficient for traveling in this part of the world. You British keep things moving."

Farrow smiled politely. The step taken, his suspicions had blown away. Now he felt exhilarated, having something to do. He was certain he'd done the right thing. He looked over at the big Jeffries rifle and winked at it.

Osher was droning, "...no bother about visa. I checked their office this morning and they're expecting you sometime before five. You won't need much luggage. You can furnish yourself in the States."

"Weapons?"

"Whatever you think you'll need."

Farrow said gently, "But I don't know the game." He waited expectantly while the other man gave it a moment's thought.

When Osher answered, his voice had an odd note behind the cool matter-of-fact words. "You had better be prepared for anything."

Chapter Two

SUNDAY, APRIL 29, 10:00 P.M.

He was used to traveling on foot through open silent country. He was un-accustomed to speed and noise and confinement. For three days—nearly eight thousand air miles—Farrow wondered uncomfortably if he was as hardy as he had assumed. Osher, his older and fatter companion, seemed unaffected by their headlong journey. He showed signs of pride each time there was no delay in their connections, but he spoke no oftener than necessary. It was a dull exhausting trip and Farrow felt like a piece of baggage.

Sunday evening they debarked at La Guardia Field, New York City. Here there was a short wait. Then Osher led the way up into another, smaller air-liner. Farrow squinted his eyes wearily and trudged after. His tweed suit, two years old but almost never worn, was rumpled. Although it had been made by the best tailor in Nairobi, he had a constant suspicion that the other pas-sengers, sleek and well pressed, were commenting on it. He glared at them un-til he finally dozed off, trapped by metal walls, smothered by engine roar.

When he awoke, it was ten o'clock by his pocket watch. "We're here," said Osher. "This is Albany." They claimed their baggage and walked to the air-port parking lot. Farrow carried his suitcase in his left hand and the heavier rifle case in his right. The rifle case contained the Jeffries, a .404 Mauser, and a light carbine. Osher unlocked a black Lincoln Continental sedan that was parked and waiting. Farrow laid his gear on the back seat and they were off again.

Osher drove as efficiently as he did everything else. Farrow gazed grimly at the unfamiliar surroundings, wondering anew just where he was headed. The broad rushing highway followed the Hudson River and its flat black wa-ters seemed to glower back at him. Then they drew nearer to the heart of the capital city and he watched the buildings grow around him, threaten to en-gulf him. Plate glass and traffic lights and upshooting rectangular masses, square-cut valleys of busy concrete, and it was all precisely ranged, as if await-ing a push, on a steep slope down to the river. Much of it was as modern as Nairobi, but even through the exhaust fumes and crowd scent Farrow thought he could smell the city's age, like the gentle dust on a museum ex-hibit.

They turned up the hill and the lights of downtown fell behind and below them. The car slid through quiet streets of elm and maple trees where rested brownstone and brick homes and an occasional latter-day apartment building.

"Pine Hills," offered Osher suddenly. "The old mansions, the first families.

Some of these houses were standing when Nairobi was just native huts, Mr.
Farrow."

Farrow grunted, unimpressed. The car slowed and wheeled through iron
gates onto a curved driveway. The house that sat behind its fence and hedges
and lawns was one of the old mansions, well kept as a gigolo. Three stories
of dull-red brick, white-trimmed doors and windows, a great gambrel roof
pierced by dormers and square chimneys. The end of the journey, and Farrow began to feel less tired.

They stopped by the front door. The brass porch lamps were on but no one
came out to greet them. "Leave your things in the car for the time being," Osher said. He had a key to the mansion's door too. As he swung it open, a black
mourning wreath suspended from the shining knocker swayed slightly, making dry noises. Farrow felt a chill deeper than the spring night.

He followed Osher through an octagonal vestibule, through a wide central
hall where a mahogany staircase curved beautifully up to the second floor. All
was lamplit; all was deserted. Osher looked into a vast living room. A fire
danced in the fireplace but no persons warmed themselves there. Osher con-
sulted his wrist watch and mused, "I wonder...." It made Farrow feel a little
better somehow that the fat self-confident little machine was, momentarily
at least, not certain of his next move.

He heard a sound above and looked up to see an elderly lady in a black dress
peering over the banister at them. She didn't speak and when she saw Farrow watching her she turned and went away.

Osher hadn't seen her. He said, "Downstairs, I presume. This way, Mr. Farrow." They went through the central hall to where another stairway led
down. Their own footsteps on the thick carpeting made the only sounds. At
the bottom of the steps was a sliding door and here Osher halted. He put out
his hand. "It was a pleasant trip, Mr. Farrow. I probably won't see you again.
Lots of luck to you."

Again the hard handshake from the pudgy soft-skinned hand. Farrow said
something polite and then he watched Osher's round body climb the stairs
again, leaving him alone before the door. From someplace near, he could hear
a muffled boom-boom-boom in rhythmic repetition. He hesitated warily,
then shrugged and slid the door aside.

He stood blinking in the light, white and blinding after the mellow lamps
of the house above. Fluorescent tubes in the ceiling banished all shadow and
reflected their brilliance off yellow plaster walls. The booming reverberation
echoed everywhere in the long low room. The noise came from a punching
bag. Farrow looked around at the wall exercisers and parallel bars and rowing machine and rubbing table in the cellar gymnasium. He grinned broadly.

For there was nothing strange about the man who battered the punching
bag with practiced strokes. He was big, older than Farrow, and showing it
far more than he had two years ago, although his crisp hair had been iron-gray

then too. Still muscular, his body betrayed his sedentary life by a thickness of waist and thighs, and by an office pallor offset by the week-end tan on his arms and on his blunt face, drawing to a V shape below the creases of his throat. Tonight his shoulders had a weary curve that Farrow had never seen before.

He looked over at the sound of the door sliding shut and he stopped hitting the bag at once. His black eyebrows shot up and a grin as broad as Farrow's carved his face, making it younger. He said with obvious pleasure, "Jacob!"

"Hello, Walt," said Farrow. "I didn't expect it'd be you. I didn't realize you might be a reference for yourself."

Walter Stennis plodded over to him, stripping off his knuckle glove to shake hands. His shoulders seemed to straighten, an obscure bitterness fading from his eyes. They both put power into the handclasp and warmth too, a pair of big men, friends sizing each other up after a long absence. Farrow wondered if the two years showed on him as heavily as they showed on Stennis.

Stennis rumbled, still holding onto Farrow's hand, "Jacob, no use going into how delighted I am to see you. And how grateful that you've come so far."

"If I'd known you were the client, I'd have come faster." Farrow chuckled, shook his head. "No I'm afraid not. I couldn't have. That fellow of yours—"

"Osher?" Stennis laughed and pounded his shoulder affectionately. "Amazing specimen, isn't he? Only person I've ever trusted completely. I knew he'd bring you."

"He can certainly keep his mouth shut."

"Orders, Jacob—and Osher always follows orders. I couldn't chance any rumors getting started. Come on, let's go upstairs. There's plenty to talk about."

He picked up his robe and draped it over his shoulders like a fighter. They went upstairs, Stennis leading. He said over his shoulder, "How's everything in the bush these days?"

"Nothing's changed since you were there, Walt."

"God, how I envy you, knowing that everything'll be the same one day to the next. This country's a madhouse, Jacob, and I'm not fooling." They crossed the central hall and started up the great mahogany staircase. Stennis lowered his voice. "I'd like to have you meet Mrs. Stennis too. I've told you about her. But right now—well, she's not meeting people."

Farrow thought of the woman in black who had peered at him over the banister. He said, "How's that boy of yours?"

Stennis climbed two more steps before he answered. When he spoke his voice was metallic with the effort to control it. "He's dead."

Farrow didn't say anything more. They went along the second-floor hall to a door that opened into a large bedroom. Stennis turned on the light and said, "Sit down and make yourself comfortable. You'll find liquor in the cabinet

there. Be right with you." He went into the adjoining bathroom and the
shower began to run.

Farrow poured himself a long gin and stretched out in a big chair before the
corner fireplace. He tried to enjoy the goodness of relaxing, tried not to think
about Steven Stennis, who had died in his thirties, and younger than himself.
He decided it must have been heart trouble; he'd heard it was a common death
in big business. "Too damn bad," he muttered. "Damn shame for both of them,
Walt and his boy." He drank. The gin was good; Stennis always had the best
there was. He rubbed his feet together. The unfamiliar oxfords cramped his
toes and he longed for his boots.

Stennis came out of the bathroom, his body nude and slightly pink from a
rough toweling. For the first time Farrow noticed the purple welt, like a burn,
under his left arm. Stennis talked in spurts while he dressed in a black suit.
Farrow guessed he was forcing out words to screen his feelings.

"Maybe you think it's odd to find me down in the gym at this time of
night," said Stennis. He was tying his tie badly. "But, honest to God, my time
isn't even halfway my own any more. Business is down to the level of a dog-
fight, and what scraps are left over the government wants."

"I had an idea you're working too hard, Walt."

"There's no choice. Oh, I admit I've overextended myself the last couple
of years, but who hasn't? You have to gamble to win. I took a bad fall on that
rear-engine auto deal—don't worry, Jacob, I won't numb you with the sad
details—but I didn't know what worrying was until I got up to my neck in
Stennisfab."

"What kind of a thing is that?"

"Well, you wouldn't know it, you lucky foreigner, but there's a housing
shortage in this country. Credit and materials are down, expenses are sky-high.
But everybody wants a home and anybody who figures a way to deliver the
goods—mass production, I mean—and still make a small profit per unit will
be sitting pretty. I think I've got the answer. Standardization down to the
last nail and a new kind of prefabrication. That's Stennisfab. Come on, let's
go."

Farrow had been on the verge of removing his shoes. Now he got up, surprised. "Certainly. Where?"

"Downtown. To the office." Stennis picked up the thread of his conversation as they headed down the staircase. "Well, to make it brief, I've tied up
everything in this mass-home proposition, trying to get government backing.
I think I'm about over the hump. But that's what's been eating at me, Jacob.
That—and the other."

"What other?"

When Stennis didn't answer, Farrow remembered he was in a house of
mourning and growled at his own clumsiness. They crossed the central hall
and he got a look into the game room as they passed the door. He saw a buf-

falo head and an elk head in the quick glimpse. The buff he had tracked himself and the elk must have come from Canada, where Stennis hunted in alternate years. Then they were going out the front door, and under the lamps
Stennis' damp gray hair shone like a tiara in contrast to his somber clothes.
The Lincoln Continental stood where Osher had left it. Stennis had his own
keys. He grunted in satisfaction when he saw Farrow's gun case on the back
seat. He started the car and then, remembering, fished a pair of horn-rimmed
glasses out of his pocket and put them on. He gave Farrow a sidelong glance,
slightly shamefaced. "I just need them for driving and reading. Getting old,
Jacob."

"It happens."

"Not to you. You haven't changed a bit, damn you. You'll never know how
I wish I'd lived your life."

Farrow snorted amusement. "Walt, you enjoy hunting money fully as
much as any other kind of game. Why not? You're more all-around and complicated than I am. Perhaps you're living twice as much, two lives actually."

"Shouldn't one be enough for anybody?"

"It's a good thing for us lazy hunters that fellows like you can't be satisfied.
I'd just let the world stand still."

Stennis let out the clutch and the Lincoln began to roll down the driveway.
"Yes," he said soberly. "That's what I insist. That's why I need you now, Jacob. I haven't been satisfied for the last two weeks."

They drove down the slope again, toward downtown and the river port.
Farrow was content to let the older man choose the proper time for a full explanation. He gazed back up at the crest of the hill where the huge French
chateau that was the state capitol loomed over the city. And beside it was a
whole tower of state offices, windows going up and up. "Always reminds me
of the high places in the Bible," said Stennis. They cruised by the larch groves
of Washington Park, and a fleeting memory of African nights reminded Farrow that he was a stranger in a strange land.

The commercial streets of Albany were nearly deserted now. Only the
street lamps and the occasional glow of a bar or restaurant front hadn't succumbed to the approaching midnight. They parked at a corner where the
street names read State and Pearl. Across the way was a mammoth brick spire
of offices and stores. The building Stennis approached was smaller, however,
only seven stories. Farrow looked up and saw the name carved in granite for
all time. Stennis Building.

The street floor on the Pearl Street side belonged exclusively to the Sunhill Building & Loan Corporation. Farrow decided there had been an accident
not too long ago, because the gleaming frontage of plate glass still had manu-
facturer's labels on it. Stennis punched impatiently at a call button by the main
entrance, grilled for the night. Presently, by the security lights inside, they
saw a man in a gray uniform approach cautiously, his hand on his pistol butt.

When he made out Stennis' face he opened the doors and the grille quickly.

"Sorry, Mr. Stennis, I didn't know—"

"That's all right, Ben. We'll be in the building a while."

The guard nodded and stared curiously at Farrow as Stennis led him across the marble floor of the main banking room, lined with tellers' cages on one side and, on the other, a low counter enclosing a herd of important-looking desks. Stennis stopped and pointed. Below one of the tellers' cages there was a white gouge in the black tile wall, like a bloodless wound. The raw scar exposed some new electrical conduit.

"In line of duty," said Stennis with no humor.

The new front window, the gouged tile wall.... Farrow began to understand. "You've had a robbery here, is that it?"

"More like a raid." Stennis' voice, though low, boomed through the lofty room. "Come on in here." He ushered Farrow back to a wide marble corridor that ended in a steel fence; through the bars could be seen the massive door of the main vault. On both sides of the corridor were executive offices, four of them, with glass doors and gleaming glass windows to the floor. It was something like an aquarium. But the office nearest the steel fence no longer had a window, only lengths of scrap lumber nailed in place. The gold-lettered name on the door was Steven W. Stennis, President.

Slowly, his lips together in a thin hard line, Walter Stennis reached out and opened the door. He stepped into the office but made no move toward the light switch. A little illumination filtered down the vault corridor and between the boards covering the shattered window. Tiny stripes of the dim glow fell across the massive desk and leather conference chairs, touched the big portrait of the elder Stennis that hung on the wall. The father had aged again, in minutes. Farrow stood beside him, waiting silently.

Stennis murmured, "I founded all this. This was his office." He was mute again for a while. "Sometimes he disappointed me. Sometimes he went beyond my expectations. I guess he was about like any son—something of me in him, something of himself."

"I'm sorry, Walt."

"Sit down, Jacob. I wanted you to see it, to hear the story here." Stennis seemed short of breath suddenly. "Here is where I saw him killed."

Farrow sat down in the gloom. The leather chair sighed under his weight. He said quietly, "I'm ready to listen when you're ready to speak. But I can wait."

Stennis shook his head. He walked around behind the desk and slumped in his son's chair. "It'll be two weeks ago tomorrow—Monday, April sixteenth." He paused as if the date had caught in his throat. Then he spoke steadily and softly. "Three o'clock in the afternoon; a little before, because they hadn't closed the doors yet. Business was heavy at closing time, particularly on a Monday, people crowding in at the last minute to deposit the week -

end take. The vault was open to put the day's receipts away. Two cars double-parked out front; that isn't anything unusual either. There were three men in one, two men in the other. Understand, Jacob, I didn't see all this myself. A lot of it I found out afterward, from the witnesses and the police.

"This vault corridor was nearly deserted. The other officials were out front. Only Steven was in his office here. And myself. I'd come downstairs—my own offices are up top—to argue some investments with Steven. That's how I used up his last minutes on earth, God forgive me—arguing. We were going at it hot and heavy and the first thing we knew was the shotgun going off out in the main room. That was to put the alarm system out of commission. You saw the hole in the tile. They knew just where to hit it, one of the few signs of planning they showed.

"Three men had come into the bank. Two of them had pistols and the third one carried the shotgun. The other two stayed with the cars. They're known as the Bocock gang. The three who came in were Clel Bocock himself, his right-hand man, Vito Duccone, and a crazy hophead called Mouse Egan. Egan was the one with the shotgun. Oh, yes, Bocock and Duccone also carried traveling bags. The whole gang was already wanted for another raid, the same pattern, over in Pennsylvania last month. They're throwbacks, Jacob, atavisms. Like Dillinger, except they don't seem to plan as well as Dillinger. Maybe more like Jesse James, although I don't know much about him. Bocock's bunch doesn't give a damn about concealment. They just strike and hit hard and throw such a scare into everybody that nobody moves—and then they get away in the confusion afterward. Brute force, not precision.

"Well, I just sat here when they shot out the alarm system, not understanding what was going on. Steven caught on right away, though. Maybe, being here all the time, he'd thought about robbery more than I had. He grabbed his pistol out of his desk drawer and ran to the door. Clel Bocock was coming along the corridor, heading for the open vault, casual as you please. He had the traveling bag in his left hand, but his right was empty. He hadn't even drawn his gun. He wore it in a holster on his hip just like an old-time badman.

"I guess that's what threw Steven, his not even having his gun out. The unexpected. Bocock operates on nerve, not brains. So Steven just stood there for an instant and Bocock crouched and drew and shot him in the face. And I still sat here, Jacob, just where you are. All I thought about was my boy, not Bocock. He didn't see me, didn't even look, simply walked on into the vault. I think he was whistling.

"Steven died quickly. That's one small blessing; he didn't suffer, he didn't know. I tried to pick him up for some reason—I wasn't thinking. Then the pistol fell out of his hand and I saw it and I grabbed it up and went out into the corridor. Clel Bocock was coming out of the vault again by that time. He'd loaded the traveling bag. He saw me and we both fired. That was when the window got smashed." Stennis paused again. "This is the part I hate to think about, Jacob. All my years with guns and hunting, and when the big thing happened, I didn't make the kill. I think I winged him. I'm sure of it; he was limping when he ran out, according to the witnesses. But his shot was as good as mine. Better. I guess you saw the mark on my left side. Just a graze, off one rib, but it knocked me down. When I could get up again he had run past me and it was too late.

"There was more. Vito Duccone and Mouse Egan heard the shots and Egan let fly with his shotgun. Wounded the floor guard and killed a woman depositor. The usual innocent bystanders. That's the score—two killed, two wounded. Most of the other loss was covered by insurance, of course. About a hundred and twenty thousand dollars. A little of it was currency that Duccone and Egan collected in the main room. The greatest part of it was negotiable bonds that Bocock was lucky enough to run onto in the vault. Plus a little vault currency and some checks and bonds that wouldn't be any use to them.

"And they got away, Jacob! They killed and wounded and stole and got away clean. Bocock in one car, the rest of his gang in the other. That was two weeks ago." His voice dropped to a tired whisper. "They're still free."

Stennis had finished. For a time the shadowy office was silent as a mausoleum. Then Farrow stirred slightly. He said tentatively, a big man embarrassed before a friend's grief, "No need my saying how I feel about it, Walt. You know how I feel about it."

"Everybody is sorry," muttered Stennis. He pushed to his feet and suddenly brought his fist down on the desk with a crash. "It isn't enough, Jacob! I want more than sorrow, something stronger than sympathy. My son is dead, but the bastard who killed him isn't."

"The law will track him. It's certain."

"Is it? And what then? Suppose the law finally does manage to corner Clel Bocock—what then? Maybe he'll die or maybe he'll only fatten up in some prison. *But Steven is dead.*" Stennis shook his head savagely. "No, I've seen too many of those sure things fall flat. I swear to God it won't happen this time. That's why I sent for you."

Farrow was expecting it. He said nothing.

"I sent for you because you're one man in this damned world who never fails at his trade. Resase Modja—I've heard the natives call you that. One Cartridge." Stennis leaned across his son's desk. "Don't tell me you haven't guessed what I want, Jacob."

"No, Walt. I've guessed."

Stennis said it anyway. "I want you to hunt down Clel Bocock. Hunt him down and kill him."

Chapter Three

SUNDAY, APRIL 29, 12:00 MIDNIGHT

The silence after that stretched tighter. Stennis broke it by saying softly, "I know it's big to think about. Let's go up. I've got some material you'll want to see."

Farrow grunted dubiously. The night guard let them out of the banking department of the building through a side door into the State Street foyer, where they rode an elevator up to the top floor. Farrow's forehead was ridged deep in thought and his eyes were distant.

Sunhill Investment Corporation appeared to occupy all of the seventh floor of the Stennis Building. Farrow followed the older man through a lavish series of connecting offices, reception areas, and conference rooms, all done in blond mahogany and hunting-print wallpaper. But behind Stennis' own executive quarters was a smaller room, almost undecorated and with a single window facing the Hudson River. The only furnishings were a couch, a straight chair, and an old filing cabinet. "My cave," Stennis explained. "Sort of a hiding place. I come in here to do my private thinking." It was more to Farrow's taste than anything he'd seen in three days.

On the wall was a single picture, an enlarged fuzzy photograph of two men standing by the carcass of an elephant. One of the men was Stennis himself, his face younger. The other was Farrow. Farrow stood and looked at the picture for a while. It had been a long time ago.

Stennis said, "Yes, that's the same elephant. I don't forget it, Jacob."

"Your chief fault, then and now. You always took too long a chance."

"You saved my life then. Will you do just as much for me now?"

Farrow turned around and eyed him quizzically. "Walt, I might as well be blunt. I think your loss has put you a bit off your rocker. I think you're doing again what you did with that bull in the picture. Rushing into a bad situation without considering."

"Maybe, maybe not. I didn't get where I am today by being orthodox, I'll tell you. On occasion I've even skirted the law because there come times when the law doesn't provide. The law isn't providing for me now. The rules of this century don't allow for a personal revenge. And that's what I want, a personal revenge. My son's death was personal and I saw it happen. I want the same for Bocock, to be caused by me. There's only one restriction I'll put on you, Jacob—when you've tracked him down, I want to see his death, be in at the kill."

"Revenge and good hunting don't mix. There are only two reasons to hunt, for food or for sport. Since this Clel Bocock is a man, he doesn't fit either category."

"No," said Stennis emphatically. "He's not a man any longer in the sense that you and I are men. That's what you've got to remember. He's an animal, nothing more. By murdering, he's forfeited his human estate. He's free game to anyone with guts enough to go after him."

Again Farrow grunted doubtfully.

Stennis said, "My God, you're not going to hold up a lot of moral objections, are you?"

"No." Farrow lowered himself to the couch and sat there, hands clasped in a single large fist between his knees. "No, I don't know that morality has much to do with it, Walt. I'm a hunter. I will admit that you're appealing to the worst side of me, I think. Every professional hunter wonders at one time or another how it would be to hunt game that can shoot back."

"But you're not sold on it."

"No, I'm not. I can't believe you're thinking clearly. There already must be thousands of police on Bocock's trail. They know their terrain and they've hunted criminals before. I'm a stranger to all that."

Stennis made a brushing gesture, as if those objections were gnats. "The metropolitan cops and the county and state forces and the FBI have all been on the job two weeks. They've accomplished exactly nothing. Could you do any *worse* than that? Bocock is a country boy, right out of the Georgia swamps. You're bound to understand him better—how he thinks, where he'll hide—than these city people who are chasing him."

"And perhaps I'd fail, Walt. My pride wouldn't like that."

"I'm gambling a lot of money on the fact that you've never failed." Stennis paced up and down. "We'd have to maintain a certain amount of secrecy, of course. Any publicity would lessen your value. I've prepared credentials establishing you as a bank investigator, but I don't think you'll need them. The man who kills Clel Bocock is performing a public service. I have traveler's checks made out in your name; they're in my desk out there. The Lincoln downstairs is the hunting car I've used in Canada. It's a beauty, Jacob. The trunk is stocked with any camping supplies you might need, and behind the rear seat is a rack for your rifles. The car can go anywhere and—"

"You think it will be a long trek, then."

Stennis' face had been like his voice, intense, anxious, striving for confidence. Now it relaxed slightly with a short grateful smile. He said, "I knew you'd agree, Jacob. It can be done, and you're the one who can do it."

"I didn't say that. I asked your opinion on the extent of the thing."

But Stennis was heartened. "Yes, it'll probably take time and travel. I know you never count on luck. The Bocock gang isn't in this part of the country, that we know for sure. A week ago they knocked over a bank in Jefferson City, Missouri. A teller got shotgun wounds from that trigger-happy Mouse bastard and the whole gang got away clean again. That's when I sent Osher off after you."

"That's strange," Farrow muttered. Stennis raised his eyebrows. "I mean, strange they'd strike so soon after making off with so much here. Why wouldn't such badly wanted outlaws be satisfied with a hundred and twenty thousand dollars for a while?"

Stennis twisted his mouth scornfully. "You'll learn that Bocock isn't noted for brains. Just ego—with a gun. Let me show you what his pack is like." From the filing cabinet he drew some bulging manila folders and some scrapbooks. "I've had the best outfits across the country researching for me. Private detectives and clipping bureaus and.... Maybe I have gone a little crazy, Jacob. I've sorted and arranged and rearranged this stuff until my eyes ached. All to find out what makes Bocock and his friends tick. But, by God, I've got a right to my obsession."

"Yes," said Farrow. He examined the first batch of pictures, clipped from newspapers, Sunday supplements, magazines. First was a blank-faced youthful member of the gang, Larry Sidell, old enough to have a sneer but not a personality. Stennis commented, "Sold papers till a few months ago, when he fell in with Bocock."

Farrow inspected the second man, who, with Sidell, had guarded the getaway cars. "Nicholas Mellick," said Stennis. "Known as Prof Nick. A confidence man, first time at armed robbery. Somehow Bocock persuaded him to change his ways." A debonair man gone to flesh, long greasy-looking hair with sideburns. It would be dyed hair, for the aging Prof Nick had vanity lined on his face.

"Number three. James Egan, Mouse Egan." He was a little fellow, pimply, bucktoothed, broad of forehead and jaw but narrow in between, as if his head had been squeezed at birth. Even in the graceless prison photos he had a wild-eyed look. "Ex-con. A killer even before what happened downstairs. Narcotics addict and a mad dog with that damned shotgun."

And then there was Vito Duccone, an ape in a pinstriped suit. "Bocock's right hand," said Stennis. "Suspected of everything, convicted of nothing. Got quite a bit on him from the Creme Agency in Chicago. Duccone is the gang's principal contact with the underworld. He's been around a long time. He probably helped found hell." Bocock's adjutant wore a broad insinuating smile in every picture. The smile only made the flat, jowly face more sinister. His bald head gleamed from within a fringe of black hair.

"Those are the assistant devils."

"Nice lot," Farrow said softly.

"Here is the head man. McClellan Bocock himself." Farrow separated the final batch of pictures carefully and spread them out on the couch. He noticed the eyes first, large and round and glittering. Yet, even at secondhand, they had a dark melting look, persuasive.

Farrow said, "I'd imagine he's hell with the ladies."

"I don't have anything on that. He's a drifter, never could find a place to light. Comes from a share-cropper family, according to the write-ups. The newspapers have made a lot of his child bride, romanticizing him and his parents. The Bocock clan like to talk to reporters about him, it seems, though I doubt if they can read the interviews."

Clel Bocock was tall and slim, twenty-five years old. He had a rather pale, willful face. Under the compelling eyes, his cheekbones were high and slanted jauntily. When he smiled, his full lips parted crookedly at the left side. His hair was thick and curly and black, and one lock seemed trained to hang down over his forehead. In three different pictures, he was wearing a black sport shirt with white piping, giving him a cavalier air. Women would consider him handsome; men would know he was dangerous. Farrow stared for a long time into the deep demanding eyes.

"And he's a pretty deadly shot," said Stennis abruptly.

"I'm not surprised," Farrow murmured. From the river a ship's whistle wailed long and mournfully.

"I know what you must be thinking, Jacob. It's really my job to do, not yours. I wounded the animal and I should be the one to follow in and finish him off. But I'm scared that I haven't got the talent; all I've got is the money to get it done. I've got too old."

Farrow was embarrassed. He growled, "Never mind that, Walt. Let me think." He wanted to do it for friendship's sake. He put that part of it aside and tried to consider the project as just another job. When he did that, he found his heart beat a little faster. The pay was good and there was certainly nothing for him in Kenya this year. Here, the terrain would be unfamiliar but speedy to travel; although, like most of his profession, he disliked hunting by car. And the quarry—a wild beast with a gun.... In the end Farrow said slowly, "Well, I've always considered myself a professional. Perhaps this is the acid test."

Stennis let out his breath. He said, "God bless you, Jacob," and touched his shoulder briefly. Then he was all business again. "The gang was last seen in Missouri. In Missouri I've got the two big branches of Global—"

"No," said Farrow. "I'm not going there. I think we can trust the local police to thresh the areas where Bocock's been seen lately."

"But you've got to pick up the trail somewhere."

Farrow leafed idly through one of the scrapbooks of newspaper clippings, a chronological history of Bocock-led crime. "I've got to find out what the trail will be like. I'll get something out of your press articles and your investigators' reports, but they're still just so much written material. I need the feel of the quarry. Men leave spoor too, you know, and Bocock will act on the basis of his habits and environment like any other animal. I'll have to begin where Clel Bocock began, get to know him and how he reasons. I can take short cuts later, but I'll have to begin in Georgia."

"That won't do," objected Stennis. "That takes time. What if in the meantime the police should capture—"

Farrow chuckled. "You haven't changed at all, Walt. Quick decision, rush directly into trouble. No, I don't believe in your kind of long chances. Bocock may well be wounded. The only way to approach wounded game is from the rear."

Stennis looked unconvinced. But he shrugged tiredly and got an atlas out of the cabinet. "You're directing the hunt, Jacob. My part is to furnish what information I can." He spread the atlas to a two-page map of the United States. "You've got the whole continent for a game preserve, all yours. Here's Albany, where we are now. Down here is Waycross, Georgia." He figured rapidly. "About eleven hundred miles, say about thirty hours' driving time. If you leave tomorrow morning you should be in Waycross Tuesday evening. I'd suggest you fly, but you're going to need the car. I'll phone ahead and make hotel reservations for you."

"No need of that," Farrow demurred.

"It's something I can do," Stennis said fiercely. "Let me do what I can. Keep in touch with me and don't hesitate to draw on any of the people I've hired to help you."

Farrow nodded. He picked up the nearest sheaf of agency reports and started to read. "Odd way to begin a hunt," he murmured.

Stennis sat down beside him on the couch. He said, "Since this is the beginning, Jacob, let me wish you—good hunting."

Chapter Four

TUESDAY, MAY 1, 9:00 P.M.

When he kicked the oxfords off his feet one of them sailed all the way across the hotel room. He sauntered after it and remained by the window, sniffing the warm musky smell of the Georgia night. It was only the first of May, but the Waycross air had a heavy summery embrace. Insects buzzed and bumped against the screen and, three stories down, beneath the streetside oak trees, Farrow watched the slow promenade of pale white-clad girls and pale shirt-sleeved men.

He remembered that Clel Bocock had once been part of this picture. He left the window and flopped on the bed with his newspapers. Last night's Virginia paper carried a story, unconfirmed, that Clel Bocock had been sighted traveling alone through Arizona. This morning's South Carolina paper had a report, unconfirmed, that the entire Bocock gang had escaped into Canada.

Only the Waycross *Journal Herald*, which he'd bought a few minutes before, seemed of value. It headlined another bank raid today, this time in Butte, Montana, and the raiders were the Bocock gang. This was no rumor or guess, for they had left behind one of their members, dead. Larry Sidell, the blank-faced newsboy, had been chopped down by a bank guard's bullets.

"And then there were four," murmured Farrow. Butte, Montana, was a long way from Waycross, Georgia. He thought of calling Walter Stennis but decided against it. Stennis would want him to rush out to Montana, just as he had wanted him to rush out to Missouri. Bad policy; you had to stalk slowly or you missed important details. Farrow wiggled his toes comfortably, relaxing from the two-day drive. Tomorrow he would visit the Bocock family. Tomorrow he would wear his safari boots under his trousers. He'd had enough of the oxfords.

His head jerked up at a fumbling scratching noise. He looked at the doorknob. It was turning back and forth erratically. He wasn't in the habit of locking doors; he hadn't locked this one. It swung open.

Farrow got off the bed quickly. He said, "I beg your pardon."

A girl stood in the doorway, holding onto the jamb for support. Her head was bowed so that her long hair hung, screening her face. It was thick blonde hair, the tawny yellow color of a young lioness; although badly mussed, it shimmered prettily in the lamplight. The girl had no dress on. From behind the screen of hair her voice muttered thickly, "I know I shouldn't have come here...."

Farrow grunted stupidly, staring at her. She seemed to have been having a wild time, although he hadn't heard the noise of any party nearby. He could smell the whisky reeking from her. Besides her dress, she had also lost one of her high-heeled slippers. The elastic of her white half-slip was canted across the soft skin of her abdomen, emphasizing the narrow bow of her hips. Her breasts were less girlish and, since the straps had drooped beyond modesty, they were only half captured by her brassiere, white silk below, white lace above.

Farrow said, "You have the wrong room, miss. Which number were—"

"Oh," she breathed, and he caught her as her knees struck the floor. He lifted her onto the bed. She was a small creature, easy to carry. She sat on the edge of the bed and clumsily swept her hair out of her face and mumbled, "I just wanted to find out."

"No doubt," said Farrow dryly. He rubbed his nose at the nearness of the whisky smell; it wasn't even good whisky. Then he ambled to the door and looked up and down the hotel corridor, perplexed. None of the other doors was open and there was nobody out looking for her.

The girl was giggling. "No shoe," she said. "No shoe." Farrow went back to her, leaving his door wide in case her boy friend should come along to claim her. She lifted her face while he was staring at her some more and she tried to focus on him. Her eyes were gray, but darker and softer than his own, and with sooty curved lashes. He said, for his own benefit, "You know, you're something of a beauty."

Her pink full mouth giggled again while her eyes blinked and fought the liquor. It was evidently her first all-out encounter, for her fine-boned face showed no signs of dissipation. Her nose was narrow and short with gently flaring nostrils. At each side of her high smooth forehead the temple indented delicately. Her chin was small and firm and gently cleft. And her throat curved downward.

Farrow flushed, then chuckled at himself. He said, "You don't know it, beauty, but I've been taking advantage." He leaned over her, making no sudden movements. "Here. Don't panic on me. I'm just being a damn fine gentleman."

The girl paid no attention while he tugged the drooping straps up onto her shoulders. When the rosy tips of her breasts were behind lace again, she suddenly hugged herself to his arm. "Don't go away!" she quavered. "Don't go away!"

Her skin was satiny and moistly warm against his bare forearm. She was perspiring, and with the female smell a faint beat of desire rose in him. He let her hold herself against his arm and looked at the open door and chewed his lip. He smiled down at her. "I wish you'd had less to drink, young lady. Where can I find your sweetheart? Who's the fellow who brought you?"

She began to sob loudly. "I want to go home. I want to go home." Tears rolled freely down her cheeks and into the corners of her mouth.

He extricated his arm and went to his suitcase. He thought he understood. A young girl, not over twenty, out on a clandestine adventure, and suddenly her fogged brain was scared, wanting to run.... He dug out his rain cape and stood her up and wrapped her in it. He told her, slowly and distinctly, "You're going home now. Where do you live?"

She stopped sobbing. She lifted her chin and whispered, "I'm an Ingram." Then she retched.

Farrow sighed. "Perhaps fresh air will bring you around." The girl managed to remain standing while he laced on his safari boots and rolled down his shirt sleeves and put on his coat. He locked his arm around her waist and walked her down the hall to the back stairs. In the hall he discovered her other slipper and fitted it on her. His rain cape still dragged a short train behind her, but in two shoes she staggered less.

He got her down to the hotel garage and into the Lincoln without encountering anyone but the garage attendant. The attendant, a yellow-faced Negro, glanced away from the girl quickly. Farrow handed him a dollar.

"I'm going out for a short time. It'd be very kind of you to forget about it." The Negro grinned slyly and put his hands over his eyes and then laughed.

Farrow drove in a circle around town, the girl huddled beside him, occasionally shuddering with nausea. Waycross was a small clean warehouse city of some sixteen thousand inhabitants and countless railroad crossings. The girl, her head hanging out the window, gave him no help as to directions. Finally he pulled over to the side and slapped her face a few times. She didn't seem to mind. He stopped the light slaps and drew back from her when he realized again that he liked to touch her smooth skin.

After she had vomited out the door, her eyes and voice cleared a little. He could distinguish the regional drawl when she asked, "Who are you, anyway?"

"A bloody Samaritan. How do we reach your home, can you tell me?"

"I don't know you," she mumbled plaintively, but she indicated a southbound highway and they drove out into the dark countryside. She leaned forward, her nose almost against the windshield, squinting at the lightless farmhouses passing by. "No," she said to each one. After several miles, she said, "Yes."

Farrow pulled up but there was no habitation in sight, only a clump of cypress trees growing close to the road. He could smell water and he guessed they were near the border of the huge Okefenokee Swamp he'd seen on his maps. The night out here was peaceful and uncivilized, rustling pleasantly and sounding of katydids and owls. He said, "I can't leave you out here alone."

The girl opened the door and slid clumsily out of the car, leaving his rain cape on the seat. "It's just around the bend." Her head ducked, voice muffled with shame. "I daren't go in the front way. I have to sneak."

He looked at her pretty, half-clad body. "I suppose you know best."

She took off her high-heeled slippers. "No, I don't know best. But you been right nice to me, anyway." She turned away in her stocking feet, carrying her slippers. Farrow watched her move off through the tall grass, fireflies milling about the pale slim shape of her back and the half-slip. Her footing seemed surer in the undergrowth, as if she were accustomed to it. He called, "Good night," but she didn't answer, and presently she vanished like a nymph among the cypress.

He turned the Lincoln around and drove back to the hotel. The garage Negro ventured a small sly smile. Farrow went up to his room on the third floor. He had left the door unlocked again, and a stranger sat in the easy chair, smoking a cigarette.

"Hi there," the stranger said without getting up. "Been waiting for you." He grinned, showing two gold teeth on one side. He was a big blond young man, beefily handsome. He was dressed sportily and on his upper lip he had cultivated a dainty mustache of silky blond hairs that were scarcely visible. It looked like a line of frost above his mouth. The hat on the back of his head had a red and green feather in the band.

"Now I've arrived," said Farrow. He didn't like his visitor's clever blue eyes or his gritty un-Southern voice.

"So I do perceive." The blond young man laughed at nothing. "I'm the lad from down the hall, Three-nineteen. Where is she?"

"She?" Farrow saw the bundle in the stranger's lap. A black taffeta dress, rolled carelessly.

"You bet. My girl friend. Here I had her all primed, and you, you dog, made off with her." Still the grin. "That's according to the lad down in the garage."

Farrow reflected stonily about the garage attendant. "A dollar doesn't buy much, does it?"

"What about my girl? Going to bring her back?"

"No, I'm not going to bring her back. She asked me to take her home and I did."

"Ooh." The blond man grimaced disgustedly, grinned some more. "One hell of a note. Not that I blame you understand. But I never thought she'd pull a runout just when she was getting going good. Just shows you never can tell about the female sex."

They regarded each other. Farrow said coldly, "Sorry to spoil your plans." All he felt was a wistful disappointment with the girl's taste.

"Well, hell, what's a night's work, more or less?" The blond man punched out his cigarette in the ash tray, stretched to his feet. "So we'll just call it a continued story. What happened was I went down for another bottle and when I came back the bed was empty. Anyway, I still got the bottle." He grinned down at the dress he held. "And part of her clothes. Here, you might as well have this too." He tossed the dress to Farrow.

Farrow caught the garment with both hands. The throwing motion brought the stranger a step closer, and his fist lashed out deftly. Farrow opened his mouth at the explosion above his ear and sank to his knees. Dimly he saw the plaited leather blackjack dangling from the man's hand. The gritty voice said, "Maybe next time you'll mind your own goddamn business." The blackjack rang above his ear again and Farrow collapsed to his hands and knees. He stayed that way a moment before he tumbled forward into blackness.

His face was cushioned in something soft that had a feminine smell. When he opened his eyes he found it was the black taffeta dress. Farrow struggled upright, head aching. The stranger was gone and the room door was closed. Farrow didn't know how long he had been unconscious. He looked in the bureau mirror, at the swollen mass over his left ear. It hadn't blued and he doubted that it would; he didn't bruise easily. But his face was crimson with rage.

He flung the dress into his suitcase and then groped deeper. His belongings had been disarranged a little, but nothing was missing. His big hands began to shake with this additional anger, that his possessions had been tampered with. Muttering incoherently to himself, he drew out his .38 automatic, his snake-killing pistol, and pumped a cartridge into the chamber. He buckled its belt and holster around his waist under his tweed coat. With the coat buttoned the gun didn't show too much.

He marched down the corridor to Room 319 and rapped at the door. No light showed; no one answered. Grimly, he strode down the stairs and routed out the night clerk. The clerk scratched his head. "Nobody in Three-nineteen now. We had a fellow from up North—Chicago—in there, but he checked out about an hour ago." He made sucking sounds over his file cards. "By name of Sam Augustine. That who you looking for?"

"I believe so," Farrow growled. "Thank you." He went back upstairs and sat on his bed holding his head. The throbbing made thinking difficult. He didn't know how to go about finding Sam Augustine, and all he could hope was that he'd come across him accidentally.

He lay back and tried to sleep. But the distant pounding of a night-shift lumber mill crept into his head like a drum. He cursed it and finally went downstairs to the garage and got out the Lincoln again.

He drove south for the second time that night. He had no trouble finding the peaceful spot where he'd let out the girl. He parked off the road and estimated the weather and unpacked a blanket from the car's trunk. He spread it alongside the looming cypress grove and rolled up in it.

Staring up at the lonely sky, Farrow felt as if he'd come home. He listened to the owls at hunt and wondered if the girl might not reappear as she had vanished, a slim-hipped desirable dream drifting out of the whispering trees. Suddenly the past week was unreal and the desire he'd felt for the helpless girl was least real of all. Even the stars, diamond chips on velvet, were strangers. He fell asleep with his hand on his gun.

Chapter Five

WEDNESDAY, MAY 2, 9:00 A.M.

A short gentle rain woke him at dawn. The hot sun came out immediately. Farrow's first act was to examine the tender spot above his ear. He decided it wouldn't be noticeable. He breakfasted on some tinned goods in the car, shaved at a rivulet in the cypress grove, and then sat in the back seat of the Lincoln, sedulously cleaning his rifles. He wanted to give the Bocock family time to do their morning chores.

At nine o'clock, having stored his pistol and holster belt in the car's glove compartment, Farrow sauntered out onto the highway and hailed a produce truck coming from Waycross. The driver, a sallow youngster chewing tobacco, thought he was joking at first. Then he said, "You've parked your car on Bocock land, mister. The farm itself is just around the bend. You'll see a postbox says Campbell Grey Bocock on it."

"Thank you." When the truck had pulled off, Farrow turned around and stared wonderingly at the cypress grove. Here he had brought the drunken Ingram girl home—to Bocock property. He had spent the night on it. He shook his head, puzzled, as he drove around the bend to the postbox.

He could see the farmhouse from the road. It was a newly painted white frame box with a pitched roof and a veranda, far nicer than the news reports had led him to believe. He estimated it had four rooms on each side of the dogtrot, the open-end tunnel through the middle of the house. The dwelling sat on low brick pilings amid about four acres of cultivation. No more than a half acre was devoted to any one crop. As Farrow drove into the lane, a grove behind the farmhouse came into view, with several rows of whitewashed box hives.

A thick lazy drawl said, "Hold up there a minute."

Farrow braked the car. He was at the end of the lane, fifty yards from the house. He looked around for the speaker. A small skinny Negro had been squatting behind a screen of tobacco plants and now he got up and poked the twin barrels of a shotgun in Farrow's direction. Two leather leashes were wrapped around his left wrist, leashes strained tight as they held back a pair of vicious-looking beagles. The dogs didn't growl but their fangs were bared and ready.

Farrow kept his hands in sight. He said, "Good morning. I've come to see Mr. and Mrs. Bocock."

"I'm Des," the Negro said. "Get out so I can look at you better." Farrow carefully let himself out of the car and the two men looked at each other. Farrow thought the black, with his wiry frame and lean shanks, would make an excellent bearer.

"You was foolish to come here," Des said. "I know you're the man been causing us trouble." He whistled sharply. From among the beehives in the grove of tupelo trees another man came running. He pulled off his thick gloves as he came and then the netted hat that protected his face and neck from stings. He was an elderly white man, gaunt and leathery, with bushy white hair and a mouth distended by false teeth. And from the farmhouse itself emerged a big-busted powerful woman of about the same age, wiping her reddish hands on her apron as she crossed the veranda.

She stared at Farrow grimly while the man from the beehives closed in. He stopped several paces away and stuck his thumbs in his overall pockets and looked Farrow up and down. Then, without turning his head or shifting his yellowish eyes, he called to the woman on the veranda, "I think we got him, Mother!"

Farrow said, "I'm afraid you've made a mistake. I've come here from—"

"Shut your mouth," slurred the bee man. "Mother's saying something." He called, "What did you say?"

The woman on the porch appeared to be listening to someone within the house. Then she shouted, "Marget says no, Daddy."

Des murmured, "Then he ain't the one, after all." He lowered the shotgun and clucked to the dogs. They subsided watchfully. The elderly man wiped his hands on his work gloves. He nodded to Farrow. "I apologize for telling you to shut your mouth. I reckon we've acted poorly and through no fault of yours. Can I help you locate anybody you're looking for?"

"Perhaps your name is Bocock."

"I'm C. G. Bocock." The yellowish eyes had frozen over. "Clel's daddy. Might I ask if you're another law man?"

"My name is Jacob Farrow. I'm a journalist."

Farrow was not practiced at lying; even as he spoke it seemed preposterous that anyone would believe him. But the elder Bocock grinned slowly and then straightened his round shoulders to shake hands formally, he drawled, "Come into the house, Mr. Farrow. It's our pleasure and my wife is probably dying of curiosity by now."

Des settled down behind the tobacco plants, again on guard. Farrow and Clel Bocock's father walked to the house and up onto the porch. The mother waited there, formidably, her fat freckled arms folded. She was broad of face and body, taller than her husband, with sandy gray hair bunned in back. Farrow looked at her and saw Clel Bocock's eyes, deep and magnetic, and Clel Bocock's full-lipped mouth. When Farrow was introduced, she smiled genially and it was the same crooked smile.

Farrow said he was from Reuters. "Roy-ters," she repeated. She didn't understand, but she wasn't going to ask what it was. He added quickly that is was the British news agency.

Her round face beamed with delight. "British! I wondered why you're so different from the others been hanging around here. So now Clel has like to have got himself internationally famous. Come in, come in, please."

There was no question about whether the Bococks would discuss their son. They were childishly proud of Clel. Farrow, an utter stranger, became an honored guest as soon as he'd said he was a newspaperman. Mother Bocock ushered him into the cool dogtrot and opened the first screen door to the left. "Come along, Daddy. Did you tell Mr. Farrow we're sorry for what happened with Des? We thought you might be a meddler."

"Or a cop," said Daddy Bocock softly. "Neither kind is welcome on our land."

The living room was neat and dim and full of respectable old furniture. "Please take the big chair," urged Mother Bocock. "We ain't people to make trouble, but there's a stranger has been pestering Marget, she says. We been hoping he'd show his face out here. A big man with a mustache, Mr. Farrow, like you. I hope you excuse our mistake. Marget, we got company!"

Across the room, the girl stood stiffly by a window. She was sober this morning and her tawny yellow hair was combed impeccably to her shoulders. Her dark gray eyes, apprehensive but not afraid, clung to Farrow's. He nodded solemnly and sat down as soon as she sank primly into a straight chair. They couldn't keep their eyes off one another and Farrow thought he remembered every line of her full-breasted body under her cotton print frock. He said, "How do you do, Miss...." Then he waited for somebody to fill in the information.

Mother Bocock did it. "Mr. Farrow, this is another Mrs. Bocock. This is Marget, Clel's wife."

He blinked but no one noticed it aside from the girl. She flushed faintly but greeted him politely. It was plain that she remembered last night. Farrow guessed that she hadn't told the Bococks about that drunken adventure. But he couldn't make sense of her actions. She had apparently claimed to have been annoyed by Sam Augustine, a big man with a mustache.

Yet last night she—Clel Bocock's wife—had been romping in a hotel room with the Chicago man. Why?

Mother Bocock noticed Farrow's scrutiny. She chuckled heartily, settling in a rocker. "I reckon you're surprised to meet Marget, Mr. Farrow. I reckon you've read those worthless made-up lies of some of the other reporters, about her being a child bride and the like. Lord, she was eighteen when Clel married her. And she's an Ingram from Folkston." From the way she said it, it meant a great deal.

"Judge Ingram's daughter," Daddy Bocock added. His false teeth clicked slightly as he talked in his soft fierce voice. "We resent some of the things that have been written about us, Mr. Farrow, although the stories have done right well by my son, which is as it should be. But none of us is white trash or share-croppers, as you might have read. Marget is a daughter of Judge Ingram, who used to have a place down the road. She and Clel grew up together, mostly."

Marget smiled, a little woodenly. "I'm sure that Mr. Farrow didn't come all this way to hear about me."

"Might as well git it right," Mother Bocock said stubbornly. "We don't want folks in foreign countries reading the wrong things about us. We ain't share-croppers, Mr. Farrow. Bococks have always owned this land."

"Finest bee farm this side of Waycross," said Daddy Bocock. "Forty hives making the best tupelo-blossom honey in Ware County."

And they talked together. Farrow had been uncertain as to his prowess at deception, but his worries proved baseless. The Bococks were country people and so was he. He sat relaxed in the warm dim living room and listened to Mother Bocock tell about her son, and sometimes the father drawled a re-mark. The farmers had no trouble talking to the hunter because none of them was afraid of comfortable silences.

And yet Farrow didn't feel right about it. He hadn't expected to like these people, but he did, and, what was more, they trusted him. He was their kind, which the other reporters and interviewers hadn't been. He felt like a new Judas. He preferred Marget's attitude. The girl watched him constantly; if not openly hostile, she was at least wary.

Once she interposed, "Mr. Farrow, why are you interested in Clel's where-abouts?"

Mother Bocock laughed. "Lord, Marget, the whole world would like to know where Clel is. And Mr. Farrow's writing his story about Clel, ain't he?" Marget sat in her private silence once more, her eyes on the intruder, and Farrow began to fear her intuition. Perhaps the wife was closest of all to Clel Bocock, flesh of his flesh; perhaps Marget alone could sense the death that stalked with Farrow.

"Not that I'd say anything, if I knew," Mother Bocock went on. "But frankly, none of us know where Clel is. I'll tell you this—no cop will ever catch him. So long as he stays out in the open, under God's sky, he won't be seen no more than a lizard on a rock. Like all of us around here, Clel grew up poaching in the swamp"—a lazy gesture to the south—"and there never was a cleverer brush-hunter heard of around here."

"Of course," began the old man wistfully, and then worked his mouth con-templatively over his teeth while the others waited patiently, "we'd have rather he'd stayed in this locality, with us."

"I'm not saying Clel is perfect," Mother Bocock chided him. "None of us is that. He was always restless, even as a boy, and maybe too fond of excite-ment. He could never settle down like our other boys. They all live in towns now, Mr. Farrow, some of them even up North. But Clel liked to keep on the go. And now he's made the whole United States of America his swamp. Yes,

it seems strange to a mother, not knowing where her own boy is. Always before when he was away, he used to write regular and often. That was a lot of
comfort."

It was hard for Farrow to remember they were talking about a bank robber and murderer. He listened to anecdotes about a handsome youngster who
was always well liked and not easily satisfied. A quiet-walking boy with
dreaming eyes....

"You're not taking notes, Mr. Farrow," said Marget. "All the other reporters took notes. May I get you a pencil?"

She knew. Somehow she knew. Farrow said, stammering slightly, "No,
thank you, ah—Mrs. Bocock. I find this method more effective, at least for
me."

"It certainly suits me," said Mother Bocock. "I wish the +others had been
as gentlemanly as you, Mr. Farrow."

Farrow's eyes were deep in the girl's. Involuntarily but with instinctive
meaning, his gaze dropped to the cotton material holding her ripe bosom,
lower to the slight gully of the frock across her lap. The girl stiffened almost
imperceptibly, tightening her thighs together, and when he brought his
eyes up to hers again, a sort of electricity between them shamed them both.
It was as if they sat before each other naked.

Mother Bocock was saying, "About the next thing was when Clel came
home from Chicago. Two years ago, September. For once he was tired of traveling and all he wanted was to settle down here and farm the land and maybe
take a few furs out of the Okefenokee. He would've made a good living and
we were all right pleased."

Marget said she would see about getting dinner and left the room. Farrow
watched her go. He thought about last night when she had undressed for Sam
Augustine, ready to make love to him, but she had drunk too much.

Mother Bocock said warmly, "And that was when Clel and Marget got
married. Not that it was anything sudden. They'd been promised all their
lives. She's a fine girl, and loyal. She left the university to come back here and
live with us just because she thought Clel's folks might need her. No mother
could ask for a finer daughter-in-law and no husband could ask for a more loving wife." Suddenly, "You will stay for dinner with us, won't you, Mr. Farrow? Marget's setting a place."

He hesitated and Mother Bocock said, "Afterwards I'll show you something about Clel, something the rest of them ain't ever seen or suspected."
That settled it. The dining room was directly behind the living room and they
all ate around a huge circular table. It was a leisurely filling meal, and the Negro Des ate the same fare in the kitchen. Afterward Des returned to his vigil
and the two women did the dishes while Daddy Bocock and his guest sat in
peace in the living room. Daddy Bocock showed his scrapbook of news clippings about Clel and Farrow examined it politely, unable to forget that Wal-

ter Stennis kept the same kind of scrapbook.

Then Daddy Bocock had fallen asleep in his chair and the rattle of dishes ceased from the kitchen and Mother Bocock returned, wiping her hands, to usher Farrow out into the dogtrot. Marget had vanished. Mother Bocock said, "I hope you can make people understand, Mr. Farrow. About Clel, just how alive he was—is. Yet he never did anything to anybody, unless they harmed him first. He was never one to constantly be smoking and drinking and carousing around." She winked. "Not that the girls wasn't always chasing him."

The bedrooms were all on the south side of the dogtrot. She opened the door to the rear one. "Keep it just the way it was," said Mother Bocock tenderly. "He may come home someday."

Farrow didn't say anything. All the maternal love in the big old woman had blinded her to the terrible fact that Clel Bocock could never come home. He looked around the small room and was disappointed. The place was obviously unused but as scrupulously neat as the rest of the house. A spool bed, a dresser, a single-shot rifle on the wall, dungarees hanging in the box closet. But there was nothing special that Farrow could see; any of the Bocock sons might have grown up here, the older brothers who had become honest citizens of various towns. In the frame of the dresser mirror were wedged a couple of snapshots of young Clel. One was a publicized crooked-smiling picture in the familiar black sport shirt with white piping, the curly black lock self-consciously emphasizing his pale forehead. The other showed a ten-year-old boy with a spoiled round face, thick lips unsmiling, looking childishly savage. He wore a little cowboy hat and a bandanna around his neck and—already— a toy oilcloth holster on his hip, his chubby hand on the cap pistol.

"This is what I mentioned, Mr. Farrow," said Mother Bocock. She had opened a bottom drawer. "You're the first to see these—outside of the family, of course. All the picture postcards Clel ever sent me. I get them out and look at them right often."

Farrow untied the string with rising interest. Despite what Mother Bocock had said about Clel writing frequently, there weren't many cards and the messages were brief hasty scrawls. "Dear Mother…. Your loving son, Clel." No two cards came from the same place. Farrow examined both sides of all of them, especially those from places that the news stories hadn't given much play as part of Bocock's past history. One card had a picture of a Chicago hotel where he had worked as a bellhop; Farrow couldn't remember the hotel's having been mentioned in Stennis' clippings and reports. Another showed a municipal building in Cedar Rapids; Bocock had worked nearby on a wheat combine, according to the message. Another, with a desert scene, claimed that Clel Bocock had got a job as geologist with a Standard Oil field expedition. The postmark on that one was Barstow, California.

The messages were nearly all in the same vein: "Feeling fine and hope that you and Daddy are the same. Got a swell job now. Soon as this deal comes through I'll be sitting pretty.... Your loving son, Clel."

The final card was dated nearly a year and a half ago, after Clel had married Marget Ingram and then wandered off again. It was postmarked Cleveland and its tone was less breezy than before. "You know nobody is going to push me around for long. Have been thinking I need a change of luck (ha-ha!). Maybe try it with Little Jumbo again. Had fun in those days and I still think there is my fortune to be made."

"Who or what is Little Jumbo?" Farrow asked.

Mother Bocock shrugged. "I don't remember he ever got around to telling any of us. Clel often had a pet name for people he liked." She chuckled a little self-consciously. "Around home here he used to call me Sugar."

Again Farrow felt the pang of dislike for what he was doing to these people. Then he heard Marget's step along the dogtrot, walking rather heavily for her. Farrow moved to get a window view. He saw her crossing the back fields toward the south. She wore short boots and a denim skirt and a shirt. She carried a light rifle and she glanced back toward the house as she disappeared among the tupelo trees.

Mother Bocock, tying up her picture cards, hadn't seen. Farrow took the opportunity to thank her for her trouble and to make his good-bys. She was reluctant to see him leave, wished he were going to be in town more than a couple of days, and walked with him as far as the veranda. Daddy Bocock still slept in the living room, his false teeth making faint rhythmic noises.

As Farrow got into his car, Mother Bocock called, "Now, you do right by Clel, mind! Come back and see us!" Farrow waved.

He drove south on the highway until he was out of sight of the farm. Then he parked off the road and plunged into the undergrowth. He moved swiftly, but silently too, with all his veldt-bred caution.

He crossed the girl's trail as he had planned. The marsh grass was still slightly bent where she had walked moments before. He followed the track until it ended at the edge of a silent lagoon. There were marks on the bank where a narrow boat had been launched and poled away. For a long while he crouched by the spot, waiting. But Marget didn't return and there was no expedient way to follow her. Not today.

Thoughtfully, Farrow returned to his car. For the first time he could feel the excitement of the chase warming his blood, hurrying his pulse. And he no longer felt so bad about his treasonous meal with the Bococks. He had a strong happy idea that they had fooled him up till now, and that Clel Bocock had come home to the swamp, after all.

Chapter Six

THURSDAY, MAY 3, 2:00 P.M.

Farrow was a patient man. The next day, Thursday, he returned to the lagoon on the edge of the swamp and seated himself behind a rampart of wild muscadine. Through the viny tangle he had a good view of the duck punt dragged up on the bank, a long slender boat that drew only four inches. He began his wait in midmorning. The sun blazed higher and higher and he sat immobile, moving only to brush away chiggers.

He had spent the night before in his Waycross hotel room, remembering to lock the door. He had slept despite the lumber mill. Today he didn't much resemble the tweedy British journalist who had visited the Bocock farm. He wore a battered felt hat, a faded khaki shirt mottled with old sweat stains, and waterproof breeches. His moccasins reached to his knees. They were more silent than boots, better than boots for this soggy *vlei* country, as he thought of the swamp. He had hunted the Rufiji River delta for hippopotamus, and this region was much the same. From his neck hung binoculars and across his lap lay his light carbine.

As the humid afternoon approached two o'clock he heard Marget coming. He smiled a little. He hadn't been certain that her excursions into the swamp were a daily occurrence. If she hadn't appeared today he would have kept his vigil the next day and the next. Every hunting instinct told him her movements had a purpose.

He watched her pole the duck punt onto the still waters of the lagoon. A few yards from shore she stopped propelling the boat and let it drift. She stood there gazing back the way she'd come, head slightly cocked, listening. Farrow felt satisfied. She had no intention of being followed, which meant she had a destination in mind. He sat like a big brown cross-legged statue, mottled by leaf shade, hardly breathing at all. Yet, unaccountably, he had a strong and strange desire to take deeper breaths as he looked at her, suck coolness clear down into his belly. It angered him, even as his loins warmed esoterically. He couldn't understand why the mere sight of the girl should make him feel like an animal. She was pretty and well made, but he had seen many more deliberately carnal women in his lifetime. But his hands tingled with perspiration as if he were caressing her thick yellow hair, and he watched the rise and fall of her breasts against the loose white shirt she wore. She was dressed in the same light-blue denim skirt and low boots he had seen the day before, and again she carried her small-caliber rifle.

Finally Marget tossed her head and leaned into the stern pole of the punt.

She had convinced herself she was alone. The shallow boat darted silently over the lagoon and Farrow was glad to learn, from the length of her strokes, that the water wasn't more than waist deep. As soon as she was out of sight around the first bend, he got to his feet and began to follow along the bank, bending low to take cover advantage of the high marsh grass. He reached the bend in time to see her disappear down a sluggish channel to the side. He approached the channel even more cautiously, followed its sinuous course through thicker undergrowth, and sighted her again. She was halfway across another smaller lagoon, her punt pointed toward a narrow gap in the dahoon holly trunks growing out of the water on the opposite shore.

Farrow circled and located her exit through the holly trees. But the next lagoon forked, and there was no indication which route Marget had taken. He wasn't perturbed. He looked around for an observation point and chose a moss-hung cypress that was taller than its neighbors. He swarmed up the thick trunk. When he was straddling a suitable crotch, he unslung his binoculars and scanned the tangled tropical vegetation.

He didn't expect to sight the girl herself. He was looking for signs of her passage along the labyrinth of waterways, a freshly broken branch or a boat trail through the white and gold lilies that mantled the lagoons in many places. He searched through the glasses for a while and then, magically, the punt with her yellow-haired figure glided into his circle of vision from beneath an overhang of cypress and tupelo. Marget poled onto the clear expanse of a small circular lake. She was headed for an island on the other side, a flat spit of white sand covered with scrub growth.

Farrow climbed to earth and began to trot along the southern fork of the lagoon. When it narrowed, he leaped across, plunging into black mud up to his ankles. He left the lagoon, traveling across marshy land in a direct line for the tiny lake. When he was nearly there, by guess, he climbed another tree, angering an industrious woodpecker. From here he had a clear view of the island, less than a hundred yards away now.

The sand spit was thickly grown in saw palmettos and slash palms; along the richer marginal ground there stood an occasional live oak or magnolia tree. Marget had beached her punt near one of the oaks, a dead gray giant blasted by some long-ago lightning bolt. She was standing at the water's edge, listening again. Farrow's heart beat with quick even throbs of expectancy. His binoculars brought her face so near that he could see the wary pucker of concentration between her eyebrows, the taut lines of her throat.

Then she turned to the cleft oak and groped her hand into its hollow, searching for something within. After a moment her hand came out empty. She started to turn away. And at that instant a man's hand reached around the trunk of the tree and closed over her wrist.

Farrow saw her mouth screaming before he heard the wail of terror. Then his body went rigid as he watched her struggle with the man who had seized her. A big blond man, his dapper sport suit muddied about the ankles—Sam Augustine of Chicago. Augustine was shouting at the girl as they wrestled, perhaps trying to calm her. But Marget broke out of his arms, kicking madly, twisting toward the rifle she'd left in the punt. Her flying skirt caught on a gnarl of oak trunk and held her trapped for an instant while Augustine caught her by the hair. He jerked her head back and cuffed her viciously across the face. She fell backward on the sand.

Farrow let his binoculars drop against his chest. He raised his carbine, his face a mask as it strained toward the V sight. Augustine stood unaware over the unconscious girl, scowling down at her while he got his breath. Farrow lowered his sight from Augustine's heart to his leg and deliberately put a bullet through the blond man's calf.

The clean crack of the carbine and Augustine's scream of pain mingled in echo across the swamp. He reeled and fell but was up again at once, dragging his left leg, trying to escape what he couldn't see. Farrow didn't fire again. Augustine, floundering with panic, careened into the palm growth and across the island, out of Farrow's vision. In a moment Farrow could hear him splashing through the water, then the crackle of underbrush as he reached the lake shore. Marget lay unmoving.

Farrow slipped to the ground, and waded into the lake. The cool water, dark brown from the acid of decaying vegetable matter, came only to his hips. A mat of dainty floating white-heart flowers broke about his legs as he slogged across.

He knelt on the sand by the girl. Her eyelids were beginning to tremble as she came close to consciousness. A faint pink color glowed on her cheek and lip where she'd been struck. She was sprawled on her back, sand in her hair, one knee upthrust. The oak gnarl had ripped the denim skirt nearly to her waistband, baring the bent leg completely. Farrow thought he'd never seen any flesh so helplessly nude as her round thigh, as pale and fine skinned as her forehead. He growled, "Damn you," and shoved her knee down so he could cover her leg with the skirt. Then the girl was staring up at him and he was embarrassed, seeing himself through her eyes, a clumsy foolish hulk.

But she didn't know what he had done. She whispered, "I don't know—" She sat up quickly, her eyes narrowing with recognition.

He said, "Don't be alarmed. I wasn't the one who hurt you."

"I know that. Where is he?"

"He ran off. I—ah, frightened him away."

"Oh." Marget dropped back to her elbows and a leftover sob of fear caught in her throat and then they stared at each other fixedly. She said slowly, "I reckon I should say thank you. But I don't know. I don't know about you."

He didn't say anything.

She said, "What you told us yesterday wasn't true. I could feel it then. You could no more be a newspaperman than you could fly. I knew you weren't even if he hadn't said you weren't."

"Sam Augustine told you that?"

"Just now. He sneaked out here. You sneaked out here. You all watch me all the time." She had a temper and it was beginning to redden her cheeks. But her voice remained soft and easy. "Who are you? How do you know him?"

"I've told you my name. I learned Augustine's name the night I took you home."

Marget blushed and glanced away for a second. "Well he tells me you're after Clel. He claims I'm selling Clel out to you. You are after Clel, aren't you? I can see it in your eyes. You've got the same look in your eyes that Clel has sometimes."

The comparison made Farrow uncomfortable. He sat back on his heels and said coldly, "I did save you from him, you know. Twice"—a deliberate foul—"if you choose to count the other night. But you prefer to believe what he tells you."

She blushed again and shook her head irritably. "I'm sorry. I'm grateful for what you've done. *Both* times, I want you to understand."

The torn skirt had slipped away again. They both became aware of it at the same instant and Marget sat bolt upright, covering herself quickly. But the gesture was more damning than the exposure; the idea lingered, encompassing them against their wills, an aura of sensual compulsion that clung and grew. The wild solitude they shared at that moment had an almost insidious freedom. The half-recumbent girl, the man squatting over her…. Farrow drew back sharply, but it didn't alter the primitive contrast between soft flesh and hard.

She tried to smile casually. "I have kind of bad luck with my clothes whenever you show up." It didn't sound as lighthearted as she had intended. When her words trailed off they were alone again, in the swamp's silence, which wasn't a stillness but instead the faint booming of a hundred natural sounds, the sough of embracing trees, the splash of water fowl, the singing of birds, and the distant bellow of an alligator, all mingled in a waiting, yearning spirit whisper that might have been the sound of the blood in their two bodies.

Farrow, afraid of the knowledge of his own fierce heat, got to his feet.

The girl said sharply, "Don't touch me!" She had given herself away; they both knew it.

He towered over her, his shadow across her quickened breast. He said, "You know bloody well I haven't touched you."

"I know. But…."

"But what, Marget?" He hadn't meant to use her name.

"I don't know what you think." She dropped her gaze to his feet. "Sam Augustine. He called me and asked me to meet him in town. He said he was Clel's friend. I went up to his hotel room that night and he said he wanted to mar-

ket the bonds Clel took from that Albany bank—so Clel would have hideout money, he said. He wouldn't believe I don't know where Clel is. He gave
me a drink. I only took a couple of sips, but the next thing I knew I was ready
to pass out."

"He drugged you?"

"He must have. I've had more than that before. He kept asking me over and
over where Clel is, and he got right angry when I couldn't tell him. Then he
had to go downstairs to make a phone call he had promised, a long-distance
call, I think. He said something about not wanting it to go through the hotel switchboard. I don't know whether he thought I was passed out or not.
He kept talking to me while he took my dress off saying he was making sure
I wouldn't run away." She shivered, hugging her arms about herself. "I did
run away, though. Then there was you. That's the God's truth, no matter
what you've been thinking."

For Farrow it was; he couldn't stomach any other possibility. "I never
thought you were malaya," he muttered. When her eyes came up, questioning, he added, "That's what they call a woman of the town in Kenya, where
my home is."

"Kenya," Marget said. "Africa. Then you're not from England—no more
than you're from Reuters. Why did you lie to us?" She shook her head hastily.
"No, that's not a fair question. I've had to lie sometimes. I used to at the university when the girls asked me where my husband was. I lied the other night
about why I was going into town, and the next day about why I hadn't
brought my Ford home. But what do you want with Clel?"

He stood above her silently.

"I asked a question, Mr. Farrow."

He said slowly, "But that's not the question. He's a murderer. The question is why should you protect him?"

"I'm his wife."

"Yesterday they told me you're also the daughter of a judge."

Her mouth trembled suddenly. Farrow had an abrupt glimpse of her con-
flict, as shocking as a physical contact between them. She was the daughter
of a man of law, a scrupulously fair-minded young girl—and her husband was
the most wanted criminal in the country. Marget closed her eyes tiredly, shut-
ting Farrow away from her secrets. She said, "I'm his wife. Should I stop loving him because of what he's done?"

He kept his teeth clamped over his answer.

She opened her eyes and asked, "Tell me, Mr. Farrow, would you like the
sight of me turning in my husband? *Answer me!*"

Instead he said, "You're expecting him here."

"You wouldn't understand."

"I might understand." He smiled bleakly toward the great dead oak tree.
"You and Clel grew up playing in this part of the swamp. I'd guess that this

pretty little island was your special hideaway, a private world for just you two children. Once upon a time you left secret messages for each other in that hollow tree. Once—"

Marget had risen quickly. She backed toward the tree. "I'm afraid of you," she whispered. "Only Mother Bocock and I knew about the tree."

"And now that Clel's in such trouble and the police are reading all your mail, you think that somehow he'll get a message through to you." Farrow grimaced. "But Clel's world can't be a private one any more. He's killed a man. And for God's sake, Mrs. Bocock, you're not a child any more."

"Don't," she said. She leaned back against the trunk of the oak tree, joining her gaze with his again. "Please don't talk to me like that. I reckon I've a right to daydream. You're right about the island, but it spoils it to hear you talk about it that way." Her voice was husky. "We used to play farm here. We were always going to get married, the families knew it, the neighbors took it for granted. Then Clel left high school and went away and I sort of got over the idea. Two years ago he came back. He—but you don't know what a woman sees in a man's eyes, Mr. Farrow. Clel has eyes that make you want to read poetry, and he carries himself different from other men. He came back because he couldn't stand to be away from me any longer, and he was going to settle down. He made me feel more complete than any of the other boys I knew did, and so...." She was tugging it out of herself, word by word, but suddenly a startled gleam came into her eyes, a spark that diffused as her eyes widened. She whispered, "I thought he was the only man who could make me feel that way."

At Farrow's feet was the imprint in the sand where her body had lain. A step away she leaned against the tree, head back and throat exposed, her arms tense at her sides. They stared at each other, the sensation between them again. Her full breasts were strong against the front of her shirt and the ripped skirt was apart over the taut slim length of her leg. She was half surrender, half defiance. She knew he wanted her, despite whose wife she was. She knew he intended to kill her husband. Farrow was gripping his carbine by barrel and stock, and he held it tightly across his hips, a metal barrier against his body. But all that was needed was a single step forward, across the mark of her body in the sand. He didn't take it. He growled, "Go home, Marget. Stay there. No message will ever come here."

She put her knowledge into words. "You're going to kill him."

"Yes, I'm going to kill him."

"I'll have to stop you," she said. "I'll have to find a way."

"No," said Farrow. "Nobody's going to stop me." He walked around the tree without looking at her again. Through the palm growth the trail of the wounded Sam Augustine was broad and plain. He followed it swiftly, not certain whether he was pursuing a man or escaping from a woman.

Chapter Seven

THURSDAY, MAY 3, 4:00 P.M.

The trail was too easy. Farrow, a distracting female memory still speeding his pulse, had to force himself to use more caution. He had a crazy desire to plunge ahead as Augustine had done, if only to release the passionate energy that had expanded in his big body. But, once off Marget's island and on the lake shore, he trod slowly, carbine ready.

Sam Augustine had left signs enough in blood spots. In addition he had battered through the brush like a wounded buffalo, leaving broken and crushed vegetation to show he had passed by. He had kept his head enough to angle north instead of floundering deeper into the seven hundred square miles of swamp.

Farrow trudged patiently after, walking nearer the sheltering cypress trunks than had his quarry, wading the same lagoons. A cool evening breeze had already sprung up, shivering the silver veils of Spanish moss. The sun still slanted hotly through the foliage, and where it touched the water it became rippled brass. Farrow listened to every sound, tested every smell on the breeze.

At last, on a muddy bank, he crouched quickly. Augustine's track led straight ahead, but Farrow glided off to the right, circling. In a hotel room Augustine might trick him, but not out in the open. A moment later, Farrow heard the sound of laboriously controlled breathing. Through a break in the underbrush he could see the blond man's back. Augustine had behaved precisely as expected; like a wounded buff he was lying in wait for his hunter. Clothes torn, plastered with mud from head to foot, he was kneeling behind a clump of huckleberry bushes. His eyes were pointed back over the broad trail he had left—his clever blue eyes and a .45 service automatic.

Farrow took no chances. Less than twenty feet behind his prey, he put the carbine to his shoulder and shot the big pistol out of Augustine's hand. Augustine screamed at the shock and the .45 skidded off into a grassy pool.

Farrow still kept the carbine ready as he approached. But Sam Augustine didn't seem to have much fight left. He sat hunched over, massaging his numb hand, his hurt leg stretched out before him. Sullenly, with the tops of his eyes, he watched his tormenter come up. Farrow squatted a safe distance away.

Augustine wiped his good hand over his mouth. His delicate mustache couldn't be seen for dirt and twig welts. He said, "You son-of-a-bitching bastard."

"I could have killed you," Farrow said.

"You go to hell, Farrow."

"You don't amuse me at all. How do you happen to know my name?"

From a latrine wall—that was the gist of Augustine's reply. His meaty face knotted in helpless fury, he ranted all the filth he could think of until he was panting for breath.

Farrow heard him out, listening closely. He was always interested in first-class profanity. Then he took out his pocket watch and looked at it. "Somewhat past four, Augustine. It will be dark very shortly. I don't think you'll care for it out here then."

"I know the way back. I'll get out, and when I do—"

"You won't get out after I've put a bullet in your other leg." Farrow raised the carbine and smiled politely along the barrel.

All around them the swamp throbbed subtly, dank miles devoted to a living heartbeat. Augustine stared at the gun and the man who held it. His mouth worked loosely. "Christ, you would!"

"Certainly I would," said Farrow. "I'll leave you lying here after the sun goes down. This is a different place at night, more lively. The animals come nosing around. They smell blood a long way off. There are wildcats here, and bears and panthers. And, I understand, some of the alligators grow to a twelve-foot length. All capable beasts, a bit shy at first. They'll stay off in the dark, watching you, and you'll scream at them and some of them will scream back at you, and all too soon one will get up enough courage to—"

"Christ! Christ!" Augustine yelled. "Don't." He tried to crawl toward Farrow, imploring, "Don't shoot me again!"

"Stay where you are," said Farrow softly. "Simply talk to me. My name?"

"Read it in the hotel register."

"Why?"

"You made off with my girl the other night, didn't you?"

Farrow growled scornfully. "That won't do, you know. I've talked to Mrs. Marget Bocock. I know what you told her today. That I'm after her husband."

"Well, you are, aren't you?" Augustine saw the expression on Farrow's face and held up his hands defensively. "O.K., I won't kid a bright lad like you, Farrow. When I was in your room the other night, I shook down your stuff. I saw your thirty-eight in the suitcase. Well, hell, any gun that comes to Waycross is bound to be mixed up with the Bocock mess somehow."

"What's your own connection with Bocock?"

"Oh, strictly a business connection. A deal for a Chicago outfit." Augustine got over frights easily; now his face was greedy and secretive. "It's pretty complicated. You wouldn't understand the ins and outs."

"Try me with it, anyway."

A long hateful uneasy stare from the blond man. "Well," he muttered, "in that Albany knock the take was almost all bonds. Negotiable, understand, but Bocock's in no position to negotiate anything. Soon as I get in touch with Bocock, I take the bonds off his hands and turn them into ever loving money. For a cut, of course. Strictly business."

"That includes terrorizing young ladies?"

"So she's got to you, huh?" Augustine sneered. "A sexy little body, but don't let any wife of Clel Bocock's kid you, Farrow. She knows damn well where her husband is right now." Then he grinned, his two gold teeth glinting, an almost comradely grin. "Harder to see through a woman's lies, ever notice, Farrow? One twitch of their cute little bottoms and you go all to pieces. I learned—"

"Take off your clothes," said Farrow. "Toss them to me. Gently."

Augustine gaped. Then he obeyed hastily. When he was stripped naked, he cowered as if the effrontery was a property of his clothing. With an odd shyness he tried to shield his broad flabby chest and soft middle. He was pallid and almost hairless. The flesh wound in his left leg had scabbed over.

Farrow grunted, distastefully exploring the heap of soiled clothes with a fingertip. "Lying or not," he said, "she's far prettier than you, Augustine." He methodically searched the pockets and linings, even probed the shoes.

His single find was a folded telegram in the trouser watch pocket. It had been sent from Chicago two days before. LOCATED TERESE TYLER. CALL ME TONIGHT NINE. SMITH. It was to make the answering long-distance call that Augustine had taken Marget's dress and left her alone in his hotel room.

Farrow didn't bother to keep the telegram. He asked, "Who is Mr. Smith?"

Augustine glowered. "Fellow I work with. A securities expert."

"Terese Tyler?"

"That's another deal with Smith and me. The bitch tried to run out with some of our dough. Nothing to do with Bocock."

Farrow wondered. He knew his own shortcomings. He wasn't adroit at questioning, and he was inexperienced with Augustine's kind. Nor did he know the extent of Augustine's knowledge.

Smith, Terese Tyler, Chicago. Clel Bocock had lived there; some of the Bocock gang came from there. Farrow had a strong impulse to start north at once. He tossed Augustine's clothes back to him and blankly watched the blond man dress while he thought it over. He convinced himself that the trail certainly indicated Chicago, that he wasn't running away from Waycross because of Marget.

He stood upright. Augustine, fumbling at buttons, cried out in alarm. "You're not going to leave me, are you? Christ, I leveled with you, you heard me doing it!"

"You'll find your way, I'm certain."

"Don't leave me in this stinkhole! My leg, it's all stiff. *I can't walk!*" To Farrow's dismay, Sam Augustine began to cry. Huge tears rolled down his muddy cheeks and he tried to worm his way closer, begging with his hands.

Farrow swore in disgust. Then he shrugged. "All right. But please be quiet."
Eagerly Augustine smeared the tears off his face. Farrow leaned his carbine
against a cypress bole, bent, and hoisted the heavy burden to his shoulders.
Retrieving his gun, he headed over to the nearest stream. With the added
weight, bottom-walking would be less difficult than following the narrow
trails.

The sunlight was fading. As they reached the bank of a sluggish brown
channel, Farrow paused to adjust the blond man's weight. And Augustine
chose that moment of unbalance to grab for the carbine. His other hand clawed
into Farrow's throat.

Farrow reacted without hesitation. He threw the carbine away, rocked his
body back on his heels, and tossed Augustine over his head. Augustine
landed heavily in the shallow water, rolled, and came up spluttering, tangled
with pickerel weeds and water grass. "Why'd you let me fall?" he choked.
"How'd that happen, for Christ's sake?"

Then he realized he was looking into the carbine barrel and he began to sob
again. Farrow's face was dark with rage. But he didn't shoot. He grated, "You
know, you can wallow there till you rot. I'll never know what became of you."

He stalked back to the trail and headed toward the highway. Augustine's
piteous yells faded away behind him. Farrow thought ahead, more anxious
than ever to start for Chicago. He walked quickly, cursing the swamp and the
people in it.

Chapter Eight

SATURDAY, MAY 5, 8:00 A.M.

He slept away part of Friday afternoon in an auto camp outside Nashville. That night he drove the rest of the way to Chicago. Before eight o'clock Saturday morning he was squatting, native fashion, by a door on the second floor of a drab office building in Halsted Street. Farrow felt alone in the building, although from everywhere outside he could hear the rushing roar of the city going to work. On the frosted glass of the door by his side was the gilt legend "Raymond Creme Agency." Farrow waited patiently, feeling small and unimportant. The city was too big to suit him; it even smelled big in an acrid way. Its sky was a fuzzy gray, and an unfriendly wind blew in off Lake Michigan.

He stood up hastily when he heard footsteps trudging up the stairway. A short chunky man appeared at the end of the dingy corridor, his heels tapping more briskly as he advanced. He wore a sloppy brown suit, a yellow shirt, and a black tie. He spun his hat on his finger, paying no attention to Farrow until he had reached the Creme Agency door and extracted a leather key case from his pocket. Then he raised his alert brown eyes and said, "You waiting for this?" He had a flat quick voice.

"Yes, I am."

"Then you must be Farrow. I'm Ray Creme." He shook hands powerfully, unlocked the door, and said, "Come in. I didn't expect you this early. I was going to call you at the Knickerbocker. Mr. Stennis said he'd got you reservations there."

"Yes, I found it quite elaborate." Farrow stood just inside the hall door and watched Creme step around, switching on fluorescent lights, toeing wastebaskets into place, adjusting blinds. The suite of offices was sleek, pastel, and well upholstered, in sharp contrast with the fly-specked hall outside and the cluttered delicatessen on the street floor.

Farrow liked the private detective's looks. Despite his blocky build, Creme seemed to be a man who could think and act fast. His strongly muscled face had a beak of a nose, once broken and not set very expertly. Over his worried forehead his salt-and-pepper hair was bristlecut, giving him the general appearance of a Turk.

"Let's see—let's get the record straight," said Creme. He hovered in front of the PBX board, unplugging the night connections. "You called Mr. Stennis Thursday evening from Waycross before you left. He called me yesterday morning, so we've just had the one day to work on what you dug up. Come on inside."

Farrow trailed him into his private office and they sat facing each other across a polished desk top. Behind Creme the windows looked out onto the tracks of the elevated. The detective unlocked a drawer and rummaged out an aged brier pipe. He swiftly tamped it full, used three matches lighting it, then sighed contentedly. "Excuse my rush," he told Farrow. "Hilda'll be in soon—my office manager—and she disapproves. I pay her to disapprove." He grinned ruefully. "I've got a well-meaning doctor, Mr. Farrow. No excitement, no liquor, no tobacco. I miss the tobacco most, the liquor next."

"And the excitement?"

"Not at all. Kick the door shut, will you? Then Hilda can't see me the second she comes in." Farrow did so. Creme puffed out a huge cloud of smoke. He said, "So you're the hunter, huh?"

"How much did Walt Stennis tell you?"

"Enough to guess what he didn't tell me."

"And what do you think of it, Mr. Creme?"

"I get retained for plenty of reasons, but not for crystal gazing. If you pull it off, Stennis' idea of hiring a nonprofessional like you was a stroke of genius. If you flop, O.K., Stennis was crazy all along, That's the way it goes. Outcome is everything." He chewed his pipestem reflectively. "Stennis phoned me about you while you were still flying over from Africa. He asked me then what I thought and I told him. No opinion. I'll tear up the sidewalks helping you, but no opinion. I gave up opinions way back when I was a cop."

Farrow smiled. "I'll venture one opinion, that Augustine lied to me from start to finish."

"I'd like to hear about him in your own words." Farrow told about the two encounters and Creme pondered. "No, his story sounds straight. He was holding back, naturally. For one thing, we haven't found any plausible hookup between him and anybody called Smith. Smith's just an empty name, so far. But what Augustine spilled about the bonds makes sense. Over a hundred grand of bonds—somebody's got to cash them, and Clel Bocock sure can't do it. That's where the fence comes in. Bocock gets about a quarter of their face value and the fence makes the rest—clear profit. You see, crime does pay for Augustine and his boss, this unknown Smith. But not for the gunners like Bocock."

Outside there was the sound of the hall door being opened, and then people conversing, one of them a woman. "Hilda's here," murmured Creme, and inhaled smoke deeply. "I notice there hasn't been a rumble on the Bocock gang since May Day, that job out in Montana. Five days of quiet." He chuckled. "Just occurred to me. Since the first of May—moving day. They moved right out of sight."

"No Smith yet," said Farrow. "Is there any local person known as Little Jumbo?"

"We tried that. Thought it might even be the name of some poolroom or bar. No luck yet." Creme twisted a dial on the interoffice communication box. "Hilda, bring in the Stennis account, if you please."

When the door opened Farrow could see two burly men in business suits seated at desks in the main office. One was talking on the telephone; the other was searching through a stack of grimy old ledgers. The woman who came in carrying a sheaf of papers was lanky with mouse-colored hair and a nondescript dress that hung slackly on her flat-chested figure. She gave Farrow an incurious glance.

"Anything on Terese Tyler?" Creme asked. "Wasn't Jorgenson out on that one last night?"

"Jorgenson turned up nothing. He's at the morgue this morning, hasn't called in yet. Nothing on Smith or the Little Jumbo alias. More coming on Augustine." She read part, told part, all emotionlessly. "Samuel W. Augustine, W. for William. Address Six-seven-one-seven Winthrop Avenue, North Side. Hasn't been seen there for several days. Mike bribed the janitor and shook down the apartment. Nothing of interest, no names written down. Augustine isn't working now—opinion of neighbors. Last job was greeter at—"

There was a din in the distance, growing rapidly nearer and louder. Farrow sat up straight. The woman stopped talking. Outside the window a string of railway cars shot past on the elevated tracks and the building trembled. Neither Creme nor his office manager paid any attention.

"Last job," continued Hilda as the noise died away, "was greeter at a night club on LaSalle Street. Quit six months ago...." There were many more details but Farrow heard nothing he could use.

When the woman had finished, Creme mused, "He must have made a connection somewhere. We know he did—with Smith. The hell of it is that Smith's real name might be Jones or whatever. Anything else, Hilda?"

She nodded. "The pipe, Mr. Creme."

He winked at Farrow and knocked out the ashes into the ash stand. "Keep the bunch digging, Hilda." She nodded and faded away into the outer office, leaving the door ajar. "Well that's the works, Mr. Farrow, so far."

"It would seem to be a good day's labor."

"Something'll break. I'll keep in touch with you at the Knickerbocker. You can take it easy for a couple of days while we feel around. You'll have a chance to see something of Chicago. Believe me, there's nothing like it in Africa."

A handshake, a nod, and the conference was over. Creme saw him as far as the hall and a moment later Farrow was standing on the sidewalk, being jostled, the morning traffic of Halsted Street stampeding by him. He got into the comparative privacy of the Lincoln and headed back for his hotel to wait for Creme's organization to uncover the trail. He had no desire to explore the city.

He turned east across the Lake Street bridge trying to get his bearings, crawling into the teeming Loop between mountain ranges of masonry. He gawked like a child at the brazen commercial heights, the sky almost lost among the windowed monoliths. He stared at the bedecked façades of theatres and the insistent show windows of mammoth department stores and a whole civilization in a hurry. And because he was looking at everything he saw the familiar name Albion Hotel, spelled in dusty light bulbs on a stubby structure squeezed between two

grander buildings. When he had seen that structure before, heavily retouched and in brighter colors, he had been looking at Mother Bocock's picture postcards. Clel Bocock had worked there as a bellhop. Farrow braked the Lincoln suddenly, raising an indignant howl of horns behind him. Flustered, he killed the engine. Then, down the block, a parking place emptied magically. He managed to get there first. He blew out his breath and thought the situation over. It was barely nine o'clock in the morning and he had nothing to do.

He walked back down the sidewalk and entered the small sepulchral lobby of the Albion. The hotel was slowly dying of middle age and middle class. The desk clerk, like his surroundings, clung to a certain turn-of-the-century dignity. "Terese Tyler?" He could find nothing in his dog-eared register.

Farrow laid a five-dollar bill on the counter. "I know it's quite a bother, but she may have been a guest here two or three years ago. I'd appreciate knowing." Clel Bocock had been at the Albion at that time too.

The clerk hated his own need of the money. He pocketed it uncomfortably and went into an anteroom. When he finally returned, he said haughtily, "I fear I'm not the one you wish to talk to—sir." He tapped the bell before him. "George probably can help you. He's been with us some time."

George was the bell captain, withered and sly, like a trained monkey in his wine-colored uniform. After a muttered consultation with the desk clerk, he grinned and led Farrow aside. "I take it you're a stranger in town. A rancher, I'll bet. I can size people up just like that."

Farrow said, "That's very interesting. But do you remember a Terese Tyler?"

"I might."

A sudden silence, until Farrow remembered to pass over another five-dollar bill. George winked. "Lonny should know—over at the Bellamette. Know where that is? In the Loop here, go down to State and turn right, four, five blocks. Big roof sign, Hotel Bellamette."

Farrow went back to his car, feeling a surge of excitement. And a touch of superiority too. In fifteen minutes he had done more to track down Terese Tyler than Raymond Creme's trained operatives had in twenty-four hours. Then he reminded himself that he'd had private information—a remembered picture on an old postcard. He located State Street and, a few moments later, the Hotel Bellamette.

Lonny wasn't on duty yet and Farrow had to wait an hour. The Bellamette

was a larger hotel, not quite new, not quite first-class, but ostentatiously pretending. Lonny turned out to be another bell captain, younger than the Albion's George, but toothy and skeptical. "Tyler, yeah, about a year ago," he
mused. "Damned if I know what happened to her. None of my business, know
what I mean?" But five dollars bought Farrow a reference to a taxi driver
named Zamperini whose stand was a block away.

"Like a bloody parlor game," Farrow growled to himself. But he had started
the game and he was determined to play it out. He changed a twenty into a
fresh stock of fives and sought out Zamperini.

The taxi driver was a young pockmarked Italian. He listened placidly, picking his teeth with a thumbnail. "Nope," he said finally. "Out of my district.
I'm not crazy."

"I haven't asked you to do anything," said Farrow doggedly. He toyed with
one of his magic bills. "Information is the most I'm after."

"Sure, what if you're a cop?" Zamperini studied him and then reached over
and took the five. "Nope, you ain't got the look. O.K., info's what you want
and info's what you're going to get, but I ain't riding you nowhere, not a hot
week like this. There's a fellow named Dick at that fancy Pendragon Arms
up on the North Side."

It was nearly noon when Farrow found the landscaped grounds of the Pendragon Arms. A graceful granite tower, it dwelt aloofly by the bleak vastness
of Lake Michigan. It occurred to Farrow that he had trailed the elusive Terese
Tyler up a social ladder of hotels. Whenever she had lived at Pendragon Arms,
she had been in the money. It also came to him—he was weary from being
shunted about the city—that the Tyler woman might never have heard of Clel
Bocock except from the headlines. But he had to know.

He felt ill at ease and shabby in the grandeur of the lobby. His tweeds
needed pressing and he was afraid the deep carpeting had never been trod by
boots before. The desk clerk wore pince-nez. He directed Farrow into the dining room, where, amid glances of luncheon guests, another inquiry located
Dick. He was a waiter, a greasy Adonis in a crisp white mess jacket.

And Dick replied acidly, "No soap, buddy. Get on your horse."

Farrow's face hardened. He said, "Not a single damn soul speaks to me like
that. Furthermore, you blinking wart-hog, I've come too far to—"

The luncheon guests were slowly turning to look at the pair. Dick drew him
hastily around a corner. "Not so loud, for Christ's sake," he hissed. "Why'd
you barge in here? I don't know anything. I don't know *you*."

"A cab driver, Zamperini, told me—"

"Hey, can I help what some screwball hackie says? It's hot now, buddy, the
heat's on." He paused. "What'd you specially want with Terese Tyler?"

"Personal business." Farrow remembered to add, "I'm willing to pay, of
course."

"No kidding?" Dick snickered. "Zamperini huh? Well, maybe he's all right these days and maybe not. Tell me more, buddy. Who else do you know?"

Farrow considered, then tried a shot in the dark. "Perhaps the name of Sam Augustine would mean something to you."

The shot hit. Dick began chuckling with relief. "God, yes, everybody knows Sam's a right guy. Terese, huh? What's *your* name?" Farrow told him and Dick said, "Wait right here," and went away. Farrow's spirits began to rise, wondering if the waiter had gone to fetch her. But Dick returned in two minutes, alone. "All right," he said, "I made the call. You're in luck, buddy, seeing it's a Saturday night. You be in the Fallen Angel on Randolph Street, down in the Loop, tonight at seven. She'll be on the lookout for you."

Success. Farrow couldn't believe in it for a moment. He grinned happily and said, "Thank you very much," and started to turn away, but Dick's hand held his sleeve.

"Hey, buddy!" Dick raised his eyebrows. Then he put it plainly in low tones. "The hundred bucks. *You* know. I'll take it now."

For the first time it made complete sense to Farrow—the undercover referrals, the sly glances, the doubts as to his motive. He had not only caught up with Terese Tyler. He had hired her body for the night.

Chapter Nine

SATURDAY, MAY 5, 7:00 P.M.

His tweeds had been pressed and, as a concession to Chicago, Farrow squeezed into his oxfords. Before seven that night he was slumped in a booth at the Fallen Angel, a small blue-lit cocktail lounge in the heart of the Loop's entertainment district. He fingered curiously the imitation leopard-skin upholstery and half listened to the frenetic pluckings of the piano and electric-guitar team installed above the bar. Business was slow at this hour. Farrow looked relaxed behind his straight gin—to his disgust, it contained an ice cube—but he wasn't. He was conscious of his heartbeat as he steadily watched the door, and of his .38 automatic in his coat pocket. He didn't know what to expect, but he thought he was prepared for anything.

He was wrong. As the clock hands approached seven, the door swung open hesitantly. A woman came in out of the chill night, unescorted, and Farrow felt his mouth drop open.

It was too much for coincidence. While he sat stunned, Marget Bocock came directly across the room and slid into the booth beside him. She said quietly, "Hello."

Farrow just looked at her. She wore a suit of subdued plaid and a short coat. Her tawny blonde head was bare, and her glistening hair made a soft whisper against her shoulders whenever she moved slightly. She dropped her eyes, and, suddenly less bold and self-assured than when she had first sighted him, began drawing off her gloves.

Farrow said finally, "No explanation needed, I suppose."

"I don't know. Is there? When I got into town today I went around to all the biggest hotels until I found where you were staying. I waited in the lobby all afternoon. When you came out this evening, I followed you."

A waitress rustled up but went away again when Farrow said, "No, the lady's not staying." He glanced quickly toward the door. If his amazing good fortune in tracking down Terese Tyler should be negated by the presence of the Southern girl.... He said coldly, "That's not the explanation I meant, as you damn well know. Why did you follow me to Chicago?"

His tone brought her head up. "That afternoon in the swamp—we hadn't said everything, as you damn well know. I went looking for you. I found Sam Augustine."

"And I've no doubt he blubbered some more and you helped him out of the swamp."

"As a matter of fact, that's exactly what I did," she said defiantly. "He was shot clean through the leg—I hadn't known that before—and what else could I do? I know he's not much good, but—well, I couldn't just leave him to crawl."

Farrow flushed angrily. "You mean, the way I left him. Yes, it's perfectly clear why you've come a thousand miles. To instruct me in humanity."

She drawled savagely, "You'll kindly not shout at me, Mr. Farrow."

"I'm far from shouting." That wasn't quite true. He stole another look at the door. "Did Augustine specifically tell you I was coming to Chicago?"

"He said probably. He said you'd probably look for Clel here next. I had to come for Clel's sake. I have my own car and I simply left without telling anyone where I was going—the family or the FBI or anyone."

"You've wasted your time. You can't stop me."

"I reckon I shall."

Already it was after seven. He glared at her. "Do you propose to have these quiet chats with every policeman who's after your husband?"

"No."

"I suggest you leave now."

"No."

"Please do. You can't save him. He's an enemy of society and he's got to be put out of the way like any other man-eater."

Her eyes were troubled. She stuck out her lip as she played with her gloves. "But you're not a policeman," she said finally. "You talk high and mighty, but you've got a crazy streak in you that scares me. I have a terrible feeling you're going after Clel just for the sport." She searched his face anxiously. He made it masklike, but she saw the truth. He took a quick swallow of gin, mentally damning her intuitions. What existed between them that she could see inside him? When he set his glass down noisily his hand accidentally brushed hers on the booth table and she shuddered.

She whispered, "Oh, my God, no, you can't! It's not human. It's not any kind of justice at all."

"Go away. You're not wanted here," he growled at her, while the door of the Fallen Angel loomed large in his thoughts. It rested ominously motionless, awaiting the push from without that would bring the Tyler woman to their rendezvous.

"Why?" Marget insisted. "Why are you doing this? I've got to know."

"Please get out of here." He was fervently conscious of time slipping by him, time and luck—and the soft round of her hips was next to him on the booth upholstery. If he should move his leg, their thighs would press together, sealing them. They were as alone in the bar's blue dimness as they had been on the swamp island. The other customers were disembodied murmurs. Farrow clenched his hands so he wouldn't touch her.

"Jacob," Marget breathed. She didn't seem aware she'd said it aloud. A second later, she said, "Mr. Farrow, if I had come up to your room this afternoon...."

"No."

"I didn't dare."

"I know it. Now get out of here!"

"We've got to talk sense. Please don't touch me, no, but please talk sense to me so I—"

"Get out before—" Farrow broke off. The door had opened at last. The tall slim woman who paused in the entrance of the cocktail lounge had to be Terese Tyler. She looked around and her gaze passed by him because she was looking for a man alone. She was sleek and sinuous as a python; a dark green dinner dress draped her firmly conical breasts, clung to her long waist, and hugged lustfully about her hips. Her heels were extremely high and she wore a silver-gray fur jacket. Nestling on her short black curls was a scrap of green velvet with a frivolous wisp of veil.

She began to look annoyed. Farrow shoved halfway to his feet, trying to muster a smile, feeling sick about all the things that might go wrong with Marget there. Then the woman saw him and smiled back and strolled toward him slowly, the dress moving across her legs with the effect she wanted.

Farrow, "How do you do?"

She gave off sweet smells; her voice was warm and husky. "Of course—you're Jacob Farrow." When they touched hands, he held onto hers. "I want to call you Jake. May I?" He managed a full grin and drew her into the booth beside him. A woman on his left, another on his right. They pretended to notice each other for the first time and nodded with cold indifference. Marget's eyes dropped to their joined hands and Terese withdrew hers and commenced to strip off her gloves as if preparing to undress or to fight or both.

She said, more coolly, "I didn't expect you'd have company already, Jake."

"Nor did I—Terese." He shifted toward her slightly and Marget was clearly alone. "It was entirely unexpected. This is—well, probably a Miss Smith."

"Oh-ho." Terese smiled broadly, forgiving him. Her complexion was dark, her upper lip long, and in the blue light her deep-red mouth was as black as congealed blood. She had a handsome heart-shaped face without much forehead and a thin perfected line of brows turning up at the ends. She was about thirty and she considered Marget with large blue-black eyes older than Marget would ever be. "Smith," mused Terese. "So many girls in bars are named that. So sorry I'm late, Jake. I didn't mean to throw you to the wolves. But what does the cute young thing want with you?"

"She wants to sleep with me," Farrow said.

He thought that would do it. But Marget, after she had reddened and set her lips in a flat hurt line, didn't budge. She sat there and Farrow could feel her eyes on him.

"Oh, my goodness!" said Terese. "What an embarrassing spot for you, poor darling. I'm so tickled I came along when I did to rescue you."

"So am I." He took her hand again and started to suggest leaving. Marget was too stubborn to be driven away.

But Terese was having fun. "Wait, wait," she said, and pretended to study the girl analytically. "I said she was cute, and she is, here and there." Marget stared back at her stonily; Farrow knew she had sensed what Terese Tyler was. "A trifle young, maybe, but it's hardly Miss Smith's fault that she had slow parents. Really, though, I think she should be in school somewhere—at this hour, I guess, staying *after* school with some lewd old teacher. At any rate, she doesn't quite fit here...." She waved her free hand around at the dim coziness of the Fallen Angel.

Marget's eyes had become a little glassy and unbelieving. Terese cooed, "A cute enough face if she'd touch it up. But goodness, Jake, that hair! Look at it, no style and too long. It might have got by back in—where was it, dear? Nebraska?—but in Chicago there's too much competition."

Farrow kept from hitting her; he needed what she might know. Marget was shrinking deep within herself. Her gaze, like a trapped gray bird, fluttered to Farrow and then slid helplessly back to Terese.

Terese giggled at her. "But let's be fair and not overlook her really cute points. Her *two* cute points, I should say. You suppose they're nature's work?" She was completely confident of her own streamlined charms in comparison with the younger girl. She leaned across the table and pinched Marget's fuller bosom quizzically. "Oh-ho, the genuine home-grown—"

Marget shot to her feet, trembling. She seized her gloves as if to strike and then turned and walked away unsteadily. Terese cocked her head and asked with mock innocence, "Do you suppose it was something I said?"

Farrow laughed, loudly enough for Marget to hear. Inside, he was on the verge of nausea. The cruel baiting had got the girl away, but it was nothing to be proud of.

"These amateurs," Terese said, patting his hand. "Don't they make themselves ridiculous? But it was an enjoyable way to break the ice with us, don't you think? Now we can relax and enjoy ourselves."

Farrow doubted it. He couldn't forget what he'd let the girl in for. And to his surprise, when he looked around, he found that she hadn't left the cocktail lounge at all. She had only retreated to the bar, where she perched unhappily, still watching the two of them. He muttered, "Let's leave, shall we?"

"Of course, Jake. What have you planned? Dancing? A show? There's a new fem vocalist at the Blackhawk I'm dying to see."

Farrow said, "No, I thought we'd just talk."

Terese gave a faint sigh of disappointment, a sigh that complained, this is the way it usually goes. But she took his arm without objection; she had been paid for his pleasure, not her own. "Perhaps dinner in my apartment?"

To leave, they had to pass close to Marget, and Farrow didn't look at her.

He was glad to get out in the biting night air. He drank deeply of it. Terese lived at the Pendragon Arms, where he had purchased her that noon. She chattered gaily about the latest popular records as he drove through the North Side. He understood nothing of what she said, and his mind kept going back to Marget, wondering what she would do with herself now.

He found out quickly. As they waited for the elevator, she came through the lobby doors from outside. She stood stock-still when she saw Farrow. Her mouth had retained its hurt look but her chin was tilted up willfully. Terese, talking busily, didn't discover that they had been followed. Marget made no attempt to join them in the elevator, but her accusing eyes stayed on Farrow until the doors glided shut.

Chapter Ten

SATURDAY, MAY 5, 10:00 P.M.

"Oh-ho, you're not drinking, Jake sweet!"

"No, thank you. I've had plenty." He didn't like champagne and his goblet was almost untasted. While Terese was pouring herself still another, he wandered over to the south window of her sumptuous sitting room. He was ten floors up, and the black pin-lighted ocean of Chicago seemed to lap at his feet. He could see the heart of the city where, worn like medals, glittered the showiest skyscrapers, the Board of Trade spire, the twin horns of the Wrigley Building, the Tribune Tower, and the floodlit Palmolive Building with its blinding flash of beacon. Everywhere below, the million eyes of traffic wormed sluggishly, meaninglessly, as if crawling over ancestral trails by instinct, not desire.

Nor had Farrow felt desire yet. The remains of a good dinner sat on the sideboard; Terese held her liquor well and behaved gaily and provocatively, but.... He sighed moodily. He had the whole night to find out what she knew.

And then she had come up close behind him, one incredibly pointed breast pushing against his coat sleeve. "What's the matter, Jake? Lonesome for that big old farm of yours?"

Terese blithely assumed he was a wealthy farmer from somewhere out west—with a Boston accent. Not being very smart, she made no attempt to equate the two assumptions. Farrow supposed he did look like a farmer to her. He said, "Not particularly. Simply reflecting on what a monstrous thing this city is. I can't believe it does anyone good to feel small."

She giggled and gave him a slanting gaze. "Don't worry, I'm sure *you're* big enough." Then she drank some more, looking over her champagne at the view. "Isn't it a gorgeous hunk of something, though?" Her voice changed to brittleness. "For some people, it's really like that, you know. Right at their feet— and some of them a bunch of no-talents, too."

Suddenly she tossed off her drink and crossed purposefully to the console combination of television, radio, and record player. She selected a record and set it spinning. "Listen to this," she demanded. The music turned out to be a piano accompaniment, recorded specially for vocal practice. Terese began to sing huskily across the room to him. She closed her eyes and looked intense and rubbed her backside against the console as she performed, waving the empty goblet in slow rhythm.

"Right from the start
I wanted your heart
but all that I got was the go-by...."

Farrow applauded politely when she was finished. "This one's jumpier," she said, and turned the record over. She opened her eyes for the faster music and revolved her hips more and smiled insistently.

"You thrill me in the tummy,
You thrill me in the head,
And when I stand up close to you
I know that I ain't dead.
Oh, ba-bee!...."

Her voice was no better than the popular prattle she sang. Farrow said, "Why, that's really splendid, Terese. I didn't realize you sang professionally." "You really think I sound that good? Tell the truth, now." She glowed with self-approval as she refilled her goblet. "That's the way I feel about it too. Might as well be candid, I think I'm *good*. I haven't done anything with my voice yet, but I think I'm as good as most of the top singers. Don't you?" "I can't believe you haven't had years of experience. Really." She was silent, sipping her champagne sternly. She grumbled, "I need a break, just one break. I need the reputation, that's what counts." She sulkily lit a cigarette and said between puffs of smoke, "I want to be up there. *Be* somebody. Get my chance at all the money...." After a moment she switched off the whirring record player and drifted toward Farrow. She had returned from her jealous dream world to the base realities. She forced a giggle. "Wouldn't it be nice if we never had to think? Imagine how happy we'd all be, not thinking. Oh, why do I always seem to be broke, just living from one day to the next?"

Farrow doubted it. The rich overdone apartment... a hundred dollars a night... but Terese Tyler wasn't the kind of woman ever to be satisfied if she knew there was more to be had.

And she obviously fancied Farrow was a source. She leaned against him while she chattered about a jacket she had bought that morning. "I went into Carson Pirie Scott just to browse around and there it was and I simply fell in love with it, Jake. It's the cutest thing, absolutely my personality to the T, and—just on the spur of the moment, you know women—I took it. Of course, it's way out of my budget." A sigh. "But I love it so and I so hate to return it." A pretended thought, a slow shy gaze up at his face. "Perhaps, Jake—perhaps if I modeled it for you, well, you might like it so much you'd want me to keep it."

He knew he was going to be overcharged for something she'd bought herself weeks ago. He said, "Perhaps I might, Terese," and settled himself on the divan, smiling at her. Money seemed to be the key to her soul; enough of it might buy what he was after.

"Oh, you're a darling! I'll change right now." She widened her eyes, touched her forehead. "Whoa, that champagne! It's doing things to me. You're such a sweet boy, would you be so sweet as to unbutton me? I don't think I can make my fingers behave."

"Are you certain that I can?"

She giggled and slapped his face lightly and brushed a moist red kiss across his mouth. Her breath was faintly rancid with wine. Then she presented her back to him pertly, a row of cloth buttons curving down her spine. "Now, be your gentlest, Jake. I have the kind of skin that bruises so easily."

He worked at the dress, opening it narrowly to the small of her back. As his fingers intermittently touched her flesh he thought of Marget, whose skin was so much paler, and he cursed the memory away, wondering what was wrong with him. Being disrobed by his own hands was a lovely woman, skilled in every kind of sexual response... but where was the soaring excitation he'd fought in the swamp?

Terese hunched her shoulders a little, widening the aperture in her dress, revealing the black elastic of the brassiere. She wore no slip. "Don't stop now, darling," she said. Obediently he unsnapped the band, and when she turned slowly the profile of her bosom wasn't quite so conical as before.

She slid onto his lap and trailed a finger across his bristly upper lip. With a practiced heavy-lidded smile she murmured, "A mustache excites me so." One arm draped itself around his neck; with the other she began dragging her dress up her legs. When a glimpse of bare ivory appeared above her stocking tops, she stopped and her mouth rounded coyly at her daring. "I don't know what's come over me," she whispered. "You're such a quiet boy. But so big—and so helpful."

He slowly stroked up the sheer nylon of her posed legs. When his hands reached the wine-hot nakedness high on her thigh, he let them linger for a moment before he began to unfasten her hose from the garter belt.

He smiled into her parted lips, whispered back at her, "A mere jacket for all this. What would I have to give you for Clel Bocock?"

Terese didn't stiffen or look surprised. Her passionate smile only broadened. Softly she said, "A whole lot, Jake."

He was the surprised one. He stammered, "Then you know where he is?"

"Did I say that?"

"Almost. Where is he?"

Terese looked down at her lap and Farrow released his anxious brutal grip on her thigh. She held the leg out straight, toe pointed, admiring her sleek slimness. "My stocking, honey. Do it in slow motion." He pulled it down, taking his time. She said, "Why do you want to know about Clel?"

"I've been hired to kill him."

She accepted that calmly too. She rolled in his lap a little so he could undress her other leg. She reached down and patted the outline of the pistol in his coat pocket. "Then that explains the gun. I hoped it wasn't for me, Jake. I'd rather do business other ways."

He let the second stocking slip to the carpet. "I have money, too."

"On you?"

"No. But I can have a sizable check cashed at my hotel any time you give me reason to."

"Um." She rose from him and stood barefooted, crossing her arms to hold the dress on her body. She looked down on him lovingly. "I promised to model my jacket for you. I won't be a minute, Jake." She padded sinuously toward the bedroom, a tantalizing smile over her bare shoulder. "Your proposition fascinates me." She shut herself in.

Farrow immediately got up and moved silently to the closed door, listening to every sound. He wasn't satisfied with the way the evening was going; she had made it too easy for him. But he couldn't hear anything amiss. Terese was crooning to herself and making the customary undressing sounds. Then he blinked. From behind the door had come an unmistakable click like the magazine of an automatic pistol being shoved home.

He put a hand on his own gun and quickly opened the door. He felt like a fool at once. The metallic click had come from a suitcase being closed; Terese still held the bag in her hand, ready to put it away in the closet. "Jake! I wasn't ready yet!"

She had put on an expensive lounge jacket of quilted crimson silk, high-collared and long-sleeved. It scarcely reached her nude thighs, and the game was to imagine whether she wore anything at all beneath it. Even Farrow, beyond the erogenous tonight, succumbed momentarily to the suggestive length. At the other end of her long bare legs she wore high-heeled black shoes.

"Sorry," he said awkwardly. "I was looking for the lavatory."

She giggled, pretending to make every effort to tug the jacket lower on her hips. "You sure that's what you were looking for, honey?" She eyed him smugly. "Since I've led the way in getting relaxed and comfortable, why don't you at least take off that hot old coat?"

"I'm comfortable, thanks." Farrow retreated to the divan again. He was glad he had broken in on her. He had got a quick look at her closet. The floor had been stacked with luggage and the rods held only empty hangers. Terese Tyler was completely packed for a trip to somewhere. *Where?*

Terese emerged, leaving the bedroom door open. She moved around the sitting room, turning down the lights, showing off her legs from every provocative angle. "Like the jacket?" she asked demurely.

"Quite distracting. A less lovely creature wouldn't dare wear it." She smirked. He said, "But I'm still curious about that other matter. Did a man named Smith ever call on you about it?"

She looked blank. He tried the names Sam Augustine and Little Jumbo with the same effect. She said, "Oh, what's all this hurry, Jake? We've got all night, haven't we?" She poured herself a goblet of champagne. "And you're still dressed up so formal in your coat and everything." Her eyes widened mischievously as she stood over him and she said, "Oops!" and upset her champagne on his sleeve.

Farrow said, "You've won. I'll take it off."

"Why darling, you surely don't think I—"

He removed his coat. Then he took the .38 from its pocket and placed it plainly on the seat cushion beside him. Terese didn't seem to mind. She murmured, "Now we're beginning to get really cozy," and sat down in his lap again and wriggled around until she was settled.

He said, "Tell me about Clel."

"Tell me about money."

"If you can deliver the goods, you can virtually name your own price. But I must be convinced first. Why should you know his whereabouts when no one else does?"

Again her smug smile as she tickled his mustache. "Why shouldn't I know where Clel is?" she asked. "I'm his wife."

If she had suddenly turned into a full-grown lion, Farrow could hardly have been more amazed. He was certain he had misunderstood her. She repeated herself, giggling at his astonishment.

"When? I mean, how long? When did he marry you, Terese?"

"Three years ago next month. Right here in Chicago." She added, "I can show you the official paper if you really want, but I hope you'll take my word because I'm not sure which suitcase it's in."

Three years. At least a year before Clel Bocock had gone home to Waycross to marry Marget Ingram, a marriage that had no status at all, had never had any save in Marget's ignorance. Anger began boiling in Farrow. He said thickly, "Tell me about it."

"Oh, I don't know there's so much to tell. I met Clel when he was a bellhop at the hotel where I was living then. It was an antique dump down in the Loop, nothing as nice as this."

"And you married him—why?"

"You don't know Clel. Those big wet eyes of his can make a woman do just about anything," Terese said thoughtfully. Farrow gritted his teeth, remembering that Marget had told him nearly the same thing about Clel's charm. "And I guess he figured that living off me would be easier than bellhopping."

"Did you love him?"

"Of course, darling! He's a very easy guy to love. He's got that something— God, yes."

"You know he's got another wife down in Georgia?"

She snorted. "*I'm* his wife, Jake honey, the one and only. That Southern gal was just a sucker play, a coverup." Terese had no idea she had been face to face with the other Mrs. Bocock that evening. "You see, one night Clel got into a little trouble at the Albion. I was—well, entertaining a male friend, and when Clel pressured him for more money there was a fight and Clel hit the guy a little too hard. The guy died." Farrow understood the setup. Clel the pimp drunk-rolling one of his wife's clients; the victim not drunk enough and coming to unexpectedly. "I was in the clear but Clel got noticed dumping the guy in the alley. So he had to get out of town. He lammed back to that little hick town he came from, making out he'd gone home to marry his barefoot sweetheart." Terese giggled. "Well, I guess the farmer's daughter got a good time out of it during the couple months he pretended to settle down. But when I wrote him the heat was off, he sure hustled back to my bed."

Farrow couldn't trust himself to speak. Terese cuddled against him and after a moment she threw back her head and laughed loudly. "Oh-ho, can't you just see Clel as a farmer! That must've griped him. They used to call him Buck Bocock around town here—behind his back, naturally—because he always thought of himself as such a big bad gunman, even when he was a bellhop. I don't think that guy ever missed a cowboy picture."

"Why did he leave *you?*" Farrow asked finally.

She rubbed her cheek against his to pay for the supposed compliment and then said, "I don't know," indifferently. "He got in with Vito Duccone after he came back, breaking into warehouses and other things I didn't have much use for. Clel never liked to stay in one place and so he wandered off and now he's knocking over banks."

"You don't seem to care particularly, Terese."

"Why should I? You got to keep your eye on number one." Though she lounged in his lap, next to naked, an affectionate arm twined around his neck, she spoke brusquely. Her call-girl routine was forgotten. "Clel never supplied me with anything that any man couldn't. Sure, I loved him, but right now I'd love him a lot better dead." The grin coming over her face was slow and cold. "When Clel baby gets his, then I figure on getting mine. I'll bring this notary-public marriage out in the open. Terese Tyler Bocock—the great Clel Bocock's widow. Can't you see the splash *that'll* make? Personal appearances, and the night-club contracts will really pour in. Because I'll have a reputation then. *Be* somebody."

"Why wait? You'd have a reputation now."

"I'm scared of him," she said simply. "He's got a mean streak and he might not like me bringing up this bigamy business. He might come back and—not kill me—just scar me up." She mused, "He's like that. He always did like to slap me around."

Farrow gently petted the curve of her leg. He said softly, "Then we can help each other, Terese. We both want him dead. Suppose—"

She straightened, suddenly coy. "Jake, I couldn't just up and tell you where he is. That wouldn't look right. Clel's still my husband." She worked her mouth around on his for a sticky excited moment, then whispered, "But you saw I'm all packed. If that check is big enough I might let you follow me."

"Exactly how large does big enough—" he began.

And a key grated in the hall door behind them. Farrow swung his head around and his hand darted for the gun beside him. But Terese moved faster. She slid off his lap and sat squarely on the pistol. The crimson jacket slipped up, a tardy answer to whether she wore anything beneath it. She didn't.

Farrow stared into another gun. Raymond Creme was pointing it at him. Behind Creme in the doorway was the familiar blond head of Sam Augustine.

Chapter Eleven

SATURDAY, MAY 5, 11:00 P.M.

While Augustine limped around the room turning the lights up full, Creme said in a flat tense voice, "Get over against the television there, Farrow. Don't make any funny moves, now." And to Augustine, "Take his gun, Sam." Terese giggled. "Ray, I'm sitting on it."

Raymond Creme grinned, feeling safer. "I knew that pretty tail of yours would be some good to us. Now put your clothes on. We're late already." Terese got up sulkily. "Everybody's in such a hell of a hurry. Another hour and I'd have got him to fork over some more dough." Farrow stood in front of the console combination. As she swayed into the bedroom, she gave him a small sneer. "Smart like an ox," she said.

Both the chunky private detective and the big Sam Augustine wore topcoats and hats. Creme held the only gun, a .45 automatic. Augustine went over to the divan, favoring his bad leg, and picked up Farrow's pistol.

Farrow said to Creme, "Then I presume you're Mr. Smith."

"I signed a telegram that way, yes. I'm the fellow who sent Sam down to Georgia. He's one of my boys—my best. Now if you'd taken my advice, Farrow, and stuck around your hotel—"

"Didn't your doctor advise you to avoid excitement?"

Creme smiled. "Times when it can't be helped. You've got to admit I did my best to avoid this kind of thing but you wouldn't co-operate." A thoughtful pause. "Or maybe it was Terese. She was supposed to gimmick your champagne."

He spoke pleasantly enough but, through the open bedroom door, Terese heard the underlying menace. She said quickly and defensively, "Now look, he just wouldn't drink any, honest to God. I took care of his gun, didn't I?" She was pawing through a suitcase for other clothes, nude except for high heels. None of the men paid any attention.

Augustine spoke for the first time. He stood before Farrow, hefting the .38 in his hand. A smile began gradually to lift his silken line of mustache. "That's my boy," he murmured.

Creme said, "Don't play around, Sam."

Augustine didn't turn. He studied Farrow. "Nice gun," he remarked. "Fair trade for mine that you wrecked in the swamp." He drew back his hand and slapped the barrel above Farrow's ear, at the same spot he had hit him with the blackjack.

Lightning flashed inside Farrow's head and he staggered back with his elbows on the console cabinet, but he didn't fall. He saw a gleam of gold teeth as Augustine laughed. "This is a habit I could get to like."

Then Creme's voice was telling the blond man to stop it and there were no more blows. When Farrow's vision cleared, Augustine was leaning against the hall door and Creme was sitting on the divan, his hat beside him, his cropped head bare. Both guns were held steadily at Farrow's middle. Creme said, "Better my way, Sam. We don't want to carry a big load like him down ten flights. I'm not supposed to exert myself."

"He might fall out of a window. Ever think of that?"

"Sam, grow up," said Creme disgustedly.

Terese flounced into the room. She had donned garter belt and stockings and panties. "None of that noise, Sam!" she snapped. "Plenty of people saw him come up here with me. I had one close call with Clel and I'm not letting myself in for another."

Creme said, "You'll let yourself in for a fat lip if you don't get those clothes on." She retreated, muttering. He told Augustine, "But it's better my way, Sam."

The blond man shrugged. Then he bowed low to Farrow. "Put your jolly old coat on, what-ho?"

Creme thought that was funny. He went to the bedroom door and said, "Terese, we're going for a little jaunt with your friend. Say, fifteen minutes each way—which means we'll be back in half an hour. I want you and your luggage in the lobby waiting for us. Understand?"

"All right, all right," she said sullenly. "I speak English." Then an anguished yelp. "Goddamn that strap! Why'd it have to break now of all the...."

The two men got in back of Farrow and guided him out into the deserted hall. Creme said, "Don't try anything with us. It'll only make the same out-come sooner." They both carried their hats with their guns inside. Farrow glanced back at Terese Tyler, but she was angrily threading a needle and did-n't even look up to see him go.

Farrow walked obediently along the hall. He was still dazed, both from the blow and from the abrupt change of circumstances. But at the sight of the el-evators his brain began to function again. Plainly he was going to his death and at the moment he was helpless. But he remembered Terese saying, "Plenty of people saw him come up here...." Among them was Marget.

Was she still waiting in the lobby below? It was over three hours since he had come upstairs. Had she seen Sam Augustine arrive? Obviously, Augus-tine had not seen her. If she was still stubbornly waiting and if she put two and two together, Farrow thought she might be of some help to him in his desperate predicament.

Then he thought, Would she want to help me?

They rode down silently to the main floor. The questions burning in Far-row's mind didn't get answered. Instead of turning out across the lobby,

Creme and Augustine nudged him into a narrow hallway leading to the rear of the hotel. Farrow's heart sank and for a blind moment he held back. Augustine dug in deep with his masked gun and growled, "Just keep walking, Tarzan."

They went out into the night and down some steps into a parking area where a blue Buick sedan waited. The wind had increased in velocity, scudding pieces of newspaper across the asphalt and probing icily through Farrow's clothing. Augustine shivered and put on his hat. There was no one around to see the guns. "Going to snow again, Ray, bet you. Damned if I won't be glad to head out of here. Maybe we'll get a little sunshine out west."

They got into the sedan, Creme and Farrow in back, Augustine driving with Farrow's pistol in his lap. The blond man wheeled from behind the Pendragon Arms onto Lakeshore Drive, pointing south toward the center of town.

Farrow had no desire to talk. He sat in his corner of the back seat, his eyes roving about, searching for an opening. Creme sat opposite, his .45 low and aimed across his knee, difficult to snatch. But he was keyed up, anxious to keep conversing.

He said, meaning the traffic, "Saturday night's always busy like this."

Farrow grunted. Creme said, "Frankly, Farrow, I didn't foresee any trouble like this when Stennis first phoned me about you. I thought all this mighty-hunter business was crackpot stuff, a bunch of crap. This morning, even, I couldn't see you as anybody I had to worry about."

"Yeah?" muttered Augustine from up front. "After I'd told you different? Look at what the bastard did to my leg."

"But then you tracked down Terese in such an unbelievably short time. So I had to revise my thinking about you. I just can't afford to have you interfere."

They rolled onto Michigan Avenue, the buildings rising higher on every side. Presently they stopped behind a dam of other cars that waited for the slow-descending drawbridge across the Chicago River. Augustine revved the engine impatiently while they sat on the brink of time. Farrow wanted to try for the door but the other automobiles were packed so close that he was afraid he couldn't open the door far enough to squeeze his body through.

The herd of machines began to move forward again. Creme asked, "What are you thinking about?"

Farrow had watched a police motorcycle hurry by like a false hope. He said, "Some four million people in Chicago, and Walt Stennis had to hire a detective who's working for Bocock."

Creme said, "Oh, I'm not, working for Bocock. I'm working for myself. I told you mostly the truth this morning, actually. I want those bonds, Farrow. That's part of my business—securities, lukewarm to hot. And then Vito Duccone is an old friend of mine."

Across the river, south of Randolph Street, the vista changed. On Creme's side rose the sheer cliff of skyscrapers. But through Farrow's window, the lake side, he could see the formal grass and trees of Grant Park. There were monuments and geometric avenues and lifeless museum buildings too, but it was the sweep of darkened parkland that gave him a thrill of hope. It was open country, his kind of country. He tensed his legs and inched forward on the seat. Creme peered sharply, not certain whether his captive had moved or not, and Farrow said easily, "Where is Clel Bocock, then?"

Augustine snorted. Creme said, "Well, he isn't in Chicago, that's certain. On the other hand, I wouldn't let it worry you, Farrow. As far as you're concerned, Clel Bocock is ancient history."

The stream of automobiles was now spaced out on the boulevard and Augustine made the sedan pick up speed. They passed the stone lions of the Art Institute and behind it Farrow could hear the puffing of a switch engine; the Illinois Central right of way ran along a twenty-foot ditch through the park.

Augustine said, "Yes, Farrow, another ten minutes and you'll be—" and a taxi popped out of Eleventh Street into their path. Augustine jammed on the brakes. The Buick swerved heavily, throwing Farrow off balance. But then Creme turned his head to shout at the taxi driver and Farrow scrambled for the door handle and leaped.

He rolled on the pavement and bounded up, hearing the Buick's second scream of brakes. He vaulted over the traffic island in the center of the boulevard and raced among horn blasts for the shelter of the park. Behind him, he heard Augustine yelling. But there was no shot.

In the shadow of a wind-whipped tree, he paused to take his bearings, fear panting in him. Now he knew what it was like to be hunted. He heard men's feet rasping on the sidewalk. They were coming after him and he had no weapon to match their guns. He crept to another tree, then another, but the few poplars offered little concealment. He had taken cover in a small rectangle of park, three sides bounded by street light. Behind him, toward the lake, was the dark sink of the railroad right of way.

He heard Augustine's voice: "...still got him. Move in...."

Farrow broke for the deeper darkness, zigzagging. There was a yell in back of him. He reached the embankment over the tracks. A shot cracked by his right hand. Farrow leaped into space. Ten feet down his feet connected with the dirt slope and he slid the rest of the way, slamming to a halt against the side of an empty cattle car. He crawled under it, looking around for a good hiding place.

He was in the vast pit of the marshaling yards, laced with the steely gleam of tracks. To the south was the grim old-fashioned bulk of the main station but that way led across a dangerously barren prairie. Above him on the embankment he heard whispers, then the sound of men letting themselves down the slope.

He crawled over three pairs of rails and got behind a string of idle tank cars. The puff-puff-puff of the switch engine to the north reverberated in the empty drums of the tankers. And he heard Creme, by luck or logic, tramping nearer. Despite his bad heart, the detective was moving faster than the limping Augustine, and he was growling at the blond man to hurry.

The rear spotlight of the switch engine limned Farrow for an instant and he scrambled out of the glow. It was difficult to move silently over the gravel. He rolled into a culvert just as Creme fired again. "...saw him! Over here!"

Running feet. The chug of the switch engine became louder. It was backing leisurely into the yards. It began to pick up speed. Farrow began groping out of the shallow ditch before a turn in the locomotive's route brought the light glow on him again.

And his hand closed over a rusty iron bar. It was a yard length of one-inch pipe, ax-handle size. Before its discard, it had served as a brake stick to supply extra leverage in turning the outmoded brake wheels atop freight cars.

The stalking crunch of Creme's feet was almost upon him now. He peered out of the culvert and saw the searching figures of his pursuers. Neither saw him. Farrow ducked down and collected a handful of gravel.

He bobbed up again to throw it. His target was the half-open door of a boxcar standing alone two tracks away. He heard the gravel rattle inside the car and then Augustine's tense shout, "Ray! Down here!"

Both men angled south past Farrow, running for the boxcar. Farrow crawled rapidly north toward the advancing switch engine. He was the hunter again now.

Behind him Creme hollered, "Get around to the other side of the car! Cut him off!" Then the switch engine was backing abreast of Farrow and he stood up and ran for it. He reached its side, caught a hand grip, and jerked himself up onto the broad fender. The engineer was watching his rearward path and failed to see his new passenger. Farrow worked himself hurriedly along the hot metal side of the engine until he was perched on its front ledge under the huge glaring headlight. He readied the brake stick, gripping it one-handed like a tennis racket. Holding on with the other hand, he leaned out from the other side of the locomotive.

The switch engine returned him to the boxcar he had used as a decoy. Creme was out of sight, guarding the other side. Augustine stood facing the car's half-open door, waiting for the switch engine to pass behind him before attempting to flush their quarry. He didn't even have his gun out.

As the switch engine rolled by, Farrow jumped and swung. The brake stick glanced off the back of Augustine's head. He toppled forward, bending at the knees. Farrow stood over him, the iron pipe ready again. But the blond man lay like a sack, breathing heavily, blood glistening down the back of his neck.

One to go. Farrow crouched down and discovered Raymond Creme's stocky legs on the other side of the boxcar. He was still guarding the opposite door. The switch engine had slowed to a halt a hundred yards south of them, the beam of its headlamp barely missing the duel on the tracks.

Creme called, "Sam! What the hell you waiting for? Go in and shoot him out of there!" When he got no answer, he called again, his voice rising with nervousness, "Sam! Damn it, you hear me?"

Farrow crept silently around the end of the boxcar, trying to reach the detective before he realized the truth. He was too late. Creme looked under the car for Augustine's legs at the same moment Farrow came into view. Creme whirled, his hand flung out, and a shot splintered the planking a foot from Farrow's ear.

Farrow howled and charged like a rhino, swinging the heavy brake stick above his head. The onslaught was too much for Creme. He forgot he had a gun and began to run. He vanished around the far end of the boxcar and when Farrow sighted him again he was racing along the next track. His overcoat flapped about his short legs but the energy of panic gave him surprising speed for his build. Farrow broke into a loping sprint, the ungainly brake stick slowing him only a little. He began to close the distance between them.

Behind them hooted the whistle of the switch engine. It was heading forward now, returning north across the marshaling yards. Suddenly its spotlight glow fell around the two running men, grew in glaring intensity.

Creme's hat flopped off as he turned his head. His mouth was strained open with exertion and his face was chalk-white in the brightening spotlight. He didn't see the ground falling away on either side of the rail bed. He was headed out onto a low trestle over a drainage ditch. He took two more strides before his foot plunged between the ties. He sank to the knee, sprawling forward cruelly. He floundered about, trying to get his leg free. His scream was lost in another wail from the locomotive.

Farrow cast the brake stick aside and tried to reach him to pull him loose. But Creme was already a black and white figure in the terrible glare and Farrow could almost feel the heat of the headlamp on his own back. He jumped off the track bed, trying to call to the engineer through the roar of the engine. He couldn't even hear his own voice.

Creme waved his hands frantically at the looming monster, face twisted in a soundless cry of horror. Farrow stood helpless, the breath of the locomotive hissing warmly against his body as it shot by.

And as it thundered past, the juggernaut rumbled over a Y switch, veering across the ditch at a slight angle. Farrow stared at his first miracle. The switch engine had rolled over another trestle, next to the one where Creme lay. And Creme was invisible in the dark again, the engine's cone of light hurrying on north.

Farrow ran out onto the trestle. His heart was thumping from the noisy passing by of death itself. He almost fell over Creme. The detective lay on his back, eyes staring up. Even before he touched him, Farrow knew.

Raymond Creme's heart had stopped. He had been frightened to death.
Farrow loosed the dead man's leg and rolled him off the trestle for someone else to find. He felt nothing toward Creme as a fellow being, but he was
deeply shaken by the way a huge machine had killed him without touching
him. He hunted around for the .45 but couldn't find it in the darkness.

He turned and ran back to where he had left Augustine. But the gravel
alongside the lone boxcar was bare. Augustine had recovered consciousness
and fled. Farrow thought he knew where. He scrambled up the embankment
toward the park, hoping that he could return to Terese Tyler first.

Chapter Twelve

SATURDAY, MAY 5, 12:00 MIDNIGHT

The blue Buick was nowhere in sight. Farrow brushed most of the grime off his tweeds and waited a cold five minutes on Michigan Avenue before a cruising taxi answered his hail. The cab took him back over the route he had ridden with Creme and Augustine, to the big glass doors of the Pendragon Arms. He knew he wasn't in time.

He saw neither Terese Tyler nor her luggage in the lobby. He rode the elevator up to the tenth floor, blaming himself. During the struggle in the rail yard he had violated one of his own hunting commandments—to dispatch completely one animal at a time—and now he was paying for his error. He should have made certain of Sam Augustine before commencing to stalk Creme.

He went to Terese's apartment. Then he began to squint hopefully. Light from the sitting room seeped under the door. He tried the knob and the door eased open. He stepped in, spirits bounding. Within the bedroom he could hear the woman crying softly, choking off little moans. Three strides took him to the doorway.

But it wasn't Terese. It was Marget Bocock, her plaid-suited body curled up on the bed, her hands pressed to her groin. When she saw Farrow, she turned away, burying her tear-streaked face in the red satin coverlet.

He asked, "Are you hurt?" She didn't answer. He stood still a moment, listening to be certain there was no one else in the apartment. Then he went out to the telephone. He called the desk, claiming to be a friend of Miss Tyler's. The clerk said that Miss Tyler had left a few minutes before on a vacation trip; he didn't know where she could be reached. Farrow sighed and hung up and roamed, scowling, into the kitchenette. He found a bottle of bourbon and poured a stiff shot for the girl. While he was at it he took one himself.

Marget huddled away from him when he carried in the liquor. He said, "Don't be a fool. A peg of this'll make you feel better."

"I don't want it."

"Then bloody well don't drink it," Farrow snapped.

He plunked the glass down on the dresser and jammed his hands in his pockets.

His change in tone made Marget sit upright. She jerked her skirt over her knees and flared, "What's so wrong with you? I reckon you didn't have such a high old time with her, after all. Wasn't she worth the money?"

He stared at her in surprise. Her lip began to tremble and she looked away from him. He growled, "How in hell does it concern you, young lady?"

"I don't know," she muttered. "It's certainly none of my business."

"No, it certainly isn't." He fumed to himself. She was acting just like a wife. Then he remembered that she was nobody's wife. She had been tricked into open adultery and she still didn't know about it. The thought made him sick all over again. The very prostitute she had blazed up about was the rightful Mrs. McClellan Bocock. He found himself looking down at her more tenderly.

She said, "Why are you gawking at me like that?"

He chewed his mustache and looked at her in a mirror instead. There were too many mirrors in the bedroom, one on every door and on almost every piece of furniture. He said gruffly, "I wanted to tell you about—ah, tonight. Apologize, as it were. I'm sorry for that nonsense I let her say to you in the bar. It was all a business proposition and I was afraid you'd interfere. You'd said you would. The woman meant nothing to me, nor I to her. In any way. I mean—well, the bed's made, isn't it?"

He had never heard a stuffier speech. Apparently Marget hadn't either. She laughed softly at him. She said, "If you can forgive a fellow fool, I'll take that drink, after all." She tossed it off solemnly. It was good smooth whisky and Farrow was glad to see she didn't pretend a shudder simply because the peg was neat.

"Better?"

"Yes, thank you."

"Then tell me why you happen to be here."

She said slowly, "I don't know why anything any more." She arranged her long blonde hair while she talked, glancing from one mirror to another. "I was still waiting down below in the lobby when I saw him come in—Sam Augustine. He had another fellow with him, a short man with a broken nose. They didn't see me, of course, but I came near passing away. I thought first they must be friends of yours—like I thought of that woman."

"Much obliged," he said dryly.

"Well, when I really got to thinking, I knew that couldn't be so. Not after what you did to him in the swamp, I mean. The boy on the elevator told me what floor you all had come to and then I came up. The door here was standing open and everybody was gone—all except that woman." She flushed faintly, not from the whisky. "I reckon I said a few things and she said a few things and we got to scrapping right good. Until she hit me with a suitcase—here." She pressed her stomach, considerably higher than where Farrow knew she'd been fouled. "While I was almost being sick she left, and some time later you came. I thought you were coming back for her because, as we agree, I'm a fool."

"I was," Farrow said.

"Oh."

"She knows where Clel is hiding."

Marget's eyes flashed. She swung her legs off the bed. "Don't you lie to me! I don't believe it at all. Why should she know? Why should that—why should *she* know when I don't?"

Farrow did lie. He muttered, "I don't know," because he was afraid to tell her the truth. Marget had been hurt by everybody concerned, himself included, and he saw no reason why he should be the one to hurt her further. Right then Clel Bocock's cowardly marriage fraud infuriated him more than the murder of Steven Stennis.

He added lamely, "Well, perhaps she doesn't know. But she seems to know where to start looking."

"I don't believe it at all," she repeated with less confidence.

He turned away and opened the closet door to survey the bare floor, the empty hangers and shelves. Then he prowled around, inspecting the equally barren drawers of the other furniture. Nothing personal had been left behind. He met with the same result in the bathroom and kitchenette.

Marget came to stand in the doorway and watch him while he searched the sitting room. "What are you looking for, Jacob?"

"Everyone leaves tracks of some kind. Terese hasn't—not here." He shook his head, frowning. "West. Augustine said they were going west." He hadn't the slightest doubt that Terese and Augustine had left Chicago as planned, only without Raymond Creme, of course. "But where west? How far?"

Marget watched him and played with the clasp on her purse. She fidgeted and Farrow vaguely wondered why. Finally she said, her nervous compulsion to speak so strong that she almost stuttered, "Is it so important to you?"

"Yes. Simply because—well, I've never got used to failure."

"Pride, then. In what?"

"In my trade." He knew her next question and he was tired of keeping the truth inside him where it might rot. He faced her squarely and told her that he was a white hunter and that he had been hired to hunt her husband. He told her about Walt Stennis and his dead son. He put it all as baldly as he could, and when he had finished he could see no change in her. Her skin was already so creamy white that it was difficult to discern any additional pallor.

"Yes," she whispered. "I believe you would do it. You will do it and I'll despise you for it. We're two different kinds of people. I'd give anything to be able to stop you."

He shrugged. He'd told her the facts and he had no desire to hear any commentary on them. "Let's see, Iowa is west of here, and Clel worked there once, near Cedar Rapids. An animal takes cover in familiar country when he can. I suppose I must beat the bush there before...."

Marget was still gazing wonderingly at him as if she'd never beheld such a curious sight. He said irritably, "You're going back home, you know. All this talk of stopping me is nonsense."

"That's what I'm afraid of most."

He felt unclean, the way she was staring directly through him. But he was ashamed of having spoken sharply to her. "Marget, I'll— When I return afterward, perhaps I'll be able to stop over in Waycross—"

"You won't want to come then. You'll feel that way, I promise you. And I promise you I won't want you to come." Then she straightened, a small crooked smile on her mouth. "I reckon that one like you is enough in my life."

She was comparing him to Clel Bocock again, just as she had in the swamp. To Clel Bocock, who had bedded her by trickery and then run away. To Clel Bocock, when he, Jacob Farrow, was willing to treat her fairly—after he had completed his present assignment fairly. The anger came up in him simultaneously with the passion. If he'd learned anything tonight, it was that the tawny-haired Southern girl was a woman he could desire permanently. For the first time in his life he admitted the possibility of curtailing his own freedom and taking responsibility for this soft-bodied, slur-voiced creature.

And she bloody well wouldn't have him! His face was red with the thought. He said thickly, "I suppose you know what you're saying."

Now she was angry. Her chin came up and she drawled, "I do, Mr. Farrow. What's so— Don't you touch me!"

She fought like a cat. He put his mouth over hers and tried to drink her in to satisfy the rest of his life. His free hand groped over the plaid suit while she struggled, found the live cushion of her bosom, descended blindly to the warmth of her skirted thighs. Then he released her.

He wiped the blood from his lip where she'd bit him and growled, "That was good-by to you." She spat names at his back, the few weak words she knew, as he stalked out of the apartment.

He rode down to the lobby and retrieved his Lincoln from the parking area. Back at his hotel, the Knickerbocker, he composed a long ambiguous telegram to Walter Stennis, telling of the day's developments. Then he packed quickly and changed into his boots and drove west out of Chicago.

He was wheeling through dingy slum streets when he heard about it on the car radio: "Police learned tonight that Mrs. Marget Bocock, child wife of the notorious gangster, disappeared two days ago from Waycross, Georgia, where she was living with her killer husband's parents. FBI officials state that she has undoubtedly gone to join her husband in his secret hideaway. Exact whereabouts of bank robber Clel Bocock and his gang are still...."

Chapter Thirteen

SUNDAY, MAY 6, 6:00 A.M.

He crossed the Mississippi River into Iowa shortly before dawn. The highway looked deserted to the edge of the world but Farrow strained forward, his eyes seeking into the dark as he pushed the chase to the limit. For it had become a chase again. Fueling at a gas station on the outskirts of Aurora, Illinois, he had idly inquired if the attendant had seen anything of a late-model blue Buick sedan, driven by a blond man accompanied by a brunette woman. To Farrow's surprise, the youth had noticed such a car, principally because of the glamorous short-curled woman who had visited the rest room about an hour before.

But at the first light of dawn Farrow had still not caught up with Sam Augustine and Terese Tyler. The sky changed from soot to lead. Fat dark clouds soared overhead, propelled by an icy wind that sneaked into the Lincoln and made Farrow shiver.

A sign shot by, "Hargath County." Clel Bocock had once worked on a combine around here. It was mainly flat land of fields, huge but precisely fenced off. At this time of year it resembled a giant formal lawn because the fresh green of corn and wheat had not pushed far above ground. There were sudden dips in the monotony, however, where wide river courses snaked between low irregular hills. Now and then Farrow would see the window lights of a farmhouse, large boxlike structures of red or white, dominated by a tall silo and sheltered in groves of maple or birch.

Except for those few friendly windows he was alone on a prairie of budding crops. Then, as he streaked over the crest of a tree-studded hill, he braked hard to avoid running into the rear of a parade of slow-moving automobiles and trucks, strung down the highway for nearly a quarter mile. At the head of the line Farrow saw the red warning light of an official car, facing the westbound traffic. Several men on foot were examining each car. It was a road block.

Farrow swore at the delay but there was nothing to do but endure it. He had not slept since his nap the afternoon before, and with the sudden halt of his forward progress, exhaustion sank down upon him. And his stomach reminded him to be irritable, besides; he hadn't yet drunk his customary early morning cup of hot tea and milk. He rolled down the car window and stuck his head out into the chilly wind to look down the creeping row of cars ahead. He immediately forgot his troubles.

Three hundred yards in front of him, nearly ready to pass through the road block, was a Blue Buick sedan.

As the Lincoln crawled forward in low gear, Farrow debated his next move. Once through the road block he could catch up with Augustine and Terese in a matter of minutes. What then? Would it be more expedient to capture them and apply force to get the information he wanted? Or should he be content to follow behind and go where they led him? By the former method he might be misguided by one of their lies; by the latter method he would chance losing them again....

When he looked out once more, the Buick had passed through and was gathering speed westward. Still inching forward, Farrow was forced to watch his quarry diminish to nothing on the flat horizon.

Then he was at the barrier himself. Two unshaven drowsy-eyed men with riot guns were posted on either side of the highway while a tall skinny man with a sheriff's badge pinned on his fur-collared jacket walked curiously around the Lincoln and finally stopped by the open window.

"Name?" he asked nasally.

"Jacob Farrow."

The sheriff bent forward slightly and then the long barrel of a .38 revolver was pointing at Farrow's face. The sheriff grated, "Get out of that car. Don't get rambunctious and keep your hands in plain sight."

Farrow blinked his astonishment. "I beg your pardon?"

The sheriff said, "You get out of there before I shoot." He pressed the button that opened the car door and backed away to let it swing outward, still keeping the revolver slanted at Farrow's head. The two men with riot guns came trotting up.

Farrow got out slowly, bewildered. "There's been some mistake. I'm certain that—"

"You made the mistake, Farrow, I didn't. Didn't think you'd have the sand to give your real name. But I'd recognized the car all right, anyway." He jerked his head at one of his deputies. "Charlie, let the other folks go on by. We got our man."

The deputies, wide awake now, blew their whistles and gestured officiously and the clot of cars and trucks began to pull out around the stalled Lincoln, their occupants staring avidly at the mysterious goings-on.

Farrow said, "Yes, my name's Jacob Farrow. I have plenty of identification to prove—"

"Well, mister, you've driven right into the hands of Sheriff Loob, Hargath County," the skinny man said. "Consider yourself a prisoner." He was about Farrow's age, in his thirties, with a lean hatchet face under a mop of brown hair. His sharp-pointed jaw moved by ropy muscles. He licked his chapped lips as if he'd never tasted success before and his protuberant eyes glittered. "The charge'll be aiding and abetting—when we get around to it. I got a wire from Chicago last night saying you were on your way to join up with Clel Bocock. I been out here ever since, just waiting for you to show up."

"Chicago?" echoed Farrow. He had a sinking feeling. It showed on his face and Sheriff Loob grinned.

"Know about it, don't you?" Loob said. "Know who crossed you up. Well, we'll get that out of you too. You see, the viper in your bosom didn't bother to sign any name, just told what you looked like and what you're up to. These anonymous tips crack a lot of cases. Sometimes they're no good and sometimes they're mighty good. This one is mighty good."

Farrow could only stare at the tight mirthless grin. It was too easy to deduce who had sent the lying telegram. Only Marget had known his destination. She had finally interfered to save her supposed husband.

Then he remembered something else. "For God's sake!" Farrow said. "Don't let that asinine telegram fool you. It was sent by one of Bocock's friends—to keep me from catching him. The people you want are up ahead— the blond fellow and the woman in the Buick. They're the ones who know where Bocock's hiding."

The two deputies smirked and Loob laughed aloud. He scoffed, "Oldest trick in the world, Farrow. Try again. You can't shift your load to those nice young honeymooners. Trying to spoil their fun?"

"Honeymooner, my bloody—"

"Get his gun," Loob snapped to his deputies. "Christ knows I've been standing out in this wind long enough."

Farrow didn't try to resist as Charlie roughly patted his pockets. Three to one, and he was unarmed. His pistol was in the possession of Sam Augustine and his rifles were racked out of sight behind the Lincoln's rear seat. Furthermore, he was innocent; he had no cause to resist the law. Of course, while the hardheaded sheriff was being convinced, Augustine and Terese would increase their lead, might even disappear altogether, but those were the fortunes of the hunt.

"No gun," Charlie reported in a disappointed voice.

"Well, maybe these foreigners have different ways," Loob muttered. He ordered Farrow back into the Lincoln but not behind the wheel. The sheriff folded his own lanky body into the driver's seat and Charlie and his riot gun got in back. The other deputy was left to bring the official car.

While the sheriff sped the Lincoln west, Farrow got permission to produce his identification from his hip pocket. Charlie read it aloud to his boss. Loob curled his lip and shook his head. "Sounds haywire to me. Got a passport, yet you're supposed to be a New York bank detective. Never heard of an Englishman coming over to take a job like that."

Farrow explained patiently, "I'm not from Eng—" but Charlie cut in with "Never saw a white African before," and snickered.

"Furthermore," said Loob, "I never even heard of a private cop who could be trusted. Those papers don't sound very good to me."

"All that's necessary is to call Walter Stennis in Albany, New York."

Loob said with malicious sweetness, "Aren't you being kind of free with our taxpayers' money—long-distance calls and all that? I'm going to talk to you about your friend Bocock before I start spending the taxpayers' money." Farrow let the conversation die. They were coming into a small town of one- and two-story buildings, and a roadside billboard told him that this was Hargath, county seat, population five thousand. It was a farming community, whelped long ago by a railroad depot. The high way was the main street, commencing with the inevitable stock pens and grain elevator, then transforming into a gantlet of small drab stores. The spires of two churches thrust at the frowning sky; at one a minister was just opening the front doors while his wife swept out the lobby. A few automobiles crept through the Sunday-morning silence, all big gleaming brand-new machines.

Loob turned off onto a dirt side street lined with cottonwoods. They stopped. Farrow looked up, amazed. Marble steps led up to the colonnaded front of a palace, three stories high, the largest, grandest building in town. Over the shining white façade were carved the words "Hargath City Hall," and below that a motto about democracy. Bars across the windows of the third floor showed the location of the jail.

The second deputy parked behind them and then Farrow was escorted up to the sheriff's office on the second floor. There he was relieved of his belt and bootlaces and papers. Loob had already pocketed the Lincoln's keys. With no pretense of booking, the law men guided Farrow up another flight of stairs. All three of them kept their guns ready; they couldn't have been more cautious, Farrow thought, if he had been Clel Bocock himself.

And the entire building was deserted. There were lines of cell doors on the third floor and all of them stood open. "Nice clean town," Loob said. "You get your pick of quarters." They ushered him to an inside central accommodation, a self-contained little unit with a spring cot that folded into the wall, a wooden stool, and a washbasin and toilet in one corner. No window; the door was solid iron with a small grilled port.

Loob glanced at his deputies and they filed out again into the corridor. The sheriff closed the door and put his back to it, alone with his prisoner. He said, "Sit down." Farrow chose the stool. "How do you like my little project, Farrow? The jailhouse, I mean."

"It's very nice. But I'd appreciate some effort on your part to—"

"Up to date and practically never used yet," Loob said, not paying any attention. "Wangled it through at the last presidential election, with a little help here and there. Not many towns this size get a civic monument like this one." He chuckled. "Try to appreciate it, Farrow. You might spend a lot of time here."

Farrow shivered. The cell was cold.

Loob said, "That's up to you, whether you're going to be bullheaded about things. I hope you don't try to be bullheaded. Up in Cedar Rapids, the city cops been doing a lot of laughing at my expense. Simply because I got a hunch Clel Bocock might try coming here. Let 'em laugh. My law-enforcement methods are just as up to date as my city hall here."

"I'm trying to catch Bocock too, you know."

Loob got out a cigarette and lit it, showing off a monogrammed lighter. He smoked, half-smiling, a lean aloof figure, sinister in his egotism, impervious to any thought but his own. "You know why Bocock might turn up here yet? Not many people know it, but he worked a harvest around here a while back, when he was a tramp. I talked to a couple folks who remembered him, a pretty-faced young pup who couldn't hold his liquor. Talked big even in those days, said he'd been busting broncs down in Texas, all a pack of lies. One Saturday night he talked smart in a poolroom to the wrong fellow. Got the stuffing beat out of him and all his buddies gave him the ha-ha. He snuck out of town the same night." Loob smiled directly at Farrow. "But he might come back, mightn't he? He knows this is quiet country, good for hiding. I've visited every nook and cranny in my county and he ain't come back yet—but he might. Finding Bocock means a lot to me, Farrow. My luck's been bad—up to this morning."

Farrow said steadily, "I don't know where he is, Sheriff. I represent the bank in Albany. I merely came here to look for him."

Loob's protruding eyes gleamed like insect eyes. "Funny you'd know enough to come here. A lot of funny things about you. But I'm glad you came because you're going to be a help to me."

"I'm sorry, I can't. Unless—would there be a town or a farm called Little Jumbo in this territory?"

"We got places like Waubeek and Lost Nation roundabout, but no foolish names like that. That sounds more like some gangster alias you're trying to throw me off with."

Farrow's mouth tightened. "I can't help you if you don't listen. I suggest we summon a lawyer to establish my status. I don't want trouble, but—"

"You've already asked for trouble," said Loob in his sweet voice. "Just by meeting up with me. Maybe you don't understand how much Bocock means to me. I'm a fellow with plans, Farrow, big ones. If I can be the one to put the finger on Bocock—no matter where he's holed up—there'll be no stopping me. I'm the county official who built the biggest city hall in Iowa, but that's just the first step for me. When I catch Bocock the whole state and country will know about me. In the political game you got to make a splash. You got to get your name in front of people, no matter how."

The words had a familiar ring to Farrow. Then he remembered Terese Tyler looking down at Chicago and vowing much the same thing. He had a fleeting sardonic thought that no one wanted Clel Bocock for purposes of justice, only for some personal satisfaction. Did that include himself? He shook his head, not certain of where the idea was leading him.

"Giving it some thought, Farrow? Going to tell what you know about Bo-cock?"

"I'd do it gladly. But I haven't anything to add. You've seen my papers."

After a pause, Loob said, "Sorry to hear that." His narrow face was low-ered, grinning. His tongue licked across the edges of his teeth. "Sure you don't want to change your mind? You know I've got every up-to-date method at my disposal, just like the big cities." He snapped his cigarette into the wash-basin and opened the cell door, "Charlie, you better come back in. I guess he's going to be bullheaded, after all."

Outside a church bell began to toll slowly. From the pocket of his jacket Loob pulled a dirty pair of yellow pigskin gloves. Still grinning at Farrow, he began to stroke them onto his hands.

Chapter Fourteen

SUNDAY, MAY 6, 9.00 P.M.

The deep bell voice still reverberated in his head, pulsating the terrible glare beneath his eyelids. When he opened his eyes, it was even worse; he was star-ing up at the naked light bulb in the ceiling. It finally occurred to Farrow to turn his head. He did and the effort made him groan aloud and for a long time he gazed into a wiry forest of brown. It was the coarse texture of a heavy blan-ket; he was lying on the fold-down cot in the Hargath jail.

Sensible recollection came slowly. After several gritting attempts he sat up-right. One side of his face seemed detached and he put up his hand and felt the bandage there. There was a strong greasy smell of ointment. But he was fully conscious of his body; every time he took a breath it felt like an acid bath. Loob and Charlie had concentrated on his belly and groin.

Suddenly the bell stopped tolling and silence pressed in. He wondered how long he'd been unconscious. He worked out his pocket watch and studied its alternate blur and focus. The crystal had cracked under the impact of a kick, but it was running. It told him it was a little after nine o'clock. Since the light bulb hadn't been burning before, he reasoned that it was evening. Sunday evening, over twelve hours since he had lost Sam Augustine and Terese Tyler at the road block and.... But that wasn't important. He had slept from the ear-liest church service to the bell of the latest, all day Sunday in bed, but details were flooded out by the one terrifying importance. *Loob might return.*

"Must get away," Farrow mumbled. He stared at the massive iron door with its barred peephole. No eyes looked in at him. He was completely alone. Sud-denly he was baked in frightful heat and he hugged his arms over his stom-ach, trying to contain the nausea. Immediately afterward he was shivering with cold. The cot squeaked with his shaking. "Oh, God!" he moaned. The spasm was too familiar. Recurrent malaria. The strain, the lack of rest, and the vicious beating had combined to weaken him.

He staggered to his feet in a panic. His teeth chattered, "Atabrine, got to get atabrine...." Then the chill had passed away and his mind was clearer than before. He had been on the point of calling for the sheriff but he realized in time that it would do no good. Loob wouldn't be interested in saving him from delirium; quite the opposite.

Footsteps rang outside in the concrete corridor, Farrow fell back onto the cot and closed his eyes. An instant later the footsteps stopped and he could feel himself being watched. Then Loob's voice called down the corridor, "Go on home, Charlie. He still hasn't come around yet."

Charlie said something Farrow couldn't make out.

"No, never mind," Loob answered. "I'll stick around for another hour and see if he feels like talking then. I can handle him by myself." His nasal voice faded as he talked and his footsteps were strolling away and presently a door slammed downstairs.

Farrow succumbed to another chill and he gripped hard to the flat springs of the bunk until it passed. He stared at the door. "An hour," he breathed, and sat up, lightheaded. Perhaps an hour before Sheriff Loob came back. He looked around for a way out. He dug at the mortar of the wall with his thumbnail. It crumbled under the whitewash, leaving a gray gouge. Like other political buildings, the construction wasn't of the best—but he didn't have the time or strength to dig the door hinges out of the wall. Nor did he have a tool.

Then he looked down where his hand clutched the metal springs and his heart beat excitedly. The idea grew. He scrambled off the wall cot and threw the blanket aside and, kneeling, searched the spring anxiously for a wire that could be detached. When he found one, he laboriously bent it back and forth until it snapped loose in his hands, a stiff piece of wire nearly six inches long. It was the beginning of victory and he held it up and grinned at it like an idiot.

He pulled the stool over against the cell door and stood up on it, every movement causing him pain. Using the wire as a crude drill, he worked a hole into the plaster as high as he could reach above the door in line with the hinges. When, after an interminable period, the hole was deep enough, he bent the wire double into a rough sort of hook and forced the prong end into the hole. It was a tight fit and the hook didn't give much when he tugged at it.

The fever squeezed at him just as he'd finished this job and he retched miserably, almost falling from the stool. His stomach was nearly empty; he hadn't had any food in twenty-four hours. When his head stopped spinning, Farrow sat on the cold floor beside the bunk and tried to keep his hands steady enough to work on the coarse blanket. He frayed an edge and began to unravel long cotton threads, one after another, until at last he had nearly a dozen. He tied them together to form a single long knotty string.

Then his head drooped involuntarily and he had to rest. He longed to lapse into unconsciousness again and only by softly cursing Sheriff Loob in every language he knew could he keep himself awake. Finally he was angry enough to stand up and attack the hardest part of his task.

The flat rectangular springs were detachable from the iron frame of the bunk itself. Farrow lifted them out and they twisted around in his hands and clattered on the floor. The noise sounded to him like a clap of thunder. He held his breath, aching with frustration, and waited for the sheriff to investigate.

But Loob didn't come. Farrow tugged the springs across the floor and got them to lean upright against the door. He clambered up on the stool again and began lifting the springs up the wall. Sweating, straining with all his ebbing strength, he forced the unwieldy metal rectangle up, inch by groaning inch, until at last he could catch one end of the frame on the feeble hook he'd made. The far diagonal corner, slanting downward, came to rest precariously on the narrow ledge above the door, over the latch side. He took his hands away carefully, hopelessly expecting the springs to fall. But they didn't; they rested miraculously in the position he intended.

With the end of his labors in sight he could move faster. The yarn thread was knotted around the lower end of the springs, dangling down the latch side of the door to the floor with a few feet of thread to spare. The ravaged wall cot gaped emptily but Farrow spread the blanket over the cavity to conceal the theft.

And at last it was done: a deadfall. His native friends wouldn't have recognized its materials, but they would have understood its primitive principle—the suspended weight, the rope trigger. Farrow had seen it break a lion's back. Only the bait was missing, and Farrow himself would fill that role.

He tore the bandage from his face and cast it aside. Then he lay down on the cold concrete, head toward the door. He arranged his limbs so that he looked as if he had fallen unconscious from his bed. He was completely in view from the grilled port in the cell door—with the exception of his right hand. That was out of sight beneath the overhang of the folding bunk. And it clasped the end of the yarn thread.

He lay in wait. He had believed that the most arduous work was done. But now it was necessary to struggle with himself. He wanted to go to sleep. His big body in a relaxed position, his mind insidiously tried to slip away into some pleasanter region. Nothing, not escape or revenge or even self-preservation, seemed so vital as oblivion.

He fought the sweet temptation, counting off the minutes, certain that the hour had passed. The malaria racked him more frequently now, and he was alternately washed in sweat and shaken by chills. And he was thirsty, terribly thirsty. He played a lunatic game with himself. He told himself, I'll count to a hundred and then I'll give up and rest sensibly. And when he had counted to a hundred, he said, I'll count just fifty more.

Footsteps echoed in the corridor.

The footsteps stopped outside the door. Then Loob exclaimed, "Well, I'll be goddamned!" A key grumbled in the lock; the door started to swing open. Farrow turned his head as the lanky sheriff stepped into the cell—and he tried to pull the yarn trigger of the deadfall.

To his horror, his numb fingers wouldn't respond. The knotted yarn didn't draw taut; his terrible struggle of the past hour was all in vain. Farrow sobbed out in sheer despair.

And then Loob did the job for him. At Farrow's cry he stepped inside quickly and slammed the cell door behind him. The reverberation was enough to dislodge the crude hook that held the springs suspended over his head. The wire and metal framework toppled onto him, not the swinging ax blow that Farrow had intended, but like the fall of an iron net.

Stunned, Loob went down on his hands and knees, the springs teetering across his back. Farrow summoned up his last reserve of strength. Reaching up, he got hold of Loob's necktie and hauled the dazed face downward. With his hand on the back of Loob's neck he pounded the sheriff's forehead against the concrete floor again and again. He finally stopped when he realized his victim was unconscious.

With fumbling fingers he emptied Loob's pockets. The keys to the Lincoln Continental weren't there. Crawling, he got to the door and pulled himself to his feet and staggered out into the corridor. Using the wall, he reached the stairway and, finally, the office on the floor below. His belt, bootlaces, wallet, and—most important—his keys were in a heap on top of the sheriff's desk. There was no one else around.

Another seemingly endless flight of stairs and he was a tiny figure trudging across the marble of the cavernous entrance hall of the main floor. As he forced the big doors open with the dead weight of his body the wind cuffed his face roughly. It was howling like a Masai witch doctor and a thousand knife blades of sleet stung his cheeks. But the shock braced his dulling brain. Below, at the foot of the palatial steps, the Lincoln waited like an old friend. Farrow plunged down and sought its shelter.

He leaned over into the rear seat and hauled his suitcase up front beside him. He was groping through it for the atabrine when a far-off voice called his name. It might have been the wind or the fever's delirium—or Loob. "Should've killed him," Farrow mumbled. He forgot about the medicine and fought to get the car started.

He drove in a daze, not knowing where he was going, only that he must run away somewhere, anywhere. A white line appeared and led him along into the blackness... where? He kept trying to think but the answer danced around the edge of his brain, always just eluding him. Behind him glowed two great eyes that were pursuing him and he drove faster and faster, trying to outdistance them. But whenever he looked in the mirror, the eyes were still there.

Occasionally there were other eyes, too, charging at him out of the night and then vanishing at his side. He passed through shadowy places he vaguely realized were towns and once he rumbled over a long bridge where the white line disappeared. He found it again and raced on along its tightrope through a universe of freezing black. But then appeared other whiteness, falling petals that sifted through the beam of his headlights. When the petals blew into his windshield they blurred and trickled until he discovered that the wipers would brush them away. The steering wheel was cold and sticky in his fists. The white line turned and twisted now, trying to throw him off into space, and in a rare moment of reason he realized that he was climbing higher among invisible hills.

Then he thought he sighted the road block ahead and Sheriff Loob's sadistic grin and waiting hands in yellow pigskin gloves. He slammed on the brakes and his head spun with the car. When he found himself driving again, the Lincoln was bucking over a narrow rising road and the white line had broadened until it covered everything, even the trees that had sprung up on either side. The trees closed in on him until there was no room to pass through and he finally ran into one of them and stopped.

Behind him still were the eyes, climbing up to him, trying to catch him.

The Lincoln wouldn't go any farther, so he got the .475 Jeffries out of the gun rack behind the rear seat and fell out of the car. He was sobbing with exertion and panic. Everywhere he touched, his hands sank into the whiteness, soft wet fire. His car lights still burned and they pointed at something up among the trees. It was a cabin.

Dragging the rifle, Farrow floundered up to the door and pounded on it. "Jacob!" the wind screeched. He kicked at the door and it yawned open and he tumbled into a dark room.

He crawled across the rough wooden floor until he bumped into a corner. He propped himself up there, sitting cross-legged. "Come and get me, damn you!" he yelled. "Come and get me!" He steadied the Jeffries over one knee and pointed it at the receding shape of the door.

The pursuing demons screeched like the wind and one of them suddenly became a figure against the light, swimming into his vision. A slender figure with curved legs and long tawny blonde hair. Farrow squeezed the trigger and the heavy rifle boomed and thrust him back hard against the wall. Marget's piercing scream was the last thing he heard as he sprawled sideways onto the floor.

Chapter Fifteen

TUESDAY, MAY 8, 9:00 A.M.

He awoke to grayness. He was lying on his back, blankets up to his chin. Farrow turned his head wonderingly, letting his gaze creep across the small barren room, one object at a time. First, the narrow wooden bed on which he lay. Then the wide-cracked plank floor, fallen in at one corner. In another corner murmured a round blackbellied iron stove, a fire burning frantically behind its small isinglass door. Of the two cabin windows, one was broken and stuffed with a blanket.

Lethargically, Farrow attempted to raise himself. He fell back again as the room began to spin and he recognized how weak he was. Just as his vision began to clear, he heard the rifle crack and he clenched his hands convulsively. But he was no longer holding the gun. This was another time, daytime. His hands touched his body and he discovered he was naked. He couldn't understand that, or the swift passage of the night, or how he had got himself to bed. His skin felt warm, despite the drafts through the wall and the snow outside on the sill, but the fever heat was gone.

He muttered petulantly. With his eyes only, he searched for his clothing. It was folded on the foot of the bed. But he couldn't see his boots or his .475 Jeffries. The floor was dusty but he was unable to make anything of the tracks because it had been clumsily swept with a hickory branch that leaned beside the door.

The door opened with a rush of cold air and a skittering of a few large snowflakes. Marget Bocock came in, as if it were the most natural act in the world, and stamped the slush off his safari boots, ludicrously huge on her feet. "Still dreaming," Farrow sighed. Under one arm the girl carried the heavy Jeffries. From her other hand dangled a big cottontail rabbit, its head shot away. She was belted up in her own tan trench coat but she wore no hat. Her cheeks and nose glowed from the cold.

Marget realized suddenly that Farrow had made a noise. She gave a faint glad cry and rushed over to him, still lugging the rifle and sprinkling blood from the rabbit. "Well, you're awake!" she said happily. "Bless your heart, you finally decided to wake up!"

He moved his lips but couldn't make his voice come out.

She composed herself quickly. "No, that's all right, don't talk, Jacob. Save your strength." She remembered the rabbit then and held it up for him to see. "Isn't he a beauty? I had to shoot high or there wouldn't have been any left of him. Lord, that big gun of yours sure has a kick, though."

Evidently she hadn't discovered the smaller rifles racked behind the rear seat of the Lincoln. Farrow whispered, "Tinned food—in the car."

"Yes. Don't talk." Marget deposited her burden, eyed his face anxiously, rested her hand on his forehead briefly. "I've emptied your car trunk pretty thoroughly—that's where the blankets came from. Did you notice I had to wear your boots? I didn't bring anything except pumps, and I thought fresh broth would be better for you than canned goods. You see, I kind of expected you'd wake up today."

"Today?" he managed.

"Yes, this is Tuesday. I guess you wouldn't know. You've been out for almost a day and a half. It's nine o'clock Tuesday morning, May eighth." She smiled brightly, unbuckling her coat. "Still the same year, however."

Farrow watched her move about, extracting pans from the heap of camping equipment she had stacked at the other end of the room. He tried to reconcile the date with his own certainty that he had only closed his eyes for a moment. Monday had passed without his having lived it, and Monday night—and when had he eaten last? Saturday? No wonder he was so weak. He asked, "Was I bad?"

Marget, in a blue knit dress but with the coat still over her shoulders, had seated herself on the floor by the bedside. She was busily skinning the rabbit and she knew how to do it. She said, "I should say it was a pretty bad attack. Malaria, isn't it? I thought I recognized the symptoms. Then I found the atabrine tablets in your suitcase and I dissolved some and forced a little down you and just generally did what I could."

He grinned feebly. "Convenient—your coming from swamp country."

"Don't you talk!" she insisted. "No, we have mosquitoes in the Okefenokee, all right, but they aren't anopheles. I learned about malaria in a home-nursing course at the university." He lay peacefully, watching her deft movements as she cut the rabbit into crimson chunks, occasionally tossing her hair back out of the way. She said, "It's only snowing now and then—last bit of winter, I reckon. Lucky you found this old cabin, Jacob, because we're sort of snowbound. The road down from here looks terrible. I found chains in your car but I couldn't figure out how to get them on." She grinned up at him. "I've never been in the snow before. It's fun."

His eyes dwelled on her face and she busied herself with the rabbit again and he was content to gaze at her glistening fall of hair and the soft edge of one cheek. She was being a different person, some friendly stranger. She was refusing to be the female creature whose body strained toward his, or the girl he had brutally kissed in a harlot's apartment in Chicago. Except that she was tenderly caring for him, they had never met before—that was her pretense, and he was too spent to resist it just then.

She mused, "From the direction we headed, I reckon we're someplace in Wisconsin. All I can get on the car radios are Wisconsin stations, anyway."

She rose to her feet and wiped her hands clean. Not looking at him, she said briskly, "No news about us, either of us. The picture they ran of me in the Chicago papers wasn't anything you'd know me by. There, we'll have your broth before long." She turned to the stove, humming softly to herself.

How had she found him? Farrow couldn't hold onto the question. He listened to her music and the water boiling and presently the pungent broth aroma began to caress his nostrils and he went off to sleep again.

When he opened his eyes, it was night and the only light in the cabin glowed from the isinglass door of the stove. The wind that romped in the stovepipe made the flames dance from side to side and sent huge shadows careening over the rough walls. Farrow watched the interplay of black and yellow for a while. He felt less numb, more like a human being.

Suddenly he turned on his side and looked for the girl. "Marget," he called. She was seated on the floor by the stove, head nodding drowsily. "Yes, Jacob." Her eyes were enormous in the firelight.

"The other night—whenever it was—I shot at you."

"Uh-huh," she agreed calmly, and got up and stretched. She had put her own shoes on. "Hungry for that broth now? I didn't want to wake you up special."

He said slowly, trying to make sense of it, "But you're all right."

"Oh, you missed me a mile." She put the pot of broth on the stove top and adjusted the damper. "I'm lucky you were so ill. Though I don't suppose you'd have shot at me at all if you hadn't been so out of your head with fever."

Farrow tried to recall that instant's emotions out of the past. It was too much for him; he couldn't be responsible for his nightmares. Watching Marget work, the proud way she held her head, the trim fire-limned line from shoulder to haunch to ankle, he couldn't actually believe he had ever fired at her in hate or fear. But as he watched her body move and turn, unwanted memories began to come back to him, the serpentine truth that lay between them. *Clel Bocock's wife.* No, not even that, simply a woman Bocock had used to his advantage. And to his pleasure. Farrow scowled. Marget didn't know the truth, of course, but she did know that he was bent on destroying the man she loved as a husband. His empty belly tautened with confused passions. Vaguely he felt both grateful and humiliated. Why was Bocock's woman here now, nursing him, aiding him? He had no illusions about his condition; without her he would be dead, from exposure if not from the fever.

She brought the steaming pot over to the bed and helped him into a half-sitting position and began to spoon the broth into his mouth. Their nearness and his hard stare made her self-conscious. She spilled a few drops on his bare chest and, as she wiped them away, she murmured, "Why are you looking at me like that, Jacob?"

"Wondering." He made a short gesture at the room they had come to live in. "Why did you bother with me?"

"Oh, I don't know." She gazed, troubled, at the broth she stirred absently. "Yes, I guess I do. It was what I owed to you. I got you into that terrible thing at Hargath, not knowing. Honestly, Jacob, I didn't know things like that could happen."

"How do you know what happened in Hargath?" he interrupted.

Added color crept into her cheeks. "When I—when I put you to bed I *saw* the bruises. They beat you. And the side of your face—it's almost healed, but you were black and blue all over when...."

There was an awkward silence while Farrow imagined her dragging him to the bed, working embarrassedly to remove his clothing, touching him with solicitous fingers. It was the reverse of their first meeting—seven nights ago, so distant—in his Waycross hotel room. There she had been the helpless one.

She glanced at him. "I sent a telegram—did they tell you?—full of lies. I thought I could hold you up a little, long enough so you wouldn't be able to find Clel. I thought maybe just the publicity would be enough to spoil what you were doing. But then I couldn't sleep with worry—I'm not used to being underhanded, please know that—and I came there just as you were driving away."

The wind calling his name, the eyes following him....

Suddenly she made herself become the tender stranger once again and she could look him in the eye and smile almost impersonally. "Here, your broth's getting cold." He shook his head resentfully; he didn't want her to be like that. He wanted to be with the real Marget, not shut away; being enemies was preferable to impersonality.

And suddenly he couldn't bear to lose their old relationship with its torture of desire. He snapped out angrily, "You still haven't answered me. Why did you bother with me? That's no way to save your sainted Clel." A strange raw emotion turned the broth taste bitter in his mouth. He shoved aside her rising spoon and got up on his elbows, glaring at her. Even as he longed to hurt her—despite and because of her help—he was amazed at this delightful pain of pure jealousy. He had never experienced jealousy before. He said, "Not that you have any business fretting about Clel. You're not his wife. He's not your husband. He has another wife, a real one, whom he married three years ago. The woman in Chicago, that call girl. When Clel married you, he was running from the police just as he is today. He ran home and used your bed to hide in. Listen to me! He used your damned pretty body as a hiding—" He shut his mouth abruptly and sank back, afraid of what he'd said and what more he might say. He was deeply ashamed.

Marget said nothing. She simply looked at him out of her pale expressionless face, still kneeling beside his bed, still stirring the broth automatically. It was as if she hadn't heard. Finally she spoke quietly, "You must finish your broth, Jacob."

"Marget," he muttered. "I'm sorry."

Again she didn't answer but continued to feed the warm liquid into his mouth. The spoon rose and fell like a slow heartbeat until the broth was gone. Then she returned the pot to the stove and opened the cabin door and peered out into the night. "I reckon the storm's over." She belted her trench coat and went out, closing the door carefully around her.

Farrow's outburst had used up his small amount of strength. He lay on the hard bed and stared miserably at the door and listened for a car engine to start. He didn't blame her for leaving; he could undoubtedly manage for himself now. "Marget," he said.

The door opened and she stepped back inside. "Did you want something?" she asked. She had only been standing on the other side of the door, to be alone in the dark.

He said, "No."

"I thought you called." She looked around and finally withdrew her small suitcase from the pile of other equipment. She opened it and took out a pair of blue dungarees and a shapeless wool plaid shirt. She said, "I left Waycross in such a hurry that I forgot to pack my night gowns. The thing is, we'll have to use the same bed, Jacob. We don't have enough blankets for two of us."

Awkwardly, he said, "That's all right, Marget." He cleared his throat. "What did you do last night?"

She was behind the stove where its flicker couldn't find her. "Oh, I didn't sleep very much last night." Farrow turned his head away and listened to the rustle of her clothes as she changed into the shirt and dungarees. The stove clanked as she adjusted its fire to suit her and then she came padding across to him. He squirmed over and lay perfectly still while she slipped under the blankets beside him. Neither of them spoke.

He hardly breathed, conscious of the stiff denim against his naked thigh and the fragrance of her long hair close to his face. The shadow glow still swayed on the wall and ceiling. Tentatively, he reached down to press her hand lightly in wordless apology. He felt her flesh go rigid at his touch and he took his hand away and let his emotions fight it out until he went to sleep at last.

Chapter Sixteen

WEDNESDAY, MAY 9, 8:00 A.M.

When Farrow awoke the next morning, he found his arms wound tightly around Marget, holding the girl against him. She lay passive in his heavy embrace, staring at the reflected sunlight on the ceiling. When he realized, he released her instantly and she climbed out of the bed and began to put on her shoes, not speaking.

Farrow said uncomfortably, "I didn't mean to disturb your sleep."

"You didn't."

"You should have wakened me."

"You needed to rest." She was busy poking up the fire. "How do you feel?"

"Much better, thanks." He did. The deadening effects of the fever attack had passed away completely and he could sense the stirring return of vitality throughout his frame. He was conscious again that his body was composed of muscle, not jelly, and he was tremendously hungry. He was able to sit up and feed himself the breakfast Marget fixed. And the world had changed to a brighter one, golden bars of sunlight slanting through the east window and warming a path across the floor.

After eating, he dozed off, and when he opened his eyes again he lazily watched Marget comb her tawny hair and scrub her pale skin with melted snow water. He frowned quizzically, a memory nudging him. Although stockingless, Marget now wore a short-sleeved black taffeta dress, a party sort of dress incongruous in the rough cabin. It zippered tightly up her front; he gazed pleasantly at the curving zipper track and her bare arms and the swirling fullness of skirt.

She looked at him across her wash basin. "I found my dress in your suitcase. I'm trying to save my traveling things." Although it seemed to Farrow to be *their* dress, the garment Sam Augustine had stripped off her and given to Farrow, she could be aloof about it, admitting no link between them.

"I'm sorry. I didn't mean to keep it."

"Of course not. It was among your things and you simply forgot." Then she warmed another pan of water so he could wash and shave, and the morning passed with only token conversation. Like all who spent their lives in the bush, Farrow wasn't given to much talk, and silences didn't annoy him. Today's silence did, however, and no matter how thoroughly he considered himself to blame, he longed to have Marget speak to him and smile now and then. It seemed the choicest memory of his life, his instant of awakening when his face was pillowed on the softness of her breast and her hair was fanned out like some wild halo. But that had been an accident that she had borne, not invited. She preferred the gulf between them and her preoccupied attitude made even the smallest physical distances between them inviolate.

The day got warmer instead of colder, and at noon Farrow decided to get up. He was alone; Marget had left the cabin nearly an hour before with no explanation. He was still weak and the simple task of putting on his clothes tired him greatly, but being dressed gave him a sense of achievement. He hobbled to the window and feasted on the ridged landscape, the sheer drop behind the cabin into a narrow rivuleted valley, crags and forest and all layered in glistening white. A northbound flock of geese triangled overhead. Presently he saw Marget returning along the crest, meandering between the snowburdened beeches and elms, her head bent in thought.

Her reaction when she saw him dressed was a startled "Oh!" and then a frown. "It's too soon. Go back to bed."

He had been proud of himself until then. He said, "I've been through this before, you know. I can pretty well judge my own resources."

"Very well," she drawled crossly. "I reckon there's no use arguing with you. Kill yourself if you want to. That's all you seem to be good for, anyway."

Farrow chuckled at her scowl, which deepened. He didn't mind her irritation with him; in fact, he rather welcomed it. Any reaction toward himself was better than her previous withdrawal. While she was banging pans around in the process of preparing lunch, she snapped, "I suppose you think you can drive today too."

"No. I don't believe either I or the road down is quite ready. This is Wednesday, isn't it? Perhaps by Friday...." He stared thoughtfully out the window.

"But that's two more ni—" Marget began and then stopped abruptly. "I mean, that's one more day." She found he had turned round to look at her and she flushed and muttered, "Well, go any time you feel able, certainly."

He smiled wryly and went back to gazing out the window. He murmured, "Snow. I'd almost forgotten. I haven't been snowbound since I was a lad."

"I didn't know they had snow in Africa. Or are you talking about England?"

"I've never been there."

"Well, you're English, aren't you?"

"No," he said, "as a matter of fact, I'm not." She stopped cooking and stared at him. "I'm an American, Marget, born here. And my parents before me."

"But your accent—everything about you—"

"A matter of environment. You have an accent yourself." He grinned at her. "I'm nearer home right now than I've been in twenty-five years—if anyone can call a place he hasn't seen in a quarter century home. I was born in South Dakota, a town called Huron." Automatically, he added, "Pheasant country," just as he might have been designating the Masai plains as lion country.

"I don't understand."

"One thing and another." For the first time in years he was discussing his origins with another person and he felt embarrassed. "I lost my parents quite early, you see, and I was shuttled about from one uncle to another. Not a very inspiring life for a growing chap. Then I discovered the book. Mostly woodcuts, titled *Wild Animals of the World*. I still have it at my house in Nairobi. Nothing before or since that book ever thrilled me so much. I got many a thrashing because of it—I'd be hiding in the hayloft, reading away instead of doing my chores. Until finally I ran away. I was twelve at the time."

"Twelve," she said softly. "I can imagine you then—that way."

"And I've never been back. It was simpler to travel in those days, not so much fuss and red tape. All I wanted out of life was to become a hunter, stand up to each of those exaggerated animals in that book, face to face. Which I've done. British territories for the most part, for the most part Africa. Simply a *shenzi*, a man of the wild. But satisfied—for the most part."

Marget's eyes were dreamy, far away. "A rolling stone. Just like—"

Farrow's own reflective smile vanished. "Just like Clel," he snapped. "You'd better pay attention to the food."

She bit her lip and turned her back on him. Farrow said cruelly, "Speaking of Clel..." and crossed unsteadily to get the Jeffries. He hadn't cleaned it in four days. His uncertain foot struck her suitcase, toppling it open on the floor. He knelt to retrieve its spilled contents.

Marget had spun around quickly. "No, I'll pick them up. Don't bother. I'll—" She was too late. She froze, looking at what he held draped across his hands.

It was her nightgown, peach-colored and full and filmy. Through its gossamer, although doubled, Farrow could see plainly the brown sinews of his big hands. He understood before he raised his head to meet the girl's defiant eyes. She had lied to him last night and he knew why. She had worn the shapeless shirt and stout dungarees not through necessity but from fear of both their bodies. He drew the soft seduction of the nightgown over his palm and her scent rose intimately from it. There was a pounding in his temples and his breath came shorter. Despite his weakened condition there was between them in the sharp air of the cabin that same sultry meaning that had risen from their first moment together, always tempestuous and ever growing as it fed on repression. They had never been so savagely alone together; Marget's breasts tightened against the black taffeta as their eyes clashed like animals.

Farrow rose to his feet. Abruptly, almost surprising himself, he flung the nightgown down in the suitcase and left the cabin, walking through the ankle-deep snow as he had seen Marget walk, head down, looking at nothing. He reached the Lincoln, where it leaned its crumpled fender against an elm trunk, and seat down in the car to rest. He dialed on the radio and tried to concentrate on what he heard. It was the news; the usual repetitious events

were going on in the world outside. There was no mention at all of the Bocock gang.

After a while he plodded back to the cabin and ate the lunch that Marget
had prepared. Neither of them spoke a word, as if they were afraid that even
the simplest remark might set off a chain reaction. After the meal Farrow fell
onto the bed as the easiest escape. He was certain he couldn't sleep. He
dropped off immediately into slumber.

He opened his eyes in the familiar darkness and stove glow. Marget was fix-
ing dinner. Farrow cleaned his rifle until she told him in a low voice that the
food was ready and then they ate in silence again. The thoughts of both of
them were on the rapidly approaching bedtime. Farrow perched on the end
of the waiting bed itself, balancing his tin plate, but he and the girl resolutely
kept from looking directly at the level suggestive surface, the wanton tangle
of blankets.

Suddenly Marget said, "Jacob."

He hastened back to the present. "Yes, Marget?"

With no preamble she said quickly, "I didn't love Clel, not like—" There
was pause as she searched out some secret within herself. "Not like I might
today, I mean. I was two years younger then, such important years. I didn't
know as much. Under the right conditions, almost anybody can love anybody.
I believe that, don't you."

"I don't know."

"There was nature and my knowing him so well, all my life. We were both
healthy youngsters, and at eighteen—especially a girl—you think about, well,
mating more than is generally admitted. I wanted to be loved, to be completed
physically, and I reckon it was natural to think I was in love with Clel, actually be in love with him *at the time!*" Her slurring voice was fierce with concentration, begging to be understood. "After he went away I'd wonder
sometimes if we'd done the right thing, but I wouldn't really let myself think
it through because it seemed disloyal. I was a wife. I wanted to be a good one."
She slowed down, picking her words more carefully. "But now, if what you
say is true, I find that I was wasting my time being so scrupulous, that from
the start Clel was cheating me dreadfully. That gives me a right to think."

"What I told you was the truth, Marget, I'm sorry I—"

"Yes, I know it, actually. I'm afraid I wasn't as shocked as I should have
been. Maybe I guessed it would come to something like that, something de-
grading." She shuddered slightly. "That hurts as much as anything, to be second choice to *her!* I don't hate her, though. I don't even hate Clel. It might
be that it's too soon to feel it deep. But—do you remember once I asked you
if I should stop loving him because of what he's done? I still don't believe so.
If that were all, I'd hold onto loyalty somehow. But I stopped loving Clel because I *outgrew* him. What little there was between us—looking back, it seems
like terribly little—passed away ages ago. That's what I want you to know,

Jacob, and understand. Not because he's a criminal, not because of what you shouted at me last night. I don't love him because I just plain don't love him." Farrow said tensely, "Why are you telling me all this?" Her eyes shone soft in the fire glow. "I'm asking you again not to kill him." "No, Marget." "Please. Can't I appeal to you as a sportsman?" "No, Marget. Don't you realize what sportsmanship is? Simply practical rules to protect the player. Do you know why a hunter shouldn't shoot a sitting animal? Because it's difficult to locate the beast's vital organs when he's in a sitting position. That's the basic practical answer." After a moment's thought he went on, "Actually, this is the most sporting hunt of my life. There is a rule that you mustn't do what the game can't do—for example, climb a tree to shoot antelope. In this hunt, Clel has the same advantages as I, the use of identical weapons to kill me if he can."

"No, no, won't you understand? Jacob, do you believe in God?"

"Certainly. Do you have a notion I'm trying to pretend I'm some deity or other? I'm merely doing my business, Marget, tracking legitimate game."

"Not legitimate. That's what I was getting at. You're insisting Clel is an animal when he's not. He's much more. Even with blood on his hands, he's more. He's a human being like us, only a little lower than the angels, just as it says in the Psalms. It's not your right to deny him that. If human beings aren't any better than animals, then everything that people have ever done, ever built up, doesn't count for anything. It's got to count, don't you see? If Clel is only an animal, what are we?"

He shook his head. "You're making too much out of a runaway murderer. He gave up his rights."

She came over to him, crouched on the floor, holding to his knees. "No." She gave him a little shake. "*You're* saying he has no rights. But he's not accountable to you or me or to any one person. He's only accountable to himself and the law. That's what I grew up with, Jacob, the law. My father—the judge—oh, he wasn't perfect any more than the best of us, but he understood how law and justice held up the world. Everything there is, the meaning of everything, falls apart when law gets taken into a single pair of hands. It's *everybody's* will that keeps the world from being the jungle it used to be. You're not a policeman or a judge—you haven't been appointed by anybody except a bloodthirsty old man back East. What you are trying to do is wrong, horribly wrong. Your Mr. Stennis is bad enough, wanting a vengeance for his son. But you're doing worse, you don't even have vengeance in mind. You've simply hired yourself out to murder a man."

Farrow rose and looked down at her. He said roughly, "And what if I did have another reason to kill him? Perhaps I want you so much that I'd kill him to get you. What then?"

She released his legs suddenly. At last it was out in the open, the passion

he felt. Her white face strained up at him, mouth parted to release her deep-
est breath. Stammering slightly, she said, "That would be murder too, but at
least it would be personal, not so cold-blooded as...." She got up quickly to
face him in the gloom. "Jacob, you don't have to kill him to get me. I'm not
even his wife."

His voice was hoarse. "What do I have to do to get you?"

"Nothing," she said. "I'm here with you."

Still he made no move, conscience battling his desire. "I won't deceive you,
Marget. All I have of any importance is my trade, and pride is part of my trade.
I don't turn back from a trail."

She, sighed and her breasts brushed his chest as she turned away. "I have
pride too, Jacob." She drifted tiredly away from him, across the room—lost
to him, he thought. Her soft voice said, "I told you that you had to do nothing to have me. I won't put a price on myself or bribe you with myself. Perhaps I should, to influence you—but, you see, pride."

He said, "Don't talk any more." She bent to pick up the wool shirt and dungarees from where they lay beside the stove. He took two steps and seized the
heavy clothes out of her hand and flung them across the cabin. "No. The
nightgown."

"Jacob—you're not well yet." But she was already clinging against him, legs
straddled, and he was murmuring with senseless fury about the nightgown
and she was guiding his hand between her breasts and whispering, "Oh, darling, help me! Over a week, Jacob...."

Over a week since she had stumbled into his hotel room, six days since he
had followed her into the swamp, four days since his brutal embrace in
Chicago, two days since she had put his bruised fever-racked body to bed, that
bed which waited. She clasped his hand to the roundness of her breast as with
the other hand he pulled the zipper down over the trembling curvature of her
stomach, and then there was only the tautness of skirt from loins to hem. She
put her feet together so that the dress would fall and her skin and underclothes
appeared out of the taffeta's blackness like the rising of the moon. They struggled together with shoulder straps and a clasp in the middle of her smooth slim
back and elastic at her waist, Farrow's breath rasping, Marget whimpering
through her low laughter and saying shakily, "I wanted to say it earlier, but
Lord, I was afraid. I never loved Clel, no, not like I love you with all my heart
and soul. Oh, Lord, Jacob, I'm so cold except where you touch me...."

Then she had kicked off her shoes and he had never felt so strong as when
carrying her to the bed and he tore at his own clothes while she tried to bring
some order to the blankets. The yellow fire pattern striped her pale flesh and
his darker hands pushing her back. Her hair spread out around her face in the
tangled flamelike halo he remembered and everything about her seemed a remembrance, the abandoned hotness of her mouth, the full resilient thrust of
her breasts, the dainty arch of her hips, now surging and frantic. She tore her

mouth free to choke, "Oh, I didn't mean to bite you, I didn't! I love you so, I loved you always!" But there was no pain to the fervent nails raking his shoulders, no effort to their pulsating search for a single identity, no consciousness of anything save the glowing yellowness that soared and sank and heightened to an engulfing sentient splendor that could be borne only because they were two combined.

Chapter Seventeen

THURSDAY, MAY 10, 8:00 A.M.

And awakening to sunlight was another remembrance, for again he held Marget tightly in his arms and again she lay quietly, staring up at the ceiling. He knew a startled instant of wonder. Had the night been another figment of delirium? Then he stirred to the consciousness of her bare flesh full length against him and he said, "Good morning, darling."

Marget turned her head, smiled mistily, and kissed him warmly and whispered, "Good morning, darling," like a sacrament.

He said into her tousled hair, "I'm relieved to find you real. Did I tell you I love you?"

"Not nearly often enough."

"I do, Marget."

"Thank you, darling. Me too. But I'm not asking for anything, I don't expect anything. Thank you for saying it, though."

"How many ways would you like me to say it?" He began to urge her toward him with gently increasing pressure.

"Wait, Jacob." She slid out of the blankets into the brisk morning air. For the first time he saw her in utter revealment, beautiful in her nakedness beyond any carnal call. He gazed at her reverently and she grinned shyly and then for an instant posed brazenly for him, laughing, before she trotted away to crouch over her suitcase.

He said, "Don't you think the nightgown would be a waste of time right now?"

When she looked back over her shoulder, her eyes were serious. "Jacob, I believe I'll ask you for something after all. I'll ask you to take me along—to Africa or any other place in the world you want to go."

"I insist on it."

"I mean now. Now—not afterward." She read her answer in the slow stiffening of his face. "All right, darling. That's the last time I'll ask you, I promise."

"Marget...."

After a hesitation, she smiled, sadness in it and tenderness and resignation. She bent her blonde head over the suitcase, rummaging through it, voice muffled. "No, Jacob, we won't talk about it. Nothing can change the way I feel about you, remember that. But I've thought a lot. You see, it's your intent that matters—not whether some accident makes you fail. If I stood in your way, made you fail, that wouldn't change your intent or change you." She was fumbling for words. "So even though I don't respect what you're going to do, please understand it's because I love you so much, Jacob...."

He sat upright. "*Do you know where Clel is hiding?*"

"I'm—not sure." She rose and walked toward him, holding something behind her back. "In Chicago, that woman's apartment that night. Before you came back, I had already looked through it. I found this in a vanity drawer."

Marget held out her hand and he snatched the brochure of heavy paper, garish with color. A travel folder, unfolding noisily in his grasp. On the cover was a spouting geyser, "Come to Yellowstone America's Greatest Park... Nature's Wonderland."

She said, "I had it in my purse that night, that first time you kissed me."

He scanned the pages with mounting excitement, skimming through the printed matter, devouring pictures of evergreen forests and purple hot springs and golden trout. "This might be it, Marget, it truly might." He clambered out of bed and from his own belongings extracted his map of the United States. "Yellowstone Park opened the first of May, precisely the day that the gang dropped out of sight. They were last reported in Butte, and that's only a little way north. And Terese and Augustine were headed west...." He looked up sharply, unable to comprehend the girl's motives. "Why did you give me this, Marget?"

"I'm your woman."

"I'm afraid I don't understand you."

She sighed. "No, I'm afraid you don't."

He tapped the travel folder against his hand. "I'll leave for Yellowstone tomorrow. It may not be too late."

"I'm coming with you, Jacob."

He hesitated; it was better in hunting to travel alone. But she was part of him now. "Of course you are. Come here. You're much too far away this minute."

"I really should fix breakfast."

"You really should come here."

She stuck out her tongue at him and he captured her and the morning spun by. In the afternoon they dressed and dined like starving persons and strolled leisurely across the countryside, hand in hand. The snow was melting fast, unveiling the sharp outlines of coulee country. They skirted deep ravines and shook private snowfalls from low-hanging branches. Reddish-tinged rocks had pushed harsh snouts above the uneven ground, and where patches of grass had reappeared they saw bird's-foot violets and the white and pink of shooting stars. They talked of little except themselves and how long they had waited for each other.

Dinner was a hurried affair, and in the friendly dark again they twined close, listening to the wood crackle in the stove and the screech of owls and the infrequent bark of a fox. And once Marget cried out, "Oh, I wish we never had to go away!" and Farrow hugged her close.

But in the morning Marget commenced to pack the suitcases without a word from him. With his bare hands he straightened the Lincoln's fender enough to save the tire from harm. He dallied with the loading of the car, pretending a weakness he no longer felt. But at last there was no further excuse to linger and he went back for Marget. Dressed in her quiet plaid traveling suit, she was absently stirring the ashes of the old stove, staring at nothing. She came with him without protest, and when he had closed the cabin door behind them, Farrow took her shoulders and said roughly, "We'll come back here someday, the two of us. You'll see."

Marget said nothing. She didn't look back.

The dirt road was still slippery with ruts of slush. Farrow drove cautiously down to the paved highway, Marget following in her own car, and turned south. Fifteen minutes later they were in the little dairy town of Richland Center. They left her Ford in storage at the town's principal garage and by noon they were out of Wisconsin, the Lincoln heading due west once again.

The land they crossed was prairie, the highway a flat infinite ribbon for the most part, and Farrow trod heavily on the accelerator. They stopped that night in Mitchell, South Dakota, left before dawn Saturday, and by evening were in Cody, Wyoming, ready to enter America's Greatest Park and Nature's Wonderland the next morning.

Farrow called Walter Stennis from Cody, reported his progress briefly, and received a grumbling complaint at his failure to keep in touch. Stennis' pettishness seemed to arise from the silence of the press about the Bocock gang; he cursed the public's short memory but had nothing else to contribute. Farrow promised again to call immediately upon discovering anything definite about Clel Bocock's whereabouts.

"Remember our terms," Stennis warned. "You find Bocock—but no kill until I'm there to see it."

"I am not in the habit of forgetting," Farrow told him curtly and hung up. Wondering at his irritation, he hurried back to the auto court where he'd left Marget. That night their love-making was fiercer than ever.

It was a bright crisp midmorning Sunday when he braked the Lincoln at the Sylvan Pass gateway to Yellowstone National Park, paid the three-dollar fee for an automobile permit, and listened to instructions from a weathered ranger in a forest-green uniform. "No firearms allowed in the park. Penalty for hunting is five-hundred-dollar fine, six months in jail."

Farrow nodded. His rifles were safely concealed behind the rear seat.

"Don't feed the animals and don't go too close to them." With a glance at Farrow, Marget burst out laughing and the ranger frowned. "It's no joke, ma'am. Lots of city folks like you forget that they're wild animals, not pets. No matter how friendly, they can be dangerous."

"We'll take care," Farrow promised solemnly. About to drive on, he held up on impulse. "By the by, we're planning to join a party of friends here. I wonder if you'd know where I might find them."

It was the ranger's turn to be amused. "Mister, there's three thousand square miles in this park."

"Two of them arrived just a short time before us," Farrow persisted. "Probably through this same entrance. A blond man with a mustache and a woman with black hair. They drove a blue Buick sedan with Illinois license plates."

The ranger shook his head, then said, "Wait a minute—seems to me they did come through here Wednesday or Thursday. Don't know where they were heading, though. Were they sagebrushers or dudes?" Farrow raised his eyebrows. "I mean, were your friends going to camp out or stay at one of the lodges?"

"They would camp out," Farrow said definitely; the Bocock gang would come here only for seclusion.

The ranger said he'd check and went into the station. When he returned, he said, "That couple was a Mr. and Mrs. Arthur—Sam Arthur. That who you're looking for?"

Farrow nodded.

"I called headquarters and it seems they joined another party of three men up on Mount Washburn."

Farrow took a deep breath, at first excited, then slightly puzzled. Three men; had Bocock lost another henchman? Then he remembered it was Clel Bocock himself who would be missing from the count. The Bocock face was too well publicized to be shown anywhere. The park authorities wouldn't know of that fourth sagebrusher on Mount Washburn. "They must like it rugged," the ranger was saying. "One of the smaller camp sites doesn't have the water and sanitary facilities like most. You even have to go twenty miles to buy firewood."

"They don't care for people about," Farrow said quietly. "We're going to surprise them." Then he started the engine.

"Well, this early in the season even the main camp grounds are practically deserted." The ranger stepped back out of the way. "Follow this road until you hit the Grand Loop, then head north. It's one-way traffic. Grand Loop'll take you right past Mount Washburn."

They left his friendly wave behind. Farrow sped toward the peaks and gorges of the Absaroka range. Marget, watching his faint frown, asked, "Aren't you happy, Jacob? Things are working out the way you wanted, aren't they?"

"Oh, yes. Merely thinking." Of what? he wondered. For a few moments he had lost himself in a moody formless sorrow he didn't understand. As lost, as bushed as he'd ever been in a wilderness. A premonition? He scoffed at himself and put the girl's hand on his leg and made an attempt at gaiety. The joke he told her she utterly failed to unravel, but then she became excited over a black mother bear and two cubs begging by the roadside and they took a few minutes to watch. Farrow reminisced about the fence that had to be built outside Nairobi to keep the game from wandering into town. "In the afternoon you may take your tea and drive out some five miles and sit in your automobile and watch them feed. Zebras, giraffes, gazelles—occasionally lions."

"That must really be exciting!"

"You'll see for yourself, Marget, one of these days."

Her smile faded slowly. "Yes," she said absently, "one of these days. Hadn't we better get going now?"

About noon they turned north on the Grand Loop road, seeing almost no other traffic as they wound steadily through the mountainous forest land. The air was thin and chill and they passed several unmelted patches of snow. They glimpsed the great yellow-bouldered river canyon from which the park got its name, and then Mount Washburn's massive shoulder hove into view, towering above its neighbor peaks, its summit crowned with brilliant whiteness. It reminded Farrow of Kilimanjaro. "The Masai people call it Ngaje Nga," he informed Marget. "The House of God." The clean air, the panorama of stone and tree, the nearness of his quarry all combined to lift his spirits. But his exhilaration aroused no echo in the girl beside him.

And at last they came to the gravel road that branched off the Grand Loop to ascend steeply to the summit of the ten-thousand-foot mountain. Farrow drove up the lonely grade until he deemed it unwise to go farther. The camp ground where he expected to find Bocock couldn't be any great distance away. He wheeled the Lincoln off the road and under the shelter of a stand of Douglas fir. He changed into his hunting clothes while Marget prepared their lunch.

She kissed him good-by, holding him tightly, then watched him hike off into the underbrush. Farrow continued away from the gravel road for half a mile, then turned at right angles and paralleled its climb. His destination was a smaller peak—in Africa he would have called it a kopje—that jutted from a little way up Washburn's tremendous side. From there he was certain he could survey most of the country roundabout, spot his game before it spotted him. His only equipment was his long-bladed hunting knife and binoculars.

The clear mountain air confounded the distance and it was midafternoon before he arrived, panting, at the crest of his chosen kopje. Above him loomed most of the mountain and, out of sight of its summit, a ranger lookout station. Farrow worked himself cautiously around to a ledge on his promontory's western side. Lying on his stomach, he began to sweep the country with his glasses.

And immediately he had found the hiding place of the Bocock gang! The camp site, a tiny ragged clearing surrounded by fir and pine and spruce, lay almost directly below him at the base of his hill. There were two tents badly pitched at the north side of the clearing and two cars parked at the open south end, their noses pointed downhill, ready for a quick getaway. One of the cars was Sam Augustine's blue Buick sedan.

Farrow let out all his pent-up emotions in one long sigh. He lowered his binoculars and assiduously cleaned the lenses. Then he took up his watch again. The Bocock camp was a sloppy one, but he was not interested then in the fine points of woodsmanship. He began seeking out individuals in his circular range of vision. Bocock had posted a guard, a small man with a shotgun who chainsmoked as he scanned the trail leading up from the main road. They weren't expecting an attack from above; Farrow could detect no vigilance in his direction.

He located Sam Augustine, easily recognizable because of his blond head and his limp. And he could make out the female shape and walk of Terese Tyler as she wandered restlessly around camp; Farrow guessed that she found the solitude particularly distressing. There was still another man sprawled under a tree, but distance and shade combined to obscure his identity; only one thing was sure—the sprawling man wasn't tall enough to be Clel Bocock.

Which left the tents. One was plainly empty; through the half-drawn flaps of the other, Farrow could see a man's legs and shoes as he lay prone on a cot. The binoculars grew cold and sticky in Farrow's grasp as he waited for the fourth man to emerge. He waited and waited but the man stayed where he was. Occasionally one of the others paused by the tent doorway to speak to the man inside.

Farrow cursed as the sun roamed west. He was almost certain the man in the tent was Bocock, perhaps still convalescing from his Albany wound. Bocock was the one person of the group who would not dare to leave the camp. Duccone or Prof Nick Mellick or any of the lesser-known faces might make an excursion to the distant stores for supplies, but not Bocock.

Long shadows commenced creeping across the clearing below. Farrow growled helplessly. He wanted the sight of Bocock's face, the penultimate thrill. His quarry lay a few hundred feet below in that tent, but the only proof positive would be the actual sight of his game.

Finally he put his glasses away disgustedly. Today wasn't to be the day; the sunlight hadn't lasted long enough. He had to think of some way to get Bocock out in the open for a clear view of him, but without arousing the gang's triggery suspicions. He pondered the problem as he wormed out of sight of the camp below and picked his way down the opposite side of the mountain. Night was upon him before he reached the Lincoln.

Marget was waiting, huddled in the front seat. By dashlight she saw the stony look on his face. "Jacob! You haven't—"

"Not yet," he muttered. "I can't be certain yet. But tomorrow...."

Chapter Eighteen

MONDAY, MAY 14, 12:00 NOON

That night they spent at a lodge cabin far to the north of Mount Washburn, at Mammoth Hot Springs, the park headquarters. Early the next morning, Monday, they were circling south, again on the Grand Loop but driving the western side of its pretzel pattern, across Gardiner River and past black Obsidian Cliff and Roaring Mountain. They saw more of the black clownish bears and some elk and once, in the distance, a few shaggy ancient bison.

By noon they had reached Mount Washburn's gravel road and their parking place of the day before. During the drive, Marget had sat affectionately close to Farrow but not speaking much. As he climbed into the rear seat to open up the gun rack, she asked hesitantly, "Jacob, are you going to attack all of them by yourself?"

He chuckled at her worried face. "I'm a hunter, not a hero, darling. I don't take unnecessary chances. I have no intention of attacking anybody." From the weapons' compartment he pulled out a long bow and a quiver of arrows. "I stole these this morning while you were still in bed. From an archery locker behind that big hotel, the one that hasn't opened yet. No, today I'm only being a bloody Robin Hood."

"I don't understand."

"I'll brag to you *after* it works. There'll be no final show today. I promised Walt Stennis he could be present for the final show." He slung the bow and quiver over his shoulder, feeling a little foolish in her eyes. He tightened the cap on the small bottle of gasoline stowed in his hip pocket. "First of everything, I must make certain that it's actually Clel resting in that tent. I can't afford to believe anything I don't see. I've got to produce him without getting his wind up. Are you going to kiss me?"

She came into his arms obediently, lips warm for him. He could sense that she was frightened. The pace of her heart hurried his own and he embraced her at length, hoping to calm her, until he began to wonder if he was subconsciously putting off the showdown with Bocock.

Was he pursuing his quarry as eagerly as he might? For the situation was incongruous; her soft lovingness, so natural and right for himself, had once been Clel Bocock's. Had it been natural and right then, too? Farrow made himself stop thinking and kissed her with a final ferocity and left her gazing after him.

The day was a bit warmer, and the going was easier because he was able to follow his own trail. When he finally crept around the promontory to yesterday's observation point, his pocket watch told him it was half past one. Farrow lay and studied the outlaw camp through his binoculars for a while. The guard was posted below in the same spot. From the shotgun and the man's slight stature, Farrow decided it was Mouse Egan. The shotgun leaned against one fir tree and Egan slouched against the next. Farrow smiled. He had counted on a certain amount of after-lunch drowsiness. He wondered if the pinch-faced Egan wasn't also fortified with narcotics.

Sam Augustine and a third man were playing cards, seated in the shade of the Buick. Augustine's playmate had a sagging face with long sideburns; that would be Prof Nick Mellick, the former confidence man. There was no sign of Terese save some stockings on an improvised clothesline. Flies swarmed everywhere in the ill-kept camp.

The tent situation was the same as before. One was deserted; the cot end visible within the other bore a man's bare legs and shoe-clad feet. But the legs were simply male legs; they might have belonged to anyone.

A stiff breeze had sprung up, cooling the hot stone ledge on which Farrow lay. He crawled around to the other side of the promontory, out of sight of the camp, and strung his stolen bow. Then he selected a tall juniper tree, a good distance below him, and tried a few practice arrows, getting the feel of his weapon. He grimaced with disappointment. His former position was obviously too high above Bocock's hideout for accurate shooting.

Reluctantly, Farrow began to work his way back around the promontory, slanting his course downward on the mountainside. He kept a cautious watch in every direction, descending but a few feet at a time. When he halted, he was scarcely a hundred yards above the camp site, on an escarpment of rock that jutted out of the sagebrush. It was a natural platform, extending around the shoulder of the promontory in both directions. A dangerously close position—although nearness was the most important factor for good shooting—but he was counting on surprise below to save him from being seen.

A single arrow was left in the quiver; one shot would be all he needed, all he would have time for. He pulled out his handkerchief and knotted it securely around the arrowhead. Then he soaked the cloth with the gasoline from his bottle. A final secret survey of the camp found the occupants still off guard. Farrow lit the dripping handkerchief. It puffed into flame. He quickly notched the arrow against the bow string, stood up in plain view, and fired the burning shaft.

Farrow dropped flat immediately, discarding bow and quiver. He fumbled up his binoculars and wormed cautiously forward on the escarpment. Again, disappointment. All was placid in the camp below. He had aimed the arrow behind the occupied tent, at the mat of dry grass and weeds that the campers hadn't had sense enough to clear away from their living area. But through his glasses he could locate neither the arrow nor any smoke. With a curse he turned away.

"Sam! Hey, Sam!"

The yelp from below brought Farrow back. The matted undergrowth had burst into flame all at once. A guy rope was already smoking, and as he watched exultantly, the rear flap of the tent began to burn merrily. Mouse Egan had grabbed up his shotgun and was hollering excitedly while Augustine and Prof Nick scrambled around.

Farrow trained his binoculars on the tent door.

Within the tent, the bare male legs came to life. The cot overturned and there was a flailing view of a shorts-clad man scrambling to safety under one of the half-rolled sides. He looked about, directly into Farrow's lenses.

Farrow's amused grin stiffened in dismay. His heart sank with a sense of tremendous anticlimax. No deep compelling eyes, no tall swaggering killer of twenty-five years. The man he'd driven into the open with such difficulty was not Clel Bocock. There was no mistaking the apish build, the jowled face, the bald scalp with its fringe of hair. They belonged to Vito Duccone. His burly half-naked body was sunburned pink even to the top of his head, which explained why he had remained within the sheltering tent. He glistened with unguent.

Farrow squinted unbelieving at the terrible truth. Here was the Bocock gang—but where was Clel Bocock?

He had no time for speculation; he had to get away. He could hear the gangsters shouting above the crackle of the tent fire. It was doubtful, but possible, that they might reason that the blaze had no natural origin and start looking for the arsonist. Farrow crawled rapidly along the rock shelf away from their voices, away from their range of vision.

The gusty breeze was at his back and the shock of not finding Bocock made him careless. He rounded a jagged corner of rock, glanced up—and stared into the astounded eyes of Terese Tyler.

Time stood on edge for a still moment. Terese kneeled in green slacks and halter over a basin of suds. She had come up here to sun and to wash her hair. Her hands were poised in the lather of her short black curls and only her red mouth moved, opening wider and wider until she finally let out a piercing shriek.

It rang in Farrow's ears like the trumpet of doom. But it saved his life, for she screamed before she grabbed under her towel, which lay to one side. And he had time to spring before she could get the revolver leveled.

Even so, the first shot burned wind across his cheek. The second went straight up as he grabbed her arm, and then they were locked in a furious struggle for the gun. Her soapy head butted into Farrow's eyes as they wrestled on the narrow ledge and he couldn't see, only feel her wiry frantic strength as she twisted and clawed and bit, and her screeches shrilled continuously. He groped up her straining arms for whichever hand clutched the revolver and his foot skidded in the basin of water and they fell backward together, another explosion blasting his ears, searing his chest.

For a moment, dazed by the tumble, he thought that he had been shot. Then he realized that Terese had stopped her shrill noises, that she lay warmly quiet on his body.

Farrow forced himself up to a sitting position, holding the woman across his lap. He wiped the stinging lather out of his eyes and saw the blood pumping from below her left breast, running everywhere across her bare stomach and blotting on her slacks. The gun had evidently fallen over the edge of the escarpment.

Her blue-black eyes were puzzled and indignant. "Jake, I've hurt myself. You better do something for me." She touched herself distastefully and then her head lolled weakly on his shoulder. "It won't—leave a scar, will it?"

Her upturned worried face was that of a painted child. "Christ, if it does, I'll have to wear...." She began to smile at him in foolish surprise. Perhaps she was realizing. Death hadn't been planned for her career. It was all right for Clel Bocock or for Farrow or anybody else, but not for herself. She didn't know what to do with it.

So she closed her eyes. "Tired," she mumbled. "Let's just go to sleep." Then she was completely relaxed. Farrow was unable to move. For the second time he held her in his lap and he couldn't actually believe she was dead. Finally he edged his legs from under her limp weight and gently laid her back on the warm rock. "Not my fault," he muttered. "I didn't—" At the sight of his trembling hands, one thumb wet with her blood, he was nearly sick.

He didn't want to look at her any more. He turned away, standing up. The shotgun blast nearly tore his head off.

Chapter Nineteen

MONDAY, MAY 14, 2:30 P.M.

With the stinging rush of noise past his face, Farrow forgot the dead woman, forgot the loss of Clel Bocock, forgot everything but his immediate safety. He dove into the sagebrush cover and began crawling upward, away from the shotgun blast.

Behind him the high cracked voice of a man—Mouse Egan, certainly— yelled triumphantly, "Winged the bastard! Winged him sure!"

"Keep after him," came a hoarse bellow from the base of the promontory. "We'll swing around—catch him coming down!"

Farrow wormed higher through the low-spreading acrid brush, trying to move rapidly without disturbing the interlocked green branches. He reached a position of temporary safety behind a tilted slab of stone and eased aside the screening sagebrush to peer back. Twenty yards below him the little figure of Mouse Egan, repeater shotgun poised, was struggling upward. His thin mouth was distended in an evil panting grin and his eyes danced eagerly, seeking. He was a mad dog walking upright and Farrow felt an unholy chill of fear.

Then he loosened his hunting knife in its sheath. From a shot nick on his forehead a narrow trickle of blood found its way to his mouth and it tasted of anger. Who was this trigger-happy little *fisi*, this hyena, to hunt him? His mounting fury urged him to charge; for an instant his blood lust was as great as that of the dope addict stalking him.

Then he became himself, all taut caution, as he sighted the other three— Duccone, Augustine, Prof Nick—circling the foot of the hill. They were getting behind him to cut off his retreat. To leave the promontory was impossible; a barren expanse of rock would expose him if he tried to cross to the main slope of Mount Washburn. He was trapped, four against one, and they were armed. A shotgun and three pistols versus his sheath knife. Hyenas they might be, but he had seen hyenas tree a leopard.

He was living quickly; seldom had Farrow been aware of such intensity in every nerve, every vein. His survival of the next few minutes depended solely on his wits. In the clearing below, the burning tent sent up a wind-fuzzed column of smoke that might attract attention from the ranger lookout atop Mount Washburn—but by the time help arrived it would be too late. No, it was up to him and him alone.

Egan was crashing nearer. Farrow resumed his creeping uphill, making no noise and easily outdistancing the clumsy gangster, who was forcing a trail with his shotgun. When he reached the summit, he checked his relative position again. Mouse Egan was still the nearer menace. The half-clad Duccone and his two companions had rounded the south shoulder of the promontory and were beginning to climb also, to catch him in a vise. Yet they had not spread out in a skirmishing line but forged upward together in a compact group, as if for protection.

And it suddenly became apparent to Farrow that none of the Bocock gang knew he was unarmed. Why should they? They had heard Terese's shots but they hadn't seen the struggle. They would naturally assume their unknown enemy had a gun. "Afraid to get too close to me," Farrow muttered. "They want first shot." He played with the possibilities of this until the idea came.

Deliberately, he stood upright, waist and shoulders in plain view above the screening underbrush. He flung himself down again as the volley of shots roared up from both sides of the hill. The gangsters shouted back and forth until Farrow heard Vito Duccone harshly ordering them to keep their mouths shut.

On his belly again he began wriggling down the east slope, away from Mouse Egan and toward the other three. This leeward side was rougher, its growth heavier, a tangled thicket often taller than a man. Farrow crawled downward, turning his head from side to side, in search of the hollow his plan envisioned. Halfway down the hill, he found it and licked his dust-caked lips happily. It was a shallow ditch—a nullah, his African mind called it—that indented the side of the hill like a girdle. Little underbrush grew in its gray rocky track.

Both above and below Farrow, his stalkers were obeying Duccone's command and not speaking. Their movements were awkward, however, and Farrow could estimate their progress without seeing them. Nor could they see him, until they reached the brink of the nullah.

And most important to his scheme, they couldn't see each other.

He worked hastily, stripping off his khaki shirt first. A young fir tree grew in the ditch near where he'd entered, its tip reaching a mere six feet in the air. He risked detection by standing up, grabbing its tip and then sinking back to earth, pulling the pliant tree trunk down with him. He held its resilient length tightly, pinning its tip to the ground with a good sized boulder so that the tree formed a bow against the earth.

Then he dressed the fir in his shirt, buttoning the garment around the tree's upper half. The trap was set. Farrow backed cautiously away down the nullah, finally sheltering himself prone between the crumbly gray bank and a low rock ridge. He lay in wait, his right hand clenching a round stone like a baseball.

Crackling noises in the sage below warned him of the approach of Duccone and Augustine and Prof Nick. Above, and much nearer, he could hear the descent of Mouse Egan. The little man was moving more cautiously now, but his breathing rasped loud and excited. Farrow shivered involuntarily as he pictured those inhuman berserk eyes, searching about for a victim. But he made himself wait, listening in both directions at once, trying by sheer will power to jockey both hunting parties into position. Finally, when he could scarcely believe that the two detachments of the gang would remain unconscious of each other so long, Farrow pitched his round stone. It arced along the nullah and crashed against the boulder he had balanced.

The boulder teetered and released the tip of the fir, and the young tree sprang upright. Its upper branches, bound in Farrow's shirt, snapped back and forth almost in front of Mouse Egan's eyes.

The inevitable happened. The keyed-up Egan let loose a blast from his shotgun, then another and another, all poured indiscriminately into the brush down the hill. And, caught in the deadly crazy fire, the trio below began shooting back. The quiet mountain slope reverberated to the slam of mingled explosions as the two panicked forces fought it out blindly. Farrow hugged the gray earth and kept his face buried and prayed.

As abruptly as it had begun, the firing stopped. Wilderness silence, then a whimpered moan, then the crunching protest of brush as a body dragged itself painfully upward. This was above Farrow; he raised his head, then eased himself out of the nullah and crawled downhill again, away from the retreating Mouse Egan.

He came across Sam Augustine first. The blond man was sprawled face up, bent backward over a clump of sagebrush that was slowly sinking and adjusting under his dead weight. Part of his head and one cheek were missing, but his dandy's mustache was still intact. Farrow grunted; he felt no emotion at all as he straightened the dead fingers and removed his pistol, Farrow's own .38 snake-killer, which Augustine had appropriated in Chicago.

Vito Duccone was a few paces away, huddled on the ground, with a hand pressed fiercely against his side. His hairy back shuddered with pain and his shorts were dripping red. He still clutched his .45 automatic, but he didn't pay any attention to Farrow's approach because his eyes were screwed tight shut as he gritted against his shot wounds.

Farrow whispered, "Put down the gun."

"O.K., copper. Jesus...."

"Where's the other one?"

"The Prof—he ran away." Like a big pink sunburned bear, Duccone rocked back and forth, squeezing himself, muttering in Italian.

Farrow crawled over and took Duccone's automatic. Then he stood up and looked around. Above, nearing the summit, he could see the puny figure of Mouse Egan inching along. The shotgun had been discarded and there seemed to be something wrong with the dope addict's legs. In the other direction, down the hill, Farrow spotted Prof Nick. There was nothing wrong with the ex-confidence man's legs; for his age, he was floundering ahead rapidly, falling occasionally but escaping from the scene of battle. He was circling back toward the camp site.

Farrow crouched a few feet away from Duccone. "How badly are you hit?"

"Bad enough. But I'll live—I always do, copper."

"I'm not a policeman," Farrow said. "I didn't want a fight. You started it." Duccone spat with amazement. Farrow said, "You've been shooting back and forth with your own Mr. Egan. How does it go in the Bible? Whoso diggeth a pit-"

"Skip that crap," Duccone grated. His flat blue-stubbled face contorted with hate. "I'll live, all right. Just for one minute alone with that Mouse bastard, that goddamn hophead. One minute's all I'll need."

"Where is Clel Bocock?"

"You're so bitching smart, you— Goddamn!"

Farrow had reached out and slapped him across the face with the .38. He murmured, "Your opinions don't interest me. I'm anxious to get home and put on a shirt. Where is Clel Bocock? Is he with Little Jumbo?"

Duccone's jowls quivered, then he ducked his head and beat his fists on the ground with frustration. "The luck, the luck, always the no-good luck! Who do you have to be to pay this lousy world back? A piece at a time, I'd do it— starting with the Mouse. No, starting with that no-good Bocock."

"Where is Bocock?"

"If I knew, do you think I'd be cooped up in this stinking woodpile? I don't know nothing about this Jumbo talk. All I know is I haven't seen that louse Bocock since the Albany job. He skipped out in the other car. We got screwed up. And he took all that vault dough with him. Every double-crossing cent he took, leaving us peanuts."

Farrow said thoughtfully, "Of course. That explains a good deal. Why you robbed the Missouri and Montana banks so soon after—"

Duccone winced with pain and hate. "We were flat broke. That Georgia cracker ratted off with the works. Over a hundred grand, the papers said— all Bocock's, wherever he is. Creme was trying to find him through his women—the damn pimp has two wives, did you know that? But something happened to Creme, and Augustine and one of the tarts came out here to help us find Bocock—after the heat died down a little—and get our money back, those bonds." Duccone spat again, then stared. There was blood in it. "Oh, Jesus...." His dark face paled and he gaped at Farrow, wanting him to see it too. "Hey, it's no good the way I'm hurt! I'm...."

Farrow stood up. "I'll see that somebody comes up after you at once."

Duccone spat again and again, experimenting. It was almost all blood now. "This isn't funny. I'm feeling sick." He begged up at Farrow. "You're a good guy, buddy. We got nothing against each other. Let me have my gun."

"Don't be foolish."

"No, no—look. Look what I'm spitting! Somebody comes up to get me, I'll be through with it by then! Hell, just give me my gun." His raspy voice soared up. "I got time for only one thing, maybe! Let me go after that Mouse bastard! *Just that one thing!*"

Farrow chewed his lip. He remembered the innocent woman who had been shotgunned in the Albany bank rail And it was Duccone's last request. The man was obviously dying; his face and his bald head were as gray as the rocks in the nullah. Farrow tossed the .45 automatic a yard up the hill from the blood-running apish body.

Then he turned and plunged away, not looking back. He circled the promontory toward the camp site, descending at a lope. Before he reached the smoldering tents, Prof Nick had already gone in the blue Buick. Farrow could hear the engine sound fading, swelling faintly, fading again as the car twisted down the camp road. And almost immediately afterward, Farrow could hear another sound—sirens. The small fire had been spotted by the lookout above and a ranger crew was on its way.

Farrow didn't wait to be found there. He cut off into the trees and ran alongside the road, keeping just out of sight. The sirens screamed past. A few moments later, another car chugged up the grade, approaching, and Farrow spied on it anxiously, afraid it might be Marget in search of him.

But it wasn't Marget. It was the blue Buick, returning. Prof Nick was huddled in the rear seat between two rangers, despair drooping his once debonair face.

Of the Bocock gang, only the leader himself remained. Clel Bocock, like a jealous lion guarding the night's kill, still hid somewhere with his loot. Clel Bocock still waited for the hunter to track him to that secret place.

Farrow trotted faster toward where he had left Marget and the Lincoln. He knew, without knowing why, that the game still waited, that the hunt was coming to an end. And far behind, from the peak of the promontory, he heard the dull booming of Duccone's big automatic. Twice it sounded, then peace returned.

Chapter Twenty

MONDAY, MAY 14, to THURSDAY, MAY 17

Marget did the driving as they headed south. Farrow slouched on the seat beside her and tried to doze. He awoke, startled, to twilight. Marget was shaking him gently as she steered with her left hand. "Jacob, you're dreaming."

"I don't dream. Let me sleep."

"But you were, darling. You were shouting. You said something wasn't your fault. What is it, Jacob?"

"Nonsense," he growled and turned away and closed his eyes again. But he still saw the face of Terese Tyler, her childish astonishment at death. He had never before held a person in his arms and watched—and felt—the life drain away. He couldn't forget. You blinking idiot, he told himself. Working yourself up into a funk. You white-livered coward. *You* didn't kill her. No, he thought, the only person you would kill is not a person any more—the animal Clel Bocock. It's right; everybody wants him dead; he'd hang anyway. Don't think about it, don't think. He clenched his fists and slept uneasily.

That night in their hotel room in Salt Lake City he got out his big map of the United States. Albany, Waycross, Chicago, Hargath, Yellowstone; he crossed them off one by one. He leaned his elbows on the map and eventually he slowly penciled a circle in the lower left-hand corner. The Mojave Desert, where Bocock had once worked as a geologist with the Standard Oil Company. No, not a geologist—that obviously had been a son's lie to impress his mother. But Bocock had undoubtedly been a laborer at one of the firm's fields in the Barstow area.

Marget was standing behind him, watching over his shoulder. "What makes you think he'll be in that circle?"

"Hope, intuition, I don't know. Mostly process of elimination, I suppose. He'll hide in open country that he knows about. If he was with an oil expedition, he's had a chance to explore a good deal of that desert. And I keep remembering that old report that Bocock was seen two weeks ago driving alone across Arizona. At that time it amused me as another wild newspaper story. But the date was right. And now that I know he was traveling alone...."

"Don't you ever give up, Jacob?"

"No." After a moment he sighed and folded the map. He grinned faintly, for her benefit. "I may be utterly wrong, you know. I suppose that sometime I must fail. Not give up, you understand, but fail—run smack into the impossible."

"No, you're not wrong," she murmured tonelessly. "I only wish you were."

They left Salt Lake City at dawn. The morning papers carried black im-
perative banners, a complete account of the end of the Bocock gang—complete except for Farrow's part in it. Only Prof Nick Mellick had been found
alive, and the police could make little sense of his jumbled story.

"Where is Clel Bocock? Although federal authorities maintain that further
developments will disclose the whereabouts of the fugitive bank bandit, a
question remains...."

And other paragraphs were full of a new lip-smacking sensation: the dis-
covery that Terese Tyler of Chicago was the real Mrs. Clel Bocock, not the
Georgia "backwoods child bride," as previously supposed.

Marget read the newspaper stories aloud to Farrow as he drove, and her
voice was steady. "To Clel Bocock's long list of crimes may now be added
bigamy," she intoned. "Although the faithful Marget Ingram apparently has
joined her quote husband unquote, no clue as to her—"

"I'm sorry, Marget," Farrow said gently.

"For what? That I'm not really Clel's wife?"

"You know what I mean. I was thinking of—well, Waycross, your home and
your friends."

"My ignorant backwoods kin?" She crumpled the paper and stared out at
the desolate countryside. Presently she mustered a smile for him. "Oh, well.
Yes, I reckon it'll be a little hard at first. There's always people who like to
feel superior, like to rub things in. But I haven't done anything wrong, Jacob.
Should I feel guilty because of what somebody else did?"

"No, of course not." Farrow scowled at the highway rushing under them.
He said suddenly, "Marget, we'll be in Nevada this afternoon or evening."

"Uh-huh."

"Well, what I'm striving for—isn't Nevada a place where one can be married quickly?" She turned her head to look at him quizzically. He flushed. "I'm
talking about the two of us. Getting married, as it were."

She patted his leg. "Thank you, Jacob."

"Will you, Marget? Marry me?"

"No." She went back to gazing out the window.

The Lincoln jerked convulsively as his fists tightened on the steering
wheel. "What do you mean, no? My God, aren't we—I mean, you've said
you loved me—"

"Of course I love you. We wouldn't be—together, otherwise. You know
that. I love you, darling, and desire you, much more than is ladylike. Yet—"
She pressed his arm tightly. "But no, I won't marry you, Jacob. I've made
my one mistake that way, marrying a man who didn't think the same way I
do. I won't do it again."

"That's no kind of future for us, Marget, without marriage."

"No."

He snapped, "Are you bargaining with me?"

"Lord, don't be stupid!" she flared. Then she rubbed her cheek against his tense shoulder. "Oh, I'm sorry. Don't look as if you hate me, darling. You know we could never live down what's going to come between us. I have my notions of right and wrong, you have yours. No, I've had you for a week, all of it wonderful. Maybe I'll even have you for another, or longer. But finally it'll be over. You'll end your hunt, and I'll go home. We're grown-up enough to say good-by. You know it wouldn't work out."

"And what if you're pregnant?"

"I don't think so. Don't carry on so, darling." She was terribly calm about it. "If I do chance to bear your child, well, I'll get along. I think I might even like that. The child would grow up to be an Ingram, believing in the things I know are important. I'm a right independent person, darling—mulish, I guess. I do love you, though, forever and ever." She stretched and yawned. "Mind if I nap a little?"

He grunted angrily. A few moments later, to his intense annoyance, she was fast asleep, blonde head pillowed in his lap. He glowered at the road and muttered to himself, every other word being "bloody" or "damn." But it didn't relieve his choked feelings any, inasmuch as he couldn't quite convince himself that he was right and Marget wrong. He was getting a taste of his own medicine. In her own fashion, the girl wasn't to be swerved by Farrow any more than he had let her swerve him. And it was a beautiful spring day.

That night they stopped at one of the smaller motels in Las Vegas. As Farrow signed the guest register, the friendly manager inquired if they were newlyweds. Farrow snorted. "Kindly mind your own blinking business." That night, for the first time since the Wisconsin cabin, he couldn't lose his doubts and fears in her arms. If Marget noticed his strangeness, she didn't comment on it. He dreamed again and she had to wake him twice in the night.

It was still dark Wednesday morning when they crossed the border into California, following U.S. 91 southwest, to reach Barstow, the hub of the great Mojave Desert. It was a flat spacious town of six thousand, sunbaked but chipper. They arrived during a violent dust storm. When their highway crossed U.S. 66, Barstow's Main Street, Farrow pulled into a modern ranch-type auto court, ever flowing streams gurgling between arcaded rows of cabins. He left Marget in the air-conditioned coolness and wandered out into the hot blast of the Santa Ana wind to pursue his search.

He met with no success.

Oil fields?

"Somebody must have been pulling your leg, mister. Only oil here is in the Santa Fe Diesel shops, biggest in the world. Lots of mines roundabout—dig up everything including borax and talc—but nobody's ever been fool enough to think this was oil country. Certainly not Standard Oil."

Little Jumbo?

"That's a new one on me. Is it supposed to be a ghost town like Calico or Bismarck? Or a dead mine like Baghdad Chase up the street? Say—sure you aren't thinking of Jimgrey?"

Strangers in town?

It seemed that eight thousand or more passed through Barstow every day, on five main highways. Finally, dusty and discouraged, Farrow trudged back to the auto court. Marget was warm with tender concern for his black depression and he let her mother him without protest. The wind died away at sunset and the evening was calm and immense. They sat outside and watched the stream ripple by their doorway and listened to the pulsing chirp of Mexican ground crickets and didn't talk. At last she said softly, "Give it up, Jacob."

"No."

"You admit that you don't know what to do next. You've already done more than any other man could do. Give up this one hunt and marry me and let's go home—to your home, Africa." She was speaking rapidly and passionately. "I'll give up too, darling—I'll pretend you understand, pretend you did it because of me. In a few years we'll both forget you ever wanted to kill a man."

"No," he said harshly. "I can't. Why, I don't know any more—but I've got to keep at it. I've gone as crazy as Walt Stennis."

She sprang up, turned away, then came back to him to stroke her hands feverishly over his shoulders. "Then come in to bed with me now. Now before we talk any more. Let me pretend anyway, just tonight, that you said yes."

But there was little pretense. They made love ferociously, even cruelly, as if they hated each other. They spoke no endearments, and when the fundamental explosions had lapsed into dull satiety, Farrow could hear her crying softly against her pillow. He dreamed fitfully, more than before. Terese died in his arms and then Marget was dying, over and over, and finally animals sprang at him out of the dark, indistinct beasts with round melting eyes like Clel Bocock.

In the morning they said only the customary things to each other, trivial affectionate remarks that ignored the barrier between them and intensified it. Farrow escaped from her with a muttered excuse of needing razor blades. He plodded aimlessly along Main Street under a bright blue sky that promised heat later. He watched the morning traffic whiz by, dusty cars, many of them with out-of-state license plates and tubular cooling units canted against their side windows and water bags dangling from their rear bumpers. Automobiles purring east and west on carefree or prosaic missions. For the moment he hated them all.

Then, loitering under the drugstore awning after buying the unwanted razor blades, he noticed a car different from the rest. It was an old Model A Ford, high and ramshackle among the newer models. It came rattling along

Main Street from the west, its radiator steaming desperately, passed where Farrow stood, and parked near the big supermarket a half block away.

Farrow eyed it with commiseration, feeling kinship for the sturdy relic, so out of place, wondering if it belonged to some prospecting old-timer.

But it was a woman who descended heavily to the curb. A tall round-faced elderly woman, with freckled arms and a broad body. Farrow felt an electric jolt of recognition and a slow thrill flowered in the pit of his stomach. He nearly called out her name.

She had dyed her hair black and she wore sun glasses, but it was Mother Bocock who climbed out of the Ford and disappeared into the market.

Chapter Twenty-one

THURSDAY, MAY 17, 9:30 A.M.

Farrow stood flatfooted on the sidewalk, gaping, until Mother Bocock was out of sight in the market. Then he cursed himself for a fool. Had she seen him? Despite his idiot lack of caution, he was inclined to believe not. Her demeanor was wary, but she was not expecting to encounter the pseudo journalist from Reuters, and what the mind wasn't prepared to see, the eyes often wouldn't.

With more care now, he moved toward the gleaming front of the supermarket and lingered by the edge of a plate-glass window. Turned half away, he scanned the interior from the corner of his eye. The big frame of Mother Bocock wasn't hard to locate. She had her back to him and was loading canned goods into a basket cart.

Farrow walked on, thinking furiously, and halted next door under the shade of a beauty-shop sign. "Marget's island," he murmured to himself. "The tree." He thought that was the answer. Somehow, by relaying through friends and neighbors, Clel had got a message through to his mother—perhaps to his childhood postbox in the hollow oak in the Okefenokee. And Mother Bocock had answered the summons, come west to help him and supply him so he wouldn't have to leave his desert hideout.

Farrow scuffed his feet impatiently, sweating more from excitement than from the dry heat of the day. By persistence and good fortune, he had finally stumbled onto the trail that led directly to his quarry. But how to utilize it? From the way Mother Bocock was throwing groceries into the basket cart, she wouldn't have to buy supplies again for some time. If he was going to follow her to her son it would have to be now or never.

The Ford was parked parallel to the curb, not quite in front of the market. Behind it, a big naval ordnance truck blocked most of the view from the store's windowed front. Farrow ambled toward the old car, covertly examining its tires. He was disappointed. The tires were as dilapidated as the automobile, all worn smooth from travel with no distinguishing tread anywhere. They would leave only an anonymous trail.

But the spare, bolted on back, still retained a semblance of tread. Farrow glanced up and down the sunny street. Nobody was paying any attention to his loitering. He sneaked out his clasp knife, selected a short sharp blade, and quickly did what he was afraid to try with the four dangerously thin tires. He carved a large X in the tough rubber. With a handful of dust he rubbed the fresh black wound until the slash marks didn't stand out so much.

Still no sign of Mother Bocock. Farrow crossed the wide pavement to the service station on the corner. From the soft-drink dispenser he got a bottle of orange pop. He went into the restroom, poured the drink down the drain, and smashed the bottle on the floor. He kicked the pieces into the corner, and when he strolled out into the sunlight again, he carried a fat razor-edged needle of heavy glass in his pocket.

He returned to the Model A. Another look around, and he squatted hastily on the curb to prop his glass needle against the thin rear tire of the Ford.

From conception to execution, the whole business hadn't taken more than ten minutes, though it seemed to Farrow as if an hour had dragged by. He retreated to the drugstore and stood under its entranceway fan, pretending to read a copy of the Barstow *Printer-Review*. Time stood there with him, refusing to move on. At last, he began to breathe again as an aproned youngster came staggering out of the supermarket with a huge box of groceries, Mother Bocock sailing close behind. The boy hoisted the box into the front seat and hurried back into the store. The woman turned in a full circle, her dark glasses scanning everything in sight on Main Street. Farrow raised his newspaper to conceal his face. He kept it there as he listened to the Model A's engine cough to life.

A moment later he heard the bang and the tragic hiss, and he peered around the newspaper to see the Ford halted a yard or so from where it had started. Its right rear tire was flat. The thick glass needle had done its job.

Mother Bocock climbed out of her car again and stood for a while beside the punctured tire, looking down on it with dismay. Then she tightened her mouth and walked across Main Street to the service station and returned with one of the attendants. Farrow withdrew into the drugstore and drank a glass of milk (he had learned better than to order tea) while the flat was being removed and the spare tire substituted. He sat at the fountain counter until he once more heard the chug-chug of the four-cylinder engine.

When he looked outdoors, he was in time to see the Ford make a U turn at the corner and come back along Main Street. It passed his observation post and he strolled out to the edge of the sidewalk to watch the car disappear west along Highway 66. Wait, he told himself. Now simply take your own good time about it. Fifteen minutes later he allowed himself to return to the auto court for the Lincoln Continental. He didn't see Marget, which suited him just as well.

The highway led southwest for about fifteen miles, then commenced angling due south. The land was mostly flat, mostly prehistoric lake beds embraced by forbidding ranges of hills and cleft occasionally by sudden valleys of sand. The shimmering asphalt coasted over a parched and repetitious plateau, spotted with stunted sagebrush and saltweed and creosote bush. Near Barstow the country was cultivated—alfalfa farms and a few chicken ranches—and so long as the highway flirted with the dry bed of the Mojave River there were clumps of willow and cottonwood trees. But soon there was nothing in view but the colossal sweep of desert.

Tracking Mother Bocock was a slow and laborious job but Farrow did it with professional thoroughness. Numerous dirt roads and lanes branched off from the main highway. At each possible intersection he stopped and examined the ground for at least a hundred yards along the turnoff, searching for the mark that the spare tire would leave. He passed the desert hamlets of Lenwood and Hodge and Helendale, and other places that were nothing more than a few weather-beaten huts rallied around a filling station.

At long last he picked up the trail. A short way past Bryman, an old road curved off to the east, two forgotten ruts worn through the foot-high galleta grass. But plainly marked in the soft dust was the X, imprinted over and over as the wheel had turned. In the distance, the road vanished among some pearl-pink hills, their backs rounded with age.

Farrow wheeled the Lincoln off the highway and locked it. He buckled his holstered .38 around his waist and slung his binoculars over his neck. On foot, he struck out for the hills. The walking was easy across the level brownish clay of the ancient lake bed. Although the noonday sun was blazing hot, the humidity was low and Farrow could enjoy the heat. He could almost imagine himself back on the veldt. Summer had not yet burned away the spring primroses and purple lupine. Grasshoppers whirred across his path, and fluttering white and yellow butterflies.

By the time he reached the slope of the first weathered hill he was alone in the world. The highway was a black tape behind him and the Lincoln only a burnished gleam. A broad-winged hawk soared slowly overhead, its shadow rippling across the ground. The bird, too, was hunting.

The man found his prey first. The two ruts wound around the hip of the hill, ascending a cactus-studded crest, dropping again. Farrow stopped there. There was no need to go farther. The trail led down into an oval valley, a sparkling sandy expanse strewn with huge boulders.

Farrow raised his binoculars. On the opposite side of the valley stood the obelisk shape of an old oil derrick. It had never been tall, and part of its planksided tower had crumbled away, but the shack at its base was still intact and enough of its stark arrogant pyramid remained to show what it was that hope had built. Pieces of drilling machinery lay about, half buried or half uncovered by the fickle sand.

The glasses trembled in Farrow's hands. He could make out some of the paint-peeled letters crudely written over the shack door: "Little Jumbo No. 1."

The desolate structure told its own story. The little wildcat company—so ephemeral that it had made no impression whatsoever in town—the eager positive sure-thing drillers, the dreadful proof each day that the earth held nothing for them yet, the money running out, failure.... Here Clel Bocock must have worked as a tramp laborer, sharing the crazy hope, drifting off again with the failure. But returning, when he needed a place to hide himself and his stolen fortune.

In the shadow of a Joshua tree, Farrow studied the scene. He wanted to run away and proclaim his victory but he stood his ground, whispering his incoherent excitement to himself, having trouble keeping the binoculars steady. He scanned the little valley from one end to the other but there was nothing to see but the all-important derrick. He could detect movement through the open door of its shack but he couldn't pierce the gloom within. Behind the decaying tower were parked two cars, one a dusty late-model Chevrolet; the other was the Model A Ford that Mother Bocock had driven.

Finally he let himself turn away and stride down the hill and across the plain to his own car. The hike took twenty minutes and the drive back to Barstow fifteen more. It was exactly one o'clock when he burst into their rooms at the auto court and, with only a nod to Marget, asked the long-distance operator to get him Walter Stennis in Albany, New York.

Stennis almost shouted. Then his voice turned husky with grim elation. "Right away," he promised. "I'll leave immediately—soon as they can gas up my plane. Osher will fly me out. Jacob, you're magnificent! Barring engine trouble or weather, I'll be in Barstow tomorrow afternoon, be right there to shake your hand. But for God's sake, don't do anything till I get there!"

"No," said Farrow. "I can wait."

"Congratulations again, Jacob. You've done the job, splendid job, just as I knew you would."

"Yes. I'll expect you tomorrow," said Farrow, and after the good-bys, he hung up slowly. He turned around in his chair and looked at Marget. He couldn't draw anything from the expression on her face. She simply stood nearby, another piece of furniture.

He wanted her to speak. His thrill of accomplishment had burned out. Stennis' words of praise had given him no flush of pleasure. He couldn't understand his own torpor; his nerves should be building, building toward the greatest peak of excitement yet. But he felt stagnant. He wanted her to speak, but he knew that the only praise he really wanted would never come.

Yet he said awkwardly, still hoping, "Well, it's almost done. It's been quite a difficult stalk."

"Yes, of course, darling," said Marget. Her voice was coolly impersonal. She walked into the kitchenette and the same voice came back to him. "I reckon it's time for lunch. I'm sure you must be hungry, Jacob."

Chapter Twenty-two

FRIDAY, MAY 18, 2:00 P.M.

It was a haggard Farrow who met Walter Stennis' shiny two-engine airplane the next afternoon. His eyes were red-rimmed; he had been afraid to sleep at all during the night. Marget's love-making had been tender, none of the hungry fury of before, but rather a slow drawn-out measure of sadness, her silent rites of farewell. And Farrow had lain awake, one hand pressed flat against the warmth of her bare hip. Keeping himself joined to her in that way, he listened to her mumble as she slept, and he stared up at the dark ceiling, seeing the world over the V sights of his rifle.

Stennis, despite the exhausting cross-country flight, was fresh as a boy. Only his double-breasted suit, the same mourning black, showed the rumpling of travel. He bounded out of his private plane, shook Farrow's hand vigorously, and cried, "Jacob, you're a sight for sore eyes!"

"You made a quick trip, Walt."

"Not a hitch all the way. I take that as a good omen."

Farrow reached out and plucked the wilted carnation from the older man's lapel and tossed it down on the sun-hot airstrip. "A bit frivolous, don't you think?"

Stennis grinned, puzzled. "What's got into you, Jacob?"

"Nothing. Sorry. The car's over here." They walked toward the Lincoln. Osher emerged from the plane and spoke briskly to the mechanics but made no attempt to follow his employer. Stennis had apparently given him his orders.

Stennis checked abruptly at the sight of Marget sitting in the front seat of the Lincoln. He frowned at Farrow, who said flatly, "Walter Stennis, Miss Marget Ingram." They barely nodded to each other.

Stennis drew him aside. "*The* Miss Marget Ingram? Bocock's missing wife, or—"

"Yes," Farrow said. "She's been with me since Wisconsin."

"Well, well," murmured Stennis. "I've wondered exactly how you did it. So she sold out her husband—or whatever the status is in those cases."

"No. It wasn't quite like that. Ready to go, Walt?"

"You bet!" They drove south from the airport, passing through Barstow, then speeding southwest onto the scorched tedium of open desert. Stennis sat in back. No one spoke and the dry heat pressed down upon them. Marget, hands folded in the lap of her plaid skirt, gazed ahead at the rolling belt of asphalt highway. Once Farrow muttered, "Please sit nearer," and she obediently moved over so that her thigh was against his khaki trousers. He was grateful. The Mojave seemed harsher, more desolate today, and he wondered if ever a hunting party had been composed of such unhomogeneous elements.

At last, south of Bryman, the rutted road was reached and Farrow turned east onto it, following the trail he had taken on foot the day before. Clouds of dust boiled up behind the jolting Lincoln and lizards scurried out of the way. A black-tailed jackrabbit bounced away into the sagebrush. All normal acts of nature, but Farrow fancied the animals could sense the burden of death borne by the sleek automobile.

Just before the crest of the cactus-warted hill he stopped the car and turned off the engine. They all sat for a moment in the baking silence until Stennis rumbled excitedly, "Is this—is this...."

"Yes," said Farrow. "A bit beyond the hill."

They got out. When the rear seat was empty, Farrow swung open the gun rack and took out the Jeffries. While the others watched, he went over it carefully. The magazine was fully loaded. He looked around at their faces. Stennis had his mouth turned down grimly. Marget's expression was unfathomable. Her eyes stayed away from Farrow's. He said, "Follow me. Don't get ahead of me."

They began walking up the sloping road, a compact group. They topped the hill and looked down upon the oval valley of sand and boulders. Nothing had changed since yesterday. The two automobiles still sat behind the crumbling oil derrick on the far side. Clel Bocock had not escaped. He would never escape now.

They surveyed the valley silently. Stennis grated, "Imagine coming all this way—to here." Farrow didn't know whether he meant Bocock or himself.

Stennis was fidgeting, breathing hard. It had been thirty-three days since the murder of his son. He took a step forward and, with no other command, the three started to descend the hill into the valley. No hail, no shot, no movement at all came from the derrick to indicate that they had been seen. When they arrived on the arid floor of the valley, Farrow led them off the tire ruts and sought the protection of the big gray boulders that were scattered everywhere. They made a slow winding advance and the only sound was the scrape of feet on sand.

But when they had crossed the valley to the open glittering expanse that lay before the dead oil well, Farrow saw that their caution had been unnecessary. They had been watched all along.

A man was seated in the sunny doorway of the derrick shack, a tall man with a black lock of hair dangling over his pale forehead. The lower part of his face was dark with beard. He wore a broad-brimmed western hat and his head was up, staring directly at Farrow.

And Farrow stepped out into the open, the heavy hunting rifle leveled across his hip. He was finally face to face with Clel Bocock. He felt no sensation at all, only a little weariness.

Then Marget moved up abreast of him and he growled, "Get back," but she didn't obey. Stennis joined him in the open, gazing at Bocock fifty yards away. Farrow said again, "Get back, both of you. A creature able to sit up is able to rise."

"He doesn't have a gun," murmured Stennis.

Farrow had already seen that the holster buckled around Bocock's waist was empty, but he didn't like what he didn't understand. Bocock sat motionless, his hands resting on the arms of his improvised chair. Farrow grunted, then began moving forward slowly. His hands dripped sweat; forty yards, thirty, twenty... ten....

Then Bocock's shoulders twitched. He turned his head and drawled over his shoulder, "Hey, Mother, I reckon we got some company." His voice was soft and unalarmed.

But the reaction within the derrick was immediate. A pan clattered to the floor and then Mother Bocock loomed in the doorway, her face contorted with fear. Her big bust heaved under her faded cotton dress. She put out her hands as if to hold the hunters off and one reddish hand still held a forgotten strip of raw bacon.

"No, no...." The frightened old face, the stark black-dyed hair were incongruous. She recognized the girl first. She choked, "Marget! Lord, what on earth—" and then she saw Farrow. "You were a cop, after all!"

And her son sat by her side, smiling crookedly out of the left side of his mouth, his teeth gleaming pleasantly through his growth of beard. He said, "Ain't you going to ask them to set down and rest a while, Mother? We got water. Looks like they come a long way."

A dry sob from Marget. "Oh, my God, Jacob! He's out of his head!"

The famous face of Clel Bocock still retained its handsome reckless outline. But the flesh was drawn tight over the jaunty cheekbones, and from the large round eyes, once deep and persuasive and demanding, death peered out. His charm, his restless vigor, his personality had already died, leaving his tall cavalier body behind for a little while longer.

The body wore a black shirt and a cheap beaded jacket, the kind sold to tourists as souvenirs of the Old West. The belt that held his empty holster was brassstudded. Dungarees and a ten-gallon hat, as in his childhood snapshot. The sight sickened Farrow. Clel had always wanted to be a cowboy.

And death's smell was already in the air. Bocock's feet were naked, too swollen for shoes. His legs were puffed tightly against the dungarees and the shirt strained across his bloated torso.

"Leave him alone," whimpered Mother Bocock. "You don't want nothing with him. He can't even move his legs." She stared vehemently at the girl. "You led them here, you dirty little spy, sell out your own man to the law. You're the one ought to die, you're the one—"

Marget seemed to shrink. Farrow rasped suddenly, "That'll be enough of that. Marget has tried to stop me from the first. She's done her best for Clel. And what is his claim on her?"

"Don't, Jacob," the girl said. "He's dying."

Bocock scowled feebly at her. His dull eyes moved on to Farrow. "Clel?" he asked petulantly. "You looking for Clel Bocock, stranger? That's me. This here's my spread...." He gestured vaguely at the rusted machine parts in the sand and mumbled something that ended, "...my fortune in it."

Mother Bocock fell on her knees by his side, patting his hand. "There, there, Clel boy, it'll be all right—don't fret about it." Her hate-filled eyes sought Farrow's. "You wouldn't stand there so cocky, Mr. Cop, if he knew what you were here for. His mind wanders part of the time. He had a bullet in his hip from that trouble up in New York State. He took it out himself, not trusting any doctor. Now he's so sick with it, he can't stand up to you. Clel, it's all right...."

Walter Stennis spoke for the first time. He said harshly, "What are you waiting for, Jacob? There's the animal. Go ahead and kill it."

Mother Bocock screamed and, on her knees, tried to get in front of her son. "You ain't going to kill him! He can't hurt you now. He don't have his gun. I took it away from him. I hid it and—"

Clel cried out loudly, "Listen to me! This well ain't dry, I tell you! There's money in it. Maybe it don't look like so much, but there's a fortune, if a guy's smart enough...."

"There should be a fortune here, quite right," Farrow said. "A matter of some hundred thousand dollars in bonds."

The old woman seized the opportunity to divert attention from her son. "Bonds?" she said, and laughed. "I'll show you the bonds he stole." She struggled to her feet and ran heavily around the derrick toward the cars.

"I don't give a damn about the money," snapped Stennis. "Finish him off, Jacob."

Farrow looked at him for an instant. Then his mouth tightened and he raised the rifle slowly to his shoulder. Clel Bocock took his gaze off Stennis. There were dim flashes of reason in his eyes as he glowered sullenly at the rising gun barrel. He made a moaning questioning noise in his throat.

Farrow steadied the Jeffries, pressed his cheek to the stock. Through the V sights he could see Bocock's chest; he found the heart. He heard the sound of Marget sucking in her breath, the old woman rummaging excitedly in the car behind the derrick. He heard the blood roaring in his head as his forefinger caressed the trigger. The waiting instant tensed, crouched....

But the shot didn't come. Instead, Farrow carefully lowered the rifle. He turned to the girl. Her eyes were closed. He said, "Marget," and when she opened her eyes, he thrust the big Jeffries into her arms.

Stennis yelled, "Jacob! What the hell are you doing?"

Farrow stammered to the girl, "Last night—I decided. I didn't know whether I could hold to it, but I have. I've had him in my sights, I could have done it—that's enough for pride's sake."

"Jacob, Jacob..." she whispered, and her arms tightly embraced the gun.

"But, Marget, I'm not certain why I was able to stop myself. I'm not good at understanding ideas. Yet I can't kill him. Because that's not the way you want it." His voice strained toward her. "Because what seems wrong to you has got to seem wrong to me too."

She began to cry and her eyes kissed him and he flushed. He wheeled abruptly to face Stennis. "Walt," he said uneasily. "We'll have to make this do. I'll pay you back whatever expenses I owe you. We'll hand the fellow over to the police. He's dying. That should be enough for you."

"The hell it is!" Stennis raged. "You've turned coward on me, Jacob! I never thought you'd do it—and you've done it to me! To me, you—"

"I'm not a coward," said Farrow quietly. "You know better. I'm sorry about our bargain. I've broken it because of a greater obligation."

Mother Bocock reappeared suddenly. Her dyed hair was in disarray and she was damp-faced from exertion. "It's been in his car trunk," she panted. She held out a battered brown leather traveling bag, open. "Look at them," she cried. "There's all the bonds that Clel stole! Look at them!"

The traveling bag was empty.

In the quick staring silence, Clel Bocock spoke. His voice and eyes were sharper, as if he was abruptly conscious of the storm around him. He looked at the rigid figure of Walter Stennis. "Hey, I know you, fellow. The papers had it wrong."

Stennis swung round. He grated, "I don't have to listen to your kind, Bocock."

"Sure, you're the old boy who winged me up in that bank, up in Albany. But the papers got it mixed up. I didn't get nothing out of that vault. Sure, you're the old boy in the glass office, like a fish bowl. First there was the young guy I dropped and then you started shooting at me and I never even got to the damn vault."

"Thank God I came prepared for something like this." Stennis dove his hand into his coat pocket, and it came out holding a short-nosed revolver. "You were right, Jacob. I wounded the game. I should finish the job myself." The gun trembled as he aimed it.

Farrow had been standing flatfooted, stunned. Then he slammed his fist against the revolver, knocking it into the sand.

Stennis rubbed his hand, grinning confusedly at him. "Jacob, what's come over you, anyway?"

Farrow shook his head. "I don't know. But something doesn't make sense, Walt."

"Don't be ridiculous. Who are you going to believe, whose word are you going to take, his or mine?" Stennis tried to look wryly amused and imperious at the same time.

Farrow said, "Are you giving me your word, Walt?"

A pause, then Stennis dropped his eyes. "How long have we been friends, now? A good many years, and...." His voice trailed off and he bit his lip. Self-doubt was melting his blunt features. Farrow had never seen it happen to the older man before.

"You lied to me. Why did you lie to me?"

Stennis muttered, "I didn't mean to." His shoulders were drooping little by little. "The bonds hadn't been in the vault for a week before the raid. I'd taken them out, credited them to the Stennisfab account so it would have better standing when I applied for a government loan. Nothing really wrong—simply a business maneuver."

Farrow breathed, "Oh, good God, Walt."

"That's what Steven and I were arguing about when—it happened, happened so fast. Steven was dead and I was the only one who knew that Bocock hadn't taken anything. It was a fantastic opportunity and I'm getting old—you can't blame me, actually."

"Opportunity," whispered Farrow. "Walt, you hired me to kill this fellow."

Stennis' head jerked up. "Because of Steven!"

"Was it? Blood vengeance—or because of what Bocock knew? Because he might have been taken alive, because somebody might have believed him despite who he was?" Farrow grimaced. "Don't think I want to believe it."

Stennis squinted at him tiredly. His voice was husky. "Don't think I want to believe it, either."

"You hired me to murder—to protect your theft."

The older man half turned away, nearly stumbling in the soft sand. His words were shaky and muffled. "I can't tell you, Jacob. Not because I won't, but because I don't know! I had it all straight and clear once. Bocock had to die for killing Steven. But—a man can't often tell what his own mind is thinking. Life itself isn't any straight clear thing. There's never a single motive for anything. Nothing's pure, nothing's uncompromised."

And then Marget screamed, "Jacob!"

Farrow whirled. Bocock was sitting up straight, eyes fever-bright, a sly grin twisting the left corner of his mouth. His right hand held a .45 Colt revolver.

By his side, Mother Bocock said through stiff lips, "I didn't want anything more like this. That's why I hid his gun. But he's got a right to protect himself."

To Farrow's left stood Stennis' head hung in aged thought, apparently oblivious of the danger. To Farrow's right stood Marget, and she still clutched the Jeffries to her bosom. The long barrel of the Colt was pointed at her.

Farrow said quickly, "Drop the rifle, Marget." She let it fall to the sand.

The Colt swung to Farrow in the center of the group. "You done right," drawled Bocock. "I'd have put one in her right now, the two-timing slut, if she hadn't put down that gun." His earlier vagueness had gone; blotches of color had appeared in his face and his febrile eyes danced with something approaching gaiety. "Damned if I don't have the say-so now. How does it feel, mister? You who was pointing that big gun in my face a while back."

Farrow said gently, "It feels quite strange." He couldn't believe it was his own voice, so level and precise. He had a cold stone of fear in his stomach. This was nothing he had foreseen, not man against man, not man against animal— but himself unarmed against a lunatic.

Bocock chuckled, a witless gargling sound. "Everybody's after Mr. Clel Bocock. Nobody gives him a chance but he gets his way anyhow. I got my way now, haven't I?" He nodded at Farrow and squeezed the trigger. The bullet touched the sleeve at Farrow's elbow, then spanged off a rock somewhere behind him.

Farrow stood motionless, staring into Bocock's eyes. "That's excellent shooting." To his left, he could see that Stennis had raised his head and was gazing listlessly at the situation.

Bocock slanted his pistol at Stennis warningly, then brought it back to bear on Farrow. "Now I got two shells to spare, two left to play with. You know, I never needed more than one shot at a target in my life. Hell, yes, that's good shooting. When I get down to three shells—three people here. Then there's a box more in the shack in case of more visitors."

"Clel," moaned Marget. "You're deathly sick. Let us get a doctor for you."

Bocock glared at her. The Colt mouth jerked slightly and Farrow's vision blurred. But again the steel barrel swung back to him like a compass needle and he could breathe. He said, "Be quiet, Marget."

"Sure, don't get me mad," Bocock slurred. He licked his lips. "I got some blood poison in my legs but I'm not dying, not by far, not at my age. I been fooling you, till I got my chance." He believed himself, yet death was etched in every line of his face. He sat there inside his swollen poisoned body, a corpse willed to life by only part of his brain. But he was still able to kill, spread the death that had half consumed him.

Farrow looked into the dark luminous eyes and began to speak. He said, "This stalemate is my fault, Bocock. One should never approach fallen game—dangerous game—without making certain it's dead. You're quite right, you're far from dead. I broke a hunting commandment." He had taken a slow step nearer the girl before Bocock grinned cruelly.

"You're up to something," Bocock said. He fired again. This shot tore the shirt alongside Farrow's waist. He shivered involuntarily at the heat of the bullet. But he took another leisurely step.

"We were discussing hunting," Farrow heard his own voice say calmly. "You used to do a great deal of hunting, I understand, with Marget. In the swamp."

He stood alongside the girl. "There are a good many rules besides the one I mentioned, all for the protection of the hunter. One slip of the memory and often a hunter is done for." As he spoke, he wondered how thick was his own body. What depth of human flesh was required to stop a .45-caliber slug hurled by a revolver at ten paces? One step....

"Quit moving," gritted Bocock. "Quit talking. I only got one shell left to play with, then I'm down to three. All it takes is those three. I don't care about rules. Nobody ever gave me a chance to screw around with rules." He chuckled again, his hot dark eyes roving over Farrow eagerly. "No, sir. All I got to worry about is who goes first. That's my choice. You with the funny stuck-up voice, or the old boy who shot me up in New York state, or that sneaking female spy who showed you where I was." His eyes flared at Marget speculatively.

Farrow took the last step. The Colt muzzle followed him once more, but now he stood between it and the girl's body.

Bocock strained forward and hissed, "Mister, I told you to stop. You don't listen to me."

Farrow said evenly, "The rules—you mustn't forget the rules. They're made to protect you." He spoke more quickly, the words metallic in the silence. He didn't dare to take his eyes off Bocock to see if Stennis heard. He had drawn the gun point far away from Stennis. He said, "You must distract the beast's attention. You must make the first shot count, for frequently there is no second chance. The hunter who wounds the animal must be the one to finish him off. That's his responsibility—to finish him off. *Never wait—*"

Bocock swung in his chair as Walter Stennis fell headlong in the sand, grabbing for his snub revolver. The Colt blasted once. Stennis fired until the revolver was empty. The thunder rolled across the valley, rebounded, returned as smaller sounds.

Bocock shuddered convulsively. He slithered to the ground, rolled onto his face, his hands outstretched and empty and curled like dead white spiders.

Mother Bocock said, "Clel," as if calling him. She sat down by her son and took his head in her lap and gazed on it dumbly. Then she put the cowboy hat aside and began stroking the curly tangle of black hair.

Farrow had dropped to earth, carrying Marget with him, shielding her. He rose slowly and the girl clung against him, sobbing hysterically. He soothed her automatically, having a faint notion that he might be babbling slightly as he collected the Colt and the Jeffries and walked toward Stennis. His ears rang and he kept squeezing her shoulder and repeating. "Thank God. I'll never let the rifle out of my hands again. Thank God it wasn't you."

Stennis was sitting up, holding his right thigh while he watched the blood soak into the hot sand.

Farrow said, "All right, Walt?"

"Yes. I suppose so. Just my leg. Is he—"

"Bocock's dead. The hunt's over."

"You gave me plenty of time. He had so far to turn, I should have hit him every...." Stennis squinted wearily at where Mother Bocock hunched over her son's body. He didn't speak for a moment. Then he said slowly, "This isn't what I wanted. I wanted something once, but I've forgotten what it was."

Farrow shook his head. "I'm not judging you, Walt. I counted on you and your long chances a minute ago with Bocock. That's what saved our lives." He sighed. "Once I saved yours. The debt's settled."

"The money," Stennis murmured. "I promised you—for the hunt—"

"No. The debt's settled. I think I'd better go for the police now, and a doc-tor. I'll let you do the talking, tell them whatever you want told."

"I hope I can make myself tell everything." The older man glanced up quickly. "Good-by, Jacob. I won't be hunting with you any more. You wouldn't want to hunt with a man you can't trust. One of your own rules." He stared down at the red-stained sand. "Something about Bocock—always be between us. Everything he touched he blighted."

"Not everything," said Farrow, taking Marget's hand.

She had dried her eyes. "Yes, Jacob, I'm ready."

They started off across the valley, toward the weathered hills. Their fin-gers gripped tightly. He said, "It'll be best if we can leave tonight."

"We," she repeated softly. "Anywhere you go, Jacob, anywhere you care to take me."

"I'm taking you home," he said. "Africa."

THE END

Devil on
Two Sticks

By Wade Miller

1

Thursday, May 19, 4:00 p.m.

There was one parking place open near the Cathay Gardens when Steven Beck came along in his Buick. A gray sedan had pulled up ahead, ready to back into the opening. Beck tapped his horn and slid his Buick coupe in instead. The driver of the gray car glared back, mouth working. Beck met his eyes and laughed. The other driver shifted gears savagely, spurted away through National City.

Beck got out of his black coupe on the curb side and walked back three buildings to Hop Kung's Cathay Gardens. His body moved as always with a quiet surety, as if convinced its every move was valuable. His was a solid medium-sized body, conditioned in a club gym, tanned by sunlamp. An afternoon breeze ruffled his hair pleasantly, taking the curse off the high May sun, the California sun he seldom had time for.

He looked younger than he was. Part of this discrepancy was his crisp brown hair, cropped short like a college man's, and part was his clothing. Beck wore a tweed suit, slipover sweater and bow tie. His eyes, light brown and thoughtful, were his softest features. Nothing immature showed in his blunt face. Patches of steel-gray bristles at his temples were clipped near to invisibility. He carried his mouth locked shut but in the beginnings of a smile.

Past the bamboo screen at the front of Hop Kung's long restaurant, Beck paused in the dim, rosy light. He knew no one at the bar and there was only one man in the booths, a dapper Filipino eating chow mein with his hat on. The Filipino nodded his hat indifferently as Beck walked by and Beck murmured, "Joe," in greeting.

Beck went on through a door at the back that was guarded by a gilt dragon spouting painted smoke and a sign that said Private—No Admittance. He trotted up a narrow flight of stairs toward a second door labeled Private—No Admittance. The second door was mostly plate-glass mirror and it opened to him before he reached it.

A burly man rose from a chair six feet inside the short hallway where the lock control was. "Howdy, Mr. Beck," he said and made the mirror-door close again. Inside, the long glass was clear—giving the doorman a full view of the stairs—and laced over with steel mesh.

Turning the corner, Beck looked around the crowded second-floor room for his man. Softly chattering people circulated under the two television screens or sat at the small bar or studied the big blackboard where the odds were posted. The room was air-conditioned and pleasant. There was no trace of the

Chinese motif.

Beck stood quietly by the door until he located Sid Dominic and then went across to him. Dominic sat with Eddie Cortes at a corner table as far away from the flashing television screens as they could get. His oily face grimaced at Beck. "Here's that man again," he said to Cortes. "Why don't you ever get lost, Steve?"

Beck pulled a chair up next to Cortes. "I thought I'd catch you here, Sid." He accented *catch* slightly. "I saw your protection downstairs. Hello, Eddie."

Dominic was a chunky man with damp reproachful eyes and a voice always ready with an apologetic laugh. "Who—Joe Zuaben? Say, why does the boss saddle me with a creep like that, anyway? I got enough on my mind, making my pickups every day, without carrying that Zuaben in my side pocket. Never even smiles or anything—enough to scare a man to death."

Cortes chuckled gently, showing his white teeth, and Dominic said, "Well, it is."

"That's the little fellow's calling," Beck said. "Nothing must happen to you, Sid. Not while you're carrying our money. What are we drinking?"

"Not me," said Dominic quickly. "Not on the job. I just sat down by Eddie until Hollypark gets over."

"It's up to you. What's that you have, Eddie?"

"An affair I invented. I call it Shady Lady."

"It sounds like an affair of yours."

"I finally got the barkeep here doing it right." Cortes explained his formula.

"Be glad to get you one, Steve," Dominic said, starting off. "And a ham sandwich."

Cortes slumped a little lower on his spine and sipped his deep red cocktail. "Rushing around slapping wrists, Steve?" He was tall and slim, a flashy dresser with a handsome olive face. His nose and his black hair were both long. He indolently riffled the bundled tickets in his coat pocket. "I should be out distributing but a wise duck like me organizes so there's no work left over for days like this. Now, tell me different."

"Not while Pat's happy. You've worked up a smooth crew, all right." He liked Cortes. Dominic, he didn't think enough of to dislike. He found Cortes grinning at him. "What's the gag?"

"The last thing I intend to discuss is business, that's what I was getting at. Not and spoil the weather. Why don't you try sitting on your tail some day just for the sake of sitting?"

"Too busy, Eddie boy. I'm caught in the wheels now."

"You are the wheels. What ticks under there?" Cortes made a pass at Beck's short hair. Beck cuffed his hand aside and rapped him in the stomach.

"I'm not just a roadside peon like certain operators within reach."

Cortes patted his stomach and belched dramatically. "You out to mate your ulcer?" Both men laughed. Cortes went on to describe Beck's Southern antecedents and Dominic came back with the sandwich and the cocktail. The room grew noisier as two races—Hollywood Park and Agua Caliente—broke loose on the screens.

Beck munched deliberately through his sandwich, tossed his crust on the plate, and took a long sip of the Shady Lady before he began studying Dominic. Then, without moving his eyes, he found a cigarette, snapped up a low flame on his lighter and blew out smoke. Dominic fidgeted, laughing a little for no reason. Cortes was watching some girl across the room.

"How long you been collection man for Kyle?" Beck asked.

Dominic shrugged. "Nine, ten months. Why you asking, Steve?"

"Like your job?"

"Sure. Sure I do."

"Want to keep it?"

"Sure." Dominic gave his laugh. "My old lady would break my neck if I quit. What you getting at, Steve? Going to move me up?"

Beck kept looking at him. "Your accounts were off seven hundred last week. About a hundred dollars a day."

"That ain't so," Dominic cried. He tried to get up but the table caught his paunch and kept him halfway risen. "Who says so?"

"The boss says so. Seven hundred bucks, he says, and you can bet seven hundred bucks it is. My check shows you drawing too many receipt books. Either you're double-slipping or you spoiled some. I'm not being coy. There's a chance it's just error on your part."

Dominic sat down and tongued his lips. "Then you've seen Kyle already."

"Uh-huh. Through him to you, in proper order." Beck sent a thin stream of smoke across the table at Dominic. "Realize that Kyle's not the top in his bookie business any more, Sid. You might as well realize that. He takes orders from the boss same as all of us."

"Yeah, I could have made a mistake in my slips."

"That's what I'm saying. Better make it up this week."

Dominic forced another laugh. "Sure, Steve. Be sure to tell him I'll make it up this week. Anybody can make a mistake, I guess."

"Certainly."

"Tell you the honest truth, Steve, my old lady's been spending so much lately I just been putting it into one pocket and taking it out the other. Maybe last week—she got a new refrigerator since the old one ran so noisy—I took it out of the wrong pocket, huh?" Laughing more heartily, he wiped his damp face.

Beck sipped and didn't answer. He nudged Cortes. "Come to the party, Eddie."

Cortes only glanced around briefly, showing his teeth. His eyes were hot. "Why? Take a look over there. Nice material."

A girl was sitting by herself at the bar, her round hips perched on a high

stool with easy grace. Simply dressed in a glen plaid skirt and pale pink cashmere sweater, she looked as expensive as anyone there. Her figure wasn't elaborate. Even from across the room Beck could make out the fragile bones of her
wrists and of one lazily swinging ankle. But something in the way her arm lay
along the bar, fingers idly spinning a martini glass, impressed him. The same
for her delicate face, tilted back to watch the screens although she didn't seem
especially interested. *Patrician* was the word that occurred to him.

"Quit slobbering," Cortes interrupted.

Beck grinned. "So that's why you hang around here instead of tending to
your lottery like a good little boy."

"Accident, pure accident. At least, she looks pure. How lucky can you get?"

"She looks bored, too," Beck mused. "I guess we got that kind of snob appeal, Eddie. I can read the quail's mind. These antics are so, so common, but
it is amusing to watch the lower classes at their sport." He put it derisively
to cover himself. He had decided he wanted her.

"No, she's looking for a thrill, my boy," said Cortes. "Life went flat on the
old estate today. The game's all shot in daddy's preserve."

"Hey, what you guys talking about?" Dominic wanted to know. He followed their eyes, then held his nose. "Too thin. Too skinny. Splinters yet.
That won't keep you warm. Now my wife—"

"You're right, Eddie."

"Probably she doesn't know it but she's looking for a full-grown man."
Cortes pretended he'd been uppercut, shook his head groggily. "She's never
been hit by lightning. Match you."

"You're on good behavior."

"Steve, the parole board didn't put women on the restricted list. Be a sport."

"I wasn't raised that way. Sorry, chum, but she's my pigeon."

"What's so special about that one dame?" Dominic complained. "Eddie's got
his eyes peeled all the time for that stuff but I never heard of you getting
steamed up over any—"

Beck's eyes shut him up and went back to the girl. She had finished her martini and was searching her purse.

"You can't help admiring a thoroughbred," said Cortes.

Dominic said, "I heard a hot one about a rich gal and a—"

Cortes said, "I don't want to hear it, either."

The girl lit a cigarette. Beck liked her motions, smooth yet intense. He
thought her long unpainted fingers shook a little. He liked that nervousness
in her. Her young body was the next thing to frail but she'd be wound up
inside, waiting furiously. Under that tawny hair her brain would be the same
way, intricate, worth matching and possessing. She would be a precious possession. He tried to tell himself that she couldn't be as desirable as he was imagining but he still couldn't remember wanting a woman this much. Not even
the first time. He thought, *Possibly this is the first time.*

Dominic was arguing at Cortes. "What do you mean by either? What makes you so positive Steve doesn't want to hear it?"

Cortes asked languidly, "Steve, dear, do you want to hear Brother Dominic's joke about a hot rich gal and a—"

"For Christ's sake, no!" Beck snapped.

"I didn't mean a thing," Dominic mumbled in fat dignity. His face suddenly looked oilier and he toed Beck under the table. Beck turned on him coldly, then saw that Cortes had straightened up off the middle of his spine.

Somebody new sat at the bar. A tall broad man in a cheap dark suit sat two stools away from the girl and Beck hadn't seen him arrive.

"Well, well," he said.

"Not playing, barely drinking, looking at faces." Cortes slipped his hand under the table. Something thumped on his shoe and was eased to the floor. "Just a pocket knife but the board often gets picky."

"Tickets," Beck said. "Give them to Dominic."

Dominic stuffed the lottery tabs away nervously. "Why the raid? I thought things were under control. My old lady won't take to me getting jugged."

"We better get cleaned up before company comes." Beck murmured swift orders. Dominic got up first, heading for the blackboard to tip the man there, then to the cashier, then to the incinerator. A minute later Eddie Cortes rose, stretched and sauntered over to the bartender, signaling the doorman on his way.

Beck went up to the bar and slid onto the stool next to the cop. His elbow bumped over the man's beer and he apologized. "A round on me, of course."

The cop said heavily, "That's a good idea."

"I'd recommend a sour." The bartender was already mixing it. "If you don't mind drinking with me."

"No, but I think I'll have a beer." A short yellow drink was shoved to him and the cop began to catch on.

"Don't knock it over," Beck warned him cheerfully.

Narrowing his eyes, the cop stared hard at him, then at some of the others. The bartender stood a step away, holding a square frosted gin bottle as if reading the label. The doorman had moved closer. The chalkman was erasing his blackboard with one hand and gathering papers with the other.

While the cop digested his position, Beck glanced back at the girl. She had gray eyes which were watching him solemnly. He smiled at her.

"Please don't wait for me," Beck told the cop.

The larger man frowned, lifted the glass to his lips and began to set it down again.

"I said don't wait for me."

Their eyes met. The cop's throat muscles moved. He hesitated, muttered, "See you in hell," and tossed the yellow liquid into his mouth.

Beck said to the doorman, "I think my friend may get a little sick. Help him make it to the little boys' room."

"This way, pal." The doorman took his arm and the cop tried to pull away angrily. He said, "I can take anything you—" and began to retch. He let himself be led. His chin was wet and he was staggering before he made it to the toilet door.

Dominic came around from the incinerator door in the wall by the bar. He had dumped his load of paper down into the kitchen fires on the ground floor. "Too late," he moaned. "They're here already."

Over the bar, a red light flashed on and off, on and off. "Get after slips," Beck commanded.

Noises came up the stairwell. Glass smashing, wood tearing.

The customers began to get on their feet. Beck weaved among the tables, soothing as he went. "Ladies and gentlemen, we're about to have some uninvited police with us. Give me all your slips quickly, please, and there will be no trouble." Cortes followed his lead.

"Police!" a man bellowed incredulously. Beck pushed him back in his chair and asked for his betting slips. Most of the crowd behaved. These places were taken care of. Beck and his help combed the room while the smashing noises continued from below. The steel mesh and the trick lock were holding them up.

Cortes waved all clear from beside the little door to the incinerator. Beck started back across the room, both hands full of wadded paper. The smashing noises had stopped.

He sprinted along the bar with the last load of slips. He heard feet slapping up the stairs, lots of them. A khaki uniform showed in the doorway.

Beck collided violently with a yielding body and sprawled headlong to the floor, the girl under him. The paper was scattered in a little circle around them. He shoved her aside and tried to gather the slips again.

The girl sat up, halfway between laughing and crying. Her plaid skirt was up around her hips. Beck noticed she had shapely legs for a slim girl and that her hose were sheer. She didn't paint her toes, either, and he saw no rings on her fingers. He thought of the nursery rhyme while he squatted at the maddening, childish task of picking up a hundred scraps of paper.

A rough hand jerked him to his feet, held him there. A plainclothesman came up and forced the betting slips out of his fist. A uniform cop took his place at picking up the paper. Beck stood quietly under the first cop's grip while the room milled in confusion. The girl was still sitting on the floor, watching him with puzzled interest. Beck winked down at her and started to whistle "The Prisoner's Song."

2

Thursday, May 19, 7:30 p.m.

The blind was pulled down over the single window to the police headquarters patio. Two wooden folding chairs stood in the bare stucco room. Lieutenant Richards, Vice Detail, had his foot up on one. He was big, lean except
for slight jowls, red-veined on cheeks and eyes. He wore the typical cop expression, angry, bored, untiring.

"Let's go over it again," he suggested.

"Let's," Beck said pleasantly. He'd been sitting in the other chair for over
two hours.

"What's your name?"

"Steven Beck, age thirty-five, bachelor, last residence Montgomery, Alabama. Presently a resident member of the Southwest Towers Athletic Club
here in San Diego."

"Occupation?"

"Life insurance underwriter."

The uniform cop leaning against the door expelled his breath noisily and
crossed his feet the other way. Richards contemplated a fluorescent tube that
flickered in the ceiling fixture. He watched it until it went out for good. He
had all the time in the world. "You know Patrick Garland?"

"Of course. I handle his insurance."

"Know Orville Kyle?"

"He's another client of mine."

"How about Larson Tarrant? How about Charles Holsclaw?"

"You must have gotten hold of my renewal list, Lieutenant."

"Uh-huh." Richards wandered around behind Beck, who didn't bother to
watch him. "If you were in my shoes, wouldn't it strike you peculiar that all
the bosses get their insurance from the same man?"

"I'm not in your shoes."

"Just a coincidence, I suppose. That's what they all say."

"You're putting words in my mouth. I've been cooperative. I repeat, may
I see my lawyer?"

Beck saw the uniform cop shoot a pleased glance over his head to Richards.
Richards said mildly, "Well, I don't believe much in coincidence. Don't Garland's boys get tired of buying insurance all the time just to keep up a front
for you?"

"You can't carry too much insurance."

"What were you doing in that bookie joint?"

"I thought it was a private social club. A client took me up for a drink."

"A mickey? Like the one you handed Ryland?"

"I didn't hand anybody a drink, Lieutenant."

"Why'd you try to destroy the betting slips when my men broke in?"

"What betting slips?"

"These." Richards came around in front of him to show a fistful of paper.

"Is that what they are? Somebody dropped them and I was helping pick them up. Are you certain those are the same papers?"

"Just plain neat," said the cop at the door.

Richards' look said keep out of this. He thought he was getting somewhere. He stuffed the slips back in his pocket and fondled them almost sensuously. "Too bad you aren't a little faster, Beck. Then we wouldn't have found any evidence at all. What does Eddie Cortes do?"

"I wouldn't know. I've only met him once or twice."

The cop at the door cleared his throat. He said doggedly, "Maybe if you could let us see what we can do, Lieutenant—"

"In good time," Richards said. He towered over the man in the chair. "Thanks to these slips, we can close up that little enterprise at the Cathay Gardens, shut it down for good. Oh, I know Pat Garland will open something else, but I want to tell you something straight."

Beck asked, "Do you mind if I smoke?"

"There's a joke about that. It goes, I don't care if you burn."

"That's very good."

Richards went over to stare at the window as if the blind were up and he could see through the dark outside. The bare dull room was a small world to wander. A block away the ferry whistled. Richards said, as an afterthought, "No, you can't smoke."

The uniform cop left the door, joined Richards at the blank window, keeping an eye on Beck. He whispered. When he had finished, Richards said aloud, "The hell you know his kind."

The cop took up his old pose against the door and Richards booted the other chair closer to Beck. He sat down and told the cop, "Go down and see if my wife has called." After the door closed, he got out a cigarette and went through extra motions lighting it. Beck examined his hands, which were still dirty from his fall. He raised his head as a puff of smoke from Richards' mouth eddied about him.

Richards spoke suddenly. "Put it to you man to man. I'll tell you what we know and don't know, Beck. We know that your Pat Garland runs everything south of the Orange County line. Everything in what's laughingly called the sporting fraternity. Everything crooked. We know who his men are. We know how they operate."

Beck smiled and nodded his interest. "I imagine this information is confidential."

"This trip we're going to do more than close up one bookie joint. We're going to roll up the whole Garland organization. Now, you're Garland's number one trouble-shooter. If there should be anything we don't know, you could fill in the blank spots. How about it?"

"How about what?"

"Beck, you're a smart cookie. You wouldn't be where you are if you weren't." Richards paused, struck by a thought. "Maybe you're even smarter than Garland. Maybe you got the smart position of being the front man's brains. Why don't you use those brains and see how now is the time to get out with a whole skin. Garland's number is up."

"In that case, I'm glad his wife is so well taken care of," Beck said. "There's a man who's used his head about a planned insurance program."

Richards laughed harshly and got up, kicking the chair backward. "Sorry if I've bored you. You'll go down the drain with the rest. At San Quentin they won't doll you up so cute." He took one end of the bow tie and gave it a jerk, untying it.

Beck looked on without expression. Softly he said, "Sweet talk and having your cop rest against the outside of the door instead of the inside—don't ever try to go on the stage, Lieutenant."

After a knock, the first cop came back in followed by another one. The second cop held an official-looking paper. One glance and Richards swore angrily. The newcomer nodded toward Beck and said, "His lawyer just brought it."

Beck commenced reknotting his tie. Richards asked, "How'd they know we had him?"

Both cops shrugged.

"Who signed it?"

The second cop said, "Yount."

"Yount." Richards snorted, a big man helpless. "Garland must have interrupted his dinner for the habeas, pulled him right away from the trough. Sort of anxious, wasn't he, Beck?" He was still trying. "I'd think about that if I were you. Big Pat was worried you might run off at the mouth."

"You letting me go?" Beck asked.

"Yeah. You can go, all right." Richards waved the other two aside and opened the door into the corridor. "I'll miss you, Buddy. Except that you'll be back."

Beck said, "Always glad to be of assistance," and started to squeeze by him. Richards grinned and drove a fist into his stomach. Beck doubled over against the door frame and the two cops grabbed his arms. He blacked out for an instant, came to looking at his hands clutching the front of his sweater. He straightened slowly and gave Richards a pained smile.

"Get out," Richards grated, and turned his back on him. The two cops led Beck into the sterile corridor and pointed him toward the distant exit before letting go of his arms.

Beck straightened his clothes and walked down the hallway. A small pensive man sat on one of the last benches. He rose precisely and turned his mouth into a sardonic smile. "Hello, Steve."

They shook hands. "You arrived like the U. S. Cavalry, J. J. Thank you."

"How is it a man of my principles is always chosen to abort justice? No, don't mention money. I was wondering rhetorically."

Beck said, "Your habeas embarrassed them. The rest were booked but not me. How'd you know about me? Got a cigarette?"

J. John Everett opened his cigarette case and Beck took one. The lawyer wore hornrim glasses and a cigarette holder tilted from the corner of his mouth. Behind this equipment his gentle, keen face went almost unnoticed, just as behind his bittersweet charm lurked an impudence which was jarring in an older man. Beck respected his brain and his air of constantly listening for something, perhaps for an answer he didn't already know. Everett said, "Anonymous tip about you. Evidently one of your insiders, which was lucky."

Beck stopped the lighter halfway to his lips and looked at him. "What do you mean, lucky?"

"Pat wants you. He's rather worried. The rest can stay put until the morning. He wanted you out immediately."

"That doesn't sound like Pat, worried about a little raid."

Everett was acting as imperturbable as ever. Beck sensed, rather than saw, that something was wrong. He expected confirmation. But Everett said, "It was probably my imagination. Perhaps he didn't want you spending a night in jail."

"Pat never thought of anyone else in his life, J. J."

Everett remonstrated mockingly, "Now, Steve. In an organization dedicated to greed and controlled by fear I wonder if it's ethical to slander the boss."

Beck only grinned.

Everett nodded toward the back of headquarters. "Did you tell them anything I ought to know?"

"I was innocent and cooperative. Also maddening."

"Were they hard?"

"They had a notion." Beck clicked his lighter twice again and nothing happened. "Out of fluid."

"Here." Everett snapped his own lighter to flame. "Pat wants you to come out to his place right away."

"Didn't he tell you why?"

"No. He wanted you."

Beck bent his head to the lighter flame, blue and untrembling in the still air. He saw the lawyer's softly aged fingers. They clenched the silver mechanism so tightly that pads of flesh pressed out at the sides. Beck inhaled deeply and said, "Thanks again, J. J. See you in court."

Everett said, "My best to Pat," and they separated. Out in the cool night Pacific Highway was crowded with cars hurrying to the ball game at Lane Field.

Beck caught a taxi. Pat Garland wanted him but it wouldn`t hurt Garland to stew a bit. And tonight he might need his car. So he rode back to National City and then headed for La Jolla in his Buick. Both ways he considered Everett, who had never shown nervousness before.

3

Thursday, May 19, 8:45 p.m.

Beck parked a block below the Garland house and waited. Nobody came by. After two minutes he walked up the hill and into the curved driveway.

The house sat on a knoll of the sloping land above La Jolla and beneath Mount Soledad, the exclusive district called The Muirlands. A low gate in the hedge opened for him as he passed the electric eye and he left the drive to walk among beds of sleeping flowers. The house was flat and modern, built in three levels to fit the knoll. Its imperial sweep of glassy front commanded the best view of ocean and city. Draperies were closed against the view.

On the vestigial porch, Beck stood beneath the overhead light and thumbed his nose at the grillwork. He didn't bother with bell or knocker.

Mrs. Garland opened the door at once, a tall cool woman, Beck's age. Her skin and figure always reminded him of flowing cream. Tonight her shiny hair was wound in a black coil on the side of her head. He thought she would look better in something more somber than her gay hostess gown.

He said, "Good evening, Leda. You're looking good."

She widened her blue eyes but smiled with her mouth only. She conserved her face. "Steve, you shouldn't make fun of Pat's gadgets. He gets a kick out of them."

"I'm just jealous. I have to open my doors to see anything."

Leda led him into the house, walking as if she were still a fashion model. "Pat likes to look first. Been keeping yourself amused?"

"Busy enough." At the other end of the sleek living room a little woman with blue-white hair was playing solitaire, pecking at the cards like a bird. Beck called, "No cheating, Gusta." Augusta Norley gave him a motherly smile and went on with her game.

Leda had a let's talk look about her. "Pat?" inquired Beck.

"Oh. Out back. He's been shut up all evening with somebody I didn't even see arrive. A half hour ago he called on the intercom to see if you were here yet. That's the first I knew you were coming." She was draping herself into a low chair, making herself cozy.

"I better not keep him waiting. I know the way." He left her, crossing through the living room, through the circus decorations of the bar, through the patio with its slide and sandbox and barbecue grill. In front of a heavy door which he rapped, Beck stood beneath another light and looked bored at the viewer until the circuit breaker buzzed and he could work the latch. Down a short hall and he entered a den of weighty, comfortable furniture.

Patrick Garland pushed out of his chair by the fireplace, came over to shake hands. "Steve," he said in a heavy voice, "I've been waiting for you."

He was large and masculine like the room, built for easy living. No gray head appeared in the shock of black hair that straggled over his forehead. The ruddy face which had added flesh lately, the slightly bulging eyes and full lips, seemed to enjoy whatever turned up.

"All I could do to tear myself away," Beck said. He looked over the seedy gray-suited man who had gotten out of the other fireside chair.

The man wore elevator shoes and twirled a broadbrim hat between his wrinkled hands. His face was also wrinkled and tanned in blotches. His mop of hair and ragged mustache were a dirty shade of white.

Garland drew Beck forward, signaled the stranger to silence. "Don't say anything. I want you to get this." He grinned at Beck. "What about it, Steve?"

"Some monkeys get peanuts before they perform."

"Huh? Oh, sorry. What'll it be?"

"Shady Lady."

Garland grimaced from behind the short bar. "Never heard of it. I thought you wanted a drink. Scotch?"

"As long as it isn't that Mexican stuff." Beck told the stranger, "Pat's got a scheme for making scotch from cactus."

The little man chuckled gruffly and sat back in his chair, still spinning his hat. Garland came back with a glass and a third chair. "Well, Steve?"

"State Senator Gene L. Wake. Some papers call him The Parimutuel Senator. Talks like a farmer, dresses like a farmer, but grew up on Main Street, L. A. Gambling lobby in Sacramento. One of the Fierro's front men before Fierro retired. In state politics for about, oh, seven, eight years." Beck tossed off his drink, went to pour another.

Behind him, Garland laughed. "What'd I tell you, Gene? Like clockwork."

Wake's twangy voice complained, "Downright uncanny, considering I don't have a name this far south. How's he do it?"

"I don't know. How do you do it, Steve?"

"Professional secret."

"You left out only one thing," said Garland. "Gene may be our next governor."

Beck sat down again, held up his glass. "God save California."

Both the men laughed this time. Wake said, "Hey, that ain't the *only* thing he left out, Pat. I got a good side, too, you know."

Beck asked Garland, "We going into politics?"

"Too nasty for me. I'm satisfied to own a councilman and let it go at that. Say, speaking of the councilman, he may get the slot machines in all right."

"Hurray, hurray."

"What's eating you, Steve? You're in a nasty mood."

"I guess I am. I don't like to be elbowed by cops."

Wake looked interested. Garland changed the subject, salving Beck. "Gene, like I told you, Steve Beck has been my good right arm for almost a year now. Right arm? Hell, he's practically my brains, too."

"What he means is that I do his dirty work for him," Beck explained to the Senator. "If brains meant anything these days, we'd all be out of jobs. Or working for J. John Everett."

"Is that so?" asked Wake politely. "How's that?"

Garland said, "Steve's got everything worked out, to hear him talk."

Wake nodded and asked how Everett was doing. Garland said fine and thanked him for sending the lawyer down from Sacramento. Beck leaned his head back and stared at the ceiling. Wake rambled on, with a little laugh, about J. J. needing more money than he could make in ordinary practice, how he'd been brought up to expect it, how he was one of the railroad Everetts.

Garland grunted at his platinum wristwatch. He'd had all this in his files since J. J. came south a year ago. He took a tiny bottle out of the pocket of his lounging jacket and popped a pill in his mouth.

Senator Wake thought to look at his watch, too, the kind that made the dollar famous. "My plane's at nine forty-five, Pat."

Garland stirred up the fire, then turned down the thermostat so it would be cool enough for a fire. Beck murmured, "Somebody either pour another drink or tell me what's going on."

Wordless, Garland flipped a square of paper toward him which Beck caught and unfolded.

The text was typewritten, apparently a letter although without salutation or signature. It was addressed to: Criminal Investigation Section, Office of the Attorney General, Sacramento, California. The date line read 45 18/5. Beck frowned once, read it through, glanced at the blank reverse side. "Nice of the Senator to risk bringing this down, Pat."

"I thought so."

Wake cleared his throat. "It was just pure chance I got ahold of it, Beck. Mistake in the mail delivery up there. That report came to my office instead of the attorney general's and my girl opened it, not realizing. She couldn't figure it out so she brought it to me." He paused. "She's safe—my secretary."

Beck nodded and said, "Very fortunate," about the letter. He read it through point by point, musing aloud. "Written by a lawyer or an educated cop from the terminology. Airmailed here yesterday, the eighteenth of May, and lost in Sacramento today. Apparently the 45 is a report number. From the way the writer refers to me, he's mentioned me before. And he seems to know all about the Dewdrop Inn transfer." He whistled a couple bars between his teeth while he stopped to consider.

Garland, having thought of nothing to say but wanting to add comment, repeated his last sentence in a different tone.

"He knows The Natchez will open Saturday night," Beck went on. "That's practically public information but he also knows there'll be a private party there tomorrow night—which isn't. And he knows just what The Natchez is and whose property." He read out a part of the report. "*License privileges of the State Equalization Board were transferred from the Dewdrop Inn, a tavern in Jacumba, owner and proprietor Henry D. Hooper. Liquor license now registered to name of Hervey Isham, Natchez proprietor. Agreement to license transfer secured from Hooper 3 May by Beck, under influence of duress.*" Beck stopped reading. "Then our boy goes on to compare this operation with the Klein business in January and the mixup with that Palomar joint. All just facts—no recommendation. You can practically hear his mind tick."

Beck sat through the short silence, idly rubbing the letter between his fingers. "Nice paper. Next thing to parchment."

"Hold it up to the light, look at the watermark," Wake suggested.

"I did. It says *Bond Supreme* around a bear, the Bear Flag Republic bear. Official stock, Senator?"

"The kind we use for special-occasion letterheads—you know, letters that might be museumed as a milepost of democracy or when we want to impress some bigger shot. Don't know whether it's restricted to state use, though."

"I can find out."

Garland said, "What do you think, Steve?"

"What is there to think?"

"That's right. Clear as a bell. We've got a snooper."

"I caught the first plane down," Wake said, and looked at his watch again. "I better be back before I'm missed."

Garland decided to busy his broad soft hands with some more drinks. Beck said, "No, thanks. I've had my quota," and Wake murmured, "Well, one more." Beck said, "I've read about this operation but I've never actually seen it in action. The attorney general can't crack us from the outside so he plants a man on the inside. Somebody pretty high up, too, from all our boy has to report."

Leaning on the bar, Garland watched the tropical fish drift around the wall aquarium. He spoke slowly over his shoulder. "Correct me if I'm off the track, Steve, but you notice he takes the Natchez business and refers back to two other license transfers—the Klein business last January and the Palomar business last fall. He doesn't go back any further. Get what I mean?"

Beck frowned. "Only maybe."

"He doesn't mention the Blue Heaven business, which smelled even worse. Same thing exactly. A year ago April. Maybe he just didn't bother to refer to it, but he sounds like a thorough boy. Maybe he's already reported enough about it. Or maybe he doesn't know."

"It slipped my mind. I remember you mentioning it once now."

Garland turned around to see if Beck figured the same way.

"Uh-huh. Someone who's caught on in the last year," Beck said. "Like me, for instance."

Wake rose and teetered impatiently on his built-up shoes.

Garland laughed silently at Beck. "Quit being so touchy. You know as well as I do that three-quarters of the circle haven't been with me more than a year. Yes, including you if you got to be so damn technical."

"Okay. Lend me a cigarette, Pat."

Garland reached in his pocket and then shook his head. "Sorry, Steve. I forgot. I threw them all out of the house. The doc said no."

"What doc is this? Galen arisen?"

The big man reddened faintly. "I found a new specialist, heart man. Just came to La Jolla from Cincinnati. If he's as sharp as his prices he—" He stopped chuckling at himself and became gruffly annoyed. "All right. So you don't think much of my doctors. Who pays for them, I want to know?"

"Lend me a cigarette, Senator?"

"A pleasure."

Beck stood up to lean over Wake's lighter and he remembered the same gesture with Everett earlier had disturbed him. After a puff, he asked, "How many people know about this?"

"You. Me. Gene." Garland shrugged. "And the plant, of course."

"The plant won't spread it around." Beck smiled thinly. "Let's keep our little secret." He warmed his smile for the Senator.

"Of course," Wake said. "The fewer folks know the better. It's your baby down there and I consider I've done my part bringing the news—"

Garland interrupted. "Was there anything to the raid, Steve?"

"With this other, who can tell? The vice detail showed off their brains all over the place. They found a few slips somebody will have to take a fall for."

"We won't worry about that," Garland said. "I can do without Hop Kung."

"Worst break was that they picked up Eddie Cortes there. He's a weekly visitor to First Avenue, remember, and if Richards wants to get rough Eddie will be back rattling his cup on the bars."

"That I don't want to see. Cortes is a comer. Well, I don't think Richards will get that rough. I've still got a few friends at court, huh, Gene?" Garland winked at Wake.

The Senator put on his cowboy hat. "You can always count on me, Pat, you know that. At the moment, though, I'd strongly advise me staying out of the picture until local efforts fail. J. J. will keep up his end, I'm sure."

"Sure," Garland agreed. "I'll call the car for you, Gene." He slid back a panel above the fireplace, pulled a microphone out of the instrument board, flipped a switch.

"Pat never had any toys when he was a kid," Beck said to Wake.

Garland finished his orders and replaced the microphone. "Steve thinks everything I own is a joke."

"Thing-happy were my exact words."

"Thanks for reminding me because that's what I'm getting at. The way I feel is—what the hell is the use of making money if you don't enjoy things?"

Wake was eyeing the paper which Beck still held. "If it's all the same with you, Pat, I'd feel safer if that report was destroyed. I know I can trust every-one here but—all the same, accidents happen."

Beck raised his eyebrows at Garland, who nodded. Beck tore a blank strip off the bottom of the page and put it in his wallet. Then he read the type-writing through once more before he wadded the paper and flipped it into the fireplace. The three men watched silently while the wad flared and blackened and grayed to ash.

Garland's voice rang when he said, "I'll walk out with you, Gene."

"Glad to have met you, Beck. Give me a call ever up north. At the house."

"I will, thanks."

"And good luck."

"See you around, Senator."

"Stick close, Steve," Garland said as the pair turned into the hall. "Matters to discuss."

"I'm sure we have." Beck listened to the electric lock of the door buzz open and then shut. He dropped his cigarette into the fire and wished he had an-other.

He wandered over to the big tank built into the wall and watched the fish, the gentle eddy of life through clumps of water grass. He thought about Pat's owning the fish for decoration and not knowing anything more about them except that they were fish. Beck had looked them all up out of sheer curios-ity. There was the angelfish, a black-striped silver dollar with trailing fins. *Pterophyllum eimekei* and generally mistaken for *P. scalare*. Even the man who had landscaped the aquarium hadn't known that, he recalled with a touch of pride. At the moment *P. eimekei* was incensed with a sooty-tailed blackamoor. *Gymnocorymbus ternetzi*. *P. eirnekei* was twice the size of *G. ternetzi* but his straight-line charges were no match for the other's quick darting deception.

Beck watched the chase attentively. Then he said aloud through his hu-morless smile, "Run, you little bastard. Run."

4

Thursday, May 19, 9:30 p.m.

Garland came back without his jovial mask, looking tired. Beck was sitting in one of the heavy leather chairs before the fire and Garland sank into another nearest.

"Well, what'd you see in him, Steve?"

"Not a lot. Obviously, he's usable. He didn't care for me, did he?"

"No. I don't think he liked your intimating J. J. has a monopoly on brains. Wake takes that view of himself, power behind the scenes, you know."

"He's got animal cunning but not intellect. I've followed his voting record. He's a skulker afraid to screw the people too much. Nothing like you."

Garland snorted. "Now you're blessing me with intellect?"

"Hardly. You're popular, intellect isn't. You're a lot higher animal than Wake, you're the boss type. You know as well as I do that you got to the top through force of personality, bulled your way all the way."

"Turn off some of the lights, will you, Steve? I feel a twinge coming on, right about here." Garland pressed around on his temples.

Beck got up, switched off all the lights, sat down again in the shuttling red glow. Garland was pretending deep weariness, putting off the trouble as usual. Garland said, "Well, you're right about us animals. Remember a sales manual I read when I was just a youngster starting in business. It said never to wear your Phi Beta Kappa key or you'll be resented. I guess I went the book one better. I never *got* a key. Like, do you want your coffee without cream or without milk. But I guess I've done pretty well selling entertainment to the masses."

"Pat, your only regret is that the cattle aren't one big cow so you could milk them easier."

Garland sighed complacently. "We're giving the folks their money's worth. Did you ever think of it this way, that we're the pioneers? Just like those characters that did nothing but build log cabins or more like the railroad boys that wrung out the country when the wringing was good. Now's the time to make the big money in gambling. One of these days Wake and the others will make gambling legal and then they'll be wondering where the profits went, just like the railroads today. Now's the time. Hey, I been thinking. What about dope?"

Beck shook his head.

"Why not? Now's the time for that, too, before they bring it within the law. I mean, prohibition is prohibition. Why should we be allowed, oh, tobacco and liquor and not be allowed the other? I bet we could make it as popular as hell on that basis, telling folks that their freedom was being abridged. Which it is. Our customers don`t know where to draw the line. Like you say, they`re cattle."

Beck said, "No."

"Why not?"

"One good practical reason. We don`t want trouble with the federal government. Not with this other. Maybe later, though."

Garland grunted disappointment.

Beck asked, "Is that straight about Wake being governor or were you buttering him?"

"Maybe, maybe not. There`s been talk—and this is California, isn`t it? Nice thing for us, if we can swing it."

"I don`t think so. You`re forgetting a rule that should have been in your sales manual under the heading of People Act Like People. Everybody`s looking out for number one. Wake will think of himself first, just like the rest of us, and no governor can stand to be tied up with Pat Garland. He`d feed you to your own pet fish."

"Uh. Think he has ideas along that line already?"

"Not yet. I like to figure ahead. You can`t go wrong if you follow the rule."

Garland chuckled, feeling better, feeling more like the fight. "Lucky you`ve standardized all the secrets of the universe, Steve boy. But you`re sure being modest tonight. Where do you stand in the animal kingdom?"

"What was it you said when I came in? Oh. Clockwork."

"Animal clockwork?"

"Jocko, the toy monkey."

"You mad at me, Steve?"

"No, why should I be?"

"I don`t know. I just thought. All evening you`ve acted like somebody stole your best girl. You ought to get yourself one. Nothing like married life, kids and so forth."

Beck laughed.

"What`s the joke?"

"You reminded me how tender the real me is. Just before the raid, I ran into quite a girl. I was honest to God impressed. I`d forgotten her till you opened your big mouth. You know what they say about propinquity."

"Like fun I do. Pour me a drink. I might as well get completely stewed. Help yourself."

Beck got to work, poured one only for Garland. The room was warm and dim. He remembered the girl, how he`d felt earlier. Now she was in jail and he didn`t even know her name. If there wasn`t so much else to do....

Garland growled sulkily over his drink, "Why can`t they leave us alone? We`re not hurting anybody."

"Wake made a bad mistake."

"Like what?"

"He shouldn't have swiped that report to the attorney general. He should have copied it down or memorized it or something and then sent it on."

"I still don't see why."

"I think Wake tipped our hand."

"You're thinking around corners, Steve. What the attorney general doesn't know won't hurt us."

"Don't be too sure. That report was numbered 45. Either 46 will tip them off in Sacramento or simply not getting a report during a specified period will tip them off. Another thing, this afternoon at headquarters Lieutenant Richards practically told me out-and-out that the raid wasn't an ordinary affair."

"I'm not afraid of one raid. Or a dozen."

"Our personal bravery doesn't have a lot to do with it. I think the special agent—the plant—knows we're on to his existence already. He's been with us a year and hasn't gotten the big thing the attorney general wants. Now his period of usefulness is shortened. He knows we know. So he's either trying to tear up as much of the circle as he can before we catch him or he's trying to stampede us."

There was a long silence. The glow from the fire tricked across their two set faces, transforming them. The glow made Garland's features look brutish, made Beck's look unsubstantial. Some wood cracked viciously.

Garland asked, "You *can* catch him, Steve?"

"Certainly."

"I'm not afraid of a raid, a shutdown here and there. I've been through that sporadic stuff before. But the AG isn't interested in picking us off one operation at a time."

"I know. He wants the books."

"Income tax is a rap we couldn't get out from under. He'd have us all in the same net and a hundred Senator Wakes couldn't help us then. The books. That's what the snooper's hunting for."

"He's had a year."

The leather squeaked as Garland got out of his chair. He opened the cigarette box on the coffee table before he remembered it was empty. He said, "I wonder if that doc has got a brain in his head," and wandered restlessly down to the bar. "Yeah, by now he's looked in all the usual places, probably every office we've got. I wish we could destroy the books, burn them up right here and now. But how can we? This is big business. I can't run it without records."

"One of the penalties of growing up," Beck agreed. "Remember the dinosaurs."

Like a juke box, Garland was making noise for himself. Beck just happened to be there. "...a state income tax rap and then a federal rap. Don't you suppose the AG man figures like this, that he can pull one open raid for the books then he's done for? Because then we'd put them where he'd never find them. So he's got to know ahead of time, be right on his one chance."

"Okay. He doesn't know they're right here in your own house."

"The most dangerous place possible. For me."

"Wasn't that the idea? Here's one place he hasn't thought of looking, obviously. Can't look, for that matter."

Garland emptied his glass, set it down with a bump. "Steve, what do you think?"

"Who else knows?"

"Gusta, of course. And Leda. That's all."

"Leave them here."

"What if he's narrowed it down to here? This may be his last resort."

"You're here to protect them. You move them some place else and you'll have to keep running back and forth, wondering. And don't forget another big item: it's not only the state would be glad to locate those books. Those accounts are your most powerful hold over the circle. The way you've got this town organized, any circle member who finds out where you keep the books is going to make a stab at snatching them and taking over your job. Those accounts are a mighty potent weapon, Pat, and it's asking trouble to let them roam around. Leave them here."

"I know," muttered Garland. "But I got my kids to think of. Patty—and Dick is due back from military school the end of the week. I couldn't face a blowup here, anyway, not with them in the line of fire."

Beck shrugged. "Ship the little darlings off somewhere."

"Oh, sure. That'd be a sure tipoff the books were here. Wouldn't it?"

"Pat, why argue about it? You've made up your mind to move the books so go ahead and do it."

Garland said, "I guess you're right." He moved slowly to the instrument panel and pressed a button. When Gusta's voice came through the amplifier, he said, "Be ready to leave inside an hour. Take what you need for a couple of weeks."

"What's up, Pat?"

"I'm moving the books for safekeeping."

Beck put in, "Tell her to bring up the folders on everybody who's joined in the last year. I'll need them."

Garland parroted the order into the intercom and came back to the fire. After a moment, he said, "Maybe I'm getting old."

"The new doctor tell you that?"

Garland hesitated, grinned wryly. "Those robbers never say anything. I don't know why I keep throwing my good money at them, I really don't."

"If you're worried," Beck said, "call in Kyle and Holsclaw and the two Tarrants. No use you should carry the ball for everybody. Let them worry, too."

"No, I can handle it by myself. Besides, Holsclaw left for Chicago this morning. Had to check at the factory on one of the new coin machines. He won't be back for a week or so, until they can promise delivery. Paul Moon's in charge. We ought to have this wrapped up in a week or so."

"Sure. I put the bee on Sid Dominic."

"Fine. Who can take his place? In case."

"I suggest Eddie Cortes. He's been palling around with Dominic, which means he's got an eye on his job. Kyle's outfit could stand a little firing up."

"Anything you say. Might as well use Cortez's push on some real money, race money." Garland snapped his fingers. "Which reminds me!" He clicked on the lights suddenly, came back to Beck's chair as if he had been recharged. "Did you know Dominic's brother-in-law owns that job printing layout on C Street?"

"Yes."

"Well, I was figuring last night in bed. We're working the horses two ways now, why not print the racing forms, too? There must be a fine pile of cash in that racket, especially if you can arrange a monopoly around here. Think you can? Get the printing dirt cheap and make the business pay proper." He spoke swiftly and surely now that he was on untroubled ground. "Subsidize what's-his-name-Dominic's relative—for whatever equipment he needs. Tie him up so he can't get loose. Then go to town. We can use our own printing layout a million ways. Offhand, I think of dogs. They open tomorrow. No reason we can't build them up and make racing forms on the dogs just as popular as on the horses. Make sense?"

Beck grinned. "More sense than that cactus whiskey."

"Oh, I miss sometimes. But just sometimes, Steve. I'm only human."

"That isn't good enough?"

Garland laughed exultantly, full of his own power. "Pity you couldn't have seen this place when I came out after the war. Not a bit of organization south of L. A. This town was tight as a drum, nothing to catch the tourist trade, and all that entertainment money going south of the border to get spent. Now Tijuana and Caliente are running full blast every day of the week trying to catch up with us. And I'll move in down there pretty soon, too. And look what I've got already: Kyle's bookies, Holsclaw's coin machines and the Tarrants' card rooms all in one package. Not to mention that lottery setup for the two-bitters which'll grow slowly but it'll grow. Plus a few other little operations here and there."

"That's the second time today I've heard the story of your life," Beck said. "Lieutenant Richards related it earlier."

The buzzer sounded. Augusta Norley's motherly face filled the viewer. Garland pressed the button that let her in. Her delicate old hands held a bundle of yellow manila folders. She passed as a governess. Under one of her earlier names she was a CPA.

"Speed of light," Gusta said in her harsh startling voice.

Beck took the folders. "Want a medal, honey?"

"I'll settle for less lip from characters." She grinned crookedly at Garland.

"You weren't serious about moving the books." He nodded. "Why?"

"I decided you needed a change of scenery. Will that do as a reason?" Gusta clucked her tongue, unabashed. "Mine not to reason why—"

"I want you to burn every piece of paper that isn't actually vital," Garland interrupted. "Pack the rest in suitcases, hatboxes or anything that looks like luggage. You can't take the big machine, take that little calculator. Be ready to leave in an hour. That clear?"

"I'm not deaf. Will I be out of touch?"

"Not entirely. I'll figure some way to get the daily figures to you, maybe only the weekly."

She swore softly at the prospect.

Garland said, "Maybe none at all. But this hideout won't last long. If the records get behind a trifle, okay. There's a bonus in it."

"You're the boss."

"Wait a minute." Beck had leafed through the folders. He handed most of them back to Gusta as she turned to go. Garland asked, "What's this?"

"No use bothering with the small fry," Beck said. "Our man's bigger than that."

Garland looked at the top folder Gusta held. "How about Joe Zuaben? He gets around."

"Not a chance. Joe has killed two men I know of personally. No special agent could go quite that far."

Garland grunted, then remembered Gusta Norley was standing by curiously. "An hour, I said."

Gusta hoisted the folders against her chest. "Keep your pants on." She left and the men were silent until the door buzzed shut.

Garland eyed the few folders Beck still held. "How many left?"

"Six."

"Six." Again Garland glanced at the top tab only. HERVEY ISHAM. He said, "I wish it would turn out to be Isham. Two birds with one stone. He makes my skin crawl. Think it might be Isham, Steve?"

Beck shrugged. "He's running The Natchez and that's where the liquor license was going."

"Six. That's not as bad as I thought. Doesn't sound like it would be too hard, does it? I think we should have a drink on that, Steve." He went over to the bar and got out the scotch again.

"No, thanks. I want to accomplish a few things yet tonight." Beck walked over to the bar, the six folders swinging in one hand. "Just a quick résumé to get things accurate."

"Sure."

"You'll get the books out of danger. I don't have to know where they go for my end of the job. I know that no one else in the circle will know. And this AG trouble will be just between you and me. I'll work my own way and dig up the snooper. I'm no cop, you know—I'm not going to round up enough material for a court trial. All we need for a conviction is a couple hints, maybe just a feeling. Is that the size of it, Pat?"

"That's the size of it."

"One more point. When I dig up this AG man—what do I do?"

Garland paused, replacing the bottle. His face was surprised. "Do you have to ask? You kill him."

"I just like to be accurate," Beck said.

5

Thursday, May 19, 10:30 p.m.

On the lower reaches of Broadway, near the waterfront, and among the sailor amusements and the Army-Navy Y, was a block-long billboard, intensely lighted. Painted on the billboard, a cartoon average man constantly smiled while a masked unshaven cartoon crook constantly picked his pocket. The red-letter legend said this was the headquarters of CHARLEY THE CHEAT—The Crookedest Used Car Dealer in the World.

Beck parked his Buick down the street and walked into the lot beneath the billboard, through aisles between shining gorgeous machines. A placard hung from each automobile:

"Belonged to minister. Has never been sworn at."

"Speedometer set back to mere 5,000 miles."

"Has Charley Holsclaw's personal guarantee—you won't like it."

A small stucco office sat in the center of the lot, both its doors opening into the same room. One door was labeled Men, the other Women. Beck went in the Men one.

Joe Zuaben, off-duty now as Dominic's protection, had his chair tilted against the wall while he scrubbed his teeth with a monogrammed handkerchief. The Filipino moved the handkerchief from in front of his dried-leaf face to bare his gold teeth in Beck's direction. He didn't speak.

Beck said, "Looking for Felix."

Zuaben said, "Yeah," and waved the handkerchief toward the rear of the car lot, his big gold watch slipping back on his bony wrist. Then he went back to wiping his teeth.

Beck walked up to him, plucked the handkerchief from Zuaben's hand and tore it in two. He stuffed both pieces of silk in the Filipino's breast pocket.

Zuaben got to his feet, his shoulders trembling angrily.

Beck said down to him, "Look, fancy—when I say I want to see a man, it means you go get him. Never forget that."

Zuaben turned away, banged his chair noisily under a desk and said, "Yeah," again on his way out.

A muscled man in a skivvy shirt loomed in the other doorway, his thick twisted features wondering about the noise. His scar-lidded eyes stared at Beck suspiciously.

Beck said, "Hello, Speed."

Speed recognized him then. Some of his reactions had been off since the second DeVore fight, but Pat Garland took care of his own. DeVore was still going great guns back in New York now and making Garland money, although he had sold most of him. Speed explained, "Heard a noise. I guess nothing's wrong."

"Joe stumbled over some furniture. You been working out, Speed?"

"I guess nothing's wrong."

"You been working out?"

Speed chuckled. "I'll get at that DeVore boy one of these days."

"Sure. Mr. Garland will get you a rematch one of these days."

Speed chuckled again and swung his fist against the wall. The little building shook. "That's what I'm waiting for, Steve."

Felix came up behind Speed, who laughed high-pitched and danced out of the doorway, his hands waving frantically. Beck and Felix laughed. After a reproachful reverie, Speed joined the laughter.

"My hand slipped," Felix apologized.

Speed said, "I got things to do." As he left, he noticed the wall again and socked it again.

Felix pulled his coat up over his head comically. "How'd you like to be that strong, Steve old fellow old pal?" He was a butterball of a man with slick hair and a small, insolent mouth.

"Not me. Afraid I might break my neck tying my tie."

"What'd you say to Joe the schmoe? He's pretty sore."

"He'll get a lot sorer unless he comes down to eye level." Beck sat down on a desk edge to tighten a shoelace. "I said it was a mistake to move him up to that protection job. I don't like little men and I don't mean in feet and inches."

"Well, I haven't had much use for our brown brothers since I got busted from the force, said chain of circumstances commencing with a dead Filipino."

"Best thing that ever happened to you."

"Who's complaining?" Felix relaxed in a swivel chair and spun his bulk around a few times. "Got anything in mind right now?"

"Busy tonight?"

"No, thanks. You ain't my type, honey."

"Quit kidding—if you are kidding. Remember assisting me at a conference early part of the month? Dewdrop Inn up in Jacumba. License transfer."

Felix cracked his knuckles meaningfully. "Yowsah."

"Who did you talk to about it?"

"Me? Who, me?" He pretended he didn't have a tongue. "Have to ask somebody else, mister. I can't talk, mister."

"Okay. Then it's that little Hooper fellow might be called upon to talk."

"We told him. He'd be a sucker to."

"I want you to go up there tonight and make certain."

"To Jacumba at this time of night? Have a heart, Steve."

Beck continued as if he hadn't heard. "No rough stuff unless it's absolutely necessary. Henry D. Hooper, in case you've forgotten. He has relatives back in Garrett, Indiana. If he'd like to visit them, get him the bus ticket."

"Something's up."

"A little interest shown in that liquor license is all. Merely get him out of the state quietly. And if you should find anyone approached him lately on the subject, I'd be interested."

Felix mused. "Jacumba. Well, it might have been worser. So happens I can shack in Tecate. A hot little thing"—his fat hands drew a picture in the air—"Steve, you'd love her. And, boy, she'd let you, too." He laughed, jowls shaking.

"Get going," Beck, said, standing up. "I'll expect to hear from you."

"In the morning sometime. Unless her husband's home." He laughed again.

Beck nodded and went out into the daylight brilliance of the used car lot. Down a row of cars he could see Joe Zuaben hunched on the bumper of a Cadillac, waiting until Beck was gone before he went back into the office.

6

Thursday, May 19, 11:00 p.m.

Beck nightlocked himself in his suite and stripped his coat, sweater, bow tie and shoes from his body. He put on sandals and a pale blue robe. Then he fried some eggs and bacon and swiftly ate them with a glass of milk. He wasn't noticeably hungry but he had been too busy to eat since noon and he would function better with his stomach attended to.

His suite—living room, bedroom, bath, electric kitchenette—was ten stories above the downtown streets, one floor above the gymnasium and directly beneath the north spire of the Southwest Towers Athletic Club. The club building had been deliberately built higher than necessary in the spacious city and its twin towers had been erected for show. They were the tallest chrome-plated towers west of the Mississippi. The sun dazzled on them by day and floodlights by night. They shone unceasingly, remarkable at first sight, commonplace to Beck.

After eating, he felt even more confident of mind. Opening a fresh pack of cigarettes, he moved his operations into his living room. Except for some antique touches sold him by Garland's interior decorator, it was furnished exactly as it had been the day Beck became its occupant.

He opened his portable typewriter and set it on a hassock by the chair under the brightest lamp. He collected an ashstand and six sheets of paper and with the six file folders sat down. Then he remembered his pocket lighter was out of fluid and, rather than take time to fill it, he got up again and brought over the table lighter. A cigarette going, he began to work.

Beck headed the first sheet of paper *Specifications of Identity*. The mechanical letters were actuated swiftly and evenly by his fingers.

I. Facts Available:

He has law background evidenced by cant. He is circle member no more than 1 year evidenced by lack of knowledge. He is circle executive evidenced by knowledge.

II. Facts Presumptive:

He has accounting background also because would be valuable in this type assignment. He has not criminal record or background because such would negate his value as state witness later.

Therefore, he has manufactured identity in circle.

III. Probability:
He is member (attorney, investigator, accountant) of attorney general staff.
(Have Wake check such retiring, resigning, canned or taking leave of absence
in last two years.)

Beck jerked the first sheet out of the machine, glanced over the specifications to fix them in his memory and burned them in the ashstand. He
punched the button which made the residue sift down into the base.
   The file material in each of the six folders followed a pattern. There would
be a photo with a description pasted on the back. There would be two printed
forms, a biography and an occupational history of the subject since joining the
circle. The fill-in information on these forms was coded. Beck had devised the
code and could sight-read it. Additional papers sometimes consisted of pho-
tostated documents and letters confirming or embroidering the biographical
information.
   Beck opened the top folder. He read about Hervey Isham. Then he ques-
tioned the assailable points in the terse biography:

HERVEY ISHAM
   Photostat proves he owned roadhouse in Springfield, Mass. (Wire Turquin-
Bloch, Boston, for complete history to corroborate reason for selling: Ashley
scandal.)
   He was forwarded to Tarrants by Chicken Joe Sanchell. Sanchell died 2
months after. (Have Pelletreau secure all info final status Sanchell.)

He put Isham aside and sifted through the folders until he found the one
on his friend.

EDWARD CORTES
   Early life in San Francisco seems OK. (Wire Johnny ask around on petty
crime counts and pimping job. Have Pelletreau verify details SF cop records.)
   Release from San Quentin last year proven by photostat. 2 year term, knifed
Doris Ebell over money: proven by newsclips. (No photo however. Check
prison said period and secure prison photo. Pelletreau.)

He was working in a smooth rhythm now, reading a man's life, doubting
the facts on his machine, scooping up another folder.

SID DOMINIC
   Independent policy job in LA until Hurley 1947 crackdown. (Wire Ace
Hurley to remember Dominic. Wire Kate for same story.)
   Letters of recommendation from Schirr, Moncey, Brown are genuine.
(Schirr, Brown both Moncey's boys, would take his word. Do AG or cops

have any hold over Moncey? Have Pelletreau check LA files Moncey dealings. Wire Driscoll's agency to scout for rumors.)
Dominic's wife is unchecked. (Driscoll.)
Dominic's wife's brother info looks OK. (Driscoll.)

He lit another cigarette. The first lay a soft gray length on the ashtray. He had sucked at it once and forgotten it since.

PAUL MOON
Assault charge, Chicago, 1940, uncorroborated. (Wire Kingsley for record photostat.)
Left strikebreak job, Detroit, Allan J. Farnsworth, Industrial Consultant, for no apparent reason. Farnsworth now in prison. (Wire Estes for Farnsworth story, especially origin of evidence, rumors.)

Beck opened the fifth folder. J. JOHN EVERETT

The phone buzzed.
Garland said, "Hi. Working hard?"
"Coming along."
"I just happened to think, Steve. You probably got the dope up there on the friend of our friend from Sacramento." He meant Everett, friend of Sen-ator Wake, but he didn't want to say so over the phone. And it was not their policy to use the message scrambler on calls through the club switchboard.
Beck said, "Just commencing on that one."
"I suggest you skip it. You have anyone nosing around in Sacramento and it's liable to get to—uh—what's his name, our friend up there. The way you outlined the situation tonight, we don't want to cause any hard feelings."
"Do that and you're making a mistake."
"Well, we better just skip it. I'm sure both of them are all right and we don't want to cause any hard feelings. Any checking you want to do right around town here would be okay, of course, but better not chance starting any sto-ries up north. All right?"
"Anything you say."
"All right. See you later, Steve." Through a yawning noise, Garland said, "Lord, I'm sleepy."
"Good night."
Beck turned back to the typewriter and the folder on Everett. His eyes spec-ulative, he continued writing on the nearly blank paper in the machine as if not to waste it.

Everett fits all points of specifications: he is attorney with access most cir-cle operations for past 7 months. His sole recommendation is Wake. (Wake's motives?)

His background is unimpeachable. (Verification would serve no purpose. Pat is right for the wrong reasons.)

Beck paused over the keys. Then as if the typewriter had asked the question:

Why was he nervous at police headquarters tonight?

He paused again. He had come upon the last document in Everett's file. It was a formal letter from the lawyer to Garland advising purchase of certain real estate in Chula Vista. Only Garland would know its purpose in the folder.

Beck rubbed the letterhead between his fingers. He held it up to the light. Then he unfolded the scrap of paper from his wallet, the strip he had torn from the report to the attorney general.

The watermarks matched. The textures matched.

Beck put both pieces of paper back in their places and shut his typewriter away. He had sat down with six blank sheets and he had written on six sheets. He had burned one and now he reread the remaining five before destroying them.

He dressed and went down to a lonely phone booth across the street in a closed parking lot. Sitting in the dark, Beck dictated concise inclusive telegrams across the country. To Johnny Torano in San Francisco, to Ace Hurley and the Driscoll Agency in Los Angeles, to Kate Doerck who was hiding in Salt Lake City, to F. L. Kingsley in Chicago, to Porter Estes in Detroit, to Turquin-Bloch Importers in Boston.

He did not ask any questions of Senator Wake in Sacramento.

With a faint smile of satisfaction, Beck went back up to his suite and undressed again, putting on his pajamas. He settled in the same chair and read through the last folder, the sixth file which told about Steven Beck. He knew every detail of its information but that never detracted from the sweetness of reading about oneself.

7

Friday, May 20, 10:00 a.m.

Pelletreau's voice filtered through the receiver uneasily. "Can't I meet you later? I'm not supposed to make private calls while I'm on duty."

"I called you," Beck pointed out. "This stuff won't wait."

"Surely till lunch. How about lunch?"

"That little bar and grill across from headquarters. Twelve-thirty."

Pelletreau whispered. "Not so close," almost whimpering. "Use some sense, for God's sake."

Beck grinned at the mouthpiece. "You name it then."

"How about the Hidalgo Café on Third below Broadway? I don't think anybody—"

"Twelve-thirty." Beck hung up, folded open the humid phone booth and walked across the lobby of the Moulton Building to the elevators. His ride ended on the third floor, a marble hall of frosted glass doors identical but for names. Three of the business cells were named Everett and the center one was for entering.

Beck entered the paneled anteroom.

A stylish woman of forty smiled good morning professionally. "Mr. Everett hasn't come in yet, Mr. Beck." She put a final letter through the postage meter and returned to her desk. "Was he expecting you?"

"That's debatable. I'll wait." He glanced across the outgoing mail. "Is J. J. very late when he's late like this?"

"I haven't been here long enough to say, really."

"True, I guess J. J. has been having bad luck with his secretarial turnover." He smiled warmly. "Up to now."

She smiled back. "I'm certain he'll be along shortly or he would've phoned. Would you care to wait in his office?"

"If you don't think he'd mind."

"One of the first things he told me was that Mr. Beck is to have carte blanche."

"Thank you."

The secretary closed the door behind him. Beck flipped a switch of the intercom box on Everett's desk, heard her begin dialing in the anteroom. She inquired of a bookstore if an order had arrived.

He let the box eavesdrop for him while he made certain the two flanking rooms were deserted. One was a small conference room, the other an extra inner office. All were paneled and soundproof and linked with intercom and telephone.

The secretary was typing now. Beck idly searched Everett's desk. He found more of the telltale paper.

Outside, the secretary laughed. He switched off the intercom and relaxed in a chair. He got up again as Everett wandered in, twinkling slightly behind his hornrim glasses, followed by the secretary. The two men greeted each other.

The woman was oohing over a puckish ball of fur Everett carried, a black kitten. After she had excused herself and closed the door, the lawyer hung up his hat and parked the kitten in the center of his desk blotter. It weaved on its tiny legs, mewing softly, peering about with weak eyes.

"The newest member of the Everett family. Paul Moon promised me one last week."

"He has plenty," said Beck. "Unfortunately, they all grow up to be cats."

"And you're on the side of the rats?"

"Aren't we all?"

Everett laughed. Opening a drawer, he wadded up a sheet off his stationery for the animal to play with. Not the best, the important paper, Beck noted. The kitten ignored it.

"He hasn't learned the value of entertainment," Beck said. "Do you suppose we can educate him up to consumership?"

"He's useless otherwise."

"No escape mechanism, poor beast. Of course, he has nothing to escape from. He doesn't seem afraid of facing himself during his leisure time."

The kitten was licking its paw.

"The only flaw in that brief," Everett continued, "is that I have probably picked a she." He fitted a cigarette into his holder, gave one to Beck and lit them both with his lighter. "What's troubling you, Steve?"

"Nothing. Does something show?"

"Heaven forbid. I did sense a difference though when I came in, a different attitude. My mind leaped immediately to the remotest possibility: that you were worried."

"Not me. I'm adjusted, J. J. What happened to the others?"

"All the innocent bystanders were turned loose early this morning with a stern lecture. I sprang a sheaf of writs on Lieutenant Richards about an hour ago which released Dominic, Cortes, Hop Kung and the other five. So that's that."

"Is it?"

"Judge Yount won't even set a high bail. They haven't enough of a case to press it."

"Cortes may have some trouble with First Avenue over this one."

"I know. I'm lunching with a member of the parole bureau." Everett smiled and moved the ambling kitten back to the center of the blotter.

"You're right," said Beck. "That is that."

"Excuse me." Everett switched on the intercom. "If Marcy should come by, have her wait for me, please. I have a present for her."

The box answered yessir.

Beck was trying to interest the kitten in his fountain pen. It persisted in staggering away, toward the opposite side of the desk. "Keeps wanting to go south," he complained, retrieving it.

"Moon's warehouse and the creature's mother lie in that general direction."

"Coincidence, J. J."

"Possibly not. Don't forget the creature does have a directional sense which it can use to the fullest." Everett leaned back, his arms behind his head. Puffing his holder, he contemplated Beck, then the kitten. "Do you?"

"No. Does that make him better off than I?"

"He uses his faculties to completion, Steve. He's less made up of leftovers, old biological residue, than we are."

Beck regarded the frustrated kitten and nodded solemnly. He always enjoyed talking with Everett like this. Something refreshing about the lawyer's odd tangents and odder conclusions appealed to an unplumbed depth within Beck. He said, "I'll go along with you, J. J. Right up to the point where you lock me on your back porch with a plate of milk and a box of sand. I could think my way out of that spot. The cat won't."

"I wonder. You know, no one's ever handed down an adequate definition between instinct and reason. Besides I'm merely pointing out how closely we're linked to this animal and making a case for said cat. He can move his ears and he can see at night."

Beck chuckled. "Okay. I've forgotten how, I admit."

"And take intuition. That's an integral sense to him, not to us. There's an animal sense we've lost except for mysterious spasms."

"Why don't you name your defendant Lucky, J. J.?"

"Good idea. Notice that Lucky walks properly on all fours, the way his skeleton is designed. He doesn't rear up on his hindpaws and drop his organs into our own distressing position. Even so, Lucky's been careless with his leftovers, too. I read somewhere that birds and lizards have a handy cleaning gadget, a third eyelid, moves back and forth. Now Lucky has a trace of that, but no more than I see in your eye, Steve."

"You know what I think? I suspect you're prosecuting the human species more than you're defending Lucky's."

"That's my unfortunate bent." Everett sighed out smoke. "I suppose I'm a Penitente, in my way. Yes, I can even bow to our reptilian ancestors in regret. You know, they actually had a sort of third eye which they undoubtedly found uses for. All we've inherited is the pineal body on top of our brains, an unnecessary gland. It's a sad thought. And to cap the climax, a good many creatures can grow new parts in case of loss. All we can manage are a

few piddling tricks with skin and hair and nails and perhaps a nub on an am-
putated stump."

"The trouble with you is that you want everything."

"The trouble with me is that I know it. Aren't we sorry heirs, though?"
Everett leaned forward to stroke the kitten with one soft finger. "I'm proud
of you, Lucky. You stopped off at a practicable station."

"All right, I'm convinced." Beck smiled quizzically. "But where did you
leave us, at the top or the bottom of the animal kingdom?"

Everett replied as if it was a real problem to him. "Well, all the returns aren't
in yet. We certainly have an advanced power we call reason. And we sup-
posedly have souls, if we haven't voided our ballots."

"I was telling Pat last night we were a pack of beasts. He wasn't beyond
comprehension." Beck paused on an uncomfortable brink. "Richards would
separate the sheep from the goats. Did you talk to him personally?"

"I wouldn't call it that. Why, Steve?"

"Oh, his attitude yesterday. As if Garland's days were numbered."

"Not much else he could say, is there? He has to believe that himself, being
the kind he is. Otherwise, psychological imbalance and throw a wheel. He's
a weary man."

"You get a feeling sometimes."

"And you have a feeling? An intuition?" Beck avoided his eyes and nodded.

"You're a weary man yourself, Steve," Everett's laugh sounded kind. "Believe me, Pat's still moving uphill, pulling us with him, and will for a good
time to come if I know anything about people. Why don't you relax, take a
vacation?"

"It's an idea. Takes money, though, and I'm a little short at the moment.
A trip might do me good—if I could swing it."

"Pat's good for it. He couldn't do without you, as you well know. You've
earned a rest. Forgive me, Steve, if I'm a bit cruelly pleased that you do tire,
the same as all of us. I was beginning to wonder. Now I can return to my old
certainties of death and taxes."

"Uh-huh." Beck lit another cigarette listlessly, inspected the glowing tip.
"Pat and I don't see eye to eye on all subjects. What do you think of his health,
J. J., seeing all these doctors?"

"Pat's the healthiest man among us. He's strong. He's so strong he has to
pretend to a weakness so we'll accept him as a real person. Subconsciously
but he's pretending. I'm no better. You can't help but notice that I always
wear a tie in deliberate bad taste. I'm inclined to be too precise so I try to offset it that way. I'm human and I want to be one of the boys. Up to a certain
point, of course." Everett chuckled to himself. "I'm quite fond of psychology.
It relieves me of all personal responsibility."

"I suppose you're right."

"I believe I am."

"Still—" Beck rose and smiled wryly. "We'll, I'll just keep that idea between Lucky and me."

"What were you going to say, Steve?"

Everett walked him to the door, carrying the kitten.

Beck said, "The advantage of gambling over actual living. If you don't like the cards, you can throw in your hand."

Everett opened the door.

Beck said, "Nearly forgot what I came for. We're going to take over a printing business. I'm broaching Dominic's brother-in-law this afternoon about buying in with some new equipment. I thought you might want to start thinking up wrinkles to finish the job."

"I'll put my mind to it. But I'm sorry you told me, Steve. I thought you simply wanted to talk to me."

"That too."

They said goodbye and Everett called the secretary into his office. Beck walked down the hall and buzzed the elevator, stood before the shafts humming.

A cage ascended, halted, flung wide its doors. The passenger it released was a familiar figure.

8

Beck was glad to see her again, the girl of the collision at the Cathay Gardens. He was glad to see her, even now realizing now who she must be.
Her pink cashmere sweater and glen plaid skirt had mussed a little and he saw faint bluish circles under her long gray eyes. Yesterday he had missed only one detail, her sole decoration: a small bronze mask of tragedy buckling a belt about her waist. He said hello as the elevator clanged shut.
She couldn't quite place him.
He said, "One step closer and I'll knock you down again."
It came back to her. "Oh, you're the man in a hurry!" She spun her cigarette into an urn of sand, studied him as she lit another from her purse.
"You're Marcy Everett, J. J.'s daughter."
"J. J. shouldn't talk to strangers. I've warned him."
"I'm not a stranger. I'm Steve Beck."
"How do you do, Mr. Beck."
It was perfectly natural to be talking to her. And they walked automatically to keep moving. They wandered down the marble hall to the window overlooking the chasm of traffic and back to the elevators, back and forth.
He asked, "I thought you were supposed to get through Berkeley this year. What are you doing down?"
"I quit. I'm a black sheep, daughter of a black sheep, you know."
"Is he? J. J.?"
"Awful. Don't you know him very well?"
"I've always thought so."
She chuckled. "Well, it's all in what you're used to. I didn't realize J. J. took your kind of client."
"He doesn't know me as well as I know him."
"You can't tell about us Everetts. I had a grandfather steal a railroad."
"I only underwrite life insurance. Men are inferior these days."
"Oh, but harder," she said. "I have a bruise to prove it."
He asked where and she shook her head, smiling. Now that he knew about her, he could see the resemblance to her father. The gray eyes, of course, but more in the delicacy of feature and fleeting tartness of speech. Marcy's mouth was a trifle lopsided, a soft mouth trying to grow up bitter. He decided not to kiss her yet.
"How was jail?"
"Ungodly," she said flatly. "They didn't let us out until just before break-

fast this morning. I've been sitting in a little place ever since, drinking coffee, trying to dream up what I'll tell J. J. You won't tell him, will you?"

"I see no reason to."

"That's a reassuring answer."

"What's Marcy short for?"

"Marcy's all there is to it. Are you one of these probers that has to find more to everything? Oh, dear, I'm out of cigarettes. Please?"

He lit a pair. Holding hers, her long fingers shook slightly, energy for which she hadn't found a use. They continued their aimless course along the hall.

She told him, "I didn't give my right name. I said I was a friend of mine away at school. I was scared to death and still not as scared as a lot of people in that cage. Perhaps they had more to lose."

"I doubt it. After all, they were other people."

"That's true. No, there's no reason for J. J. to know about my adventures. My first week down here and I.... By the by, I never did see you in a cage."

"I don't take to it."

"You're the kind that would have pull, certainly. What were you doing at the Cathay Gardens when the police rushed in? You were running up and down like mad."

Beck said, "I was destroying evidence so the cops wouldn't get it."

"Oh. You mean I had you guessed right?" They walked in silence and smoked while she thought him over. She said finally, "I ought to keep my mouth shut. Much of a price on your head?"

"A pretty penny, it's called. I'm the most dangerous man in town. When I pick you up tonight—eight o'clock, incidentally—we'll discuss the terms of turning me in."

"No."

"There's a new place opening called The Natchez. It should be an experience and we can compare prison records."

"Really no. I'm serious."

"So am I." They stood still, facing each other. He said, "Must I ask your father's permission?"

"Blackmail. Won't you even flip a coin or anything?"

"I never gamble."

She gazed at him steadily, her tongue between her teeth. "If you're what I think, aren't you used to women a little bit brighter than I am?"

"No. No's supposed to be a compliment."

Marcy grinned suddenly. "What hellish questions I ask! Why this hasty interest in me? I suspect it's merely sex."

He felt a surprising sense of relief that she'd made up her mind right. He said, "You notice I didn't invite your father."

"I'm dangerous too, knowing just how far you can be trusted."

"I'll bring a yardstick. Eight o'clock and evening dress. We'll eat there."

"Anything in particular you'd like me to wear, Mr. Beck?"

"Oh, how about one of these gay strapless affairs? They add."

"And hold my shoulders up to your ridicule?"

"That wasn't what I had in mind holding them up to."

"Ah. Well, you're ordering. I do have a very good figure except through the shoulders. I'm rather thin there. Inbreeding, J. J. says. I like to be out in the open myself but I want you to know I'm complying under duress. Oh, here."

"What's that for?"

It was a little bronze mask which she unclasped from her belt and dropped into his coat pocket.

"A token. To make me certain I'll come with you. I prize it very much and I want it back tonight. I'm pretty undependable and you might never see me again otherwise."

"Thank you."

She wound her belt around her hand and put it in her purse. "See? All is sham. The belt doesn't support a single garment. I do it all. Please may I have another cigarette ere we part?"

He lit her again and she waved her fingers and left him. She stopped by Everett's door. "Oh, the dress. I warn you—it's boned."

Beck said, "I never gamble." They exchanged smiles. She inhaled deeply on the cigarette and tossed it down the hall for him to step on. She went in to face her father and he buzzed for another elevator.

9

Friday, May 20, 1:00 p.m.

The blue-painted steel disc slid down the polished hardwood, knocked two red discs off into the gutters. Beck said, "Three blue. Chalk it up, Dan."

"That's game," Dan Pelletreau said. All his pinched clerical face showed was disgust for himself. "Don't you ever lose?"

"No." Admit chance and he wouldn't play. It was a silly game but it killed the time until the waitress brought their food. Beck played with micrometer precision, knowing what he was doing and what would happen because of it.

They left the shuffleboard table and sat down in a rear booth now that their meals were ready. Beck rubbed it in a little more. "At least, I made it easy on your pocketbook. This Spanish food is cheaper than what you ordered. Also better."

Pelletreau laughed, fidgeted and took it. He smoked through his veal cutlet special plate, halting at intervals to muffle his cigarette cough. He was ageless at thirty and unimportant. He still wanted to know what was up.

Beck asked back, "What happened in your department yesterday?"

"I couldn't help it, Steve. It was my night for duty in the file room so I wasn't at headquarters yesterday afternoon when Richards got that wild hair. I didn't know anything before. Not until I went to work at six and heard he had you out back. I didn't know what else to do but call you know."

"That was the right move."

Pelletreau beamed faintly.

Beck added, "But too bad you didn't come through on that other."

"I couldn't help it, Steve."

"What's Richards' idea?"

"I don't know. Just a wild hair."

"That veal isn't much good, is it? Should have gotten the enchiladas."

Pelletreau chewed, considering. "Yeah, I guess you're right."

The cash register clanged through their lunch. The juke box played "La Golondrina" three times running. A siren howled up Third toward Broadway and Pelletreau twisted nervously.

Beck had the view out the front of the Hidalgo Café. "Relax," he commanded. "Just a private ambulance, no one in it. It's their way of advertising."

"A crummy way but I guess they got to live, too. Sure wish I could move out a little, though, some place a little quieter. It seems like they're always tearing up the street in front of our place, laying new wires, laying new pipe. Wears my wife to a frazzle."

"It's all a matter of self-control, learning not to notice it."

"That's what I tell her, Steve, but it would be nice out a ways."

"You'd be out of touch with everything important."

"I guess you're right. I can't afford it, anyway, not on civil service."

"You'll get your money this month, same time, same place."

"Oh, I didn't mean that!"

"I was telling you. You'll earn it. There may be a little extra."

Pelletreau made a joke about scalping his grandmother for an extra buck. He waited for Beck to continue, then complained, "You're what's making me nervous. Why don't you tell a guy instead of keeping me on the hook?"

"I thought we'd eat first. But if it's making you squirm...." Beck explained what he wanted from Springfield on Isham, from San Francisco and San Quentin on Cortes, and from Los Angeles on Dominic. Then he had to repeat it so Pelletreau could scribble brief notes.

"Steve, this is going to take some doing!"

"In a pig's eye. Your department sends out a hundred routine inquiries per day. These won't look any different from the rest."

Pelletreau had his notes tucked away before it sank in. "But these are all Big Pat's own men!"

Beck said softly, "This is routine, Dan. A new angle of Mr. Garland's. Don't think otherwise. In fact, don't think period."

"Just the idea gave me a start there for a minute. I don't want to be caught in the middle of anything, believe me."

"You're not big enough for that, Dan."

"Boy, I'm glad I'm not!"

"Get that stuff to me tomorrow." Pelletreau's eyes bulged and he sought refuge in coughing. Beck repeated, "Tomorrow. No excuses."

"I'll do my best."

"Tomorrow."

"Okay. Hey, aren't you going to wait for dessert? It comes with the meal."

"Haven't time."

"So long, Steve. Be good."

He was going to spend as much of the afternoon as necessary at the printing plant Garland wanted, laying the groundwork by getting Dominic's brother-in-law discontented with his his present profits. Beck headed back for the Southwest Towers first to see if anything had come in.

He stopped off at Exclusive Florists to order a corsage for Marcy Everett. He told the salesgirl to send their most expensive single orchid. She insisted he look at it although he knew by the price it would be lovely. It was, graceful and streaked with chartreuse and brown. On impulse, with a childish grin, he had the salesgirl throw in a nosegay of forget-me-nots. He wrote a card: *In case the bruise has faded—*

The clerk at the club had four telegrams for Steven Beck, three on the coast, one from Salt Lake.

Ace Hurley remembered breaking Sid Dominic in 1947 and sent his love to Pat and missus.

Kate Doerck echoed Hurley's L. A. wire from Salt Lake City.

Johnny Torano wired the one word SURE from San Francisco. He would nose into Cortes' past.

The Driscoll Agency gave formal recognizance to Beck's message of the night before and promised daily mailed reports on Needle Moncey re Sid Dominic, on Mrs. Dominic and on her brother.

"Quite a crop, Mr. Beck."

"Yes, it is."

"Oh, there's a telephone message here, too, at the back of your box."

"Thank you."

Beck read it on the way to the elevator and again while waiting for the elevator. Felix was back in town. He had made a local call at 10:03 a.m. *Saw our buddy off for the East last might. Heard something about a mutual pal and am checking. Will phone later. Felix.*

Beck frowned and stuck a cigarette in his mouth to help him wonder. His lighter still needed a refill. He didn't feel like walking back across the lobby to the match dispenser.

He asked a stocky man reading the bulletin board, "Got a light?"

The man dug a book of matches from his coat pocket and handed them over without interrupting his reading. "Keep them."

"Thank you."

The elevator came. On the ride up, Beck looked at the match folder. It said CABRILLO MORTUARY. Easy Payments. Fine Funerals.

The elevator boy chuckled with him, then said, "Something funny, Mr. Beck?"

"Now that you mention it, son, damned if I know."

10

Friday, May 20, 8:15 p.m.

Marcy said, "You drive well, Steve. Like part of a car."

Beck was pleased.

The heavy coupe dripped over the crest of Juan Street hill, purring down toward Mission Bay. The dash flow reflected from Beck's shirtfront and the gleaming machine-weave of the girl's formal.

She had been right about her naked shoulders although *rather thin* were not the words he would have used. Delicate, perhaps. He could look at her and consider such finer details without his eye leaping at once to the juncture of her breasts. He could be dispassionate like that.

The obese petals of his orchid didn't look well against her. On her appearance tonight, he had been disappointed about the flower, half-inclined to blame her until he realized she knew it too and had worn it only as a courtesy to him. That made it right, the way he wanted matters.

Marcy nudged him. "Hey, wake up!"

"I'm sorry. I was thinking about you. What did I miss?"

"One of my sparkling statements. That you seem as complete a metropolitan as I've ever seen."

"I wasn't born in a metropolis, I'll tell you. It was a place called Lower Peach Tree, Alabama."

"You're kidding!"

"It's on the larger maps. As soon as I learned what I wanted, I went over to Montgomery, then up to Birmingham, doing this and that, and here I am. Story of a life."

"What was it you wanted?"

"A job."

Marcy chuckled and he saw it was a funny answer, spoken seriously.

She said, "I bet I'm going to have fun tonight. Oh, that's right, you don't bet. Are we on time?"

"That's an unknown dimension where we're going. This party you just pick up anywhere."

"Good, As long as I can drop it anywhere, too. Not like the Cathay Gardens. I don't care if I never see another policeman."

"You never can tell when you're with me."

"I know it. And that's probably not all."

They both grinned. She tucked her skirted legs up under her and drummed on one knee to the radio music. She watched the lighted windows flash by and began another cigarette.

He said, "Before you demand your token back, I might as well tell you I'm keeping it."

"My precious sad little copper face? Oh, Steve!"

"Bronze."

"Is it? I never looked past the expression. You know, I thought of that right after I left you this morning. I suspected you."

"You suspected right. Goes to show you: don't leave your jewelry lying around. I'm one of those gentleman safecrackers that used to run in installments."

It was, he decided, mere accident that her bent knee rested against his hip.

"Bet you I get it back before the evening's over," Marcy said. "I really haven't turned loose my wiles yet."

Beck laughed. "I thought of that. I left it on my dresser where I'm reasonably sure it's safe."

"Oh, I'm perfectly sure. But did you ever think I might have wanted you to keep it? Times I surprise myself how tricky I can be."

Beck glanced soberly at her, said, "Times I surprise myself," and returned his eyes to the highway. He felt her knee leave his side and not come back.

"In the words of the prophet," she murmured, "let's keep it just fun."

"Okay." In a second he added, "But you're wrong in principle, anyway. You can't keep things static. People, either. They develop whether you like it or not and you either have to keep up or drop out."

"I'm sorry already. I was being unduly defensive. Offensively defensive. Wasn't I?"

"No offense meant where none is intended."

"Why, that's the first thing you've spoken like a true Southern gentleman. You certainly might have come from anywhere, Steve."

"Thank you."

"Even sprung fullblown from the West Wind. I know! I bet you're one of the minor deities on a visit. In you I sense that beautiful complete kind of vanity I associate with the.... I haven't hurt your feelings, have I?"

He laughed no.

"I didn't mean vanity, anyhow. I meant pride, pride of accomplishment, with self-reliance thrown in. You always give me the feeling—I've known you so long, haven't I!—that you've accomplished something or are just doing something."

"Oh, I admit I try to act important. It sells more insurance to men like J.J."

"*That's* what I was, groping for: act! You're just the man who would change his spots on an untutored girl. Domineering this morning, charming tonight. You stole my little mask to wear sometime."

"Well, you have to respond to your environment, Marcy, or get eaten up."

"No, no. J. J. tells me on the best authority—himself—that road leads to slavery and ruin. You mustn't let environment get away with any tricks, he says, keep the upper hand. J. J. thinks man with a capital M is a gone gosling, anyway. I suspect him of a strong sense of sin."

"That'll do it. I'll make you an offer. When a side of me comes up that you like, don't drop any more coins. Leave me at two bells and an orange or whatever."

"I'll try for the jackpot. I always do."

His glance caught her lips, twisting briefly. He asked, "What's wrong, Marcy?"

"And I always lose my shirt, to put it nicely."

The incandescent stream, the aloof stranger windows, and the staring stranger headlights flashed by on her silence for a while.

She said finally, smiling steadily, "I had might as well tell you the plain old truth, Steve. So if I should get drunk tonight and start adding to it, don't believe me because I'm unpredictable. I got myself married a while back, not long."

"Oh?"

"One of those college affairs. I thought I was in love or I was in love and didn't use my head about it and—oh, you know. I think I tried but no good came of it. It didn't, it never had a chance to, work out."

"Divorce?"

"Annulment. J. J. had some reason for it being better that way. I forget what it was. I was on a stratospheric bender at the time, kicking myself all over the lot for not knowing better. So take a lesson from me: you're never as smart as you think you are." Marcy studied the fresh cigarette she had drawn from her purse. "And one of your finer points, Mr. Beck, is that you don't tell me I smoke too much."

"I own a few shares of American."

She grinned and patted his hand on the wheel. "That's the gay spirit I was supposed to preserve. Forgive all my contradictions, please, my mournful history and my defensiveness and my timidity. You set the course from now on. I sure can't be trusted. I'm surprised I had the guts to come."

"So am I."

"Well, I'm surprised you asked me, too, though I did see you and your two friends in that bookmaking place giving me the eye and a frank discussion."

"No. I was keeping them from discussing you. A little difficult, considering."

"Why, thank you, I presume. Really, why did you pick on me, Steve? You haven't mistaken me for an heiress because of the Everett name?"

"If you don't know I'm not going to tell you."

"That's a fair arrangement."

"What did you tell J. J., by the way?"

"I didn't have to tell, thank Heaven. I had all sorts of schemes to get him out of the house at the right time. But he doublecrossed me and went out himself. He probably has secrets darker than mine. See, Steve?"

"See what?"

"You don't dare turn out to be ordinary."

"It's a deal, reciprocal treaty. J. J. like it here in San Diego?"

"He's making a lot of money, as he may have told you. He represents some sort of corporation, what exactly I don't know. He's a whiz at that intricate financial stuff. He works too hard, though. Poor J. J."

The music from the radio had ended and a voice began to state the news. Beck scowled at the speaker vent suddenly. Marcy reached out and gave the knob a twist. "I hate the news, too, particularly these days. All I read any more are the funnies."

"No. Just a second." Beck swiftly found the station again.

The announcer said, "...possibly of accidental death. The body was found impaled on an ornamental ironwork gate behind the Point Loma estate of Charles Holsclaw, local used car dealer who is absent in the East on business. The body was found by a caretaker at seven-oh-five this evening. Police are investigating the possibility of an accident, since the sharp-pointed gate of death is at the bottom of a steep flight of steps at the rear of...."

"How gruesome!" Marcy explained. "Turn it off, Steve, please."

Beck shook his head.

The voice continued, "...has been tentatively identified as Felix Pavek, age forty-five, an automobile salesman in the employ of Mr. Holsclaw. This brings the accidental death list in the county this month to fourteen. Elsewhere in San Diego...."

Beck shut the radio off.

They were speeding around the perimeter of Mission Bay park. Some night-sailing was visible out on the bay, an aura lay over the distant grandstands where there was a softball game and a faint yell arose like a baby's cry, there were party lights in the clubhouse on the golf course, and, farthest away, by the ocean, glimmered the concessions of Mission Beach and the spangled roller coaster.

Marcy was looking at him. "What's the trouble? Did you know him, Steve?"

"Slightly, just slightly. We were members of the same club."

"It's a horrible way to start the evening for you, Steve. Perhaps you'd rather not go."

"Just the opposite. Now I have to go." He smiled for her. "Let's do our best to forget we heard. It's just a shock to hear a familiar name, even somebody you hardly knew, like that."

She nodded.

He wheeled the Buick off the highway into a steel-fenced parking lot alongside Mission Bay. A shadow detached itself from the other shadows and came up to the slowing car to flick a flashlight beam in Beck's face. The unknown said, "Evening, Mr. Beck," and walked away.

When Beck let Marcy out her side, she asked, "Does everybody know you?"

"Just the people who count."

She smoothed back her tawny hair and gathered up her skirt for walking.

"One detail," Beck said. He touched her shoulder as his hand closed over the orchid. He pulled the bloom away from her dress top gently, opened his fingers and tossed the pulp into the dark.

She said, "For Heaven's sake!" as she felt around to remove the corsage pin.

"You don't need a flower."

"I need the idea of a flower."

"You've got the idea and you look wonderful in it."

"The wonderful thing is that I understand what you mean. Matter of fact, I nearly wore the forget-me-nots, just to let you know." Marcy chuckled and took his arm. "We're a forward pair of brutes."

They walked toward the glistening water.

11

Friday, May 20, 8:45 p.m.

From the paved bank a gangplank led onto the middle deck of The Natchez. Marcy said, "Gorgeous! Honestly, it must be the most elaborate false front ever built."

"So far. The owner constantly outdoes himself."

She stopped to survey it all. "Boy, oh, boy, that's life."

The Natchez was a three-story showboat which could never float. Built on pilings at high tide level, it spun its neon-trimmed sidewheels in lazy display and never got them wet.

Beck gestured up. "That fake smoke coming out of the stack is scented with jasmine. You can't smell it unless the wind's right."

"Somebody must have all the money in the world."

"More is being printed all the time."

They went aboard. A tall gaunt shape lounged by the forward rail, only blond wavy hair and a white shirt front discernible in the night.

Beck called, "Did they kick you out, Paul?"

The blond man replied in his soft thoughtful voice, "Good evening, Steve. No, I just came out to see the stars. It's quite stuffy inside."

"We'll chance it."

Beck slid back the door and motioned Marcy in.

She whispered, "I see this is one of those evenings when I never do get introduced. But I've no doubt you know best."

"Yes. I'll just point, politely with my elbow. That star gazer was Paul Moon. He's in the warehouse business."

"How dull."

"Sort of."

They were into the music and noise, under the lights. They waited on the shore of the throng while George Papago, the assistant manager, emptied a secluded corner loge. The smooth young Greek had a little trouble with the bookie and his tart who were necking in it until Papago mentioned Beck's name. Then the couple vacated with some dignity and stiff smiles in their direction.

Marcy was amused. "I want to learn all those magic words."

Dinner lasted till after ten. They decided mutually not to broach the ballroom floor although Beck informed her the crowd was exceptionally well-behaved tonight, probably because of the formal dress. He explained about the public opening tomorrow night, how this was a private party for the owner's

friends. He pointed out the Tarrants and Orville Kyle and various other people.

"Certainly a lot of fascinating types," she said.

"Mostly because you're overworking your imagination. Those two men
across the way, whispering. Which peddles dope sheets and which is the
judge?"

"Naturally, it's vice versa. The shifty looking character is the judge."

"No. They're both horse trainers."

"Oh, you cheated on me!"

"Demonstrating the value of independent opinion."

"You didn't give me a chance!"

They were having dessert when Sid Dominic spotted them and broke away
from the push of dancers. His fat neck gleamed with sweat above his starched
collar. He hauled behind him a rawboned woman taller than he, his wife.
"Howsa kid, Steve!"

Beck made an answer without introductions.

"Pretty good food, huh? Larruping, I call it!"

"It *was* larruping," Marcy picked it up enthusiastically. "The first time in
my life I've had pheasant under glass."

"Trust Pat to put on the dog." Dominic's wife smiled thinly and nudged
him. "Huh? Oh, yeah. Well, be seeing you two lovebirds later." They passed
on.

Beck said, "That was Mr. Dominic, a collector," and ordered more marti-
nis.

"Of what?"

"Coins. He's independently wealthy."

"You just never can tell, can you? You're right about me driving my imagination."

"They're all just working people."

Below their loge a girl had a disaster with the halter of her gown and dashed
for the powder room, giggling.

Marcy said, "Oh, there's a prime example. Who's Pat?"

"He owns fifty-one percent of The Natchez. It's his party."

"Is he the one you've been looking for?"

"I didn't realize I'd been looking for anybody. Except the waiter."

"No, let me catch my breath between drinks, please. Steve, you know
you've been revolving like radar all evening."

"No, I didn't know that. I wonder where Pat is, though. He's a party man
from way back in G."

"Go ahead. Change the subject. See if I care. I'm breaking trail to the little
girls' room and I may never return." She picked up her purse and went off
in a pretended huff.

Beck watched her course across the room. He started to get up when one of Kyle's men reeled after her, trying to throw his arms around her, but there was no incident. He summoned Papago, told him he said for the punk to go home and that was that.

The orchestra was playing faster now, loosening up, bearing down on the drums. Around the edges of the ballroom, couples were dancing the music halftime, their bodies melted together in an affected privacy. A circle of spectators had formed in the center of the floor. The smoke was beginning to win its battle with the air-conditioning system. Too many people, like all of Garland's parties.

Marcy came back. "Made it, partner. A lot of sick lassies in there, I'll tell you. I'm glad I'm in training. One girl was sitting there, bawling at the top of her lungs, saying she was nothing but a blankety-blank tramp over and over. Or words to that effect."

"Well, there's nothing like a good cry."

"I felt so sorry for her."

"How about another drink now?"

She patted her stomach the way Dominic had done. "Ooh, I'm so full! You don't like the people here very much, do you, Steve?"

"Oh, I don't dislike them."

"Canaille. We just ignore them, don't we? Hey, what's going on out there?" She waved toward the ring of people out on the dance floor.

"A member of the theatrical profession is showing off her act."

Marcy stood up on her chair to look and hurried down again. "For Heaven's sake!"

"I told you so."

"I'm beginning to mistrust your euphemisms. You just wanted to see if I blush. Did I?"

"As far as I could see."

Marcy hitched up her bodice on general principles. "I keep noticing people disappear into that elevator over there. Where does it go?"

"Up and down. It's slow to learn. I'm ready for another."

"Poor little elevator, a slave to the system. What's up?"

"Luxurious staterooms, where one can capture the enchantment—"

"That's enough said. That why you've been pouring glasses of enchantment down me all evening? Not a chance, my friend."

"As a matter of fact, it hadn't entered my head."

"Oh, please don't look hurt, Steve. I'm sorry it entered mine." She took his hand. "Why am I always saying I'm sorry to you? I never had to other men. Simply thousands of other men, as you can imagine."

They sat in their own precious quietness for a few seconds, hands clasped.

Marcy said, "Oh, damn them for playing faster and faster! I definitely want to dance now. With you, to make up for me being such a neurotic clown."

"Some other time. It's a promise."

"A promise. Did any other beautiful woman ever tell you how strong you seem? Like you were steel through and through. It's very intriguing, especially to an all-around weakling like me. You're like a weapon. Tell me, am I making sense? I shouldn't be drunk yet."

Across the floor someone was having a laughing fit.

"I'd like to think you were making sense." Beck tugged at her hand and they came to their feet together.

"Where we going?"

"Down."

She bowed her head meekly. "Yes, sir."

They made their way to the elevator and Beck punched the demand button. The doors slid back finally and a mussed couple got off, the woman half-carrying her drunken escort.

Beck said to the man waiting behind him. "Next trip, Jerry," and closed the doors in his face.

"Not a very big elevator," Marcy said.

"It's a small world. I might mention in passing that when this club opens tomorrow night, this particular button will not be exposed to general view."

Beck pressed the button in question. They buzzed down a few feet and he pressed another on the regular panel. The car stopped.

"Where are we?"

"Halfway. Cigarette?"

"Are you supposed to smoke in elevators? Oh, I forgot. You do what you want to do."

"Privacy's suddenly taken on an added luster after that free-for-all upstairs. This is the freshest air I've smelled for hours."

Marcy took a cigarette. "So let's pollute it."

"I think I should quote J. J. right back at you. He told me once that people are prone to make sweeping observations about anything bad and say, well, that's life. I've watched ever since and it never works in reverse."

"Oh, dear. Am I like that?"

"You're not like anything."

"Isn't this exciting, this being halfway? I don't know where I'm going and I don't have much idea where I've been." Marcy leaned back against the wall and grinned. "Well, that's life. I'm having a wonderful time, Steve. I bet we're on our way to the original Hell."

"So you wore a red dress."

"I had to. It's the only one I have that stops here, where you wanted it to. This is my temptress dress, obviously bought during a discouraged moment."

"I like it. Not to mention the temptress."

They both looked embarrassed suddenly. They both knew they were going to kiss.

Marcy said thank you, nervously. Beck said yes, hesitated, then drew her away from the wall. She dropped her hand with the cigarette and lifted her face. It was short and sweet, a first kiss.

Then she snuggled against him, he imagined she fluttered, and they clutched at each other. Time was a mystery. He had never been so glad to hold to any-thing on earth.

Eyes still closed, Marcy freed her mouth to whisper uncle. They ground their cheeks together fervently and he took his hands off her. Her cigarette shook as she put it to her lips automatically and he noticed it looked only as burned as when he had seen it last, as if no time had passed at all and noth-ing could have happened.

They looked at each other questioningly, waiting for the other to comment. When she saw he wasn't going to speak either, she got out her compact.

He said inanely, "That's a good idea."

Marcy chuckled and kissed him again, gaily. "Not so glib in a pinch, am I?" She used his handkerchief to wipe off his face and then repaired her own.

He pressed the buttons that sent them on down. When the doors slid back, she nodded wisely.

Beck grinned. "Just as you suspected? This is the engine room. I thought you'd like to watch the machinery."

"Oh, I'm not completely innocent, you know. I've been to such places."

"That's right. The Berkeley kids go to a place called Pagliacci's, owned by Johnny Torano."

"How do you know everything like that? You must be a gambler, despite your virtuous line. I bet I find you taking a chance one of these days."

"Look me up in the city directory, Marcy. Insurance underwriter in black and white."

She squeezed his hand. "They must have had the decency to add a small warning in parentheses."

"Like danger, soft shoulders?"

"It just came to me. You're the devil come to earth to lead poor foolish vir-gins astray."

"Since when did he ever leave?"

Marcy was thinking of something else, solemnly. "Except I don't quite fit in that picture. I keep forgetting."

"You are, in your own way, sweetheart."

She tucked his arm through hers. "You must have a strain of the visionary in you. Let's have another drink and then see me at that roulette. I've got a system."

"Famous last words."

They got down to the bar, spun gently on the stools, holding hands. The air was clearer and quieter here on the lower deck. The people around the ta-bles murmured, following the blur of ivory balls or bouncing dice, and glasses sat unnoticed.

Hervey Isham saw Beck and turned his table over to an assistant. He came up, a distinguished man impeccable in tails. His thin dark hair was lined neatly over his high skull like a perspective drawing. He wore a prim smile fixed on his old maid face but his chewed fingernails were his least vice.

"Steve, it's grand to see you. I was afraid you wouldn't appear."

Beck said, "Mr. Isham, Miss Apollyon."

Isham said, "I'm awfully happy to meet you, Miss Apollyon. Steve's told me so much about you. I trust you're going to try your luck tonight," while his eyes looked at the tops of Marcy's breasts and at her hips and at her crossed thighs.

"She's got a system," said Beck. "Bring all your extra money over to the north table. See you later, Hervey."

Isham hesitated, bowed slightly over Marcy's skirt and went away.

"Why'd you do that, Steve?"

"He runs this place, worked up from playing for fun to house man to here. He's a study in contradictions for you. Cold as a clam at business, a martinet in administration, but then he has his other side."

"Yes, but why didn't you want him to know my real name? I guess it isn't important but I'm just curious."

"Oh, it just amused me to see Isham made a fool of. Besides, I didn't like the way he went over you."

"Mr. Pot, meet Mr. Kettle. Well, now I know and I'm happy. He does have big eyes."

"Have a drink."

"You name it. Say, I know that man!"

The bartender looked amused.

Marcy said, "You were working at the Cathay Gardens just yesterday. Well, weren't you?"

Beck said, "You heard the lady, Caesar. What about it?"

"Yes, miss. What'll it be, Mr. Beck?"

Beck ordered two Shady Ladies and the bartender moved down to the mixing rack.

Marcy whispered, "I think I've done very well at not coming right out and asking what you are."

"I think you have, too."

The cocktails came and she wanted to know what was in them besides blood.

"Lime juice, bourbon, benedictine, grenadine. A little trifle I made up for special occasions."

"I hope they're named after the dead past. They're good, like fruit punch."

"And you can spill all you like without it showing tonight."

They drank those and got two more to carry over to roulette. Beck arranged a place for Marcy right by the wheel. She insisted on buying her own chips with a wad of bills from her purse. Isham had wandered around to the opposite side of the cloth from the girl. He caught Beck's eye and nodded back with the slightest movement of his eyeballs toward the croupier. It was all set.

Marcy pulled Beck's head down close to hers and murmured, "I got this system from a couple math students up at college. It always works or at least it always has. Watch me closely." She placed a few chips carefully and won. She played and won again. She kept playing and winning.

Beck watched the color creep up her shoulders to her cheek and then subside as she decided she was on a streak and buckled down in pale and deadly earnest. He stood behind her, looking down on the crown of her head, smiling gently. She was a gambler. In the circle, the word was sucker.

The rest of the play broke up to watch her. The croupier was letting her lose only to drive out those who tried to follow her bets. Across the table, Isham chattered to her with professional ease. She answered in monosyllables and nods, her gaze never leaving the cloth. Isham watched her flesh each time she leaned out to place the chips. He avoided letting Beck catch his eye but he knew. Beck could tell by his mouth.

He decided against trouble now. With Marcy's glass and his own he went back to the bar for refills. He saw Leda Garland sitting down at the other end, dissatisfaction curling her lips. He sent Marcy's drink back to her by Caesar and carried his own down to Leda.

She had been toying with the peach fringe that was all over her gown. Now she stopped that, stroked up her back hair and sat up straight to show off her figure. "Steve, how are you? Thanks for coming down. I'm bored to tears. Isn't this deadly?" She put out her hand.

He squeezed her fingers. "I brought you the antidote."

She said, "What kind of slow death is that?" after she'd tried his drink.

"Shady Lady, lady. Where's Pat?"

"I wish I knew. We were all dressed when a call came and he told me to come ahead." Her eyebrows arched over the rim of the glass. "You pick this up along with that girl in red?"

He shook his head.

"Who is she, Steve?"

"Everett's daughter. But what he doesn't know won't hurt him."

"Business?"

"What do you think?"

"She's not bad," Leda said critically. "Still at that awkward age, of course, but that's hardly her fault. She seems to be breaking the bank."

"Isham is giving her a hand."

They exchanged glances and Leda shuddered. "You know what Pat thinks."

"Business is one thing and that's another." Beck grinned. "I'd watch that

Pat. Still, you're an exceptional woman, Leda. With all the availables around most wives would be worried."

"Not I. Not about Pat. Who does he worry about? Well, you've done your duty now so you can run along back to her." She put his empty glass back in his hand and looked around the room aimlessly. "Personally, I feel like a long hot delicious bath after this session. If you do see my darling husband, tell him I went for a drive and not to wait for me."

"Buck up, Leda. Better days ahead."

She made a word with her red lips and they both laughed.

Beck watched her swaying walk to the elevator and had Caesar mix another. Then Isham slid in beside him.

"Did you want to see me about anything special, Steve?"

"Well, Hervey, what do you think?"

"I really couldn't guess. Isn't it a shame that this layout had to be trampled through tonight, just before the formal opening tomorrow? I hear the ballroom's a wreck. I hate the thought of facing it."

"Pat, being the owner, I suppose he can throw a party here."

"Oh, I know that, Steve, Pat and the Tarrants. Just speaking theoretically, a matter of management." Isham ordered a chartreuse. "I like your taste, incidentally."

Beck laughed. "I knew you'd get around to the subject in hand if I let you talk long enough."

"Oh, I know that nasty laugh. You're annoyed with me. The world shakes at your coming and I suppose I'm no different. I do talk too much, though."

Beck called him a name.

Isham played with the liqueur in his mouth, before swallowing it. He said, "Actually, I didn't think you'd feel so harshly about it, Steve. Allow me to make my point: that I didn't consider the young lady classified under our professional relationship. However, matters standing as they do, I've erased her from my mind." He patted Beck's shoulder, one pat too many.

"What I got out of that was that you want to keep your eyes in your head."

Isham finished his drink and bit a thumbnail even, smiling.

Beck said, "Could you have mentioned your liquor license to anyone? Such as how it came to be yours?"

"Complications?"

"Not yet."

"Not to anyone unsafe. A good many of our friends have dropped out to see the new layout and you know I love to chat and play the host. But I'm no fool, Steve."

"That's all I wanted to know." Beck picked up his cocktail and added, "I've seen everybody here tonight but J. J."

"Come, come. He's never cared for this company socially."

"Not that you blame him?"

"Very well. Not that I blame him."

"Keep your nose clean, Hervey." Beck went back to the roulette. Marcy was flushed again. She said, "You doublecrosser. You took my luck away with you."

Beck looked at her chips, at the croupier, who shrugged, and then around the room. He didn't see Isham. He would later.

"All she's been winning is me," said Eddie Cortes. His white grinning teeth lit up his olive face. In a tuxedo, he looked tall and graceful and more lupine than ever and his long hair was as sleek as black paint.

"I reserve my opinion," said Beck. "How are you, Eddie?"

"I came over to your young lady to see if her luck would rub off on me." He turned out his pockets. "No go. I'm still flat busted."

Marcy said, "I'm not quite yet."

Cortes said, "No, not quite," and winked at Beck.

"Let's cash in and have a drink on her," Beck said.

"What's wrong with the one in your hand or are you saving it for your old age?" Marcy took it for a long sip. "Did you ever have one of Steve's Shady Ladies, Eddie? Something the old genius ran up in his spare time."

Cortes laughed. "I'm going to invent a drink called the Forty Thieves. I think somebody owes me a drink."

"You'll be paid in full," Beck said. "Don't be so material."

He motioned to the croupier, who wrote out a chit. Cortes went around for it.

Marcy said, "Hell's bells, why do I reach an impasse in every system?"

"The world's all wrong."

"That's the answer. Add to my microscopic winnings Friend Eddie. I'm going to take him home and stand him on my mantelpiece."

"Good news, good news," Cortes said. "Now back to the liquor for old times' sake."

"Let's take a booth."

"Take it out to the middle of the sea, the deep blue sea." Marcy twirled ahead of them.

"Watch that floor. It's tricky. The damn thing's level."

"Hey, Marcy, did this gigolo tell you what a big operator he is?"

"Steve, nobody tells me anything, not a soul."

"Well, he's the lad who put the Mexican government to work for him. He uses their lottery results for his own trade among the lower classes around the county."

"Really? You sound pretty shifty, Eddie."

"Oh, I'm a clever boy. Tell her more, Steve, go ahead. Might I say first that you two don't take up much of the booth?"

"Go ahead, say it. I dare you."

"You two don't take up much of the booth. I'm getting cold over here."

"See, he said it, Steve. He's afraid of me."

"It's a mother complex."

"For the love of mike, Steve, when will you ever get drunk? Any man in my company who can still say mother complex—see!—at this time of night... what was I going to say?"

"Comfortable, Marcy?"

"You bet. Tell them to put out the lights."

"Waiter, tell Caesar to mix up a flagon of Shady Ladies, got that, Shady Ladies, and send them over here with his compliments. Easy on the grenadine."

"Thank you, Eddie, you're a gentleman."

"Eddie's the gentleman who thought of advertising his lotteries over the Mexican stations. They're still calling out the marines on that one."

"Boy, I'm smart! But I'm cold."

"Poor lonely Eddie!"

Joe Zuaben said, "Big Pat wants to see you." The Filipino stood there in front of the booth in his white suit and panama hat. He was chewing gum.

Beck laughed. "Sure. Tell him I'll come on a white horse."

Zuaben said, "He said come up right now."

Beck took his arm from around Marcy's shoulders and got out of the booth. She stared curiously at the Filipino. Beck said, "Sweetheart, I'll have to duck out on you for a few minutes. I won't be long. Wait for me."

She squeezed his hand. "Of course, Steve. Don't worry about me. I'm a big girl."

The shaker of drinks came. "It so happens I'm unencumbered right now," said Cortes. "I'll keep an eye on her while you're gone."

Beck took his annoyance out on him. "I'd hate to guess what happened to whoever you brought."

"Have it your way, Steve boy."

Beck said, "Okay." He saw Isham down the room, looking their way. "Okay, fine. You watch her, Eddie."

He went to the elevator with Zuaben. "Where's Pat?"

Zuaben jerked a thumb up.

"Joe, you keep saving all those words and one day you're going to explode like a balloon."

They rode up, past the ballroom, to the top deck. At the end of the corridor Speed had his huge fighter's body blocking the door. Beck went that way, Zuaben at his heels.

Halfway along, one of the side doors opened partway. A tousled sulky-mouthed girl, high school age, looked out. She wore a yellow lace slip and was barefoot. Behind her, a record player murmured silky dialogue between a man and woman. The girl met Beck's eyes and lowered her lids sleepily as he passed.

Speed stepped aside, his battered face blank, and let Beck into the end room.

Pat Garland, dressed for the party, sat on the divan facing the door, both hands around a highball. Everett, wearing a business suit, stood by the window sucking on his empty holder.

Garland said, "Take his guns, boys." Speed closed heavy fists on Beck's arms. Zuaben's hands began to pat over his tuxedo pockets.

12

Friday, May 20, 11:30 p.m.

Beck snapped, "Since when have I carried a gun?"

Zuaben reported, "No gun."

"Somebody's gone off their rocker."

Garland said, "You boys wait right outside. I'll call you when I need you."

When Speed and Zuaben had gone, Beck grinned angrily. "Just what the hell's going on?"

"You tell me, Steve."

Beck stared holes through Everett. "You look like you've swallowed the canary."

Everett frowned and went on fitting a cigarette into his holder. Garland tossed down his highball, sat the glass on the carpet and wiped his hands. Across the highway, the streamliner came into town, honking. Garland said, "Well?"

"Well what? Come on out in the open, Pat. I been having a good time up to now and damned if I'm in any mood to play footsie. Even with you."

Garland played the wearily positive king-father. "Steve, you know what I'm looking for. Somebody well up in the circle who's been with me for not more than a year. You fit."

"I fit just as well last night and you laughed at the idea."

"That was before some other things came to my attention."

"So, that's the way it is. Actually, this is sort of funny. I hadn't figured on it going off in that direction."

Everett said pleasantly, "Let me say I haven't anything against you personally, Steve. I like you and admire you. I was faced with a problem of loyalty."

Beck snorted.

"And survival," Everett added.

"Just as personally, I'd like to know how you found out the attorney general had planted an agent in the circle. You knew that was why Pat wanted me out of the can last night. And don't tell me he just told you."

"No, I knew about it before you did. Gene Wake is my old friend, which proves a trifle embarrassing in this case. He thought he was doing me a favor by phoning me the news from the airport before he phoned Pat."

"Yesterday's the first I've seen you off-balance, J. J."

"Gene passed me a redhot brick. I certainly didn't want it. I think we're all on the nervous side."

"I'm not."

Garland said, "Okay, I haven't heard anything that explains why you told J. J. you were ready to sell out. Or why Felix fell on that fence after you sent him to Jacumba."

"You mind if I sit down?"

"You can talk standing up."

"Thank you, Pat. Felix. I sent him out to the back country last night to get a possible state witness—Hooper—out of the state. He did. Those are facts and the rest is guesswork. According to a message he left at my club this morning he picked up some dope from Hooper about the man in the circle we're looking for. Felix always thought he had a corner on brains; that's why he got kicked off the force. Instead of waiting for me, I believe he began trailing our man around himself. Holsclaw left town yesterday and the AG boy thought today was a good time to search Holsclaw's house for the books. Felix tailed him, got mad and got shoved downstairs onto an iron spike.

"As for J. J.: I was playing out an angle, I tried baiting a trap for him this morning, setting myself up as willing to listen to a proposition from the state. It has flopped beautifully, and I suppose an apology is due from my end. I like you, J. J., and I'm sorry we misjudged each other."

Everett smiled back at him with only lens reflections for eyes.

Garland sighed out, "Oh, make it better than that."

"You gave me a free hand," said Beck. "My move was logical. Reason number one: J. J. acted unaccountably disturbed at police headquarters last night. Reason number two: in the circle files is a—"

"Give me those files, J. J."

Everett picked up six manila folders from behind the divan and handed them to Garland, who held them and waited silently.

Beck said, "You're getting thorough. I wonder how much of my brandy your boys made off with."

"Don't stall. It's getting late."

Beck opened the J. John Everett folder and took out the real estate letter. From his wallet he produced the strip torn off the bottom of the AG report. "There's why I started with J. J."

Garland felt both papers, held them up to the light. Then he scowled at Everett. "You better take the floor."

The lawyer was frowning uncomprehendingly. "That appears to be an old letter of mine. But what's the other, the scrap?" After Garland told him, he shrugged. "I'm simply on your mercy, Pat. I simply don't know."

"They're the same identical stock."

"I can state my innocence, which I do, but I'm at a loss to prove it. But can the paper be traced? I'm surely not the only office in town with letterheads on that bond."

Beck said, "Senator Wake tells us that bond is used in state offices. Exclusively, as far as he knows, which makes it suspiciously rare."

Everett said, "Then Gene is wrong, at least in my case. His friendship has become something of a burden to me tonight, hasn't it? No, I got my letterheads from Sid Dominic. Or rather, through him. His brother-in-law printed them at an astonishingly good price. I laid in my paper supply when I first came down here and was still watching the pennies. I suggest this—that the Dominic family has some of the state printing contracts locally, that they shortchanged the local state offices on their own paper, and that my stationery was printed profitably on the remainder." Soberly, he stomped out his cigarette butt in the ashtray, blew through his holder and put it in his pocket. "As your attorney, Pat, I recommend that as a dialetical flight."

Garland was ready for a way out. He said, "Dominic," heavily. Then he commenced bustling without getting up, holding the six folders out toward Beck. "Well, I'm sorry we three had to get in this screwed-up mess. Do you want these files back, Steve?"

"No, I don't want anything back."

"What do you mean?"

"I mean, A, I finished with those files last night, and B, I was promised a free hand by you and you broke your promise."

"Oh, for God's sake, Steve!"

"Oh, for God's sake yourself. I figure when the boss gets out the knife to cut my throat it's time to move on. I'll wire you if I want an in."

"Sit down. You're making me nervous standing."

"I can't walk out sitting down."

Garland appealed to Everett. "Did you ever see such a touchy man in your life?" He got up and strode around with his hands in his pockets. "What else could I do under the circumstances? All right, all right, Steve, I'll kiss your foot in Marston's window at high noon if it'll make you feel any better. You want a raise? Anything, but please sit down and take that chip off your shoulder."

Beck thought it over and grinned. "Well, I didn't say it was final." He sat down where Garland had been.

Everett asked, "Do you need me any more, Pat?"

"No. Thanks for coming out tonight, J. J., even if…. Say, why don't you stick around for the party? Once I get down there, it'll be good for hours."

"I have to get back to the office, believe it or not. No, no, really, Pat. I'm sorry. But the hearings on the Cathay Gardens business are up in the morning and I'm not leaving anything to chance. Some other time. Good night, Steve. Sorry we got our wires crossed. Drop in tomorrow afternoon if you get the chance."

When he opened the door, Zuaben stuck his face in to catch Garland's nod. Everett waved a hand and the door closed behind him.

Garland said finally, "Nobody's that busy. He just doesn't want to associate with the crowd."

"I can't blame him for that. They're a bunch of crumbs, Pat."

"They're a living. Personally, I get sort of a kick out of them."

"You mean you get a kick out of kicking them around. J. J. and I, we're just more of the hired hands. That makes a difference."

"I said I was sorry, didn't I? Boy, you're going to be fun to live with for a while."

"Okay, we'll both forget it."

"Good," Garland said. "Well, I suppose we're still where we stood last night that I can see. Oh, I can see your angle on J. J. all right and I don't blame you one bit. But have you got anything else since that's blown up?"

"Who said it's blown up?"

"You're kidding. If J. J. was the boy he'd hardly have gotten in touch with me with that story about you."

Beck said, "Oh, wouldn't he? I would if I were the AG man. Say J. J. is the one we want. He knows we know he's in the circle and I'm the logical guy to chase after him. He simply guessed I wouldn't sell you out, that I was onto him. Rather than take a chance on me, J. J. was going to let you put me out of the way and weaken your hand. If, when he came to you tonight, you'd seen me separately instead of spilling your guts in front of him, we might have worked seven different follow-up angles on him. I had that figured ahead, too. But—you didn't so we won't. We'll forget that and I'll start over.

"Maybe Senator Wake called J. J. yesterday and maybe he didn't. I doubt if you want to ask Wake because I'm still not ruling out the possibility that Wake's after your hide.

"Don't forget that paper *still* matches up. You know the AG man isn't carrying a supply of state stationery around with him and J. J. may have the only stock outside the state offices, thanks to Dominic. There it is."

"Sure a pity that Felix had to go playing cops-and-robbers," mused Garland. "We'd know by now."

"Yeah, a pity." Beck stood up. "Well, I'm going back down to the party. Reminds me. Leda said for you to shoot yourself, she was going out for a drive. Coming?"

"What's the rush? Stick around and talk to me. You're not still mad, are you?"

"No, I'm not mad. But my girl will be if I don't show soon."

"Let her wait. I want to hear what your next move is."

Beck said, "My girl getting drunk downstairs is Marcy Everett. J. J.'s daughter."

Garland grinned broadly. "Steve, you're a dirty word. Say, you are for me, aren't you? Because if you're against me, if you're working for the AG, I'm quitting right now." He stuck a cigarette in his mouth, pressed the button on his case so another popped out for Beck.

"What happened to your new doctor?"

"He's vitamin-happy. Drives me nuts. Now did I go and forget my lighter? Oh, here." Garland chanced on a match folder in his pocket and lit the two cigarettes. "By the way, Steve, I found one beautiful place to hide those books. I doubt if even you'd be able to find them."

Beck was looking at Garland's hands and the match folder cupped there. Then he reached in his own pocket and pulled out an identical folder. He let Garland read the printing, silver on black. CABRILLO MORTUARY. Easy Payments. Fine Funerals.

Beck said, "I'll take that bet."

13

Friday, May 20, 11:45 p.m.

Garland slammed down the phone and came back to the divan where Beck was balancing the heel of his right shoe on the toe of the left. "Gusta says everything is quiet and I told her to be ready to leave by the time we get there. What are you smiling at?"

"Not a thing."

"I don't see anything funny at all."

"That's what I say."

Garland swore. "We'll never find another place so good."

"Just goes to show you shouldn't underestimate the other side. They had a man on you, Pat."

"You're talking like I was careless. I wasn't. Just blind luck on their part. What throws me is why they haven't picked up the books already. It begins to look like they've known all day."

"They're still not sure. They've been as far as the mortuary lobby, that's all we know. Talk about blind luck—just because my lighter was empty I borrowed some matches from a spotter. That gives us two men we know of, one insider and this new outsider. No, the attorney general can afford to take his time. He knows a bungled job would be worse than none at all."

Garland felt between the divan cushions and pulled out a .45 automatic. It weighed down the pocket of his tuxedo coat.

Beck said, "Oh, boy."

Garland opened the door and told Speed and Zuaben to come on in.

Zuaben asked, "All done with him?"

"Huh? What you talking about? Steve's got a job for you. He'll tell you about it."

Beck laughed. "Sorry, Joe, but I want you and Speed to go to the Southwest Towers, cover it. Pick up a fellow who may be hanging around tonight. Short stocky guy with a bullet head, brown hair, thick neck, gray suit, brown and white shoes."

"He lives there?"

"I doubt it. He was tailing me this afternoon and I believe he'll stick in that area rather than risk it out here. If I'm back at the time, bring him up to my place. Otherwise, sit on him."

"We'll get him, sure, Steve," Speed rumbled. He banged his fists together.

"Fine. Just don't hurt him any more than you have to. I want him able to talk." Beck gazed at the Filipino. "After that, I'll have some more orders for you, Joe."

Zuaben nodded, elbowed Speed and they went out.

Garland chuckled. "You like to rub his nose in it, don't you?"

"So they tell me. I'll see you at the mortuary. Got to get my girl home first."

"Okay. See you there, then. Around back."

Beck went downstairs where the gambling was still hot. Marcy and Cortes were in the same booth, talking studiously across a fresh shaker of Shady Ladies. Their conversation overlapped but they were focusing well enough. Beck said, "I'm proud of you, sweetheart."

"Oh, Steve I was just telling Eddie—I don't think I told you, did I?—about my new little charge, a little black kitten. It's the cutest thing. J. J. brought it home from the faroff lands and I've named it Lucky. All black. Except the poor little tyke's a female."

"Believe me, the cream of all cats," agreed Cortes. "Sit down, Steve boy. You're behind."

"I can't. Ready to go, Marcy?"

"What time is it?"

"Seven minutes to twelve."

"Oh, for Heaven's sake no, Steve! Let's not leave the time of my life yet. Why?"

"Some business has come up and I have to cut it short. I'm sorry, Marcy."

Cortes murmured, "Business?" Beck gave him a side glance and he pursed his lips knowingly.

Marcy raised her jaunty eyebrows. "I'm not ready to go."

"I think we'd better."

"I'm not going. Please don't make me stubborn, sweetheart, 'cause I'm lousy when I'm stubborn. Can't you take care of whatever it is and come back to me later?"

"No."

"Then let me stay a while longer. I want to. I'm setting a new world's record. Let me stay and let Eddie take me home."

Cortes said, "Remember, I didn't say one word, Steve."

Marcy squeezed Beck's hand and gazed up at him seriously. "Really, that's what I want to do. It's up to you. I'm not going to beg."

He smiled down at her. "Why should you? Eddie will be glad to take you home." He didn't smile at Cortes. "I'll depend on you, old buddy. That she gets home. Safe and sound."

Cortes nodded gravely.

Marcy said, "You're sweet, Steve. Why are you? No one else would understand."

"Count your money and don't let him get his foot in the door. I'll call you. Miss me."

"You bet."

Beck looked back from the elevator. They both waved.

He raced across town to the Hillcrest district, parked three blocks away from the Cabrillo Mortuary. He walked a couple of extra blocks getting to it but he hadn't been followed.

The mortuary was two stories high, stucco, floodlighted, copied after a Spanish hacienda. Garland's Cadillac was parked in the dark walled alleyway around back. The door had been left unlatched. Beck went up toward where the light showed on the second floor.

Garland met him on the narrow backstairs. "You give a man heart failure pussyfooting around like that. You could have whistled or something."

"And wake the dead?" Beck grinned. "Still as a morgue, isn't it?"

"Let's get a move on." Garland was in no mood for jokes.

"Where do all these doors go?"

"Preparation rooms, I guess. The guy who owns this place owed me a favor. I didn't ask for an inventory, just the loan of a room."

They went down the hall to the small pompously furnished bedroom where Augusta Norley waited. The little old woman had on her hat and coat, her clothes were packed and she was ready with her calculator in a hatbox and two big suitcases full of ledgers.

Beck said, "You know where they take them from here, Gusta."

She snorted. "Look who rented a soup and fish! The fellow who had this room before me had been dead two days and he still looked better than you."

"I love you whether you're funny or not."

"Let's get a move on," Garland insisted. "Any suggestions, Steve?"

"Gorman Hotel."

Gusta snarled. "No sir. I draw the line there. I don't know why all this commotion, getting me up in the middle of the night, anyway."

"Gorman Hotel," said Garland. "That's not bad, Steve. Not bad at all."

"It's respectable and it's off your beat." Beck sat down on the bed.

Garland nodded that his mind was made up and lifted the suitcases to go.

"Don't I have anything to say about where I go?" the woman wanted to know.

Beck said no and handed her the calculator.

"Gentlemen to the end." Gusta's voice rasped loud in the silent building. "I wish you big strong men'd get finished playing games one of these days."

Garland said from the doorway, "Aren't you coming, Steve?"

"No. I think I'll hang around a while. Tonight may be the night, when everybody's supposed to be at the party. Our boy's got an idea about this place; tonight he may come to make sure."

"Well, good luck."

Gusta said, "Don't drop off. You might come to with your hands folded."

"Just lock the downstairs door, honey."

Beck listened to them go down the hall, Gusta laughing until Garland told her to shut up for God's sake. The downstairs door clicked decisively. The Cadillac made more door-noises and then growled away.

There was silence.

Beck got off the bed and turned out the light. He folded his lapels over his shirt front and shoved his cuffs up into his coatsleeves. Then he went down the hall and sat down at the top of the back stairs.

He waited. Around the edge of the double door below him was a thin rim of light from outdoors. It got brighter as his eyes became accustomed to the blacker night inside the building. He began to feel sleepy but denied himself a cigarette. He decided he wouldn't have drunk so much if he'd known this session was ahead. It hadn't been part of his plan for the evening.

Nothing intruded on the faint peeling of light he watched. He thought he heard a footstep in the alleyway, decided not. A long time passed. Beck killed some of it by counting the steps, the rungs of the banister, the boards as far as he could see across the wooden lower floor. He smelled the chemicals in the air, tried to separate them for identification. He reflected on Pat Garland, the strong man, and his childish fear of death and its trappings.

Eventually, he felt the breeze. At first he thought his hips were numbed from sitting but when he put his hand on the thick carpet he could feel a fresh coolness. There was a new draft in the building.

He stood up and prowled down to the stairway at the other end of the hall. The draft was stronger here, coming from downstairs. Beck went back and opened a storage closet near the head of the original stairs. He found the light pull and flashed the naked bulb on and off swiftly. With the image of the closet's contents on his retina, he reached in and selected a long screwdriver. He carried it like a foil as he went back down the hall. A palm tree somewhere outside scratched its fronds across a screen. He didn't startle, recognizing the sound instantly.

Beck traced the draft down the new stairway, which was wider and car-peted for patrons, to an office off the lobby. White curtains billowed away from an open window. There was no sign of the intruder here nor in the over-stuffed lounge across the lobby. From the lounge he drifted through a cur-tained arch into a small auditorium, the service chapel.

He edged through the blackness, then stopped with a tight smile. At the far end a narrow beam glowed, roved momentarily, then disappeared. His quarry, using a tiny flashlight or a program light, was investigating the pul-pit. Beck crept that way.

He felt his way slowly from one row of padded folding chairs to the next. He kept the screwdriver cocked before his chest in a lunge position. A spray of blossoms in a floorstand brushed across his face tenderly. He thought of nothing but catching up with the unknown.

The tiny light flashed again, moving away from him. The rows of chairs ended and Beck's shoulder nudged something. His fingers sought and touched ivory coldness. It was the banked keyboard of an electric organ.

Beck drifted around the instrument. The disembodied light floated down the dais at the head of the chapel, glinted questioningly once at the imitation organ pipes behind the pulpit.

A loop of electric cable caught Beck's foot. He knew what it was even as he grabbed swiftly for support. His hand came down on the organ keys.

A thunderous dissonant chord sang through the chapel.

Beck charged toward where he had last seen the light, stabbing for obstacles with the screwdriver. Echoes rolled around the building, dying slowly. He wasn't angry, only intent and hurried since there was no time for anger at the accident. He groped swiftly up the other aisle, returning to the lobby. He reasoned certainly the intruder had taken this easiest way of escape.

When he found the drape in the archway pushed aside, he stopped to listen, knowing he was right. The faintest of footfalls whispered on the carpeted stairs. Beck followed the sound even more silently.

He returned to the upstairs hall by the same route he had come. From the far end of the hallway, he heard a rustling noise hurry down the steps toward the rear entrance. He padded softly past the preparation rooms, past the storage closet, reaching the site of his vigil. The narrow stairway was empty.

On the floor below lay an object which hadn't been there before, an object Beck realized was vitally important even before he had time to make out what it was. Then he forgot that and opened his hands wide in front of him to break his fall as a blinding surprise rocked the base of his brain. The spasmodic warding of his hands was his last conscious reflex.

14

Saturday, May 21, 1:30 a.m.

He made his eyes open and made himself realize that he was sprawled inside the double door, the rear entrance to the mortuary, and that half of it stood open. He knew he was alone now.

Beck collected himself on his feet, his head rocked a little and then he was all right. His palms had scrape marks from his fall down the stairs and his left cheek throbbed but the skin wasn't broken. He found the bump on the back of his head where he had been sapped. It hurt only when he pressed it. By his watch he figured he had been unconscious twenty minutes.

He kicked the screwdriver out of his way and picked up the object he had seen from the top of the steps just before the blow. It was a racing form, crumpled into a ball. Beck walked upstairs again just to see how right he was. As he expected, the door to the storage closet stood half open. He let the wadded racing form roll down the steps again, listening to the rustling noise he had taken for footsteps. His quarry had gone through these same motions and waited in the closet to get behind him.

He found a washroom, snapped on the light and brushed off his rumpled tuxedo in front of a mirror. Every time Beck met his own eyes he called himself a sucker. Cold water made his face and hands feel better but did nothing for his ego.

He calmed down walking the three blocks back to his coupe. Then he got an idea and drove over to the all-night drugstore at Goldfinch and Washington. With some change he closed himself in a phone booth.

Mrs. Dominic answered. "Huh? Sid? You want Sid? He's asleep and—well, if it's important, I'll get him."

Beck waited until he heard what was unmistakably Dominic's voice in the background and then cut it off. He dialed Holsclaw Amusement Enterprises. Paul Moon picked up his receiver in midring and spoke.

Beck muttered, "Wrong number," and tried Hervey Isham's quarters at The Natchez. No answer. He tried another Natchez number and caught George Papago at the gambling bar downstairs. Papago said they were cleaning up the place and tossing out the drunks but that Mr. Isham had gone upstairs to his rooms some time back.

At the court where Eddie Cortes lived in Golden Hill the phone rang and rang.

Beck scowled at the distant sound and finally broke his connection with it. Swiftly he fingered out Everett's home number.

Marcy answered, surprised. "We just got in a few minutes ago." Her voice sounded tired. "I had a wonderful time, Steve, wonderful."

"Look, Marcy, I'm just a few blocks away. Could I drop by and say good-night? I owe you an apology for deserting you."

"That's right, you do. All right, let me get a little something on and if you notice a small beat person in the kitchen that'll be me making some more cof-fee."

"Five minutes on my hands and knees."

"Come around to the back, will you? I don't want to wake up J. J."

"Okay. See you."

He was on one edge of the big home district of Mission Hills. He drove through to the other side where Everett had leased an old house with a har-bor view. It had a long front porch for sitting through nonexistent twilights and a steeply pitched roof to shed nonexistent snow. Beck parked under the trees across the street and walked around past the kitchen windows. Marcy was standing over an electric percolator, daydreaming. Beck scratched softly on the back door screen.

She smiled drowsily as she opened the door. "I knew you'd be quick."

"I knew you knew."

"Come on in so I can close this door."

"You ought to dress warmer."

Marcy smoothed the lace around the high collar of her negligee. "Little boys wouldn't come trotting around with apologies if little girls dressed warmer. Sit down. I think the stuff's done."

She poured two cups and they sat looking at each other across the kitchen table. The circles were under her eyes again. She rubbed a sleeve across them and complained, "They itch, Steve."

"Mine generally bleed."

"Don't kid me. You don't get drunk. You're too busy."

"What's your excuse? Too interested?"

Marcy chuckled. "Never thought of it. What a night! Why do they man-ufacture so much alcohol? For my sake?"

"Hear tell it's the other way around. You drink it for the factory's sake. Maintains the economy if not your stomach."

"That was tonight's slogan, all right."

Beck said, "Well, get suspicious, sweetheart." He motioned at his cheek and held out his scraped palms for her inspection.

"I hadn't noticed your face. It is a little swollen, isn't it? Some blonde hussy, no doubt?"

"Jealous?"

"I'd have to see her first. I don't throw my jealousy around like *that*."

"Believe it or not, my foot slipped getting out of my car and I fell down."

"Oh, Steve!"

"Word of honor. It seems funny now but I didn't get the humor of it at the time. Don't you believe me?"

"Oh, I believe you. It just doesn't seem like you, falling down for no reason."

"Not so strange. Since I ran into you, and I mean ran, I've done little except fall down. Possibly there's a greater plan, after all." Beck offered her a cigarette.

Marcy said no, she'd probably gag. "Cheer me up. Tell me the coffee's good."

"It's wonderful. Tell me, what did you and Eddie do after I left?"

"Mourned, of course. No, we talked and pretty soon he drove me home. I'd no sooner gotten inside and gotten my shoes off than you called. Guess I'm popular."

"I'd say so. What'd you think of Eddie? Nice fellow, isn't he?"

"Oh, yes. A little on the oily side—I don't believe him any more than I believe you—but there's worse things. Than being on the oily side, I mean."

"He tell you about me?"

"Heavens, no! I was good and didn't ask, either. I've worked out a few things in my head, though. You're connected with gambling somehow and you're Eddie's boss in some way but there's still someone who's boss over you."

"That's pretty good. Do you mind, Marcy?"

"Don't look so holy, sweetheart. Of course not, that is, until J. J. finds out I'm running with a criminal set and leaps down my throat. Actually, Steve, I don't want to know any more. I'm sure the whole thing is more exciting— no, that's not the word but I hate to call you glamorous to your face—"

"Go ahead."

"Now I have to start over. I'm sure the whole thing is more provocative from my point of view as is. From the outside. Am I right?"

"Aren't you always?"

"You shouldn't answer a question with a question."

"Did I?"

They both laughed and he took her hands across the table. "Your hands are cold. Warm heart."

"Not a chance, doctor. My feet are like ice, too." She rearranged herself so she was sitting on them. "Is it such a cold night?"

"No, it's pretty warm out, matter of fact."

"Well, look who's here! Steve, say hello to Lucky."

"So that's the orphan you took in. Come here, Lucky." The black kitten came out of the shadows of the service porch but strolled disdainfully to the center of the kitchen. It sat down, yawned and began washing its face.

Marcy said, "I wonder if J. J. thought to give her any milk before he went to bed."

"Let's see if she wants any. Here, Lucky."

Beck got up and reached for the kitten. It eluded his hand and scampered back into the dark. He straightened and shrugged.

Marcy laughed. "I take it she doesn't. How is it you explain your attraction, Mr. Beck?"

"I don't have much of the beast left in me. Lucky resents that." He sat down and they looked at each other some more. Beck said, "Why don't you come over here and get warm?"

"All right."

She put her feet down and came around and sat on his lap. Her slightness was more substantial than he expected, leaning against him. She was soft, her breath was sweet. They kissed. She stroked his sore cheek with one finger. "How old are you, Steve?"

"Hard to say."

"It is. You have some gray hair here but I guess it's premature. Then these lines at the corner of your eyes but that might be plain old California squint. Still... there's really nothing boyish about you."

"You aren't in the same mood I am."

Marcy chuckled and rubbed her cheek against his forehead. He kissed the base of her throat where the chuckle seemed to come from and they were even.

She said, "Beast or not, you know quite too well how intriguing you are."

"Never a worry or a care." He saw her swallow a yawn and stood up still holding her. "Sweetheart, I'd better disappear and let you get your beauty sleep."

"Not that I need it."

When his mouth left hers the next time, Beck said, "See you tonight."

She looked up at him, watching. "Oh, I'm sorry, Steve. I've already promised to go out with Eddie."

He felt first that he was wearing a stupid expression and changed it. Then he felt annoyed. "Why, that double-crossing—" he grinned, a second later meant it and changed the word to "—lady killer. It looks like I'll have to ease him out."

Marcy asked soberly, "What does that mean?"

"Nothing. Just beat him out, race him for you. Well, Sunday then?" When she nodded, he added, "I'll call you."

Their bad moment was over and they drifted to the back door, his arm around her waist. They watched the insects dashing against the screen, wanting the light.

She murmured, "I suppose it's the liquor that's made me melancholy."

"Tell you what. I'll sit in my car across the street and watch your window until your light goes out."

"You don't have to do that, Steve. I'm just being silly."

"I intend to do it anyway and it'd be nice if I had a reason."

"You're sweet."

"I'll call you."

A few steps away he waved back. She had picked up the kitten and was stroking it. She couldn't see him out in the dark.

He settled himself behind his steering wheel and whistled sentimentally to himself. He saw an upstairs light go on behind a venetian blind. Once or twice her shadow loomed crossing the room. Eventually, the light went out and the big old house was dark.

He had switched on his ignition when a car growled up Henry Street, turned the corner and wheeled into the Everett driveway. Beck waited.

After a moment, a man came around to the front of the house, paused by the door selecting a key. When the door was opened, when he turned on the hallway light, Beck could see him plainly. It was J. John Everett, who was supposed to be upstairs in his bed, asleep.

Beck started his engine then, just to make Everett wonder, and drove away. He wrinkled his forehead quizzically. Not at the lawyer's actions, for that was no more than he had expected, but because he had never actually gotten around to apologizing.

15

Saturday, May 21, 2:30 a.m.

Beck left his Buick in the unattended parking lot across the street from the Southwest Towers. When he walked out on the sidewalk, Joe Zuaben was there to meet him.

"He hasn't shown," Beck stated a fact. The Filipino nodded. "How long you been on the job?"

Zuaben pushed back his coat sleeve and looked at his big wristwatch. "Couple hours."

"Where's Speed?"

"Watching the back." Zuaben jerked a thumb at the club building.

"See that you keep it sewed up."

Beck crossed the street and into the deserted club lobby. He smiled at the night clerk. Running the elevator up to the tenth floor, he let his shoulders slump wearily. Then he came out of it to stride down the hall to his suite.

He unlocked his door, his living room was dark but the reading lamp was on in his bedroom. His breath stuck in his throat.

Leda Garland called out, "Oh, darling, I was afraid you weren't coming home at all!"

She was already in bed, his pillows propped up behind her, his copy of *Fortune* open in her lap. Her stockings and underthings lay folded on his bureau but her elaborate fringed formal had been wadded up and thrown into the corner.

Leda always looked better plainer. Esthetically, she was beautiful now in the stark nightgown she kept in his closet. The severe black chiffon did the most for her skin. Her hair was in perfect order and her face was freshly made up. But to Beck the sight of her made the bottom drop out of his stomach.

He said, "Leda, for God's sake, you shouldn't have come tonight."

"That isn't any kind of a greeting, after I've been waiting so long. I did have my wonderful bath. Darling, come over here quick and kiss me."

Beck sat down on the bed and brushed a kiss across her mouth. She caught his wrist when he tried to get up again. "That wasn't any kind of a kiss. Don't go away."

"Let me go."

He went into the dark living room and peered down through the slats of the blind. He couldn't see Zuaben below anywhere and didn't know whether to hope he was still there or not. He heard Leda get out of bed and follow him.

"Steve—something's wrong."

"Plenty's wrong. When did you get here?"

"A little before or after midnight. I don't know. What is it?"

"See anybody when you came in?"

"Of course not." She laughed. "Is that all that's bothering my darling, after all this time? I did it just the way I always do. Back to the phone booth at the rear of the lobby, then sneak up to the second floor and ring the elevator. I didn't see a soul."

"Midnight. It must have been close but you might have gotten here before they did. Or maybe little Joe is playing cute."

"Joe—Zuaben? What do you mean?"

"Pat has two of his boys downstairs. Not that he thinks anything. They're watching the building for someone else to show up."

She made him turn around and twined her arms around his neck and smeared lipstick on his collar. She whispered, "Then why worry?"

"Don't. You better get dressed. We have to think of something and right away."

"Steve! I don't want to."

"Leda, they may be up here any minute. It's too dangerous for you."

"You never used to be afraid."

"Right now things are different."

He had lifted her away. She kept going as if she'd meant to go anyway and turned on the light. She sank back in the big chair, flaunting herself. "Yes, I get the feeling that things *are* different. You're different. Mix me a drink, please. What's the trouble, Steve? Have I done something you don't care for?"

"Don't be silly. You need a drink."

He went to the bar, poured some rye in a glass and dashed it with water.

"You never used to want me to go at all. I always had to be the one that said I was going."

"For God's sake, don't try to read a lot of things into the situation that aren't there. All I'm afraid of is that Zuaben saw you come in and phoned Pat. Zuaben hates my guts."

He tried to hand her the drink. She closed her warm hand over his knuckles and forced him to hold the glass while she sipped. When she released him, Beck set the glass on the chair arm.

She said indifferently, "Pat wouldn't believe it. He wouldn't believe it because it would damage his precious pride to believe it. It would be easier to skin him than make him believe it." Leda drank by herself. "I am a Pat Garland original and nobody dares touch me." She drank again. "Except you, Steve, wonderful darling. Are you getting to be just like everybody else now?"

"Don't get drunk."

"I don't intend to. Answer my question. Are you getting to be like everybody damn else now?"

"And if I am, Leda?"

"I wouldn't know quite what to do. I don't want to sound hysterical, darling, but I've told you this before. You're all I have, the only thing that belongs to me. Even the kids are Pat's, not mine."

"Don't talk nonsense."

"I guess it is nonsense, isn't it?" She finished her drink, put the glass down deliberately. "You're always right, Steve."

"I'm right about this much. We're stuck here and Pat may be on his way up right now."

She laughed and stretched and wriggled her bare toes on the carpet. "I simply want to be happy. I can always count on being happy with you. You're something delicious to look forward to. I can wear the kind of clothes I like and say whatever idiotic things I like and...."

She rose, heavy-lidded, and padded over to him. She bit him gently on the mouth and he could feel her heart beating. "Come to bed, Steve."

"Let's be sensible. I've been trying to think of a way to get you out of here while you—"

Leda interrupted mockingly with the old joke but it wasn't all mocking. She said, "You don't love me any more."

He answered patiently, "Of course I do, darling. You know better than that. It's only because I love you that I want you to go."

"Is there another woman, Steve? Somebody else. You can tell me. Is there?"

"Don't be silly."

She sighed, pleased, and rubbed her cheek against his the way Marcy had done. "Oh, I felt so sorry for you tonight, having to chaperone that skinny girl at the roulette table. I so wanted to take you away with me when I left."

"Chaperone? What do you mean?"

"I mean you didn't need to act mysterious about your motives, not to me. I always understand. And it was sweet of you to bring her even if J. J. couldn't come. She must not know hardly any boys her own age at all."

Beck stiffened and she noticed. She whispered, "Darling, what is it? Did you think you heard something?"

"No. Nerves, I guess. It's been a long night."

"Come to bed and let me baby you."

"No. Let me think."

"Always no, poor darling. You need to relax and stop worrying. I fix."

Smiling, she swayed into the bedroom and came back with his robe and slippers. She made him sit down in the chair and he watched her somberly as she knelt beside him, stripping off his tie, loosening his collar and taking off his shoes. She chattered and looked into his eyes often. "I'm so glad you wear a soft shirt. So much more sensible than those stiff fronts and all that Pat wears. There! Now stand up."

When she had his coat off and the robe tied around him, Beck said, "Now it's your turn." He took her hand and led her back to her underthings on the bureau.

Leda said slowly, "You really want to get rid of me, don't you?"

"It isn't as if I haven't told you why over and over. I think I can sneak you out the back somehow, pull some deal on Speed."

"No, Steve. I'm not going. I can't go." She sat down on the bed, leaned back on her hands and her smile was triumphant. "My car. I put it in the parking lot across the street. I can't very well go there to get it, can I?"

Beck swore. "That puts us in pretty deep. Your car. Those boys may be waiting down there all night and all day tomorrow, too."

"Don't swear when you're angry. It just sounds crude then. And don't pace around so. All you've said is that there's no rush and what's wrong with that? Come over here. I've got implicit confidence in you, darling."

"Is that our thought for today?"

"Oh, quit worrying so much."

"You could go home in a taxi. With a slight accident story. I can have a garageman pick up your car tomorrow and deliver it. Would that make sense to Pat?"

"Steve, do you really love me?"

"I just told you a few minutes ago, didn't I?"

"I know—but I keep getting this funny feeling that you suddenly dislike me simply for being here and worrying you. You're not getting tired of me, are you?"

"No. Why should I?"

"You sound like you're saying that because you have to."

"I don't have to do anything."

"Everybody does sometime," Leda said lightly. "Why are you so suddenly worried about Pat's feelings tonight more than mine?"

"That's not the point and you know it. You know what I care about Pat's feelings. I don't feel any more loyalty toward him than you do. But I do have some respect for my job."

"Oh, your job. I suppose you have more respect for that, doing Pat's thinking for him, than you do for me."

"Don't twist things around. I didn't say that. Yes, I like what I do and what I've made of the circle. And I don't consider it smart to chance smashing everything I have—we have—over some silly ideas you'll be sorry for tomorrow."

"Will I?" She came over to him in the doorway and tugged at the tie to his robe. "Come on, Steve, *prove* I'm just being silly. Prove I'm just imagining things."

He didn't move. Leda let go of his robe. She wandered over to the bureau and stared at herself in the mirror. She murmured. "This ought to be a lesson for you, Mrs. Garland. The man likes to be the one who does the pulling, doesn't he?"

Beck decided he had better go over to her, and did. He put his hands on her shoulders and toyed with the straps to her nightgown. "I've been thinking about you all evening, darling, believe me—just waiting until we could get together again."

"Have you, Steve? You're not just saying that?"

"Of course not. All I can do is say it. You have to believe me. We have to believe each other."

She turned around and clung to him. "No, you can prove it to me, Steve darling. You've acted so strangely up here tonight. Make me feel absolutely warm and happy again, that things are all right with us."

"Things are the way they always have been." He laughed, gave her a little turn and a light spank back toward her clothes. "Now get dressed."

"I can't go feeling this way, I just can't. Not back out to that godawful house and watch that big jerk play with his toys and yell around. I worry about you and me too, Steve. I'll do something reckless, anything to clear the air. I know I will."

Beck said coldly, "Is that a threat, Leda?"

"I don't know. Maybe it is."

She idly stirred her stockings into a silken whorl, just as idly picked up an object she found beneath them.

Leda said, "Oh? What's this thing?"

It was the small bronze mask of tragedy, the buckle from Marcy's belt, and she was pretending she'd just found it on the bureau.

Beck said, "Just a thing."

"A buckle. It looks a trifle feminine for you, darling. And it's been worn so you couldn't have merely bought it for a friend."

"If you know all about it, why are you asking me?"

"But I don't know all about it, Steve. Whose is it and what's it doing up here?"

"It belongs to Marcy Everett. She left it in my car and I forgot to return it to her. That is all there is to it. Furthermore, Leda, that was undoubtedly the very first thing you saw when you let yourself in here tonight. You've been picking at that same idea ever since I got here. Good God! Do we have to play these kid games?"

Leda whirled and flung herself into his arms. "Steve, Steve—I didn't mean to be like that! I love you, darling—I need you!"

"If you loved me, you'd come out and say things. You'd do what I asked."

"That's not true, Steve," she said. "And if you really loved me, you wouldn't ask. You never asked me a year ago."

They were standing together tensely when the knock came on the hall door.

Beck said, "Well, here they are."

16

Saturday, May 21, 3:00 a.m.

Leda trembled and whimpered and held him tighter. "Steve, I didn't believe you!"

"That doesn't matter. Get in the bathroom."

She whispered, "I didn't believe you. I got off the track brooding about that
girl but I didn't really think anything, darling! What'll we do? Who is it?"

"Fifty-fifty it's Pat. I'll do my best. Get in the bathroom, lock yourself in
and turn off that bedlamp. Gather up your clothes."

Beck gave her a shove toward the bathroom and closed the bedroom door.
He opened the hall door and three men were standing there: Zuaben, Speed
and the third man in the middle. The third man was short and stocky with
a bullet head and a thick neck. His gray suit was rumpled.

Beck grinned and blew out his breath at the same time. It was quite a relief. He said, "Come right in. Got a match, buddy?"

"Yeah," the other man said. "Your face and—" Speed backslapped him
across the kidneys and the trio came in out of the hall. Beck shut the door and
leaned against it, inspecting the stranger. He had a face like a low comic.

Zuaben said, "Found him looking at your car in the lot."

"Maybe he intends to make me an offer for it. Does he say?"

"He don't say."

Speed said, "He wasn't much trouble."

"Good. You did a good job, gentlemen," said Beck. He turned his smile on
Zuaben. "Actually, I wasn't sure our friend would be around at night. It's
nice you didn't have to stay up all night for nothing."

Zuaben just looked him. Speed said, "Boy, I'll say. It'd been no fun to stand
around for nothing."

"You boys wait out in the hall for our friend here. Soon as we have a little
talk you can have him again. Is he clean?"

"Sure, Steve. He won't give you much trouble."

Zuaben asked, "You got a can in this place?"

Beck opened the hall door for them. "Wait out in the hall till I give the word.
It won't be long."

Zuaben gave a glance at the closed bedroom door and finally followed Speed
out. The stranger stood with his feet apart and waited. Beck nightlatched the
door and suggested a drink.

"Don't mind if I do."

Beck put some rye in a glass and brought it over. He held it above the shorter man's head. "I think I want you to bark for it. What's your name, Fido?"

The stranger threw a right at Beck's heart. Beck blocked it and tossed the whiskey in his eyes. Then he hit him in the mouth, kneed him twice between the legs and chopped the back of his neck when the stranger gasped forward. Beck returned the glass to the bar. Then he came back to the stranger, who was on his hands and knees trying to clear his head. He lifted up the man's coattail and took out his wallet. He sat down in the big chair under the lamp and began to read through it.

By the time he had finished, the stranger had gotten to his feet and swayed toward the liquor cabinet. Beck said, "Go ahead, if you really want a drink."

The stranger poured a stiff one and gulped it down. He wiped his eyes some more and massaged the back of his neck. Beck said, "Sit down and we'll try to discuss business again. What's your name?"

"Vogel." He poured another shot and took it over to a chair. "Why ask me? You got it all there. Oscar Vogel."

"Oscar N. Vogel," Beck read off a plastic case, "553 North Berendo, Los Angeles, California. This thing calls you a private detective."

"That's right."

"I know L. A. pretty well. I've never heard of any private cop named Vogel."

"I'm not so important it's likely you'd know me."

"I'd gotten another impression. That perhaps you're not a private cop at all. Perhaps you're a real one."

"You can bet your sweet patootie I wouldn't be here if I was on the force. You came near to breaking my neck!"

"No, I didn't. If I'd wanted to break your neck I'd have broken it. Oscar N. Vogel. Oscar Neck-broken Vogel. Well, what are you doing following me around?"

"Who says so?"

"I say so. Look, Vogel, we had might as well be businesslike. I want to know how long you've been on the job, what you believe the purpose is, and some other details. I know, for example, that Thursday night and early Friday morning you were spotting the Patrick Garland home out in La Jolla. Friday morning proper you cased the Cabrillo Mortuary in the Hillcrest district. Then your superior pulled you off the mortuary so as not to arouse anybody and put you to spotting me since yesterday afternoon. We're going to agree on these facts and more eventually so let's do it now and save a lot of beating around the bush, as the saying goes. Or maybe just beating around. It's pretty late."

"Well, I'm no sucker, Beck."

"No, I don't suppose you are. How long have you been on the job?"

"Three days. I came down Wednesday."

"Fine. Now what's so special about you that appeals to the attorney general?"

"What do you mean?"

"The state attorney general's office. Why they hired a private cop to do legwork. Budget trouble?"

Vogel's grin was silly and confused. "I still don't know what you mean. This state business—I don't get it."

"Who hired you?"

"Oh. That's giving away a confidence, you know, abridging my duty to the client."

"It's up to you to decide."

"You see it my way, don't you, Beck? Suppose I tell you. Then I lose my client and I'm out a bit of pocket money. How can a guy live doing business like that?"

"Don't cry into the liquor. It dilutes it."

"Now I'm no more good on this job but my client doesn't have to know that. I can still make the motions and get my fee. But if I start telling names, I'm afraid my client will not only cut this job off but let some talk get around that's bad for me professionally. What I'm getting at is that maybe you and me could make a deal that would recompense all that."

"We've already made our deal. You're going to talk and I'm going to listen. Who hired you?"

Vogel sighed. "I don't know his name, at least not his real one. He said he was named Jones but I never went for that."

"Some people are named Jones. Describe him."

"Five ten, hundred and sixty pounds, forty-five to fifty. Sharp nose, thin mouth, makes you think of an old woman. Neutral brown eyes, dark brown hair—"

"I can finish it," Beck said. "The hair's thin, plastered back over his scalp. He wears clothes well and has a good education. He chatters a lot, cultured voice, without saying much."

"Okay, you've got him down pat. He talks like that some of the time, other times he's a cold fish that means nothing but business. What name did he give you?"

"That doesn't matter. How'd he run onto you?"

"He said he was in L. A. on a buying trip. He told me to get a room down here and I drove down Wednesday, like I said. We met suppertimes at one of those auto courts out by the ocean. How about another drink?"

"Go ahead. You're doing fine."

Vogel got it and kept talking. "He said he had a list of names for me to work over one at a time. Just watch movements and report. I started with this Patrick Garland, spotting that modernistic place on the hill. You came Thursday night but I didn't know you then. The main thing Jones liked Thursday night was when this Garland took an old woman to this Cabrillo Mortuary.

I checked the place soon as it opened, playing death in the family, you know. Jones called me at my hotel rooms mornings and afternoons, just in case. I told him about the mortuary Friday morning and he said keep away from it, leave it alone. He switched me to you. He said you were number two man. That's about the size of it, Beck. Oh, he called off our auto court date last night. Said he'd see me tonight, Saturday."

Beck got up and went to the door. He motioned Zuaben and Speed inside from where they were lounging down the hall. He told them, "Our friend here decided to cooperate and he's been quite a bit of help. Now I want you to do him a favor in return."

Zuaben raised his eyebrows and fluttered the toothpick in his mouth. Vogel said nervously, "Hey, now, I told you everything I—"

"Shut up. Take him down to the bus station and see that he gets off to L. A. That's all. No rough stuff."

"Hey, what about my car?"

"That's your worry. Send a friend down for it. But don't come yourself. I don't want to find you in this town again. Stay put."

Speed rumbled, "Get that? Stay put." He clamped down on Vogel's shoulder and led him into the hall.

Beck stopped Zuaben. "After you get him off safely, hightail it out to The Natchez and wait for me. Stay out of sight and don't go aboard—unless Isham tries to leave."

"If he tries?" the Filipino asked around his toothpick.

"Then you stop him."

Beck watched the three men get on the elevator before he shut the door. He hurried back into the bedroom, stripping off his robe as he went. The bedroom was dark. He rapped on the bathroom door. "All clear, Leda. They're gone."

Leda laughed behind him, from the bed. "But I'm over here, Steve. I know it's all clear. I couldn't resist listening through the door." Her bare shoulders stirred luxuriously in the gloom. "There's hardly a rush now, is there, my darling?"

Beck flipped on the merciless overhead light and yanked back the covers. He smiled as he stood over her and folded his arms. "You get up and get dressed and get out of here—my darling—before I break your neck."

17

Saturday, May 21, 4:15 a.m.

He had changed his clothes back to some other tweeds and another slipover sweater, green. He had driven his Buick at a high whining speed to La Jolla, not thinking of anything in particular except the wonderful solitude of the streets, and enjoying the vibrato of the engine in front of his feet and the secure hard feel of the wheel in his hands.

Now Beck was parked on a lonely cliff over the ocean. He smoked and gave Leda time to get home. He reviewed his facts dispassionately, ignoring the surf crash below. After ten minutes exactly, he flipped a freshly lit cigarette out the window and drove up the hill to Garland's house.

He pulled up in the driveway, got out and stood solemnly before the viewer. A minute later Garland opened the door, hair mussed and wearing a dressing gown over loud pajamas. Garland's eyes got wide awake and he asked, "News?"

"Big news."

From the living room, Leda called, "Who is it, Pat?"

"Just Steve, honey." He told Beck, "Hold it for a couple minutes till Leda takes off. She just got in herself and she's nervous as a cat. Being nasty over my never showing up at the party."

"I don't blame her."

"Yeah, it was a pretty rotten trick. But what with all this other—hate to miss a good party myself."

They went into the long low living room where Leda was coiled in a soft chair, drinking. Her fringed formal was unzipped over one hip and she had kicked off her shoes. They all exchanged greetings and smiles and Beck turned down a drink.

Leda found a new position in her chair and swung her feet. She was edgy and it showed everywhere but in her face. "You're an early bird, Steve."

"Pat tells me you're just the opposite. What must your husband think?"

Garland said, "Leda's one and only vice, Steve, and I don't mind humoring her if she likes to take a good long drive at night, oh, once or twice a week. Why I'll never know, but she likes it."

"I like the wind in my face. It relaxes me."

"It didn't work tonight."

Leda took a long drink of her highball. "No, it didn't, Pat. And you know why."

"Yeah, I know why, honey, but let's not air our family troubles in front of Steve here."

"I didn't intend to."

"I know you didn't intend to. Sure you don't want a drink, Steve?"

"No, thanks."

Garland glanced at his wife's glass, nearly empty, and fixed another for himself only. She noticed. While his back was turned she gave Beck a sultry smile and then made a face at him.

He thumbed his nose at her and said, "Say, Pat, why don't you ever go out driving with her? Might be just what the doctor ordered."

Garland laughed as he came back and flopped in a chair. "No, thanks. I tried that just once and it nearly scared the pants off me. You drive too fast, honey."

"It's dangerous," Leda said, "but it's worth it." She killed her drink and collected her shoes. "Well, since neither of you lovely gentlemen need me, I shall retire."

"Who said anything?" Garland protested.

"Nobody said anything." Leda pecked him goodnight, waved at Beck and passed through the archway. "See you at breakfast, Pat."

"Sleep tight, honey." Garland went to the archway and shouted after her where to find his sleep tablets if she needed any. She didn't answer and he came back and sat down. "Hell of a fine-looking woman, especially in that dress. I helped her pick it out. She does drive too fast, though."

They looked at each other and Garland said, "Shoot."

"Hervey Isham."

"Well, well, well."

"I thought it would make you happy."

"It does. That son of a bitch. I never could stand him."

"Clever boy, though. A moneymaker. The best the Tarrants have."

"Sure, that's how I got talked into letting him have The Natchez. It's personally I can't stand him." Garland laughed sardonically. "Yeah, evidently he is a clever boy. If that private life was an act, it sure turned my stomach. If."

Beck didn't say anything.

Garland laughed again. "You're sorry it wasn't J. J. Boy, you had him all scheduled, didn't you?"

"No. I'm not sorry it wasn't J. J. He still looks as bad as ever except that he's now overshadowed by Isham. I'm sorry it misled me by looking bad for him. Do you want to hear the details?"

"Not much. Anything you say, Steve. Ease him out."

"You better hear. I like to be accurate." Beck told him about the mortuary and Garland didn't believe it, Beck's being sucked in.

"Okay, then I imagined it. There were about twenty-five minutes passed between my getting sapped and my phone calls. Dominic wouldn't have had time to get home in twenty-five minutes but he was and that let him out.

Moon had time to reach the warehouse where I caught him, yes. But you know he's a claustrophobe and whoever clipped me shut himself in a storage closet. I can't feature Paul Moon doing that so that halfway lets him out, at least. I furnished Eddie Cortes with a witness who was with him all evening so he's clear. That leaves J. J. and Isham.

"J. J. had an alibi with his daughter which turned out no good. I think it was an accidental alibi because if he had a purposeful one, it would have been perfect. You know Isham left the cleanup of The Natchez to his bunch, which doesn't sound like him, and was supposed to be up in his rooms. But he didn't answer my phone call. That looks more like a purposeful alibi."

Garland asked, frowning, "Is that all you have, Steve? And what makes you sure it was our inside man who sapped you at the mortuary? We know he's got one assistant, at least one."

"No, it's not all I have. I'm coming to it. I want you to know everything I know. First, it was our inside AG man at the mortuary. Making sure where the books definitely are, so there can be an official warrant raid for evidence, is the most vital part of his job. The AG man wouldn't leave that to an assistant, particularly not the private cop crumb he's been using for legwork. Second, it was not Vogel at the mortuary because the guy there moved around quiet as a ghost. Vogel is about as graceful as a cow. I proved that with a little fistwork soon as they brought him up."

"Sounds all very clever, but who's Vogel? Guess I'm too sleepy to keep up with you."

Beck told him all about Vogel.

Garland looked judicious and said, "Isham. Well, well." He nodded. "Well, it's about over. You've sold me on Isham."

"I wasn't trying to sell you on Isham or anyone. I was just laying out the evidence."

"There's plenty there. You've done a good fast job. Okay, find him and I'll call them at the airport." He didn't like the way Beck looked. "Well, what do you want me to do different?"

"Nothing different. Just something additional."

"Well, what then?"

"Call in the two Tarrants. Isham belongs to them and he's going to be a loss, even to you, though you never liked him."

"I don't think it's really necessary, Steve."

"It's up to you. But to keep things smooth and happy in the circle, I advise you to call in the Tarrants, tell them what's going to happen to their prize package and why."

Garland got up, medium angry, just enough to be positive and stubborn. "No, sir, Steve. Isham goes now without my explaining to anybody. I'm still the boss and that's all the explanation they need unless I want to tell them more. I found out we had a state snooper planted in the circle, I had you catch him and now I'm having you get rid of him. That's enough. I'm not giving any of these characters the idea that I have to ask permission to do one single thing."

"Right you are," said Beck. "You're the boss."

"Oh, don't get the idea that I'm showing off or anything. I don't see any point in doing more than necessary, that's all, and on the other hand I know I'm not biting off more than I can chew. Okay?"

"I understand."

"You talk like you're defending Isham."

"I'm not for him or against him. If he has to be killed, he has to be killed. I don't intend to make a mistake about it in any way. For example, I wired some connections in Springfield and Boston for certain information. This equation would be more neatly balanced if I had that material, too. But I haven't, so that's that. I do want to talk to Isham when I catch up with him. That won't hurt you."

"Oh. Well, you catch him first, Steve."

Beck got up and pulled down his sweater. "I'll call you."

"All right. I'll wait up. Try to make it fast, will you? Don't feel much like sitting up around an empty house any more than I have to."

"I'll call you the very minute."

18

Saturday, May 21, 5:00 a.m.

In the deep black of Mission Bay Park only a few token lights glimmered, none out on the water. The roller coaster, the ball park, all the amusements had been deadened with switches. One window high on The Natchez still shone as Beck wheeled into the parking lot.

He pulled up alongside the other car there. Speed leaned out the driver's side and shook his head.

"We'll have to go up and get him," Beck said. "Joe."

He and the Filipino went across the gangway onto the showboat while Speed remained on watch. Beck had a key to the ballroom door. Their heels clicked across the dance floor and they ran the elevator up to the corridor on the third floor. They walked down to the room where the light was and went in without knocking.

The air was layered with sickly sweet smoke and a murmurous conversation without music was coming out of the record player. It was stacked high and the rest of Isham's phonographic collection was scattered around the room. A couple of them crunched under Beck's shoes as he walked over to the girl on the couch.

She still wore the yellow lace slip and she raised up on her elbows to look Beck over. Her pouting mouth said, "Ooh, see that haircut!"

Beck pulled the crude cigarette from between her fingers and pinched it out. The girl sat up and nearly fell over. Beck asked, "Where's Isham?"

"You really want to know?"

"If you please."

"Who wants to know, fuzzy?"

Beck told Zuaben, "Turn that thing off." The player had started the top record again as it probably had for hours. Zuaben turned it off.

The girl threw back her head and laughed. Beck waited that out and then she got angry. She rose and stalked to the center of the room. There she sank down on her knees on the carpet and scowled back and forth between the two men.

She said, hardly moving her lips, "What'd you do that for? What'd you gang up on me and do that for? I want some music around this filthy place. Turn my music back on."

"Where's Isham?"

"You don't see him, do you fuzzy? I don't know. He went out after the party. Turn on the music."

Zuaben snickered.

Beck said, "Isham went out after the party. He left you all alone and that wasn't nice, was it? Where did Isham go?"

"I don't care whether I'm alone or not. I don't care about anything. I don't know."

Zuaben moved in on her, nudged her with the sharp toe of his shoe.

The girl wound her arms around herself, reared back and studied Zuaben fiercely. Finally she hissed, "You quit that!" and spat on his white trousers.

Zuaben grunted. When his hand came out of his coat pocket it wore a set of brass rings with nail points set in them. He jerked her head back by the hair and aimed at her face. Beck stepped in and chopped his wrist so that his hand drooped, numb, and then cuffed his ear.

"You do what I say, Joe. No more, no less."

The girl began to cry without covering her face. Zuaben put his hands in his coat pockets and glared, breathing heavily. He didn't try anything.

Beck kept at the girl. He squatted and stroked her hair. "You're all alone. Nobody's going to hurt you. Why did Isham leave you all alone?"

"I don't know. He went away days ago, so long ago. Please turn on the music. He promised he'd bring me back a kitty and he never did."

Beck rose and nodded at the Filipino. The girl stretched out full-length and sobbed on the carpet and on black pieces of records. As they went out, Beck turned the player back on.

The girl bawled, "Oh, don't leave me, please don't!"

George Papago, in his pajama bottoms, had come out of his room and was standing by the elevator. His eyes were stupid with sleep and he asked what was going on.

Beck said, "Nothing. Better send that little witch home before she sets the place on fire."

"Where's Mr. Isham?"

"Send the girl home and go back to bed and forget it, George. Nothing's going on."

"Oh. Righto, Mr. Beck. If you say so."

"I say so."

Speed was yawning when they returned to the cars on the parking lot. He asked, "We through yet, Steve?"

"Not quite."

"This staying up stuff doesn't do my training any good. I'd like some sleep right now."

Beck told him he'd have to wait a little longer and Speed agreed with his friendly dog grin. Beck told them both to meet him outside the Holsclaw warehouse and not to tip their hand if they beat him there.

They went by different routes to the warehouse district by the freight yards below Market Street. Beck arrived first at Holsclaw's building, a concrete win-

dowless structure with a modest sign. He saw Isham's sedan across the
street. He parked below the truck ramp and a moment later Speed and
Zuaben pulled in behind him. The three of them walked up the incline to the
big rolling door. Beck punched out the signal on the buzzer.

Shortly, Paul Moon opened the little door in the big door. He still wore his
tuxedo but he had removed his collar and tie so his blond head looked separate from his gaunt body. His complexion was coarse and grayish and his nose
had been indented by a crowbar back in Detroit. His skin didn't go with his
hair and his face didn't go with his meditative voice.

Moon said, "Well, good morning, Steve."

"Is Isham still here?"

Moon looked at them and at Isham's car across the street and smiled. "Certainly. Come in. It's him you want to see?"

"That's right."

They stepped inside and the swarm of cats fled from around Moon's feet.
Moon closed the door. "He's in my office."

Beck said, "If you'll be so kind as to wait right here, Paul. I'd rather talk to
him alone."

"Certainly." Moon touched his arm. "I begin to have an inkling. I'd like to
keep the record straight."

"Sure, Paul. Go ahead. It'd probably be wise."

"Isham suggested at the party tonight that we get together for a nightcap.
A couple of us older men discussing his success with the new layout. He came
down here a little before two."

"Is that what you talked about?"

"Yes. His business and mine. Profits."

"Thanks, Paul. I think we'll go in and see him now."

Moon swept a large white cat up into his arms and it quieted as he stroked
it. He leaned comfortably against the wall. Beck and the other two walked
toward the center of the vast warehouse. The ceiling was lost in gloom. They
walked down ordered aisles between the machines, every device which
would take a coin: pinball machines, cigarette dispensers, jukeboxes, claw machines, candy and popcorn and ballgum vendors, girlshow viewers, one-
armed bandits. The cats scampered around them, playing follow-the-leader.
They leaped and ran and posed among the silent machines.

Isham saw the cats first and then looked out at the three men. He was sitting on the cot in Moon's office, a roofless all-glass cubicle in the middle of
the floor. He was buttoned into an expensive dark topcoat with a dark scarf
at his throat. He stood up and smiled.

Beck walked in to see him alone. He wondered what Isham was thinking
right now. Through one wall of the office Isham could see Zuaben and he
knew he carried a palmgun. Through the other wall he could see Speed, who
could get hold of a gun whenever he needed one. Speed didn't have a gun

tonight but Isham didn't know that. And straight ahead Isham could see Steve Beck, who was an unknown quantity.

Beck stopped inside the glass office and let him speak first. Isham said, "I certainly didn't expect to see you here at this time of day, Steve. By what burning ambition do you maintain your pace?"

"You're up and about yourself, Hervey."

"I never got down, as the saying goes. Here, enjoy yourself at Paul's expense." There was a bottle of green liqueur and two shot glasses. Beck let Isham get a third glass and pour a drink before he said no thanks.

"Steve, you're in a strange mood. Where is Paul? You know, if I've offended you in any way...."

Beck reached down and tapped the topcoat pockets. They were empty and Isham wouldn't be able to get inside the coat quickly enough. Beck said, "Paul's waiting until I get through."

"If it's about that girl tonight, I apologize a million times. You know that. Please, for goodness' sake, don't let it upset you if I became perhaps too flippant about your authority. Where's your sense of humor, man? I was only feeling heady because of the successful way things were going at the boat."

"This isn't about any girl and you know that, too. It was that sticky side of your life that fooled me most in your act. Don't gabble, Hervey. You've lost out so that's that."

Isham's teeth clenched so tightly that his smile became ridiculous. He looked outside at Zuaben and Speed again. He said, "What's going on?"

"You know what's going on."

"No, no, what have I done to offend Big Pat?" He still sat there, getting his face in order. "You know you can get together with the Tarrants and audit my accounts at any time. I'll swear they'll check out to the penny. And it isn't that ancient history back in Springfield, is it? I know Pat never liked that but that's fixed forever."

"You know it isn't that."

"No, I don't know, Steve. That's the point, don't you see? I don't know."

"If you want to keep acting foolish, we could wrangle all night."

"I just want to know!"

Beck sighed. "Short and sweet, Hervey. Pat intercepted one of your reports to the attorney general, report number 45, the one with all the details about how I got you the liquor license."

"I don't know what you're talking about."

"I broke your alibi for you when you sapped me at the mortuary tonight. And I caught your legman, Vogel, who found the mortuary for you in the first place."

Isham passed his hand over his face as if Beck had gotten beyond his depth. His whole face squinted while he tried to grasp a way out, and his hands found each other and twisted. Irritably, Beck wished he would stand up and not look so small and huddled. Beck knew that Steven Beck had never looked that way before Lieutenant Richards or anybody else.

Isham said, "Now, the liquor license, I may have mentioned to someone but only in the circle. You know I talk too much."

"We've gone over that before."

"But what is this other?"

"I just told you."

Isham thought some more. He looked from Beck to Zuaben to Speed and then suddenly behind him. There was no one there, only a lean black cat stalking an invisible something between the machines. Beck wondered if that could be Lucky's father.

Isham said calmly, "Look, Steve."

"Okay."

"You think I've sold you out."

"No. Not exactly. You've never been with us."

"I wish you'd talk so I could understand you. This can be fixed up, can't it? You're crucifying me because I was a little free with your girl tonight, isn't that it? I can make that up to you."

"No. Now that you mention it, this will teach you to keep your eyes off my girl, you cop bastard, but that doesn't happen to be it."

"Well, Steve, what does happen to be it? Paul asked me to come down here after the party—"

"Please, Hervey."

"God damn it! I don't know what you're *talking about!*" Isham had broken. He jumped up, then sat down again and buried his face in his hands.

Beck picked up the receiver and dialed the Garland house. "We picked up that package at the warehouse."

"Good," Garland said. "Just a second while I turn on the messer-upper." Beck switched on the message scrambler at his end, too, and then Garland said, "I was about ready to doze off. Everything's waiting at the airport."

"Okay. You want to talk to him?"

"No."

"I think you should."

"Why you letting me in for this?"

"To keep it neat. I don't want any talk getting back to you that I'm roaming around on my own. That might hurt both of us."

"Nobody's going to hurt us, either of us. You've done a swell job, Steve. Little over two days, isn't it? You better get home and get some sleep yourself."

"I could use it. You want to talk to him now?"

"How is he?"

"Noncommittal. They'll have to watch him close. Maybe you can get something out of him. I couldn't."

Garland sighed. "Okay, I'll talk to him. Let's get it over with."

Isham raised his head and took the receiver, clamping both hands around it. Beck stepped outside the office, shut the door and lit a cigarette. He could hear Isham's voice spilling out words rapidly, getting incoherent and higher and higher. He looked at Speed, who grinned. Beck shook his head and Speed stopped grinning.

In a minute Isham's squeal of words died away suddenly. Beck stepped on his cigarette and went back into the office.

Isham was holding the receiver out in front of him, staring at it. It buzzed clear line. Garland had hung up on him.

Beck put the phone back together and motioned to Speed and Zuaben. They came up and he said, "The airport. It's all set."

Isham sat there on the cot, staring at Beck now, his prim sharp face frozen in no particular expression.

Beck said, "Let's go, Hervey. We're all done here."

"What?"

"Let's go."

"Oh." He added, "Very well," without his face changing and as if it didn't really concern him.

He got up, straightened his topcoat automatically, and walked away between Speed and Zuaben.

Beck lit another cigarette and hung around the glass office until he heard the engine rumble away outside. The still air inside the warehouse was turning chilly. While he was drinking the glass of green liqueur he saw the lean cat he had wondered about being Lucky's father. It slunk across a piece of light carrying a pitiful something in its jaws. Beck decided Moon probably had a dozen black toms around here. Or perhaps only the mother had been black.

He took a deep drag on his cigarette, rubbed his cold hands together and started for the door. Paul Moon ambled down the aisle toward him and grimaced.

Beck said, "Refer anything to Pat or me, Paul. You don't know anything."

"All right."

"How do you stand it without any heat in this barn?"

"Oh, it's not so bad. Maybe I'm used to it."

"You must be. Sure turned cold suddenly tonight."

"You mean this morning."

"Yeah, I guess it is morning."

They said goodbye and Beck went out and down the ramp to where his car waited in the dawnlight.

19

Saturday, May 21, and Sunday, May 22

There was not much he could do about the weekend. It came and went. It began nothing, ended nothing, and left nothing.

Saturday, Beck woke up a little after noon, feeling in-between. His neck had stiffened from the blow or from the fall down the mortuary stairs. He showered and shaved and phoned. Presently, the usual bellboy arrived with the usual breakfast—orange juice and black coffee—said good morning and went away with the usual tip. *The Sentinel*, however, which always came up on the tray, was a later edition than ordinarily. Beck read it through while Jimmy, the club masseur, worked the stiffness out of his neck. The police had released no new information on Felix's death but implied confidently that a solution would be forthcoming soon, although disclaiming it was more than accident. The Tarrants' full-page ad for The Natchez grand opening tonight had a line saying *Under the management of Mr. Hervey Isham.*

After Jimmy left, Beck read the three telegrams and two letters which the desk had sent up. He read them slouched in a chair pushed over by the window. Outside was a thrilling May day. The telegrams lacked the usual vitality of such since the matter they concerned was over and done.

Turquin-Bloch Importers had nothing to offer from Boston on Isham's connection with the Ashley scandal. Beck smiled over the last sentence: DIRECT IMPLICATION APPEARS IMPOSSIBLE TO SECURE.

F. L. Kingsley of Chicago wired that he was forwarding a photostat confirming Paul Moon's old assault charge. From Detroit, Porter Estes insisted that Moon would be the last man to have anything to do with Farnsworth's imprisonment and not to let Moon try anything so foolish as attempt to re-enter the state of Michigan.

Those were the telegrams; they had the smell of old old business about them, and the letters were no more urgent. Johnny Torano gossiped of Eddie Cortes' earlier career in San Francisco: *Always told E. he was wasting his time peddling quail and am sure glad he is making an honest living. Nothing can make you get mad like those quail and when E. loses his temper—watch out!!! At least quail ought to watch out—guess a fast boy like you don't have to, Stevie. Say hello to the skunk for me, will you?*

Beck skimmed through the first Driscoll Agency report on Dominic and family as known in L. A. and tossed all the material in his bureau drawer. He fingered Marcy's bronze buckle for a second, then dressed himself slowly. He tried to whistle away his lethargy, pulled a gay yellow sweater over his head to see if that would raise his spirits. Then he took a laxative and went down-stairs.

As he stepped out of the elevator into the lobby, he saw Pelletreau leave the registration desk and saunter nervously toward the street, walking faster and faster. Pelletreau didn't see Beck, who had an inclination to say boo.

Grinning, Beck took from the clerk the sealed manila envelope which Pelletreau had left. He opened it on the ride back up to his rooms. Again the information was all in order. As pertained to Isham: the Springfield police revealed that Chicken Joe Sanchell had died of bullet wounds and pneumonia, his last month being spent in a county hospital under guard. Vague, but it fit in nicely, Beck thought. There were also some true copies of L. A. police records that indicated Moncey hadn't pulled anything by recommending Dominic, some similar material from San Francisco that bore out Torano's information on Cortes, an official record of Cortes' activities and behavior during two years of San Quentin, and a prison photo. Beck got another grin out of that. Cortes, with short hair, looked amazed. Beck automatically passed a hand over his own crew cut.

He left the envelope in his rooms and started into the afternoon again. First, there was an appointment with two maritime union officials regarding the pay scale of Garland's water taxi fleet. Garland had acquired the small boats over a year ago when he had planned to open a gambling ship three miles off San Diego. The state had killed this by injunction but Garland had held on to the water taxis. He was keeping a stubborn eye to the future more than enjoying the revenue they brought carrying sightseers around the harbor.

Beck stuck to policy, softsoaped the union men and settled for their second offer. By three o'clock, he was hinting back and forth with Dominic's brother-in-law. What the printer needed most was a highspeed press. Beck thought a private loan could be arranged and promised to send around his attorney. The printer shook hands warmly when he left. So did Beck.

He considered a drive down to Agua Caliente to start a wedge into the dog men but decided to put that off till tomorrow night when he would be down there with Marcy. He stopped by the Grand Theater. The burlesque house, along with a string of third-run movie outlets, was a Garland enterprise. The city was considering more stringent censorship laws and Greissinger, the Grand manager, had run off at the mouth for publication. Beck bullied him, told him to keep shut up in the future and let Garland handle the city.

He stopped off at a bar to use a pay phone. Garland answered out of breath. "Been out throwing the football around with the kid. He just got down from military school today."

"Don't let the medical profession see you."

Garland laughed. "Don't worry, never felt better. Lord, how that kid has grown! Think I'll start seeing about entering him at USC. They've got good football teams there. We could go up and see him play."

"What's the angle?"

"What's the— You're kidding, aren't you?"

"Sure." Beck told him briefly what he'd done about the union, the printer, and Greissinger. Garland said fine.

Beck asked, "Have you talked to the Coronado people?" Meaning the Tarrants.

"Yes. As much as I felt like. Not the whole story."

"How about that other package?" Meaning Gusta Norley and the books.

"I haven't gotten around to them, what with the kid coming home and all."

"Well, let's let them stay put over the weekend. Just in case that group up north has anything up their sleeves."

"H'm. Well, we'll see."

Beck went back to the Southwest Towers Athletic Club, wanting to call Marcy Everett for absolutely no reason, but not. He turned eagerly when the desk clerk said there had been a call for him. "Four calls, sir. All the same lady, a Miss Black."

"Oh." Beck frowned at his own sag of disappointment. He laid a dollar bill on the desk. "That, Henry, happens to be a business deal I don't want to consider before Monday at the earliest. Suppose you forget you gave me the calls. And when Miss Black calls again, I'm not going to be in this evening."

Henry smiled. "Certainly, Mr. Beck. The dollar really isn't necessary."

"Henry, you're a dreamer." Beck went up to his suite, changed into a darker suit and came down again. He passed up his usual before-dinner drink in the club bar for fear Leda might get it into her head to drop around.

Maybe he could walk it off, whatever he felt. He left his Buick where it was and walked two blocks to the John C. Fremont Hotel. Saturday night and people were coming out on the sidewalks in couples, going somewhere. Or he would see packs of young sailors or marines, either eyeing the passing girls wistfully or talking and laughing loudly to cover their loneliness. He thought kindly: get to work, suckers, don't let them all just pass.

Beck went into the hotel, perched on a stool in the Trail's End Bar and gazed unseeing at the murals portraying the glorious West, its past. He had two more before-dinner cocktails than he generally did and ate so many cheese sticks that he decided he didn't want any dinner at all. He watched the couples come into the dim small room, have their drinks and go out again. He watched for someone he knew and who never came. Beck let himself be lulled by the romantic music that played constantly, music from a central outlet that was piping the same sensual tunes to bars like this all over town.

He bought an evening paper just before the bar auditor kicked out the crippled ancient newsboy who had sneaked in. This time the Tarrants' ad for The Natchez read *Under the management of Mr. George Papago.* There was also a minor item about the fines levied at the Cathay Gardens hearings that morning.

Eventually, Beck bought a fresh pack of cigarettes from the machine and went to a movie. He climbed up palatial stairs to the loges where he could smoke continuously. The second feature was half over but what had gone before was obvious. It was about a dog. He leaned his head against the soft back of his seat and dragged at his cigarette and drifted off into a sort of half-comfort. Close around him were unknown companions seeing the same as he and doing the same as he. The main feature was a musical in gay colors concerning a singing dancing loving tropical paradise where no one worked. Beck idly watched the magnified dollfaces, so clean, go through their paces and guessed ahead that it would all turn out to be a dream. It didn't but he mostly enjoyed it, anyway. He also sat through a brutal cartoon and a stagnant newsreel. When the lights came up he went out with the crowd and there was another crowd in the lobby, impatient to enter.

He had the beginnings of a headache. He wondered how Marcy had come through her hangover. He decided he might as well eat, having nothing better to do. Up at the Patio Club, he chose a booth on the edge of the roof garden and had a steak. The night air was clear and balmy and in the sky of the city below the neon could probably be seen for miles. A loudspeaker plane bellowed overhead for a moment about some indistinguishable kind of bread, and was gone. The dancers laughed and commented and went back to dancing. Beck had another drink and then another, not certain whether he wanted to go back to his rooms.

Then he saw Marcy. She was dancing with Eddie Cortes. They didn't see him.

Beck drew back in his booth and watched her over his last drink. He noticed the light glance off her tawny hair and that she wore a dress which covered her shoulders. She looked sprightly, as though she had felt no consequences at all. Cortes appeared to be going out of his way to look dashingly handsome and he showed his white teeth a lot. They went well together, Cortes strong and dark and she so fragile with her own private radiance. Nothing Beck could put his finger on but the picture they made annoyed him. He paid his check almost angrily and wished he hadn't seen them. He didn't like the smooth gigolo way Cortes danced with her. He didn't like to see their bodies close in that flowing graceful motion.

He walked slowly back to the Southwest Towers and most of the people were off the streets now. The desk clerk told him that Miss Black had phoned and gotten his message. Leda had not phoned again. Since he didn't feel sleepy, Beck bought a copy of *Life* and went up. He made a drink and sat down to read. He found he couldn't even get interested in the pictures of what was going on in the world although there were shattered tanks and refugees and sinking ships on a good many fronts. He let the magazine fall and drank until he did feel sleepy.

Lying in bed Sunday morning, he thought about where he would take

Marcy that evening. The dog races, of course, since he had business there, and then probably to the Jockey Club. That was a nice romantic setting.

He grimaced at the window where the sky was mottled gray. After his orange juice and black coffee and after going through the Sunday *Union* from one end to the other and discovering nothing new, he got out of bed. The radio offered nothing but choirs and sermons and frenetic bands so it got turned off again.

For a while, unshaven and unlike himself, he padded sloppily about in his pajamas, doing nothing special. He came across the *Life* he had dropped last night, which had fallen open to a deodorant ad. He sat down in the big chair and looked down on the floor at it for a time. The girl in the ad was a blonde but she didn't look sterile like most models and something of her piquancy made him think of Marcy. Of course, the ad girl was posing in girdle and brassiere but that didn't apply to his thoughts. For one thing, Marcy didn't wear a girdle; that aspect faintly revolted him like the time he'd discovered his first gray hair. And it was disagreeable to find a likeness in a deodorant ad but it was better than no likeness at all. He would have to get a picture of her at the first opportunity. He dreamed over the silly page of the magazine in a great many ways, remembering even the four-color presses that must have smashed the delicate ink face onto the paper.

No, he thought, it isn't the passion. The ad girl was undressed to catch the consumer's eye but that had nothing to do with Marcy. It wasn't the passion, although that would be another secret beyond. He tried to figure out just what it was, then.

It was that he wanted to take care of her. Beck growled to himself at the unconscious vulgarity in that.

Care for her. That was better.

Cherish.

His phone buzzed and, miraculously, it was Marcy.

Beck said, "You'll never believe this, but I was just thinking about you."

Her voice was apologetic. "Steve, I called to tell you I don't think I can go out with you tonight."

"Oh." Pointlessly, he knocked the magazine aside with his foot.

After waiting, Marcy said, "I'm really sorry, Steve. Please say something."

"I'm sorry, too. It's the worst news I've had this year. What's the trouble, Marcy, or is it any of my business?"

"Oh, nothing serious. Not very, anyway. I just feel I'm about to come down with a vicious cold. Maybe you can hear it in my voice."

"Not particularly, but I really am sorry. Is there anything I can do?"

"I don't think so but thank you. I think I'll stay in bed all day and try to lick it. So I didn't think it would be very sensible...."

He sighed. "I guess not. Maybe I'll drop out and see you. My bedside manner is heartily recommended."

She chuckled. "I'll bet it is, at that. But don't bother to come out. I still haven't told J. J. about you and I don't feel up to explaining things today."

He salted his wound by asking if she'd had a nice time last night and she said fine and when they hung up, Beck realized he had fixed no other definite date with her. He didn't call her back. He rang up a florist who stayed open Sundays and ordered a dozen red roses sent out with one word on the card: *Hurry!* And since he was on the phone, anyway, he told the florist to locate Felix Pavek's funeral services and send something appropriate.

Now it was noon or so. Beck cleaned up and got out his car. He went for a drive about the city, mostly sticking to the speedways so he could travel fast. He kept his eyes on the road ahead and watched it slip under him at whatever speed he willed. It felt good to drive but it remained a dismal day. He knew a great many people but no one he especially wanted to see. He thought how nice it would be when tomorrow came and he could get back on the job. Again, he postponed crossing the border to see the dog men. He had planned to go down with Marcy.

He ended up at the ball game at Lane Field. Beck got in at the first of the third and managed to get a box all to himself. He watched the game studiously, remembering he hadn't been to a sporting event for sheer enjoyment since early college. After two innings, he was bored. There was nothing at stake. Pat Garland didn't own any part of either team and hadn't yet been able to get a hand in the box office. Beck felt like doing something but couldn't figure out exactly what. In the eighth the rain finally began to fall in fat drops. He was soaked before he got back to his car.

There was a phone message slip at the Southwest Towers from Pat Garland. Beck called him after he had stripped off his wet clothes. "Why don't you come out and have dinner with us?" Garland wanted to know.

"Sorry, Pat," Beck lied, "but I've already got a date. Suppose I take a rain check on that."

"Any time. You know you're practically one of the family. And Leda feels the same way. In fact, this was her idea."

Beck had the dining room send up a dinner to him. He ate moodily from the cart in the silence of his suite. Halfway through, he rose abruptly and turned on the radio. He allowed the rasping voice of a comedian and the empty laughter of a studio audience to fill the silence. He finished his dinner and took some time dressing himself in pajamas, robe, scarf and slippers. He got out a deck of cards and played through the twenty-odd different kinds of solitaire he knew, reshuffling occasionally so that every game came out. The radio kept up its gaiety and he heard it now and then. When it stopped laughing and began posturing grimly with crime dramas, Beck snorted and turned it off.

He glanced around, saw the bar and downed a stiff drink as if it were medicine.

For a while, he stood by the window, listening to the rain beat and watching it ooze down the glass. He couldn't see any of the lights of the other windows across the city.

He checked the nightlatch on his door, had another swift drink and wandered toward his bedroom and his empty bed. He went that way hesitantly, as if trying to remember something he had forgotten.

He looked at his watch. It was ten minutes past nine. He stood in the doorway of his bedroom and surveyed his Sunday. The morning paper folded under the end table. The sprawled magazine still open to the deodorant ad. The wet tweed suit drying out on a chair. The dinner dishes. The playing cards scattered across the table top.

Beck's mouth twisted. He said softly, "And so to bed," and turned out the light.

20

Monday, May 23, 1:30 p.m.

The redhaired man, a club member named Smith, crouched behind the service line and panted. Sweat dribbled down his naked chest and darkened his trunks. He fiddled with the black handball, trying to gain time. "I shouldn't have eaten lunch first," he complained to Beck. "I can't move."

Beck grinned. "No alibis. Serve up and take your beating." His better shape was obvious in trunks and gym shoes. Behind them on the hardwood floor, two other businessmen played badminton and another wheezed on the rowing machine.

Smith said, "Used to be able to beat you one-handed. Don't know what happened to my game."

"I decided to learn how to win. Serve up."

Smith swatted the handball. It spun trickily off two walls but Beck had gauged it and arrived to slam it into a corner. Smith nearly fell down tipping it with his left hand and Beck charged in for a kill shot. The ball bobbled away across the floor.

Beck trotted after it. He saw Pat Garland standing in the spectator entrance up in the amphitheater watching him. They waved. Beck threw the ball back to Smith. He called, "That's it for me. Got to get to work."

"Hey, just as I was getting hot."

Beck strolled up to Garland, mopping his neck with his sweatshirt. Garland said, "Go ahead, finish your game, Steve."

"I had it won. I'll take a shower in my room."

"Could have called, then decided I better see you."

They rode up one floor in the elevator and went into Beck's suite. Garland talked about the sun coming out in La Jolla and Beck let him talk.

Garland said from the living room, "Say, nice place you've got here."

"That's right, you've never been up before." Beck stripped off his gym clothes in the bedroom and inspected his body before the mirror.

"You're in trim," Garland said critically from the doorway. He wandered in and plumped down on the bed. "Me, I've had a bellyache ever since I got up. Don't know what the trouble is. Ulcers, probably. Know of any good stomach men?"

"You need a drink. Help yourself." Beck left the shower door open while he attacked his skin with a cold needle spray and his bare hands.

"I doubt if that's the answer. Or maybe it is. Maybe I better cut down for a while."

Garland watched him take his shower, scrub himself with a coarse towel. The big man seemed to want company.

"How was your date last night, Steve?"

"Huh? Oh. Plenty smooth."

"Glad you're getting around more. I was beginning to worry about you. All work and no social life."

"Don't worry about me."

Beck came out and began dressing.

Garland asked, "The Everett girl again?"

"Oh, no. Somebody you wouldn't know."

Garland got up and drifted around the bedroom. He looked in the closet. He laughed and lifted out the hanger with Leda's severe black nightgown. "I thought you wore pajamas!"

"Christmas present for a friend of mine. I shop early."

"Oh, a good idea. Ought to have your friend try it on now and then so it won't get mildewed."

"Never thought of that."

Garland held the nightgown up in front of his face and looked through it at Beck. "Not much to it, is there?"

"That's on purpose, if you didn't know."

Garland wrinkled his nose and hung it back in the closet.

"No, can't see it. I don't care how sexy it is, every time I see black I think of funerals. Give me something with life in it any time. Some colors and a few doodads here and there, that's what makes a woman look in her class. Look how Leda dresses."

"Possibly I'm jaded."

"Every man to his taste. No, sir, I certainly wouldn't let Leda break out in something like that, though."

Garland lapsed into silence while Beck finished dressing. Beck was looping his bow tie in front of the mirror when Garland said casually, "I had a phone call about an hour ago."

"And?"

"It was Gene Wake, from Sacramento. He heard something."

"Such as?" Beck tugged a blue sweater over his head and smoothed it.

"The attorney general is dispatching two planes to look over the mountains south of the border. Wake found out about it when he ran into the Mexican consul up there."

Beck turned slowly. "No kidding."

"No kidding."

Beck went into the living room and sloshed drinks into two glasses. He brought one back to Garland. They tossed them down staring at each other.

"Well, you know what that means, Steve."

"Yeah. Isham was not the man."

"No, he wasn't. We've made a mistake, a damn bad one, and the attorney general's man is still with us." Garland glared miserably at the glass in his fist. "That's the only possible way they could've found out on such short notice exactly what happened to Isham."

Beck swore caustically and walked around. Then he noticed Garland and put a hand on his shoulder. "Well, let's not mourn about Hervey Isham, Pat. Not when the main job's still to be done. Isham was on the up and up, sure, but he was still in a business where there's a certain amount of risk involved."

"Oh, I don't give a damn about Isham! But what happened to him may cause a little trouble, on top of this other. Mistakes make a man look bad."

"When did the AG send down the planes?"

"Yesterday. I'm not worried about them finding anything. Rough country down there and if there was anything left of him after the fall, the birds undoubtedly took care of that. His clothes were burned first, of course. It's just that we're right back where we started or worse."

Beck said, "The wires from the east on Isham's background, they fit the situation either way, guilty or not."

"Well, he wasn't."

"No, he wasn't. I wish we had called in the Tarrants first. Be handy to share the blame."

Garland said savagely, "Yeah, you said that before, too." He gazed deadpan at Beck. "Steve, for some reason of your own, you didn't let me just go ahead and make that mistake, did you?"

Beck blew out his breath. He set the glass aside and after a moment smiled icily. "Well, if that isn't just the ideal thought at this time!"

He walked over to the window and watched the traffic. There was a long silence. Garland finally grumbled, "I guess I'm going out of my mind. I don't know why I said that. You understand."

Beck whirled on him. "I understand I better not turn my back on you any more! Sure, I get a hell of a bang out of you looking crosseyed at me every time some little thing goes wrong. You want to hire another boy, Pat?"

"Now, Steve."

"Well, what is it? Let's get it out in the open, explore it. I'm getting afraid you'll get too much gas on your stomach one of these nights and I'll be in Isham's spot. So what is it? You think I'm trying to snatch the books myself so I can take over the circle myself?"

"Oh, for Christ's sake! I'm sorry I—"

"I just want to know, Pat. You've got some idea I like to make mistakes better than you do. I'll claim my half of this Isham mess here and now if that's what's eating you. Sure, you should have called in the Tarrants beforehand, like I said. But I fed you the wrong information on Isham. Somewhere along the line I made a mistake and I don't like to do that. All I want to do is do the job and do it right."

"I'm sorry, Steve. I really am. I don't know why I said it." Garland sighed. "I suppose everyone lets some stupid remark pop out of his mouth at one time or another."

Beck said, "I suppose so," softly from the window. In a moment, he snapped his fingers and went into the living room. He phoned the desk downstairs to send up an L. A. city directory. Then he came back and grinned cheerfully at Garland.

"It's all a matter of getting to work, Pat. We flubbed up once but don't you see what's happening? If you and I can get mad at each other, there are some parts of the circle which can really explode—if we let them. We're doing the AG man's work for him that way."

"Yeah. He could just sit back and let the circle tear itself apart. If we let him."

"I don't think we're going to."

"You bet we're not, Steve. I guess it's that I can always tell what most people are thinking. I never can with you. Why I let a little thing like that annoy me, I don't know. Upset system, I suppose."

"Well, let's drop it."

"Sure. I don't really know why I'm worried. You'll keep clicking away like a machine and pretty soon you'll have the right answer."

Garland had another drink and a bellboy brought up the L. A. city directory. Beck thumbed through it.

"First matter is to check on this Oscar N. Vogel who said Isham hired him. That's...." He stopped.

"What's the trouble?"

Beck shut the thick book with a slam. "No such name and no such person in the private cop business. That's where I got taken. Vogel was a bona fide AG man himself, of course. He had a good story and a good act ready in case we ever picked him up."

"Well, we played it right down their alley. Isham's gone. There's one case they won't have to prosecute."

Beck thought. "You left Gusta and the books at the Gorman?"

"Right. Room 319." Garland flushed. "Fellow named Drew there. I did trust you enough to give him your description, so you can get up to see Gusta if necessary."

"Cheer up, Pat. I'm not mad."

"Well, that's good. You know, you've got me thinking about Senator Wake. So far he's given me just enough information to make himself look cooperative and keep us jumping."

"Nothing we can do about it, Pat. He's probably absolutely cooperative while still keeping his own good name out of the fire. I see your point all right about not stirring up anything in Sacramento right at this moment."

"You've got something on your mind." Garland's frown was hopefully inquiring.

Beck said, "Yes. J. John Everett."

"J. J.? How about the others?" Garland ticked them off. "Dominic, Cortes, Moon?"

"And me."

Garland swore jovially at him. Beck smiled in return and went to the bureau. He got out his Saturday messages and the police material which Pelletreau had brought. He tossed it all in Garland's lap.

Beck said, "I've checked. Dominic, Cortes and Moon are exactly who we think they are. J. J. is the only member whose background is in doubt. All we know about him is what Wake has told us."

"Well...." Garland grunted and leafed through the papers without reading them.

"Maybe Wake is being fooled by J. J., too, or maybe he isn't. Be that as it may, I believe that J. J. is exactly what we've been told up to a certain point: a brilliant Sacramento lawyer except he's what they call an honest citizen. I doubt if he was a state employee, probably a friend of the AG or something like that. He strikes me as the kind who would take this assignment down here out of a sense of civic duty."

"Possibly," said Garland. "But we don't want another Isham."

"I'm not trying to sell you anything. That's the only answer I see."

"I know that. But didn't you say J. J. has a daughter? What about her?"

Beck shook his head slowly. "No. Not a chance, Pat, that she's in on this. She's the real thing and she doesn't know what her father is doing."

"There ought to be some way you could clinch this."

"There is. This time I'll fix it so the mountain comes to me. The once I tried it, I used myself as bait. This time I'll use the books themselves. Or at least the spirits of same. I'm telling you this so we won't cross our wires again."

"Okay, Steve, anything you say. Going down now?"

"I want to mull this over a little before I make an appointment with J. J. I want my idea to be as simple as possible. Undermaneuver him rather than outmaneuver him."

Garland rose as if he were lifting weights. "Well.... You are sold on him, though, aren't you? Hope you're right. Be glad to get this over with."

"I know I'm right. See you, Pat."

"Oh." Garland stopped in the doorway. "Nearly forgot. I'm having a little dinner tonight. Kyle, the Tarrants, and Everett. I'd like you there to back me up."

"Back you up?"

"Uh-huh. Like you figured, the talk has started around the circle already. About Isham. So I decided I might as well set everybody straight before it went too far."

"Good idea."

"Seven o'clock. Don't dress."

Garland left, gloomy despite himself. Beck lounged around the room, thinking. He thought about what he was going to do and about Garland's dinner idea being spur of the moment. The club cleaner brought up some of his clothes and took away others; he came at two on Mondays, the same man never-failing.

After some irrelevant monkeying with Marcy's buckle, which still lay on the bureau, Beck reduced his plan to essentials. He put on his coat and went out to his telephone to call Everett. It buzzed before he reached it. He said hello and then raised his eyebrows at the receiver.

Everett said, "Well, happy to catch you, Steve. I was wondering if you might drop over to my office for a moment."

"I have an appointment," Beck lied, "but I'd just as soon put it off. Ten minutes all right?"

"Really no hurry. I merely suddenly decided you were the man to discuss my problem with, hence the impulse."

"No, I'll put this other off, J. J. Maybe a chat with you is what I need to open my pores after lunch. See you shortly."

"Fine. I'll appreciate it. Tell my secretary to interrupt me."

"Any time." Beck hung up and smiled across his room at no one.

21

Monday, May 23, 2:15 p.m.

The windows to Everett's offices were on the west side of the Moulton Building. Beck cruised under the windows twice until a parking place opened up on Sixth Avenue directly across from that side of the building. He paid the meter for some time. After locking the Buick coupe, he walked around it, testing both doors and the turtleback. Then he loitered on the sunny corner for a minute, keeping an eye on the passing traffic. Finally, with pretended satisfaction, he crossed the street. All the while he thought what an obvious strategy it was, yet not so obvious it could be safely disregarded. He did not glance up at Everett's windows.

The secretary swiveled away from her electric typewriting when Beck came into the reception room. Her practiced voice asked, "Would you please sit down for only a moment, Mr. Beck? Mr. Everett has just begun a consultation with a client. It will—"

"He phoned me," Beck said. "I'm to tell you that I'm an interruption."

"Oh," she apologized, and flipped the switch on the interoffice communication box. She told it, "Mr. Everett, Mr. Beck is here," and Everett's voice answered, "I'll come right out. Thank you."

The secretary looked at Beck to make certain he'd heard, they exchanged smiles and she returned to her typing.

A brief time passed.

Everett opened his office door and said, "I'm sorry you had to wait, Steve."

"I hardly noticed." Beck went in and looked around. "She said you had a client. Push him out the window?"

"I'd never be that unthrifty." Everett slouched behind his desk and gestured toward the door to the inner office. "On ice. But don't worry; the walls are soundproof. I'm glad you could come."

"You sound like it's something personal, J. J."

"Why don't you sit down?"

"Thanks, but I'll stick here by the window. Always a good show." Beck stood and looked down on the stream of shoppers going by the shiny roof of his car.

Everett sighed and rose and came over with the cigarette box. He touched the inner office door on the way to make sure it was properly shut. They each had a cigarette and lit up, gazing down on the people. The lawyer stood behind Beck and Beck could hear the slight sounds of his breathing and his polishing his spectacles.

Everett said, "You know, it was simply dodging the issue, but I've been thinking black thoughts since last night. I think the dignified term is soul-searching."

"I didn't know you were that old fashioned, J. J."

"You mean the dignity or the other? It's all the same. There used to be a time when a man's soul was his most valuable possession. A good many of the old great writings and the old great fears concerned the loss or barter of that article, a very real article then. What's happened since, Steve? Selective breeding?"

"Tell you the truth, I haven't given it much thought."

"Actually that's one solution. When we stopped believing in them, souls stole away with the elves. Along with individuality." Everett fitted his spectacles over his eyes and thoughtfully squinted them in place. "Well, I don't mean to be nostalgic."

"Not much you don't. Even granting we've discarded some parts these days, then we're incomplete and that's that. Right?"

"Yes, specialization must have its due, I suppose. And, after all, we are no longer valued for ourselves but for our products. I could offer as proof of that our universities which teach occupations rather than virtues."

Beck said, "Besides, I feel complete enough to suit me. I admit I don't have such refinements as a musical ear but...."

"No, I've long suspected you had developed more of the virtues proper to this age than the rest of us. And I am nearly the opposite."

"That's a kind of backhanded compliment, J. J. Wasn't it just last week you said the greatest achievement of these present times was higher bridges to jump from?"

Everett chuckled. "Oh, dear. Well, let's put that down to jealousy. You're built to fit in these times and I'm not. It happens today that I'm mightily discouraged with me and the law. Now there's one prop we've substituted for the soul. The law, the average conscience for the individual conscience."

"I'll let you in on a secret, J. J. The world isn't round; it's pyramidal, everyone leaning on everyone else. The trick is not to be down at the bottom where you get stood on."

The lawyer listened to him intently as if hoping to learn something. Then he shrugged absently as if he hadn't.

"But, Steve, my point is that even machines have laws. We supply them that much, fondly believing the natural law we've invented is the limit of all knowledge." Everett rummaged in his pocket for a paper handkerchief and began cleaning the tar from inside his cigarette holder. "Of course, I shouldn't slur the machine by speaking of it as a lower order when actually it's a higher order."

"Everything looks warped on Mondays, believe me."

"Well, don't we appear to be enslaved by the damned things? I'm chained to whatever device turns out cigarettes, for example, and that telephone over there and that talkbox next to it. And I'm beginning to believe you're in love with your automobile from the way you're watching it. That is your car across the street, isn't it, Steve?"

"Huh? Oh, yes. It is."

"You keep watching it as if you were afraid some rival would kidnap it. There are people starving for such affection."

Beck said, "No, I was just looking out at the traffic. And listening to your troubles. Are you sure they're your troubles, incidentally? Don't forget you did away with individual responsibility a minute ago."

"I'll make a sophist out of you yet, Steve. Or a hypochondriac like myself. I like to think I'm more honest than pat about it. I mean, take a look around at our culture. Doesn't that impress you with the popularity of hypo-chondria?"

Beck turned from the window a second so Everett could see him smile. He said, "Your only trouble is a weekend of debauchery, J. J. You're constipated."

"Quite the contrary."

"Then," Beck echoed Marcy's words, "you must be suffering from a strong sense of sin."

"What a strange diagnosis from you, Steve, and I don't think so, anyway. Sin and Hell and tragedy have gone out of style. Those ideas imply strength on the doer's part. That's a little too positive for the world as I see it today, Monday. I don't consider us so evil as spineless."

Beck laughed. "What are you after, J. J.? You're passing out an undue amount of praise today."

"As a matter of fact, I've been using you as a yardstick to some of my own private fancies. You happen to come out very well. I, well, I find I am a vic-tim of the psychological trends. The trends demand adaptation to environ-ment. I completely dislike my mechanistic environment. Hence, I have the choice of going mad fretfully or being chewed up peacefully. You know, well over a hundred thousand of us enter the insane asylums annually. But we have developed sugarcoating into such a splendid science that those entering the asylums are no longer insane, mad, lunatic, or even mentally ill. They are now suffering from personality disorders.

"I've been considering"—Everett tapped his spectacles mockingly—"trad-ing in these old hornrims on a more modern pair. I see they decorate eyeglasses beautifully now and I can't think of anything more appropriate than a deco-rated crutch."

"You keep leaving out one point," Beck said. "What do you intend doing about the world this afternoon?"

"Oh, nothing, Steve. I'll merely continue talking about poor mankind. I grant you I'm a weakling but think how safe I am in such a popularized sta-tus. I wouldn't be arguing with myself so much today if I didn't feel a lack, though. I do have a bit of soul trouble and I could use your help, Steve. Why don't we sit down now?"

"Pull a chair over here. From all you say, we should practice spaciousness." Beck grinned blandly and swept a hand to include the extent beyond the window.

Everett showed some surprise, hesitated, then shoved over a client chair for himself. He looked, Beck thought, as if he was taking fresh stock of his guest, as if he hadn't expected Beck to grasp his opinions. Beck was amused and pleased.

The lawyer put his fingers together and said, "As you've probably heard, I have a daughter. Marcy Everett. She's an only child and her mother has been dead for nearly fifteen years. Marcy has been away at college until recently."

Just her name jolted Beck. He hadn't foreseen this turn of the conversation. But he did not forget himself so much as to face altogether away from the window.

"...an unfortunate experience," Everett was saying. "She plunged into marriage with another youngster whose principal merit, so far as I can reconstruct it, was an ability to dance well. Naturally, that union didn't last. With her full permission, I had the marriage annulled. Am I boring you, Steve?"

"No. You're not boring me. What is it you want me to do?"

"I wanted to give you this background first because I think it important you understand what sort of a person Marcy is. She's twenty. She is more intelligent than her years would indicate and she is highstrung and, well, original. I consider her entirely good and honest. On the debit side—and I don't believe this is mere looking down on her from another generation—Marcy is impetuous, overly impressionable and emotionally unbalanced. Isn't it cold to discuss a person you love in such miserably limited terms? For, above all, Marcy is a good and actual human being and I do love her. Can you picture her, somewhat?"

"Yes."

"She is here in San Diego now, since she quit Berkeley. She is here with me and, Steve, somehow she has struck up a friendship with Eddie Cortes. She told me, not knowing I'd know him. That, as you might guess, is the problem."

Everett sighed. Beck didn't say anything. Everett continued.

"Marcy and I haven't discussed this, although she knows I disapprove. Perhaps we're both afraid of crystallizing the situation. For my part, I don't believe it's oversimplification to regard their meeting as a contact of guilt and innocence. Both Saturday night and yesterday afternoon and last night, Marcy was out with him until all hours. What's wrong, Steve?"

"Nothing. Yesterday? She was out with him Sunday?"

"And Saturday. Knowing both their natures, I'm badly worried. You can guess what a father feels looking on a situation like that. I've tried to describe

Marcy, and you know Cortes as well as I." Everett got up and went over to fumble through the papers laid out on his desk. His tired shoulders shrugged. "Well, anyway, you know. Cortes and his life are messy, even written down on these various parole documents. In San Francisco, he was nothing more ennobled than a pimp. He knifed one of the sluts who worked for him in an argument over a few dollars she had or hadn't earned."

Beck was conscious of his face. It felt cold as stone and set in old lines that would never disappear. Between his teeth he asked, "What do you—do you think she likes Cortes?"

He suddenly disliked Everett for looking thoughtful over the question. It wasn't an abstract question. Everett mused. "I don't know. I worry but I don't know the facts. I suppose Cortes has some persuasive charm about him that a man wouldn't see. It's a professional characteristic, you know, in his former business. I suppose a good many details, unfortunately." The lawyer cast the documents aside and came back to stand with Beck at the window. He added, "And when it comes to moral values, who am I to censure Cortes?"

Beck snapped, "Well, let's not dissect morality. What's the point?"

"The point is that I don't want Marcy to associate with Cortes, or Pat Garland, or even you, Steve, if you'll forgive me. I wouldn't want her to associate with me but there remains the mechanical difficulty that I am her father. I would rather Marcy didn't know that such a social level as the circle exists, except in the newspapers."

After sucking in his breath, Beck smiled. He was in charge of himself once more. "I wonder if you can live two lives?"

"I have to do my best to protect hers. I want your help. I think you understand because you're something near my own age. Give you a few years and you could be Marcy's father yourself."

Beck's laugh barely showed its harshness. "You want me to have a heart-to-heart talk with the girl then?"

"Hardly. She scarcely listens to me, much less someone she doesn't know. No, I only wish you'd tell Cortes to stay away from her for good. He would have to do what you said. You wouldn't even have to give a reason."

There was a silence. Beck asked, "Will I see you at Pat's dinner tonight?"

"Of course. He called just before you came. From the roster of guests I imagine it's about our problem of the other night."

"Have you heard anything yourself?"

"I only know what Pat told me then. Unless what Sid Dominic hinted at this morning is appropriate. He phoned to ask if I knew where Isham was lately."

"What was his hint?"

"Just that. Well, how about the favor, Steve?"

"I think it can be handled."

Everett touched his elbow briefly and said thank you. "Are you interested in why I asked you to do this for me? I wasn't completely hiding behind a mask of friendship. Nor do I think you would be weakened by pity. No, I thought you'd be taken with my dilemma as a tactical matter."

"It may turn out interesting. I'd better be on my way now, J. J. Thanks for all the confidences."

He left Everett by the window, smiled at the secretary on the way through and went down to the street. Overhead an airplane was writing a smoke message about soda pop across the infinite sky. Beck didn't look up at the Moulton Building to see if he was being watched. He glanced over the locks on his car, got in and drove away.

He parked in the lot across from the Southwest Towers Athletic Club in a place which could be watched from his suite all afternoon if he chose. The trap was set; only his mouth smiled about it.

Beck was waiting for the elevator when the desk clerk said he had a call coming in. He took it in a lobby booth. It was Marcy.

"I was wondering if you'd like to take a poor girl out this evening?"

"Always willing to help the poor." That sounded light enough. Beck was certain she couldn't tell anything about his voice over the phone. "How's your cold?"

"Oh, it's virtually disappeared. I feel much better—all due, of course, to those lovely roses. Thank you, Steve."

"How was bed yesterday?"

"Wonderful. Exactly what I needed."

"What time did you get up and go home?"

"Please!" She laughed. "What time tonight and what shall I be prepared for?"

"Well, there's a dinner engagement I can't escape, Marcy. Business, but it shouldn't last too long. Suppose I pick you up about nine, we catch the last dog races and then go dancing somewhere."

"Sounds like fun. I'll see you at nine then. I think J. J. will be out."

Beck got out of the phone booth slowly after she had rung off. He went up to his rooms to wait and see.

22

Monday, May 23, 7:15 p.m.

Steven Beck seldom arrived late for anything. But, with no purpose, he let himself be late for Pat Garland's dinner conference. He let himself be late exactly fifteen minutes. He felt strange, he didn't know what about, and tried to forget it.

Nothing more had happened that afternoon. From his lofty window he had kept a casual watch on his coupe below but it had not been molested. He had amended his theory: if he were the AG man and now believed the books were in the car, he would steal the car in such a way as to appear an ordinary theft. He would let the police return the car, books and all if they proved to be in it, and meanwhile procure the warrant if needed.

So when Beck parked his car in the Garland driveway, he left it farther away from the house than the Tarrants' black Packard and Everett's sedan. He locked it but that was all; it was to remain unguarded.

Garland was already waiting in the doorway of his slick geometric house. He had a disappointed look on his face.

Beck said, "That's a fine greeting."

"Oh, I just thought it might be Kyle. I heard a car. Come on in, Steve."

The living room was empty. "Where's the crowd?"

"We're eating in the patio." Garland led the way through the circus bar into the patio. A long table waited under one arbor, its buffet service pushed aside for hors d'oeuvres and liquor. Beck let his host pour him a martini from the electric mixer.

Everett was stretched out contentedly in a lawn chair, absorbed in a brandy. He waved as if it would be his last effort. He was playing at getting tight but he could not conceal his usual listening air.

Larson Tarrant perched on the second step of the children's slide with his pointed shoes braced against the edge of the sandbox. He got down and strolled over to greet Beck, shifting his martini from one elegant hand to the other. Tarrant was a gambler who had gotten ahead, a slim neat man with a sharp-angled face and an incipient pot belly. "Haven't seen much of you lately, Steve."

"Hasn't been much to see, Larson."

They smiled back and forth and Beck said, "Have you been a good girl, Ulaine?"

Ulaine Tarrant, shapelessly weighting down another of the lawn chairs, simpered at him, "Why, Steve, I didn't know you cared."

Her husband said, "Who does, darling?" and returned to his perch on the slide.

Ulaine was fat and gaudy and hennaed. She insisted on dressing in ruffles. A good many years before, Tarrant had charmed her away from one of San Diego's first families and married her for her money. She still had it. They were a clever business team; the county was dotted with their draw poker rooms and illegal stud layouts. They hated one another almost affectionately.

Garland called, "Anybody ready for another?"

Ulaine sucked an olive pit clean and flipped it at Tarrant. "Me."

Garland fixed up her martini and got himself a fresh whiskey.

After a pause, Beck said, "Well, how's the weather?"

Only Everett laughed softly. Ulaine said, "Cold as hell over in Coronado."

Tarrant said, "It's that drafty stable we live in."

His wife glared at him just so it wouldn't pass. She had inherited the big house.

"Been nice here in La Jolla," Garland reflected. "Nice in town, too, I understand."

"Orville Kyle hasn't shown up yet?" Tarrant asked.

"Oh, he's just a little late. Long way down from Del Mar."

"Fifteen miles," said Ulaine. "Pretty drive. I wish we'd get out more."

"We get out enough as is," corrected Tarrant.

Garland grinned amiably at both of them and looked around at the drinks again. He poured Everett some more brandy and came back to tower within talking distance of all four guests. "Say, Steve," he asked, "did you see the paper this morning?"

"Local sports was all."

"This was on the front page, down at the bottom."

"Isn't the government giving us a royal screwing, though," said Ulaine.

"Well, this was about DeVore, that pug I used to own," Garland related. "He fought some bum named Lopez in New York last night and, get this, he killed Lopez in the sixth. Killed him! Cracked his skull. I wish I hadn't sold so much of that DeVore boy. He'll have a name now."

"That's a shame!"

Beck said, "Easy come, easy go."

"That's the truth."

Garland grinned at Everett. "Where was *your* good advice, J. J.? Why'd you let me sell that boy?"

Everett squinted unpleasantly. "As I remember, you ordered me to let you."

Garland thought that was very funny.

Tarrant asked, "Where's the lady of the house tonight, Pat?"

"In the kitchen. A few last-minute jobs. You know how these things are," Garland said with good-natured contempt for however dinners came about. He waved the same way at the gas-fitted barbecue grill. "It's going to be a barbecue but Leda's doing it all in the kitchen. The damn cement thing's more trouble than it's worth."

"I haven't noticed any servants. Not even the governess—what's her name?—Gusta."

"I gave them the night off."

The Tarrants exchanged glances and Larson Tarrant said, "Then we'll be able to talk."

"That's exactly the reason for this get-together," Garland agreed. "Of course, I'm always glad to see you, too, and just talk. What's new over in Coronado?"

"Not a thing."

Beck winked at Everett as he went by for another martini. He wished dinner would come and go so he could pick up Marcy. He hoped they wouldn't wait on Kyle. He sipped his cocktail and ignored the pointless conversation and comforted himself by remembering that Garland wasn't the kind who waited for anybody.

Leda Garland came out with two silver-covered dishes for the table. She wore a long rustling skirt of green, silver and scarlet stripes and a loose white blouse cut low. Her face was a fixed party face until she saw Beck and then it brightened gaily. "Steve! Just the man I need to help me carry in a few things."

"Oh, I'll help you," Garland offered.

"You have to stay and be hospitable." She held out soft fingers to Beck. "Come along and earn your dinner, now."

Beck didn't take the fingers but he smiled obediently and followed her toward the kitchen. As soon as they were out of sight of the others Leda turned to be kissed. He went through the motions and then moved away to clean his mouth.

She said, "You didn't put much into that, darling."

"This isn't the place to put much into it. Too much of a crowd."

"That isn't what you used to say. Remember back when Pat was buying all those complicated cameras, the night he was showing movies in the game room?"

"We were lucky we weren't caught. Let's not risk our necks again."

Leda sighed and went on into the magnificent kitchen and posed for him. "Do you like me tonight, Steve? I wore this just for you. Pat doesn't like it one bit."

"Why not? It's bright enough."

"Not the skirt, the blouse. He thinks it's too, shall we say, advertising." She hunched one shoulder so the blouse could sink far down on that side. "What would you think?"

"That I'd better get back before he really commences thinking."

"I wish it were over. That ghastly Tarrant woman! If it were only just you here. Why couldn't you come last night, Steve?"

"Oh, one thing and another. This goes out, I take it." Beck picked up the platter with the steaming roast on it.

Leda said, "Don't go yet," but he kept walking as if he hadn't heard her. In the patio, Everett and the Tarrants were watching Garland politely as he tried to master a toy from the sandpile.

"What do you call this affair, Steve? I've been trying to think of the name for it."

"It's called a diabolo where I come from." Beck put down the roast and took the two slender rods from the big man's hands. "I used to have one of these when I was a kid. Mine was homemade, though. See, the object is to get the spool spinning on the string between these two sticks. The faster the spool— that's the diabolo—goes, the easier it is to balance it. Then you can make it do tricks." He demonstrated, tossing the plastic double-cone high in the air and catching it again on the string.

Behind him, Leda clapped softly. Garland said immediately, "Here, let me try that again. Of course, I never was much good with my hands...."

After Garland's wry failure, the toy went around the circle with no success. Everett said, "You're undefeated champion, Steve. To what do you attribute your success?"

"Clean living."

Leda said, "Perhaps because he's so good at walking a tightrope himself."

Everybody laughed. The child's toy had relieved much of the tension. Garland looked at his wrist watch. "Well, we can't wait much longer for Brother Kyle. The food's getting cold."

"Suppose I give him a ring," Beck suggested.

"Good idea. He's probably on his way but go ahead."

Beck went into the dark and deserted living room and got on the phone. The voice that answered from Orville Kyle's Del Mar estate belonged to a manservant. Yes, Mr. Kyle was in. No, Mr. Kyle had left word he was not to be disturbed by anyone. Beck didn't insist. He sat down on a voluptuous chair and thought it over in the gloom.

Garland strode in, impatient. "You mean he hasn't even left yet?"

"Pat, I don't believe he intends to come."

"It can't have slipped his mind."

"No, it can't have slipped his mind. Kyle is simply not coming."

Beck couldn't make out Garland's face. He heard his breath come hissing out and finally Garland muttered, "Well, well. What do you suppose all that means?"

"I can't say what it means. The facts are: A, Kyle is refusing to cooperate and, B, he is refusing to explain same."

"Yeah. So maybe he's gotten tired of taking my orders. Maybe he thinks I made him what he is so he can cut loose for himself. Maybe so, Steve. I guess

Mr. Godalmighty Kyle has forgotten what a two-bit character he was when I came out here and made him, him and his string of scared cigarstore bookies, him letting all the big money go down to Tijuana."

"You could send a couple boys up to escort him down. Or I can go myself."

"To hell with that! Let him sit at Del Mar for as long as he wants. Great little organization he's got, anyway, him and his petty chiselers like that Dominic. No, sir, Mr. Kyle can't get along without me but I can without him and it's time he realized it. Mr. Kyle is going to have to come to me."

Beck said, "Let's talk this out a little further. Somebody has something in mind."

"So have I." Garland expelled a harsh laugh. "Kyle will come soon enough, on my terms, with his tail between his legs. Same for all of them. I was doing these crumbs a favor, letting them know what's going on. Now they can whistle."

"Pat, calm down."

But Garland stomped back to the patio, Beck following. "Let's eat," he growled at his wife, "before all the damn food gets cold."

Larson Tarrant asked, "How about Kyle? Isn't he coming?"

"No," Garland said. "He's not coming. Let's eat."

Everybody circulated around the long table, collecting plates and silver and food. Garland had given up all pretense of sociality and sat a little distance from the others. Leda squeezed in next to Beck on a wheeled lounge, thigh intimate. Everybody began eating and said something about how lucky Garland was to have a wife who could cook like this. After that, nobody said much of anything.

Leda was taking plates away again when Tarrant mentioned Charles Holsclaw.

Only to keep talk going, Beck asked, "Has anybody heard from him since he left for Chicago?"

Tarrant helped. "Not I. He was supposed to look into this matter of automatic dealers for all our outlets. That will make a sizable contract for somebody."

"That's the way my money goes," Ulaine sighed viciously. "If you had your way, dear, our customers would bring their own cards."

"You always carry your own, dear." Pointedly, Ulaine looked around the patio. "Holsclaw. That's two missing tonight, isn't it?"

Garland raised his head at that but Everett, who had been a dreamy spectator till now, spoke up swiftly. "Larson, when you do get those dealing machines, I'd advise you to keep an eye on them."

"Why?" Ulaine asked at once. "Don't you think they'll be worth the money?"

"Certainly. Everything's worth money. But don't be surprised to find them inviting in other machine friends until eventually there'll be no room for your mortal customers and—what then? The end of the Tarrant chain. There'll be hardly any need for you to cater to your machine clientele when you don't understand them as well as they understand themselves."

Ulaine gave a loud laugh. "You're kidding me!"

"No, I'm not. I'm warning you. Just this afternoon I was lamenting with Steve the decline of humanity."

Beck said lightly, "That's right. Mentally, morally, spiritually, physically, emotionally. Have I left anything out, J. J.? You accept that hypothesis, Ulaine, and you're a goner."

"Well," she said, "I'll admit things have come to a pretty pass."

Everett smiled loosely and swept his spectacles like searchlights over the group. "There, that's all I need. We are all goners. I'll tell you how and why."

"Mentally, morally, et cetera." Larson Tarrant whistled. "Now there's a side of you, Steve, I've never seen. How deep can you get?"

Without showing his resentment, Beck laughed politely and measured off two inches between thumb and forefinger.

Everett repeated, "I'll tell you how and why. Homo sapiens, the wise animal, has evolved from the more bestial, more *complete* animals. We are weakening because of the mixture we've made of ourselves lately. I'd say we had abandoned humanity almost entirely in order to breed the machine and we can't survive, half-animal and half-mechanical. You see, the next evolutionary step is the pure complete machine. So let's reconcile ourselves to making way."

Leda, rustling by Beck, murmured, "What's he talking about?"

Beck shrugged and said, "Somebody has to."

She glanced toward her husband's morose bulk and bore out some more dishes.

Everett said, "We were goners, you know, as soon as we accepted machine ideals as our ideals. And don't think we haven't. We even believe that human nature is inferior to the machine which is perfection. We admire its accuracy, its speed and strength, its impersonality, and its standardization which is the machine word for our own beloved conformity. Especially we envy the absolute neatness and comfort of predestination. That's the basis of all machinery."

Beck gazed stolidly back at him. He felt irritably that the lawyer was making fun of him in some obscure fashion. Now that an explosion from Garland had been averted, he wished that Everett would shut up.

"See? It's predestined, paradoxically, to predestinate. In that way, it's rid of all responsibility, despite its power, and lack of responsibility is certainly an attractive feature. So attractive that we may overlook the coefficient, lack of soul."

Tarrant said, "Very interesting," in a cool voice.

Everett took a drink, chuckling over some private joke. "Nevertheless, your heirs have brass guts, Larson. Your automatic dealers are merely one more step, one more machine which replaces muscle of some sort. Oh, I'd never advise against buying them. It's always a wise investment to be in tune with the times. The increase in that sort of machine power has jumped five hundred percent since the turn of the century. And this wonderful century is just beginning to witness the expansion of cybernetics, the science of machinery to replace brains. Our brains, they happen to be."

"So what, is what I say." Ulaine said it.

"You're right. So we'll watch." Everett mastered a hiccup, smiling. "We birthed the machine and worshipped its virtues. We're getting our husks out of its way as quickly as possible by grinding ourselves up in the mechanistic society we conceived to emulate it. There's no escaping...."

On the other hand, Beck thought, it was possible that Everett wasn't talking so exclusively to him as he imagined. Everett might be prattling on to amuse himself at all their expenses. That idea irritated Beck, too. He didn't like being lumped in with the Tarrants.

"...just before our time, the vital industries were those which fed, clothed and sheltered us—people. You know the vital industries of this generation: to feed or build machines. Machines beget machines beget machines. They take great pride, not in the job, but in doing the job. There's another mechanical virtue I left out—pride in doing something no matter how ridiculous, although perhaps that falls under predestination. However, we've seen to it that we are no more free than they."

From his shadows, Garland grumbled something that sounded like, "Oh, for Christ's sake."

Beck covered with, "So you see, Ulaine. According to this drunken existentialist, you just can't take it with you."

"It would melt," said Tarrant.

Leda came back from the kitchen, looked around and came over to sit close to Beck. She told them all, "I really think we should all set about mastering this contraption before the night's over." She lifted Beck's hands. He hadn't realized he had picked up the diabolo and was holding onto it.

"Show me first, Steve," Leda said. She took the two sticks and the double-cone and leaned back against his knees so he could put his arms around her.

Beck said, "If I start giving lessons I'll lose my amateur standing," and shifted away from her.

"How is it you keep it on the string?" Leda insisted. He reached out and moved her bare arms up and down slightly.

Pat Garland got up and moved silently to the table to get another drink. He said, without looking around, "Can't you understand, Leda, that nobody is interested in that damn toy? Throw it away."

Leda sat staring at his back. Then she bit her lip and carried the diabolo over to the sandbox and dropped it. She went off to the kitchen, smiling stiffly.

Garland looked at his guests over his drink.

Tarrant said, "Well, now that that excellent dinner is gone forever, suppose we settle down to business, Pat."

Garland grunted.

"I understood this was to be in the nature of a conference."

"Then you understand wrong. It is just a social dinner." Garland tossed off his drink and poured another. "Dessert will be along in a few minutes."

Tarrant considered his smooth hands. Then he reached over into the sandbox and pushed a little dump truck back and forth.

Ulaine grated, "What about Isham?" and shattered a tight silence.

"What about him?"

The woman's little eyes were glittering. "It just seems to me when our most valuable hired hand gets picked off the least we're entitled to is a little explanation, that's all."

"Isham got in my way. Is that little enough for you?" Garland inquired.

Beck started to speak but Garland said, "Never mind, Steve." Beck shrugged and sat back and Garland said, "Well?" to the Tarrants.

"Just like that, eh?" Larson Tarrant said.

"Yes. Where the hell's that dessert?" Garland tramped away toward the kitchen, shouting for Leda. Beck got up and followed him, catching up with him in the passageway.

"Pat, don't fly off the handle just because of Kyle."

"It isn't just because of Kyle, my friend," Garland snapped. "These monkeys got to remember who runs things around here. I don't owe anybody any explanations."

"Is that all of it?"

"Yes, that's all of it. You're thinking I don't want to admit making a mistake but I wouldn't say it if I were you, Steve." He put both hands to his forehead and rubbed it fiercely. "Now don't get me mad at you. I've got a splitting enough headache as it is. Don't you heckle me like the rest of them. I'll run this damn business the way I see it."

Garland went on into the kitchen and Beck could hear him quarreling with Leda about her blouse. After a moment, Beck walked back to the patio and sat down.

Everett said softly, "Pat doesn't seem himself tonight."

"He's in a bad mood. You know how bad days come along."

Ulaine mused, "He isn't sick or anything, is he?"

"Pat has an army of doctors but he's never had a sick day in his life."

"It wouldn't be the best thing for Pat to get sick," Tarrant said and his voice was silk. "If he lost his grip...."

Beck said, "I certainly wouldn't worry, Larson. There is no danger."

Leda came back, cheeks flushed. She still wore the white blouse. She put long-stemmed glasses of mousse in front of each of them. She leaned so close to Beck that he could smell the sachet he knew she wore between her breasts. He saw Ulaine looking at Leda and him curiously.

Pat Garland did not reappear. The rest of them sat around the patio and said nice things to Leda about the dessert. When Beck's glass was empty, he set it aside and stood up.

"Don't rush off, Steve."

"Have to, Leda. Sorry to break up the party but that's business."

"Business like with Isham?" asked Ulaine.

"Just business, Ulaine. Mine. Nice to have seen you all. Larson. J. J."

Everyone was standing and saying they'd better run along, too.

"Oh, stay around and say hello to the children," Leda urged Beck alone. "They'll be home from the show any moment."

Along with the others, Beck expressed his regrets. Leda sighed. The Tarrants went off after wraps. Leda followed Beck to the front door and managed merely to squeeze his hand as he left since Everett was close behind them, weaving slightly, pretending probably.

"Good night. Wonderful dinner."

Everett caught up with him by Beck's coupe which was still there. The lawyer asked, "Have you acted any on that matter we discussed earlier?"

"Not yet."

"Oh. Well, Steve, you know how soon I hope you'll make it. I've had a dreadful premonition all evening that perhaps Marcy was seeing him tonight." Everett chuckled woozily. "Of course, it was a dreadful evening."

"You may be happy to hear that's my business tonight. I'm going about it from a little different angle." Everett smiled and nodded and watched Beck unlock his car. He waved as Beck drove away.

23

Monday, May 23, 10:30 p.m.

Below on the track the sleek narrow-brained dogs ran round and round again and again, chasing the mechanical lure they believed to be desirable. The crowd yelled them on.

"Little damn!" Marcy commented after the race and she marked her program and heaved a mock sigh. She had Beck hold the program while she searched for her cigarettes.

He asked, "Aren't you going to bet the next one?"

"Only mentally. I have to make up for the gouging that quiniela just gave me. Why'd you talk me into that, anyway? If I can't win with one dog, my poor money certainly didn't have a chance on two!"

"I talked you into what? I told you the facts. Numbers one, two and eight win the most often, the inside and outside of the track where the bunching is less apt. One and eight or one and two combine to win and place oftener than two and eight. But the quiniela odds are high for a good—"

"All right, all right." She laughed. "Don't rub it in. You sound exactly like a professor I didn't like at college."

"Dogs are exactly what the name implies. Dogs."

"They aren't as exciting as horses. But they're daintier." The entries for the next race were parading. Marcy said, "You're rather subdued tonight, Steve," and leaned forward to watch the dogs.

Beck watched her. "I'm enjoying myself quietly." He was. He had put Garland's dinner and the rest of it out of his mind, forcibly. Marcy, in brown wool, looked especially alive and apart, not from him, but from all other people. For him, her slim hands moved uniquely in commonplace gestures. He was smiling at nothing as he looked over the crowd in the Caliente grandstand, comparing the other women to Marcy. He felt happy she sat next to him, making the others shabby.

Marcy saw his eyes roaming and inspected the crowd with him. But she said, "They always make me a little sad, as if I should be doing something important instead of wasting my time here with them."

"Aren't you having an exceptional evening, sweetheart?"

"Oh, yes, of course. I guess mentioning that econ professor put it in my mind. He made me think of the old union organizers and the men who invented labor-saving devices, they lopped something like eighteen hours off the work week in the last forty or fifty years. I guess it was just propaganda but they made so much lovely talk about people having more leisure time to perfect the arts of peace. Well, here's the leisure time and here we sit."

"We all like to get away from ourselves once in a while. Can't condemn everybody for spending their time the way they like."

Marcy grinned at him and then looked up the race ahead in her program and said, "I suppose. Say, here's a natural. Dreamy Weamy! A dog named that has to win or be the laughing stock of the kennels. Let's go down."

They went down into the concrete cavern beneath the grandstand, to the parimutuel windows. Beck said, "I hope your system's better here than it was at roulette."

"I understand that lucky streak I had for a while wasn't true. You had everything fixed."

"Only for your initial plunge. When did Cortes tell you all this?"

"That initial plunge was fun, anyway. I must see that Mr. Isham again and thank him."

Beck murmured, "That's a good idea."

Marcy waved goodbye and stepped into line at the five dollar window. They looked at each other's eyes across the short distance and she tossed her cigarette over for him to step on, the way she had the first time they'd met. He liked that. It was the absurd ritual of having known each other well for a long time.

Then he saw Sid Dominic sweating in the twenty dollar line. Beck went up behind him and said, "Sucker."

"Oh, hi, Steve." Dominic laughed apologetically. "You said it. You working late?"

"Just pleasure, same as you."

"Pleasure, schmeasure. I'm behind seventy-five already yet and I cleaned up on the sixth, at that. I don't know what the old lady'll say but I got a good idea."

"You'll never make up that seven hundred bucks this way, Sid."

"What seven hundred bucks? Oh, I got you. *That* seven hundred bucks. Yeah. I'd forgotten about that."

"Oh, I wouldn't do that. Pat Garland hasn't forgotten. He doesn't forget anything."

"An elephant, a regular elephant," said Dominic and put a damp palm on Beck's elbow. "Steve, you know the fact is, though, I was talking to Kyle today and he said—well, he's really my boss when it comes right down to it—and one thing and another I thought maybe Big Pat'd let that ride."

Beck smiled pleasantly. "I know what Kyle told you. What you don't know is what Pat told Kyle."

"I ain't trying to start any trouble, Steve, believe me."

"Of course you're not, Sid. You're just trying to get along, the same as all of us. But don't make the mistake Hervey Isham made."

Dominic licked his lips and shook his head.

Beck said, "Seven hundred," and left him.

Marcy was waiting and watching. She said, "You're angry. Don't be, Steve."

"No, I'm not. Merely some business that cropped up."

She slipped her hand into his. "Well, don't be angry tonight. Surely that little fat fellow can't affect you."

They strolled slowly up to the stands, close together. "You're right," Beck confessed. "But it wasn't him, it was the idea of him and...." And all the cut-throats waiting for big men to fall within reach. Everybody out for themselves. Selfishness. He didn't finish what he was saying because he didn't even want to think about anything that would tarnish the evening.

The bugle blew post.

Marcy yelled her head off for Dreamy Weamy and then sadly tore up her tickets. "Well, that marks the end of a beautiful friendship between capital and me. I'm down to my mad money." Beck had turned around to survey the tiers of spectators up behind them. "What's wrong, Steve?"

"Guilty conscience, I guess." He grinned for her. "I had one of those weird feelings of being watched."

"For Heaven's sake!"

"Maybe I'm getting allergic to all those field glasses staring down my neck."

"Maybe you're getting allergic to people."

"Had enough of them and dogs?"

"You bet."

They left the stands and crossed the dark parking lot to the Jockey Club. On the way, Beck looked back twice and Marcy chuckled. "You better take something for those wrought-up nerves, old man."

"It's past my bedtime, that's why," he passed it off.

The headwaiter found them a small table off from the crowd and they settled back to hold hands and watch the dancers and the little orchestra. It was pleasant here and the gaiety was suave but it wasn't the right place. No, Beck decided, he would tell her tonight that he loved her but it would have to be somewhere less artificial. Up to now, he had automatically associated romance with nightclubs but touching Marcy seemed to give him a new sense of proportion. These places were contrived, they were hollow artifices which held nothing for the two of them. Somewhere else he would tell her he loved her and had to have her. He would forgive her for lying about her date with Eddie Cortes, undoubtedly a foolish whim for which she was already sorry.

Somewhere else.

But not in his car. They would have to be away from people but a parked car was a lewd setting. He wondered why that had never occurred to him before in all his life. Marcy, apparently, made the difference. Beck smiled as he thought of the right place. They would get out, away from everything including the Buick coupe, and walk along the beach. Not the crashing ocean beach but a lapping beach where the lights were far away across the water. Say, one of those stretches along the bay side of the Coronado strand.

"Awake, awake," Marcy whispered and drummed her fingers on his wrist. "I'd give a lot to know what thought put that satisfied expression on your face but I haven't a penny to spare."

"Matter of fact, I was thinking about you. You and a great sacrifice I'm about to make for you."

"Oh, wonderful! What is it?"

"See that fellow all alone at the bar? Bald head and mustache?"

"Yes."

"I had planned to see that man tonight, and about dogs, come to think of it. My crass intention was to combine business and pleasure down here."

"And I've cast such a spell that you've forgotten all but pleasure."

"That's it, sweetheart."

Marcy grinned happily. "At last. You've just fulfilled my greatest womanly ambition. To change some man in some way. If you'll free my hand, sir, I'll give you a great round of applause."

"Suppose I keep your hand and settle for a great round of drinks." The waiter had arrived. "Shall we send over the instructions for Shady Ladies?"

"Plain old 7-Up for mine, please."

He frowned at her, unbelievingly, and she nodded for emphasis. So he ordered that and a bourbon over ice for himself. "Don't tell me you're on the wagon?"

"Uh-huh."

"Firmly? Or back where you can bounce off easily?"

"Firmly," she said. "I reached the conclusion that I was drinking too much and making a fool of myself. Or at least abetting nature's efforts. I don't care to see people make fools of themselves so why shouldn't I take my own medicine?"

"When did you decide all this? Or was it you?"

"That night you invaded my kitchen and we—" Then Marcy was no longer bantering and she had pulled her hand away. "Certainly, it was I who decided. Who else would it be?"

He was sorry that last had slipped out. He lied, smiling, "I suspect your father of an iron hand. Come on, let's dance. We've waited a whole three days for this opportunity."

As they reached the dance floor, she murmured, "You caught me off balance, when I was feeling so noble and independent."

They danced. The music was right and they had enough floor to themselves but they didn't dance well together, after all. Their rhythms didn't quite jibe and their consciousness of that only made it worse. They concentrated and only spoke twice. When the music stopped, they clapped briefly and smiled like strangers. When Beck started to lead her back to the table, Marcy asked if they weren't going to dance any more.

"Why? It's not for us."

"I know. It's my fault, Steve. I'm not a very good dancer."

"No, it depends on the man, as a rule. Perhaps I don't lead you strongly enough."

She sat down. "That would be the last thing I'd think about you."

"That has all the earmarks of a profound judgment."

"Has it? I didn't mean it to."

Beck swirled the ice in his glass and they both watched it go round. He said, "Seriously, what do you think of me?"

Marcy said, "Why, you're positively fascinating, Mr. Beck," with a pitiful attempt at their former gaiety.

"Seriously. What do you think I'm like?"

"Well... Steve, you *are* fascinating, like a dynamo, or something like that. You're strong and you're ruthless, I should think, and you're direct. And you're self-confident. Even self-sufficient, I suppose."

"But what do I lack?"

"I haven't noticed you lacked anything. Of course, I don't know you as—"

Beck said swiftly, "You know me as well as anyone. If you were going to change me, Marcy, what would you change?"

"I don't know. I don't know what the word would be. Perhaps if you had a little bit more—oh, call it tenderness, if you like—"

"Like Eddie Cortes, for example?" He took a drink.

Marcy drew back a little way from the table. Her young mouth pressed together. Then she said, "You have been making nasty little cracks about Eddie all evening. Very well, like Eddie Cortes, for example, if you want to bring personalities into it. Steve, what's the matter with you tonight?"

"There's nothing the matter with me tonight. I merely wanted to find out what it was that made Eddie Cortes a better dancer with you than I am. It's tenderness."

"Have you been spying on me, by any chance?"

"No, I haven't. That was just accident, pure chance. And it was just pure chance that I found out how bad your cold was yesterday."

"So that's what's bothering you!" She tossed her hair defiantly. "All right, I stood you up last night. I did it because I wanted to go out with Eddie and I fibbed to you because I didn't want to hurt your feelings."

"Thanks for being so kind, so tender and kind."

"I felt bad about it and that's why I called you today, to make it up to you tonight but instead you've been just miserable all evening." Suddenly Marcy's anger left her and she reached across the table, pleading for his hand with hers. "And I'm being miserable, too. I'm sorry, Steve. Let's not quarrel. Don't be jealous, please."

Beck rotated the ice cube and said doggedly, "It's not as simple as jealousy, Marcy. I don't think it is. It's more that I can't let you get mixed up with a guy like Cortes—"

"Oh, can't you, really?" she cut in icily. "And what about Eddie doesn't meet your approval?"

"I'd rather not say, specifically."

"Do. I'd forgotten my friends had to pass your tests."

"Please, Marcy. Won't you take my word for it that Cortes isn't a person you can trust?"

She looked amazed while she laughed. "That's splendid, coming from you, Steve. Just splendid. Let me tell you, I happen to *know* I can trust Eddie a lot further than I could ever trust you. It's possible to *know* Eddie, you see. He's very different from you."

Leda Garland said, "Mind if I join you interesting people?" She set her binoculars on the table and stood there at Beck's elbow. She had been drinking enough to make her smile a reckless one.

Beck got up slowly, trying to read her eyes, and said, "Why, no, Leda. Please sit down." He got a third chair and Leda took his. She let her fur jacket drift down behind her and her beautiful shoulders were bold above the white blouse.

She asked Beck, "Aren't you going to introduce us, darling?"

"Miss Everett, Mrs. Garland. Marcy, Leda."

The pink anger hadn't left Marcy's face and her eyes were round with surprise at the interloper.

Leda sipped at Beck's drink and batted her lashes at Marcy over the glass. "Miss Everett, is it? I'm frankly a little surprised. I was sure you'd be somebody's wife, since Steve is an admirer of proficiency. You told me that yourself, Steve."

Marcy said, "Oh?"

Beck said, "This is hardly the place to talk like that, Leda."

"It's quite a wonderful place. Here we are, all members of the same cozy little club and who could I offend? Not Miss Everett, surely. How old are you, Miss Everett? Nineteen? Twenty? Steve, I'm ashamed of you! Really, the youngster's hardly had a chance to grow up and here you've caught her and smudged her like the rest of us."

Beck said sharply, "Leda, quit it. You're wrong. We'll settle this later."

"Oh, won't we, darling!" she crooned. She leaned her model's shoulders toward Marcy confidentially. "Tell me how it came about, youngster. When did he get your charming little buckle—"

He caught Leda's wrist. He was afraid she would touch Marcy.

She said, "Now slap me, too, Steve. You know how I love that."

Beck took his hand away. All three of them watched the marks appear on the creamy skin of Leda's wrist. She said, "Just another of those things you lie about to your husband in the morning. You get rather proficient at that, too." Leda's laugh was blurred and her hand knocked against the binoculars. "Oh, yes, I've been out watching the dogs, the dirty dogs. Isn't it one hell of a shame that I happen to be in love with a dirty dog?"

"Leda, go on home. Dominic's around somewhere and so are lots of others."

"Go on home, he says," she repeated for Marcy. "He means, go on home before your husband misses you and comes gunning for Mr. Beck. He almost came the other night, didn't he, Steve? The night we were at The Natchez. Oh, that's right!" she laughed again. "I forgot. We were all there, weren't we?"

Marcy sat still and pale, looking at Beck, while the slow tears started down her face.

Beck said to Leda, "You're only embarrassing all of us. You're not solving a thing."

"I am, I am." She finished his drink and swayed toward him. "This is the place and time to be frank, my darling. I've got you in just a hell of a position, did you ever stop to think about it? I never did until I suspected you were playing around."

Marcy tried to say, "Let me clear up one thing—"

"Wipe your nose, youngster," Leda said carelessly. "Steve, you're tied up nicely. You can't do a thing unless I let you. You come back and be a good little man or all hell will break loose. You know exactly what I mean even if Miss Everett doesn't."

In the silence, the orchestra seemed to blare like the end of the world. Beck whispered, "I can't stand threats, Leda."

"So you've told me, my strong darling." She stroked his cheek and dropped her hand to caress her own shoulders. "But this time what does it matter whether you can stand them or not? I don't have anything to lose. But, oh, you do."

She stood up and hung onto her jacket by one sleeve. "I don't expect to be seeing you again, Miss Everett. Don't anybody get up. You wanted me to go. Now I'm going." She swept her binoculars off the table into Beck's lap. "Bring me my glasses tomorrow, Steve."

The order was confident, almost contemptuous. Leda looked down on him and then she strolled away toward the door, letting the jacket drag behind her.

He couldn't make himself look at Marcy. Sickened, he stared down at the tablecloth. He heard her moving about, getting her handkerchief out of her purse, the click after she had put it back. He took the binoculars out of his lap and put them on the table, trying to set them down noiselessly.

Marcy said, "I'm going now, Steve. Goodbye."

Then he had to look up at her calm face. And he asked stupidly, "Where?"

"Home. I want a cold shower or something. Please don't bother with any explanations."

"Marcy—"

"Please!"

"I'll drive you back."

"No. I'd rather get a cab outside." He didn't know how she managed to smile so sweetly and cruelly. "Don't worry about me any more, Steve. I'll pick a cab driver I can trust."

She left.

Beck sat at the empty table. After a while the waiter came up, and asked about two more drinks. Beck paid the check and started out. He was nearly to the door when he stopped, turned, and, smiling bleakly, came back for the binoculars.

The last race was winding up and headlights were flashing across the parking lot. Beck walked along the row where he had left his Buick, reached the end and then turned back. After a moment, he stood still and let the idea sink in.

There was only an empty rectangle of gravel where his Buick should have been. His car had been stolen. The trap had sprung.

Beck stood there staring at the empty parking space. Now that theory was fact, he began to see the joke. He hadn't let himself see it before, since his brain was under strict control and he could keep Marcy in one part and her father in another. But here it was, summed up in an empty space of gravel and funny as hell. Somehow he had to regain Marcy because he had to have her. Yet here was her father as good as dead because that was his job. Oh, he was doing his job very well. He laughed shortly and even to his own ears it sounded more like a sob.

24

Tuesday, May 24, 12:15 a.m.

The Mexican cab dropped him off at Charley the Cheat's used car lot on lower Broadway a little after midnight. Beck woke up Speed and got the keys to the souped-up Ford station wagon that was always available.

He sat in the car a few minutes before starting it. Across the street, through the steamy window of an all-night hamburger joint, he could see the deadly little figure of Joe Zuaben, hunched over a mug of coffee.

Beck thought, *I can walk across Broadway, twenty yards, and give him the orders right now. I have the power.* There was no reason to wait or compromise but he did. He had to see Marcy again before he ever did anything else, tell her what he had planned to tell her. Tell her what he was truly like.

He drove out Kettner to Five Points and then up the hill to the Everett house. Marcy's bedroom light went out as he pulled up across the street. Beck saw that happen before he noticed the taxi idling in front of the house. He stayed in the station wagon and waited.

In a moment, Marcy trotted down her front steps wearing a coat. She got in the taxi and gave an address and was taken away. She didn't glance in Beck's direction.

He swung the station wagon around after her. The taxi was easy to follow, down to Pacific Highway and back through downtown. Beck's face grew stonier as the taxi climbed into the Golden Hill neighborhood and stopped in front of a flat eight-unit court. He stopped a half block behind. As if through a haze, he watched the taxi drive off and Marcy's silhouette go up the walk between the little stucco bungalows. Swinging in one hand was the shape of an overnight bag.

Beck stared at the dark ahead long after she had disappeared. He realized he had to quiet himself down. The station wagon engine was still running. He turned his attention to the ordinary mechanical things. He flipped off the ignition switch so that the engine stopped and turned the key and put it carefully in his pocket. He twisted the headlights off. He shoved down the door handle so the door would open and he got out on the curb. Finally, he started walking. He was walking more steadily as he turned up the sidewalk between the houses of the court.

Eddie Cortes' olive face was a blur of surprise through the screen door. "Well, Steve," he said first. He unhooked the screen and grinned. "Taking up insomnia, boy?"

Beck didn't say anything. He walked into the living room and looked it over.

He had been here before, drinking, kidding around. The place hadn't changed. Cortes had it furnished in rich soft things, a little gaudy, a little effeminate. Cortes was a ladies' man.

Beck inspected the room. The bedroom door was closed. He inspected Cortes, his black too-long hair and his handsome wolfish teeth. He had a white silk robe, expensively made, on over his pajamas. Cortes asked, "Something going on? You look a little sick."

"I'm fine. Nice place you got here."

"You talk like you'd never seen it before. What's on your mind, Steve? Got time for a little nightcap?"

Beck said, "No. I'm here to take Marcy home."

Cortes closed his lips over his teeth. He got his eyes away from Beck's and glanced around the room himself. "What gave you the idea she'd be here, anyway? Thanks for the compliment, chum, but—"

"She's here," Beck stated.

"Oh, you're out of your head. What've you been drinking, tell me that?"

They faced each other in the center of the little room, neither smiling, though their voices still were pleasant.

"Indeed?" said Beck. "Let's see about it, then." He took one step toward the bedroom door and Cortes caught his arm. Beck sagged toward him, lashed out and twisted the taller man across the room.

When he turned again to the door it was open. Marcy stood there, arms straight down, her body taut under the lacy modest-immodest negligee she had worn that night in her kitchen. Her hating voice said, "Is this what you want?"

Beck said, "Get your clothes together. Put on your coat. We're going home."

"Listen, Steve," Cortes said, "you might dish out your orders most of the time but this is where it stops. Right here. This isn't business. You better get out of here."

"Shut up. Put on your coat, Marcy."

"I'm not going to. After all, I've a free will, Steve. I'm staying here."

"Are you coming or do I have to carry you?"

Cortes said, "Don't let him scare you with that talk, Marcy. He doesn't dare touch you and he damn well knows it."

"Oh, I'm not afraid, Eddie." Her eyes burned at Beck.

"Steve, don't you know why I came to Eddie tonight? Don't you know why? You sent me. Learning what you were like inside made me see how much I cared for him. You made up my mind, Steve, I came because of you, because I had to get the filthy taste out of my mouth."

Beck slapped her. The sound cracked through the small room. Marcy's mouth fell open as far as it could. His fingers had left a dead white spot across her cheek. Uncertainly, she began to put her hand up there and then she seemed to forget. Her eyes flickered blankly from Cortes to Beck and back.

Nobody moved. Beck growled, "Get your coat!"

Marcy began to shake with crying as she turned and stumbled into the bedroom.

Beck said softly, "Eddie, I could kill you."

"You can't stand to lose, can you?" said Cortes. He had opened a drawer in an end table. His hand slipped in and slipped out again with a heavy pocket knife. The blade popped out.

Cortes spoke between his teeth, "I think you getter get it through your thick head that this time you are losing. As long as Marcy wants to stay, she's staying."

Beck put his left forearm up vertically before his chest, on guard. He said, "I've got no gun, Eddie. I don't need one. If you want to try to stop me, go ahead. Come on."

"She's staying."

"I'm not one of your tramps you can scare just by waving that knife around. I've broken guys in two that tried that stuff. You can try it if you like but you won't. You're not the type. No greasy coward who cuts up women is the type. Come on."

Cortes breathed hard. "Maybe you're wrong for once. You're going to be wrong sometime, you know."

"You're talking too much, Eddie. You know all I have to do is pick up that phone and you'll go the way Hervey Isham went. I can fix that up. I don't have to give any reasons, all I have to do is say so."

They stared at each other then Beck snorted and looked into the bedroom. Marcy was huddled on the far corner of the soft bed. Beck said, "Tell her, Eddie."

Cortes sighed. His mouth twitched as he closed the knife and put it back in the drawer and closed the drawer. He went as far as the bedroom and said to Marcy, "Honey, I guess you'd better go home with him."

She choked, "No, no, Eddie! I don't want to!"

"It'll save trouble for everybody all around, Marcy. Please, honey."

After a while, she stirred dully and got up. She collected her things in a little pile and put them in her overnight bag. She put on her coat over her negligee and fumbled through the buttoning of it, keeping her streaked face away from Beck. Finally, she came out into the living room and stood before Cortes helplessly. They kissed and murmured back and forth and said good night.

Beck had her go out the door first. Cortes had his fists jammed in his robe pockets and looked pale and shameful. Beck murmured, "You're right, Eddie, I'm not a nice loser." He went out and followed Marcy down the walk.

25

Tuesday, May 24, 12:45 a.m.

They didn't speak for some time after driving away from Cortes' place. Marcy looked at the windshield of the station wagon and didn't wipe off her face although she didn't cry any more. She didn't seem to notice he was driving a different car. Beck glanced anxiously at her now and then, at her defiant dreaming profile or at the incongruous hem of her negligee extending beyond her coat.

Finally he muttered, "Marcy...."

She regarded him.

He said, "I'm sorry I hit you. I didn't mean to do that; it just happened. It was the last thing I ever wanted to do."

Her voice was clear and controlled and he felt in some way she had the advantage of him. Somehow he was at her mercy. She said, "That was the smallest part of it. You couldn't stand being hurt, having anything said against you. I meant to hurt you. I'm glad I could use the truth doing it."

"All I'm glad about is that you stopped crying. It was killing me to see you cry. You're not the type for crying. Neither of us are."

"No, please don't lump us together, Steve. We haven't anything in common."

"We have, Marcy!"

"No." They cruised down Broadway, through deserted downtown. Suddenly, he wished she'd go back to staring at the windshield instead of keeping her solemn bitter eyes on him. She said, "God's own vicar on earth. In complete charge. Well, I don't care to be regulated."

"This is going to sound funny to you, Marcy, but don't laugh, please. I'm really doing this for your own good."

"I won't laugh."

"You still don't understand."

"Yes, I do. I understand you. But the rotten things you've done tonight you did all for your own good. You have to make things suit you, yourself. Can't you understand that you're constitutionally incapable of doing anything for anyone else? Steve Beck is the one person in the whole wide world you give a damn about." She was talking a little faster now and he hoped that was a good sign. He had so much to tell her, to make right.

"Oh, that's not true, Marcy."

"It is. Jealousy was why you followed me tonight, nasty sneaking little jealousy. You can't stand my escaping from you. Well, you've lost me, or rather you never had me. Oh, not that I think I'm so much worth having but whatever it is human beings have to offer one another, I could never have that for you. I could never mean anything to you."

"That's not true."

"Perhaps it isn't. Then I could never mean anything more to you than an article, say. I'd be just another article to swell that ludicrous conceit of yours."

"At least you admit I want you."

"Yes, you want me," she said wearily. "Oh, I'm sorry if I ever gave you any ideas, you'll never know how sorry and disgusted I am. I thought you'd be fun to play with. That was my silly foolish cheap way of being worldly. I'm so glad I was snapped out of it because I want to live so much more than that."

"Marcy, I want you more than anything I've ever wanted."

"We're not talking about the same things. You'll never see."

They drove down Kettner, passing from streetlight to streetlight and the only other lights were their own. It was like reliving the same emotion over and over.

Beck's face burned as he searched his knowledge for ways to make her understand but he held himself in check. He inquired, "Do you think you've fallen for Cortes?"

"Can't you put it more crudely?"

"Do you think you've fallen in love with Cortes?"

"I went to him tonight. Apparently you can picture me doing that whether I loved him or not."

"I didn't mean it that way. I've just got to be sure of the facts, how you feel."

"You believe so much in facts, don't you? I'm a research project to be computed. Steve, facts change where ideals don't. I like to consider my feelings as something better than a page of your damned facts." Beck could feel her watching him as she slipped farther and farther away. Marcy said, "I love Eddie deeply. There aren't any facts to explain why. I couldn't believe in it myself at first but he feels the same way. You'll have to kill me to keep me away from him."

"I notice he gave you up tonight with something less than a struggle."

She said, "You can't shame him for me. He was afraid for me, not for himself. I thought what he did tonight was wonderful. Being in love means sacrifice. Eddie sacrificed some of his pride for me tonight, something you could never do."

Beck snorted. He suddenly pulled the station wagon over to the curb and braked it.

"What do we go through now?" Marcy asked coldly.

"I'm going to tell you some facts I thought I could save you the trouble of hearing. You don't know one thing about that oily bastard, Marcy. He's sucked you in with that professional charm of his. He's just playing with you until he breaks that soft body and that clean innocent mind of yours. No, let me finish. Your tender gentleman Eddie Cortes has a prison record, two years of San Quentin. He's on parole right now. Do you know what he was before he went to prison? He was a lousy pimp, making girls fall in love with him and dirtying them and having them go out and work for him. Do you know why he got that jolt of prison? One of his girls tried to hold out part of her five bucks a throw or twenty bucks a night or whatever he was marketing her for. Eddie cut her face up with his knife."

She only chuckled scornfully. "Oh, Steve! Why do you want to make a pitiful little fool of yourself with lies like that? I know what Eddie's like and you can't degrade him."

Beck stared at her calm enemy face incredulously.

Then Marcy shook her head at him, mocking his expression, and commenced laughing at him. She said, "I hope you will always be very happy with yourself."

His blister of anger burst. Beck grabbed her and pulled her over close and forced her back across the front seat. He heard himself shouting down at her frightened face, "Damn you, I love you!" He ran his mouth over her face and his strong hands over her body.

Then he discovered she was not struggling at all. He raised himself a little away from her and she stared up at him and shook her head again, denying him. Marcy whispered, "Go ahead, have things your way. But you can't change anything any more, than you can change yourself. Go ahead. You know I can't fight back. Use all the power you can. I understand you, that you don't know anything else."

"You don't know me, Marcy," he pleaded. "I love you. I want you. I'll do anything for you. Don't leave me alone."

"You're too late. You don't know anything but force. Use it, Steve. You don't know anything about me or any other people, that's why I can almost feel sorry for you. But then you're not people, you're scarcely human, so how could you know anything? Go ahead and make it up to your pride now. But I'm thinking of Eddie and wishing it were Eddie and—"

"Shut up!" Then he wiped his forehead as if she had struck him and said again, dully, "I love you. I won't hurt you." He looked out of the curbside window and they were parked by a scabby vacant lot. It scared him, it was such an unclean hopeless place, nothing like the setting he had planned for.

He let her sit up, she put herself in order and he stomped on the starter. With the engine beat, the anger throbbed in him deeper than before. They drove on.

Beck said to the empty street ahead, "You've been making talk about sacrifice. That's kind of funny because I've been thinking about that same idea all evening."

"No, you haven't."

"Listen to me, Marcy."

"What do you intend to do? Give up that Mrs. Garland of yours?"

"Listen to me! Suppose I had the power to hurt you very much. Suppose I had to hurt you or lose everything I've had up till now, my job, my ambitions—"

"Steve!" Marcy's hands clenched in her lap and she leaned toward him. "Steve, if you do anything to harm Eddie, I'll kill you! Believe me, I'll kill you, I'll find a way!"

He shook his head to clear it. The station wagon was purring up the slope into Mission Hills. "You won't try, you won't help me," he said, tired. "No, it isn't Cortes I'm talking about. I've been tossing a coin in my head all night. One side, all I've got. The other side, you, Marcy."

"Oh, no," she said. "You can't scare me with that kind of force, either. I imagine you're lying again." He stopped the station wagon in front of her house. He didn't open her door for her but he didn't stop her from opening it. She slid out of the car and said back to him, "Besides that coin will come up whatever way is best for Steve Beck. Depend on that."

She turned toward the house, not bothering to say good night or goodbye. Beck thought, *No, it isn't that kind of coin.*

Then the porch light flashed on and Everett came out on the porch, dressed except for his coat. His worried voice said, "Marcy! Where have you been!"

Marcy let her little overnight bag fall to the walk. She ran like a child up onto the porch. "Oh daddy!" she wailed and let his arms shelter her.

Everett didn't even look down at the station wagon or Beck. He stroked his daughter's hair and murmured to her.

Beck could hear her sobbing and he couldn't stand that or seeing them up there together. He saw Everett as if over the sights of a gun. He saw him as a dead man. He saw Marcy already mourning. Mourning and hating.

He couldn't stay there any longer and watch them together. He stepped on the gas and raced away recklessly. He turned corners at random, heading nowhere. He drove faster and faster because he was running away.

26

Tuesday, May 24, 10:00 a.m.

Beck walked out of the bright May morning into the lobby of the Southwest Towers Athletic Club. He had been driving the station wagon around all night. He was unshaven and his eyes were bloodshot and his throat felt raw from the night air.

He went automatically to the desk to get his mail. It was only another report from the Driscoll Agency in L. A. on Sid Dominic and family. He stuck it in his pocket unread and decided he'd better shut off those useless reports or they'd keep coming to the end of time now that he's started them coming.

Henry the clerk looked curiously at Leda's binoculars swinging in Beck's fist and at his drawn face and grinned. The grin meant quite-a-night. Henry said, "I just finished taking a telephone message for you, Mr. Beck."

"Okay."

"About your car, Mr. Beck. Apparently it was stolen last night or I suppose you know. At any rate, the police have it impounded down at headquarters. The officer who called supposed that you had been down to Tijuana and some sailor took it to get back across the border. At any rate, the police found it deserted in Palm City early this morning and brought it in."

"Sure," Beck said. "Thank you." He turned away.

"It was a Lieutenant Richards who called. Of the traffic detail, I suppose." Beck looked at him. "No, he's not of the traffic detail."

"Oh. He spoke as if he was an old friend of yours. He said to be sure to drop in and see him when you came down to pick up the car and you could have a chat."

"Yeah. Send one of your club boys down to get the car, will you, Henry? I got some sleep to catch up on. Here's the key."

"Very well, Mr. Beck."

Beck went up to his suite and directly to the little bar and took a long drink out of the first bottle. Then he stumbled into the bedroom and flopped on the bed. He closed his eyes. He got up immediately and put the binoculars on the bureau next to Marcy's belt buckle. He sneered at them side by side and at his tired face in the mirror. He thought he'd better clean up and get to work. No time to sleep, after all. This was Tuesday and there were some things on his schedule for Tuesday, various jobs to take care of for Pat Garland's circle. At the moment, he couldn't recall any of them but there was always something to do.

Trying to remember, he swore dully. He was tired of thinking. To hell with work and to hell with Pat Garland's circle. He fell across the bed again and wrapped his head in his arms.

The telephone buzzed. Beck swore at it but it didn't stop buzzing. He shoved himself up finally and plodded out to answer it.

Dan Pelletreau hacked out a cigarette cough and then whispered, "Hello, I wanted to—"

"For God's sake, talk out loud!" Beck snapped. "I can't hear a goddam word!"

Pelletreau nervously raised his voice a little. "I don't dare talk very loud. I'm in a phone booth right here in headquarters. I thought I better call you. Something's going on down here. I don't know what."

"Okay, Dan. You're doing fine. Shoot it to me quick."

"Well, I don't know much except that Richards—that's the vice squad Richards—has been locked up with the chief all morning. And they just sent through an order to put a couple of the colored patrolmen in plain clothes. Mean anything to you?"

Beck was standing over the phone alertly now, eyes narrowed. "It means quite a bit. And Richards wanted to see me, get me out of the way...."

"Huh?"

"Never mind. You won't be forgotten for this, Dan."

"I just hope nobody finds out where you—"

Beck hung up. He took another swift drink out of the brandy bottle and ran for the elevator. He walked fast across the lobby and out into the sunlight, heading for the station wagon across the street. He didn't have much time on this job.

He almost didn't see the flashy convertible sedan waiting at the curb, its top folded down as always. Behind the wheel was a coarse gray face with an indented nose. It was Paul Moon and the sun shone prettily on his blond hair. Moon called, "Oh, Steve."

Beck paused in the gutter. "Say, I'm in a rush on some big business, Paul. I can't talk to you now."

"That won't do," Moon objected mildly. "I'm sorry but it's going to be now."

And Beck felt the blunt point shoving hard at his spine. He turned his head slowly. Joe Zuaben stood close behind him, his eyes like a reptile's.

Moon reached across and opened the curbside rear door. Beck let the unseen gun guide him over to it. The Filipino slid in after him warily and shifted the gun from Beck's spine to his kidney.

They drove away, no one speaking. Besides Beck and Zuaben on the back seat there sat also a large blue Persian cat which regarded them aloofly. After a block or so, the cat leaped over into the front seat and coiled against Moon's thigh.

Beck chuckled. "How is it they trust you, Paul?"

"I feed them well. This particular specimen has a longer pedigree than any of us. His first name's Darius. Darius, you know, was king of—"

"I've read a book, thanks."

Zuaben ground the gun into Beck's side and snarled, "Don't be cute, smart bastard."

Beck twisted his mouth at him and looked down to where the gun was and snickered at it. Zuaben cursed him.

Moon said, never turning his head, "Don't be angry, Joe."

Zuaben calmed down. "Okay."

He made little jabs into Beck's flesh with the gun. Beck sat there and took it. He could wait. He wasn't going to take a chance on getting shot. The Filipino's weapon was a palmgun which he'd made himself. Only an inch of .32 barrel protruded between his two middle fingers. The rest of the gun was balled in his brown fist, out of sight. No butt, just a disc cylinder of seven bullets and a squeeze lever instead of a trigger; it was an assassin's weapon.

From downtown, Moon sped silently up through Golden Hill and out into ramshackle gully country. This was still within the city but most of the homes lay a mile away on either side and hadn't closed in on this rougher ground yet.

Finally Beck told Zuaben, "Joe, relax on that toy. I'm ticklish."

The Filipino glared but kept his mouth shut.

Beck said, "Relax or I'll spit on you, like that girl the other night."

Zuaben hissed, "Just too bad you're not running things any more."

Beck said to Moon, "I've been waiting for somebody to come right out and say that."

"Well, I suppose that's what it comes down to, Steve," Paul Moon admitted reflectively. "I'm taking over the circle as of now. Pat Garland is out and I'm in. Yes, that's about it."

"It sounds splendid."

"Oh, don't laugh at it, Steve. The idea's a good one for you to think over. Big Pat has really been out of things for some time but I'm the only person who had brains enough to see it. Pat's been depending too much on handshakes and what he considers charm. He's been going too slow this last year, acting too much like a damn society leader or something. I intend to give this town a real shaking up, actually put the screws on. Pat's been pretty halfway about rough stuff. Oh, perhaps he was tough enough in his time but you've been doing all his thinking for him and don't try to tell me different."

"Paul, tell me something. Is this a sample of your thinking? Entertainment's big business. You think these old-fashioned thoughts and you won't last ten minutes."

"You amuse me. I have some help from Detroit on its way. Hell may pop slightly but Garland has already slipped. You know that, Steve, you're clever. Orville Kyle's fed up with the setup and Sid Dominic has promised to bring him in. There's one example."

"I didn't think Dominic had the guts to follow through."

"Oh, he's smart like you. Then, Charley Holsclaw's going to be left out along with Big Pat. Dear old Charley's back in Chicago for at least another week and if he's smart he'll stay there. He's got nothing left to come back to. Also, the two Tarrants didn't like Pat dumping Hervey Isham. Isham—" Moon laughed.

Beck said, "I begin to see the light about something."

"That's right. The night you came after poor Isham. I had invited him down to the warehouse to talk over this very matter. That's the closest I've come to trouble with my arrangements yet. But I imagine you had him too scared to think of giving me away."

"You're a sweet kid."

"Anyway, the Tarrants will join me, which takes care of the big operations. The little stuff, like the lotteries, can't help but come along. I'll shove some of Garland's piddling stuff like those theaters and expand in ways he's been scared to, dope and the girl racket, for instance. After all, this is a border town and we can get away with murder. We can move right on up the coast after a while."

Beck smiled and nodded, "You've forgotten J. John Everett."

"Oh, that's up to him. We can always use a lawyer."

"So that narrows it down to me, doesn't it?"

"I'm two minds about you, Steve," Moon confessed. "You've been Garland's pet boy all along. But I could use you. That's why I thought we ought to get together for a small talk."

Beck looked out at the countryside. "Long way around to get to the warehouse."

Moon glanced swiftly for the first time, a look of mock surprise. "What do you know about that, Joe? I got so interested discussing this with Steve I forgot where we were going. Well, we can talk out here, too, I suppose."

"Yeah," said Zuaben.

"Let's keep at it," Beck suggested. "You may have the Tarrants and Kyle and Holsclaw's setup all wrapped in pink ribbon, Paul. But you know Pat Garland has the clamps on you as long as he has the account books. Those books are handy things to have. You can send any individual or the whole damn circle to prison with the books, if you care for extreme measures. And without them, you don't know exactly who, where or how much. Prima donnas like Kyle and the Tarrants aren't going to listen to just talk."

Moon didn't answer. He turned the convertible off the pavement onto a narrow dirt road, past a sign that said CITY DUMP. They jounced down the dirt road into a dead-end canyon. Moon stopped the car at the bottom and shut off the engine and got out. The blue cat followed him, stepped about fastidiously and then bounded back onto the front seat. On three sides, piles of refuse rose like mountains, glass and tin and automobile remains and waste paper mostly, but with a thousand other castoffs mixed in, the debris of the city.

Moon said, "Get out and stretch your legs, Steve."

"Don't mind if I do."

Zuaben backed out first, keeping his little gun ready. His heel caught on a length of rusty chain and he nearly fell.

Beck laughed at him again.

"That's all right, Joe," Moon said softly.

Beck got down and faced them. He sized up the situation. They were isolated, out of sight of the main road. He knew Moon seldom carried a gun and he didn't seem to have one today. But Zuaben did and he was good at it.

Moon said, "Steve, you're right. I need those books."

"Don't ask me for them. They're Garland's books."

"You know where they are."

"I suppose I do."

"I know you do. I've found out that Garland keeps them at his house."

"Go get them, Paul."

"But Garland's gotten nervous lately. He's moved them somewhere. Where?"

"If you know so much, well?"

Seriously, Moon told him, "Don't waste my time, Steve. I'd rather you'd cooperate of your own free will."

Beck stopped smiling at him. He said, "Let's stop acting silly. You wouldn't have brought me out to this godforsaken place if you really intended to bargain with me. I've got important business in town and you can save your neck by taking me back now. You might as well save your talk, too."

"Come here, Steve."

Beck looked at Zuaben's gun and at Moon's thoughtful face. He shrugged and stepped away from the car, one step toward Moon.

Moon kicked him in the groin. Beck gasped and tried to grin again. Then the littered ground got closer in his agony and he felt Moon's knee catch him in the face on the way down. He bounced against the fender and rolled down into the dust.

Above, he could hear Zuaben swear at him rhythmically in time with the foot he swung against his body.

He heard Moon murmur, "Easy does it, Joe."

Moon dragged him erect and leaned him against the car again. Beck shook his head to make the dark go away.

Moon asked, "Where are the books, Steve?"

Beck managed to spit out, "See you in hell." Moon knocked the remaining wind out of his belly. Zuaben grabbed his throat from behind and they both bent him backward until his cheek was against the hot metal of the radiator, his head upside down. Beck bit his lip until the blood ran down into his eyes. He couldn't find any strength to struggle.

He got picked up again. He hardly felt Moon sock him where the hot steel had scorched his face. He lay on the ground and tried to let the dirt and salt blood drool out of his mouth but he couldn't even do that.

Then Beck found himself propped up against a car wheel, sitting in the dust. Moon asked, "Can you hear me?"

He nodded by letting his head fall forward.

Moon asked, "See this?"

Beck focused, taking all the rest they would allow him. He saw what Moon had in his hand. It was a beer bottle he'd picked out of the mountain of trash and broken off so the neck was a handle to a rake of sharp glass.

He nodded again, saving his wind.

Moon ground the sharp end into Beck's stomach, cutting his sweater and shirt and scratching his skin. "Understand, Steve? If you got careless, you could blind a man with this thing. You could put out his eyes for good. Now, would you like to spend the rest of your life selling pencils on a corner somewhere? Not a clever boy like you, surely."

Beck looked at him and Moon brought the jagged glass up to eye level, rested it against his nose. "You decide, Steve."

Beck said hoarsely, "Okay, Paul. You win. Let me rest."

They gave him another minute. Moon still played with the broken bottle. He asked, "Where are the books?"

"Lakeside."

"Where in Lakeside?"

"Ranch out there," Beck's breath sawed in and out. "Called Happy Vale Ranch. Friend of Pat's."

"How do I get there?"

"Out the main drag, couple blocks past the bridge. Road there that turns off to the left. Down that a mile or so—"

"Wait a minute," Moon commanded. "I've lost you. Start again with a couple blocks past the bridge."

"Hell, I'll draw you a map. Saves wind." He slipped forward on his hands and knees and began to trace a map in the dust. "Here's the road into Lakeside. Here's the town here. The road turns like this."

Both Zuaben and Moon bent over him, studying the crooked lines his forefinger traced.

"Okay. I know the town," said Moon. "Get to the important part."

"Then here's the bridge. Off over here is a hill. The road winds around past the bridge over to this little hill." Beck's finger slowly neared the length of chain the Filipino had stumbled on. Part of it was buried and he wondered how long it would be. He hitched up his knees a little more under him.

Beck said, "Then here's a grove of pepper trees and a fork in the road. You take the fork to the right." His finger touched the first ling of the chain. His hand leaned on it, closed.

Moon was opening his mouth for a question as Beck leaped up and whirled. Beck saw the two faces close together. Moon's mouth hung open stupidly and Zuaben's eyes were wide and blank.

The chain, four feet of it, made a whistling sound through the air. It reached the Filipino's head first and bent savagely around it with another sound. The free end flew against Paul Moon's face as he tried to come forward.

Before Beck's arm had completed its swing, the whole thing was over and he was the only one standing. He let the chain slip out of his fist and sail on into the dump heap.

Zuaben's hat had been knocked over there. Zuaben himself lay unmoving, face down in a spreading puddle.

Moon was down in the dirt beside him but he writhed and rolled over and over. He was screaming on one note and not very loudly. His fingers tore frantically at his eyes.

Beck leaned back against the side of the convertible, gasping, watching dully. Moon stopped rolling finally and making the noise. He lay collapsed in unhuman repose, his dead hands still tending his face. Beck felt no relief, no reaction but weariness. It was as if the two men on the ground had stepped too near a machine and had been dragged into it. There were no emotional consequences for the machine.

When something moved behind him, Beck looked around. The big blue Persian made a dainty leap down to the dust and stood there attentively, head thrust forward, the nose twitching at the scent of blood.

27

Tuesday, May 24, 11:00 a.m.

He took Paul Moon's convertible and backed out onto the main road and raced back toward downtown. Beck thought of Pelletreau's information and how he'd have to hurry to act on it. Thinking that way, he didn't ache so much.

He drove in behind the first filling station he came to and parked by the rest-room door. He got inside without the attendant getting a good look at him. Hastily, Beck began to repair himself. The water stung. In five minutes, with the blood and dust washed away, his face didn't look so bad. The burn on his cheek was tight and smooth and he still needed a shave but he could pass in-spection. He brushed off his clothes and buttoned his coat over where his sweater and shirt had been ripped by the beer bottle.

In his right-hand coat pocket was the palmgun he had taken from Joe Zuaben's limp fingers. Except for that, Beck had paid no more attention to the two men he had cut down. He had wanted the gun just in case.

He sped the convertible into the city proper, steered it down Market Street to the busy second-rate district dominated by the Gorman Hotel. The hotel was a four-story brick building with patched awnings. Beck drove around its corner twice, studying the parked cars and the loiterers near the entrance. He found himself a parking space not far from the iron fire escape that rambled down the drab side of the hotel.

Casually, Beck sauntered to the corner, lit a cigarette and looked over the passersby. Then he went on into the lobby. A cluster of three Negroes in the wide doorway gave him surprised glances and then spoke low among them-selves. One of them laughed musically.

Beck strode up to the desk, conscious of looks from the men and women sit-ting around the lobby. The clerk was lanky, well dressed and the color of weak cocoa. Beck asked him, "Mr. Drew?"

The Negro nodded.

Beck said softly, "I want to see the woman in 319."

Drew inspected him, matching him with Garland's description. He smiled and said, "All right, Mr. Beck. Shall I ring Mrs. Johnson or do you want to go right on up?"

"She's expecting me, thanks." The elevator was clanking somewhere above so Beck took the stairs. Walking up two flights gave him time to remember his physical being; his muscles were beginning to stiffen from the beating and lack of sleep. The third-floor corridor was as plain as any middle class hotel.

319 was midway down.

When he knocked, Augusta Norley said nervously, "Who is it?"

Beck put his head close to the panel. "It's all right, Gusta. It's Steve."

She let him in quickly and locked and bolted the door again. The little old woman looked worn out. She was fully dressed in a blue suit that made her hair whiter than ever. Even her harsh laugh was jittery. She asked, "Who got at your face? Not that you don't deserve it."

"Fell asleep in the oven." Beck looked around at the fading wallpaper and the furniture. "Not such a bad place."

"Okay."

"What's in there?" Beck indicated the closed door.

"Bedroom and the john."

"Trust Pat to get a suite, even at the Gorman." Beck watched Gusta shuffle aimlessly around the room. "Something bothering you, honey?"

She snapped, "How'd you like being cooped up here for four days?"

"You got a chance to catch up on your reading."

"I didn't bring that kind of books." Gusta kicked the suitcases that stood under the window. "This joint gives me the willies, honest to God, Steve."

"That's the idea, isn't it? We like to keep you in unexpected places. You're important."

"Sure, sure, but I still get the willies. Every time that clerk brings up a meal I can see him wondering just what I'm doing here. That gets you after a while."

Beck allowed himself a moment's rest in one of the chairs. "Is that all that's bothering you, Gusta?"

"Why—sure it is, Steve. What else?"

"Then let's see a big smile. I've come to take you away from all this."

She didn't stir. "You on the level?"

"Get your coat and calculator together. We're moving."

"Fine. That's swell, Steve. But maybe it isn't so smart moving out in the middle of the day like this. I mean, somebody might be watching the hotel—"

"Nobody's watching the hotel. Yet. I thought you wanted to go, Gusta."

"Oh, I do," she protested. "I was just trying to see all the angles, that's all." She hesitated. "I'll get my coat then."

Gusta went into the bedroom and closed the door. Beck moved swiftly over to the two suitcases and hefted them. Then he smiled and shrugged and sat down again. He was tired; he was seeing things that weren't there. He waited. From below came the constant mutter of traffic and an ice cream truck went by playing "Yankee Doodle."

The telephone rang.

Startled, Beck listened to the bell sound die away. Then he jumped up and stood over the instrument, frowning, while it rang again. He pulled the receiver up to his ear and said, "Yes?"

There was no answer. The other end hung up at once. Beck planted the receiver back in its cradle and his punished face grew colder.

He stalked to the door to the bedroom and said against it, "Gusta! That was your friends the cops. What do you suppose Pat will say when he finds you've tried to sell him out? What kind of bargain did you try to make with Richards. Or did you talk to Everett directly? Speak up, honey. The cops are slow as ever and I'm curious."

The old woman didn't answer.

Beck put his hand in his coat pocket and kicked open the door, dodging to one side. But the room was empty. He flung open the remaining doors, closet and bathroom. Augusta Norley's clothes still hung in the closet but she was gone.

The window was open, a warm breeze fluffing the curtain. Beck looked out at the fire escape that led down the outside wall to the street. He didn't see Gusta's white hair anywhere. She was gone for good now.

Beck swore and ran back into the living room. He grabbed up the heavy suitcases, hesitated as he considered the fire escape. No, too much chance of some passerby thinking he was a hotel thief and raising a yell. He pounded out into the corridor and down the way he had come, taking the steps three at a time, the suitcases banging against his legs.

28

Tuesday, May 24, 12:00 noon

The girl behind the counter hardly bothered to look at him. A quick glance at Beck's bus ticket and she selected two baggage checks. She wired them to the handles of the two suitcases, tore the tags on the perforated line and, using the stubs, transcribed the numbers in her register. A husky youngster came out of the luggage room, swung the suitcases down and carried them out of sight. Beck watched them go.

"Here you are, sir." The girl handed him the two stubs and the ticket. "They'll go straight through to Yuma and you can pick them up immediately upon the arrival of your bus."

"Thank you," Beck said. "What time does my bus leave, miss?"

"Six minutes." She smiled mechanically over his shoulder at the next man in line and Beck moved out of the way.

He bought a newspaper at the magazine stand and pretended to read it. He sat on a waiting bench and watched the minutes jerk by on the depot clock. The loudspeaker bawled the departure of the Arizona bus. Beck drifted with the crowd. He watched the passengers board and didn't see any faces to worry him. He saw the two familiar suitcases loaded into the luggage compartment and saw the porter lock the steel door over them.

The loudspeaker called again and finally the bus had gone, rumbling up First Avenue toward Highway 80. Beck folded the newspaper neatly and shoved it in the nearest trash receptacle. He drove Paul Moon's convertible uptown, parked it in front of the library and wiped away all traces of himself. He left the car there for the police to find. Then he walked slowly back to the Southwest Towers Athletic Club.

As soon as he had reached his rooms, he sagged in the big chair and phoned Pat Garland.

But it was Leda who answered. "You just missed him, Steve. Pat isn't here."

"When'll he be back?"

"Tonight, unfortunately, darling. He went up to Del Mar to talk to Orville Kyle."

Beck was dead silent so long she had to ask if he was still there. Then he said incredulously, "You mean Pat went to Kyle, after all? You're joking, Leda, he wouldn't do that. Kyle didn't call him or anything?"

"No, I don't think so. Pat just went. Why? Is something wrong?"

He slouched lower in the chair and said, "No, I guess not. I don't know."

"What time today are you bringing my glasses back to me?" she asked. When he grunted, her voice changed subtly. "I trust you haven't forgotten what I said last night. I meant it, Steve. I still mean it."

"Leda, I'm worn out. Let's not discuss it now, please."

"Let's do, though. You think I'm being a bitch, don't you, darling? I suppose I am but then you're hardly a gentleman, either, Steve. We're the same kind of animal and that's just why we belong together. I deserve some happiness, don't I? We'll be happy together, I know we will. We have been happy up till now, haven't we? Haven't we?"

"Yes," he said wearily. "Yes, Leda."

"That youngster of last night, she's *not* our kind. Would she ever understand you the way I do?"

"Leda, for God's sake, leave me alone!"

"No, no, precious darling, I'm not going to leave you alone. I want you, I have to have you, and I'm going to. Really, I'm only treating you the way you treat everyone. You don't show other people any mercy, Steve. You wouldn't show me any if I gave you half a chance. Would you, Steve?"

Beck rubbed his closed eyes. "No. No, we're alike."

The telephone chuckled in his ear. "That sounds more like it. So long as we understand each other. You get a good rest, Steve. You'd best not bring my glasses out this afternoon because I'm having bridge club this afternoon. But I'll expect to hear from you, see you, this evening. Say goodbye, darling. I love you."

"Goodbye."

"Goodbye, *darling!*"

"Goodbye, darling."

For a long time he stayed there in the big chair with his eyes closed. Then he thought, work to be done, and got up to pour part of a bottle of rye into a glass. Gulping some of it by the window, he saw that his Buick coupe was back in the parking lot, ten stories below.

Beck went into the bedroom, stripped himself naked and showered and shaved. There were blue bruises on his tan body that throbbed to the touch, pretty as they were. His lip had swelled a little from where he'd bitten it inside. He spread a thin unnoticeable film of unguent on the pink taut burn across his cheek and felt glad about his toughness. He dressed in a dark-blue double-breasted suit with sweater and bow tie to match, as if he were going to a wedding or a funeral.

Looking at himself in the mirror, he decided he looked pretty good considering. He locked his jaw shut and put on the enigma of half-smile he liked to see on himself. Steven Beck, the big operator. He said aloud, "All dressed up and only one place to go," and then snorted at people who talked to themselves.

On the bureau, by the binoculars, he saw Marcy's belt buckle looking sadly up at him. Beck touched it; it was cold and he warmed the little bronze mask in his fist. He dropped it in his coat pocket but he didn't like the clink it made against Zuaben's palmgun so he transferred it to his other pocket with the bus ticket and two baggage stubs. It merely whispered there.

In a sudden hurry he escaped from his empty suite and rode downstairs. The club bar looked cool and dim and lonely, fitting his mood. He wandered in. Nick the bartender was building a pyramid of highball glasses. Beck got onto a stool and stared at the bottle rows rather than in the mirror.

Nick pushed the cheese and crackers nearer. "What you got, Mr. Beck?"

"Nick, what is a gentleman?"

"The man who says thank you, dear, instead of how much, honey," the bartender answered promptly. "What's the good word?"

"Make it a Shady Lady." Beck had to explain about the lime juice, bourbon, benedictine, easy on the grenadine. Nick put one together and Beck tasted it. "Keep them coming." It tasted almost, not quite, the same.

Beck was the lone customer. He had another cocktail and smoked and drank and fiddled with the sweaty keys in his pocket, keys to various Garland enterprises. Leda is an animal, all right, he thought, nothing in her body but an appetite. It must run in the Garland family. Wild animals, Leda treeing him with her desire and Garland treeing him with the job he had to do. Except that Pat Garland had lapsed into compromise today because he didn't listen often enough to Steven Beck. But for that, the Garland pair rather refuted Everett's view of people being patched together with brute leftovers. No, the Garlands were completely animals, instinctive, unreasoning, and they had never had souls.

The liquor was making him warm and tired. "Oh, hell," Beck moaned. If he had a strain of the visionary in him, and Marcy had said so, long ago, then the name of Everett could certainly roil up the visions. J. John Everett with his barbed pessimism and his precise mocking face. He talked like a weakling misanthrope and yet he had come down from Sacramento to join the circle and risk death every day of the last year. He must be a pretty tough boy himself to choose a job like that.

And Marcy, in her mistaken way, was also choosing, using that free will she claimed she had. I choose Eddie, like a kid's game. Beck gritted his teeth. How could she get sucked in by that greasy pimp Cortes? No, he thought sardonically, Cortes the tender gentleman.

And just what was he: Steven Beck? Well, he was a fellow sitting here waiting for nightfall with a gun in his pocket and a job to do. He couldn't picture doing the job exactly but he could see Marcy's twisted crying face afterwards. He struggled to imagine her face some other way and couldn't. Of all the daughters in the world why did he have to love Everett's daughter? Why did the enemy have to be someone *she* loved? And Beck wondered painfully why *he* didn't have a choice in this matter.

Brooding, he had another. A trio of businessmen came in and had beers, being heavily jocular. Beck paid them no attention. They were people he'd seen around but didn't know their names. More of the same arrived. The afternoon was getting older. A trim young lady sat at Beck's elbow for a little while, humming to herself and eyeing him in the mirror. She went away finally.

Nick said softly, "Say, those cocktails are mighty sweet, Mr. Beck. I'd go easy on them."

"She said once I was too busy to get drunk." Beck laughed. "What you trying to do, Nick, spoil my day?" So Nick made up another and Beck asked, "And what are *you* going to do tonight, Nicholas?"

The bartender shrugged. "Get off in an hour, home for dinner, there's a double bill at the Fox my wife wants to see. That's about it."

"That sounds good."

Nick snorted. "Just between you and me, it doesn't. Some lousy love picture I don't want to see at all and, you know, it gets sort of monotonous. You know how a fellow is, likes to kick over the traces now and then. A shame that women can't understand that."

Beck said, "Don't be so damn silly."

"Maybe, maybe. Guys like you never know how lucky you are. No ties and all."

Beck had Nick make up a whole shakerful of Shady Ladies on the mixer. He carried them over to the darkest booth he could find. Then he bought a fresh pack of cigarettes from the machine and slid far back into the booth, looking out of the dark like a cat from a cave. He tried to think pleasant thoughts. He said Marcy's name to himself over and over.

Another drink and he went back to the bar and asked if Nick had a pin. Nick rounded up a corsage pin and Beck said, "Thank you, dear," and carried it back to his booth concealed in his hand. He fumbled Marcy's little bronze buckle out of his coat pocket and, smiling cleverly, pinned it on his lapel like a badge. He put a finger up to the mournful mask every once in a while and tried to feel good.

She didn't love him.

She didn't want *him*.

He tried to figure that one out. He wasn't an animal, yet Marcy had told him he was scarcely human, that he wasn't people, so he didn't know anything about her or people. He thought about her and Everett and maybe it was the liquor, but he began to get scared. Maybe it was the liquor but his brain seemed to stir. Like when he was a boy running a race he had to win and suddenly his lungs had opened up for him, a sweet biting expansion, and there was the adult breath he had needed. He had won, of course.

Along with the frightful expanding feeling came a sensation of falling, so sharp a daydream that Beck grabbed the edge of the table for a second. He giggled nervously. It was as if he had tumbled into black unknown depths within himself. Yet there was a sort of light down there, approaching.

Then just what was he: Steven Beck? The bursting light of answer he could believe burned around him and through him. He was clockwork. He was caught in the wheels so he was caught in himself.

No, he couldn't see any difference between himself and a machine. He had all the same virtues. He liked to be accurate. Why? He stuck the question into himself viciously. What was so wonderful about facts when they had gotten him into this position? After all, two plus two only equaled four because the whole world had agreed that they should. What was so wonderfully worshipful about that?

Oh, he had strength and power, too. No wonder tenderness hadn't been included in his blueprint; he was steel through and through, like a weapon, a dynamo, clockwork. He was always right and how could he help that since he was predestined. His dials were set to eliminate error so he couldn't gamble. He *had* to have Marcy, he *had* to win.

Beck laughed softly and unevenly. He even laughed at himself. Here your girl wanted a human being, no matter how crummy, and here you were clicking away with nothing more tender than electrical impulses where your emotions ought to be. Where your soul ought to be. Poor human Marcy wanted a being who didn't have brass guts, whose controls weren't set already and couldn't be changed. She had said he couldn't change. Why should he change when he could thrill to the marvelous vanity of predestining things, manufacturing his product time and again, whatever his product was.

He had such pride of accomplishment. Beck patted his own hand around the glass of red cocktail. You proficient grand machine, doing your job proudly and never asking what the job is. Never look at the product, that's not your responsibility, just keep at your work until you rust.

He giggled and said, "My God, but I'm drunk" then looked around suspiciously to see who had heard. Nobody had. Only the other machines noticed him and they were on his side, the cash register and the cigarette vendor and the electric mixer and the telephone. The juke-box didn't notice because it was busy singing a song it knew.

Beck shook his head at them consolingly because they were only *that* kind of machine, not as fine a device as he. For J. John Everett had been wrong with his cynic fantasies about mankind dying away and the machines inheriting the earth. What ridiculous kind of evolution was that?

In another flashing fright, he took his hand away from around the stem of the glass. His fingers felt stiff and he flexed them anxiously to prove they were still flesh. No they hadn't turned to metal. Of course not. It wasn't flesh or metal that meant the difference between man and machine; it was the controlling virtues. Everett had been wrong about the path of evolution. Evolution was not building machines to replace man. It was developing man into a machine.

For he, Steven Beck, was the world of tomorrow. He was the metropolitan who might be from anywhere, the city man living in mathematical squares. It all came true dialectically. There was a human thesis which manufactured a mechanistic antithesis. Thesis versus antithesis and what came out of it all but their synthesis: Steven Beck. The Beckian synthesis. Synthetic Steve Beck, the most dangerous unwanted man in town. He was all the best of man and machine: the brain and the power. He was the climax of a million years of mankind. Out of the Pleistocene into the here.

Boy, oh boy, am I going to be sick!

He squinted at whoever had slid into his booth and slapped him on the shoulder. It turned out to be Smith, the redhaired club member he had learned to beat at handball. Smith said jovially, "Just the speed merchant I've been looking for. How about a game of handball before dinner?"

Beck kicked back at him. "Shove off."

"Huh? What'd you say?"

"Shove off. Beat it. I'm thinking."

"Hey, what is this? Remember me, your old friend Smith—"

"No," said Beck coldly. "I don't have any friends. How could I?" He turned his head the other way and had another drink. When he peeped back, Smith was clear over by the bar describing something unbelievable to a couple other men.

Beck got up and stalked by them to the restroom. He locked himself in a booth and was hideously sick. Then he slumped into a sitting position on the cool tile floor and held his head in his hands. "Oh, Marcy..." he whimpered.

She didn't want him, didn't love him. She loved Eddie Cortes, the gentleman. Where, in God's name, had she ever gotten that idea? The first night she'd met him, the second night, the third night, last night?

The thought nagged at Beck until it began to clear his head. The first night.... He sat up straight and stared at the blank door.

Eddie Cortes couldn't be Eddie Cortes. Not if Marcy *knew* she could trust him.

And if Cortes weren't Cortes, why, there was another identity waiting to receive him. The blank faceless open identity of the AG man. The attorney general's plant.

Not Everett but Cortes.

Trembling with haste, Beck began to assemble facts. Marcy had been Cortes' alibi their first night, the night Beck had been tricked at the mortuary. Beck had seen her in her kitchen right after Cortes had brought her home. She had gulped down what she called *more* coffee. Her eyes itched, her hands and feet were cold, and her breath smelled sweet.

Because Cortes had doped her with chloral at The Natchez. Not an entire mickey, just the chloral part. Cortes had known Beck was up to something and wanted to get there first, but with an alibi.

So all the while Cortes searched the mortuary, Marcy had been his alibi, lying unconscious somewhere nearby in his car. Afterwards, he had brought her to with coffee and hurried her home. She wasn't likely to brag about how she had passed out on his hands, made a fool of herself. In fact, she had given up drinking entirely. And she knew that she could trust Eddie Cortes because she had been at his mercy.

Beck got to his feet and staggered out to douse cold water on his face. The rest of it was easy now, now that he was clicking away like his old self. He couldn't blame himself for falling for that faked prison record. But he could blame himself for baying after Everett so hard that he had overlooked the main whereabouts of that official state paper. Most of that paper was in state offices. Cortes visited a state office once a week, the parole bureau. And the intercepted report to the AG was numbered 45. One report a week for nearly a year.

And the stolen car, the trap for Everett? Now that Beck remembered, Cortes' parole documents had been suspiciously handy that afternoon, right out on the lawyer's desk. Eddie Cortes had been the client in Everett's inner office and he had listened to Beck's hints over the intercom. It was like Everett to maneuver it that way: let Cortes overhear Beck's agreement to keep away from Marcy.

Beck took his hands off the washbowl and nearly fell down. He was still drunk. But he suddenly scorned Marcy's father and his fine critical flights. What a piddling way to be clever, yapping from behind a desk about the curses of environment. Everett was actually degenerate, making a virtue of despair. With Marcy in danger, the brilliant coward had called for Steve Beck, he had presented him with Marcy as a tactical matter. Beck growled in disgust.

Rinsing his mouth once more, he left the restroom, walking carefully. He tried to open his mind to that free swooping knowledge it had had in the bar. He loved Marcy. Marcy loved Cortes who wasn't Cortes. Cortes, whatever his name was, had stolen Beck's beloved and was out to destroy Beck's life. The idea was a whirling nebula that never presented a surface long enough for him to take a swing at it. But this was a time for action. It must be nighttime by now.

It was nighttime. Beck could see it through the door of the Southwest Club. He made his way across the lobby to the registration desk and got his car keys back from the clerk. He also bought a stamped envelope and painstakingly addressed it to Patrick Garland. He put the bus ticket to Yuma and the two baggage claim checks in the envelope, sealed it and watched the clerk drop it in the outgoing mail slot.

A newspaper rack stood by the registration desk. The headlines of the orange-sheeted *Journal* blared at Beck. TWO BRUTALLY SLAIN IN CANYON MYSTERY. He looked down on them listlessly and didn't bother to pull a copy out. The clerk was gazing at the bronze buckle pinned to Beck's lapel. Beck scowled at him and turned away. He made his way across to the pay phones and closed himself in with one.

He could feel the palmgun jabbing into his hip through the lining of his coat pocket. His head swam and he had to wipe his eyes clear. Beck picked out the number to Cortes' court in Golden Hill. When that didn't answer, he used the same coin to dial the Everett house.

29

Tuesday, May 24, 9:00 p.m.

The Presque Isle of Coronado was ablaze with window lights but the strand which was the long road to the mainland stretched darkly into the night. Beck cruised his coupe down the highway slowly, searching. A few people swam at the main aggregation of floats and diving boards but he didn't stop. He drove on until he saw a familiar car parked alone by the road. He swung his Buick in front of it to block it and got out.

He put his hand in his pocket and clasped the palmgun so that its barrel protruded between his two middle fingers. Then he trudged across the sand to the bay.

From the lapping beach an old boat dock ran out into the water for twenty feet. At its far end was moored a swimming float lighted by one foodlamp high on a pole. Holding to the dock rail with his free hand, Beck made his way toward the light.

Marcy was splashing around out in the bay and laughing. She wore a white swimsuit. Eddie Cortes, in trunks, sat on the edge of the float. He sat there, his back to Beck, and dangled his feet in the water and shouted things at his girl.

He didn't hear Beck until Beck was standing behind him on the float. He twisted his head and his grin faded. He said, "Well, Steve."

"Don't get up." Beck crouched by his left side a little behind Cortes' dripping back. "How's the water?"

"On the cold side," Cortes said casually. "How'd you happen to find us?"

"A little bird." Beck chuckled. "A gabby little bird I bullied into telling where his daughter was, poor foolish little bird. I got tough. I get awfully tough, Eddie, when I'm at my best."

"Steve boy, you feeling all right tonight?"

"You know damn well I'm not. I'm drunk, I'm babbling drunk, and I haven't slept for a long time and I got the hell kicked out of me this morning. But I can still think. Oh, how I can think."

Marcy came up from a surface dive and swam toward them. Then she saw Beck and stopped paddling and floated, staring at him. His face was rigid as he looked back at her, trying to see into her eyes. Then Marcy turned silently in the water and stroked off in the opposite direction.

Cortes said, "Steve, why don't you get wise to the setup? You're not wanted. Leave us alone, won't you?"

"So sorry if I'm interrupting anything." Beck made his mouth grin broadly.

"But I didn't come after Marcy this time. Matter of fact, I came all the way to see you, Eddie. Eddie. What's your real name?"

Cortes stiffened. Beck's hand shoved into his back, holding the palmgun against his spine.

"You're drunk, Steve. Watch that stuff."

"Answer me. What was your name in Sacramento before the attorney general sent you down here?"

Cortes' olive body turned gray. He tried to laugh and make, "I don't know what you're talking about," sound as if he meant it.

Beck snorted.

They looked in each other's faces through a long silence. Then Cortes sighed and shivered with cold. "Yeah. I suppose you finally got me. But I came close to you and there's always somebody to pick up where I leave off."

"Sure, sure. I'm just curious about your name."

"William Joseph Allison. I guess there's a lot of details you'd like to know."

Beck turned on his half-smile. "If you're stalling for time, don't be silly enough to move around, Eddie. See? Eddie. I can't call you anything else since we've been friends so long now, Eddie. Whatever happened to the real one?"

"He died in the Sacramento drunk tank the night he was sprung from San Quentin. Couldn't take the celebration." Cortes talked impersonally, as if describing a good golf match. "We'd been looking around for a setup like that so we could get at you boys down here. I had a Mexican grandmother, I looked Latin enough, so I got the part."

"Why?" Beck demanded. "Why'd you make it your responsibility?"

"I was in legal research, AG office, but I thought I'd like undercover work." Cortes had missed the point. "Well, I thought we had every angle fixed. We went back and substituted my picture and prints in the San Quentin files in case you checked that far. We have a cover on every friend of the former Eddie Cortes in San Francisco so if one of them ever came down this way, I could leave town for a few days. The parole bureau here even thinks I'm the real thing. They think I'm a stoolie and that's all. That's where I make out my reports and mail them, I guess you know."

"That's right."

"And—well, we overlooked something. That's what bothers me. I don't think you could have worked it out from that report 45 you intercepted."

Beck looked wise. "Don't underestimate me, Eddie. And don't move. I guess you like nice things. You made your reports on the state's best paper."

"Oh, there must have been more than that."

Marcy was swimming back and forth fifty feet out in the bay, at the edge of the circle of floodlight. She waved at Cortes to come into the water.

Beck said, "Wave at her, shake your head no. Then put your hands back in your lap."

Cortes did. Then he asked, "Well, what was it? What got me?"

"Why are you so interested in details? Aren't you scared?"

Cortes shrugged. "Yes. Yes, if that makes you any happier. But on the other hand, I've been living with this act for almost a year now, expecting this every day. By now, I'm sort of numb. After the first month, the question got kind of academic, whether I'd catch you or you'd catch me. You can't be scared for a whole year consecutively. I was scared the other night in the mortuary, though, and when you fell into that organ I nearly passed out."

Beck squinted thoughtfully, as if that might be important. "Funny, the mortuary didn't bother me at all. Do you suppose it should have?"

Cortes stared around at him, not understanding what he meant. Then he asked again. "What was it got me, Steve?"

The metal of the palmgun was slick in Beck's fist but he kept it steady. He strained his eyes to see Marcy out there in the water. He said, "Marcy. When you doped her so you'd have an alibi while you checked the mortuary. If she'd only been genuinely passed out—well, what do you suppose the real Cortes would have done with her unconscious on her hands? That started me thinking, Eddie."

"Yeah, that's once I dropped out of character. At the time, I didn't think it would ever make any difference."

"Eddie, what would you have done if you'd thought it would."

Cortes clenched his hands on his bare thighs. He stared out at the girl's graceful body as she swam in circles. She was watching them constantly. At last Cortes admitted, "I don't know. You just don't know those things."

Beck swore at him softly. He said, "Comes a time when you've got to know those things, when you've got to face yourself. You've always got a choice, don't let anybody tell you different."

"Okay, skip it," Cortes said. His skin was its normal color now but he shivered more often with cold. He said wearily, "The idea's just beginning to sink in. How soon can we get this over, anyway? I'm not the bravest guy in the world, Steve, so don't kid around like I am."

"I'm not. Tell me, do you really love her?"

"Don't."

"Eddie, do you love her? Say yes or no, damn you, that's the only detail I'm interested in."

"And I say don't. Don't, Steve, because I don't want to do anything rash and have anything happen right here in front of her. You got me, isn't that enough? You don't have to drag out the best part of me and wallow in it."

"All right," Beck said, and added, "Thank you."

Cortes glared dully at him. "You might as well get a kick out of tonight while you can, though. You haven't won much, Steve. Your goddam circle is breaking up under your feet, can't you see that? You've gotten rid of me but your

Pat Garland is on his way down, too. Killing Hervey Isham, the members did-
n't like that. They've all got the jitters now. They figure if Big Pat can do
that to Isham then nobody's safe. The only reason for the circle is to make
business safer. When Kyle and Holsclaw and the Tarrants see that Garland
isn't doing that, why, it's all over."

Beck nodded gravely. "That's very true." It was terribly true. Only one person could keep the circle from rolling over the brink like a thrown wheel. The
one person was himself. The Holsclaw organization would be weakened
badly by Paul Moon's death. And there had been three others in the last
week: Felix and Isham and Zuaben. Gusta Norley had broken, had tried to
sell out, had run away. The Kyle and Tarrant organizations were already re-
bellious. And at this worst possible time, Pat Garland was compromising, skid-
ding out of control. He wouldn't even find any support in his own home, in
Leda. Funny how Garland could live this long without discovering there was
no solution in compromise. "I'll tell you an open secret, Eddie. What you said
has started. Pat has got the biggest jitters of all. There's a nasty war brew-
ing."

Cautiously, Cortes said, "Listen a second, Steve. You're the smartest one
of the whole bunch. Why not be just a little smarter and get out from under
the wreckage while you can? Tell me where the books are and I'll see how
easy I can get you off."

"No. Whatever I am, Eddie, I'm not that treacherous. I've done some pretty
bastardly things, but they mostly consisted of meeting people halfway. No,
the books will stay right where they are. Pat gave me two jobs. To save the
books and to kill you. I've gotten the books away from you."

Cortes' breath became audible over the murmur of water against the float.
"That kind of narrows it down, doesn't it? To me."

Beck said, "Listen to me, Eddie. I want you to understand something. I'm
not running away because of the pressure. I think I could save the circle any
time I wanted to. I put a lot of myself into the circle and I was proud of the
way I handled things. You get that, that I was proud *how* I was doing and not
what I was doing? That's a very important point."

He groped for expression, rejecting most of the ideas he had unearthed in
himself since last night. He could never make Cortes believe in the disgust he
suddenly felt for the circle and the lives within the circle including his own.
He could never make Cortes see Marcy as a catalyst. He could never tell anyone how he feared facing a future of last weekends. He said, "Now don't think
I'm drunk, just concentrate on these things. I don't want you to feel sorry
for me because I've got plenty of money put away and I'm going to be physically safe any place but California. I could be safe in California if I liked but
that would mean killing you. I hope you know how easy that would be. One
little squeeze...."

Beck sighed and stood up awkwardly. He kept the gun pointed down at

Cortes and kept his secretive half-smile in place. He said, "But I have a choice. That's important, too. Remember I had free will in this matter. I am not an animal and I am not a machine. I'm a human being." He looked down at Cortes plaintively. "Don't you understand? Marcy loves you, you're hers. I'm not going to hurt you. Marcy thinks I could never make a sacrifice for anyone. She's wrong and that's her prerogative. I can't blame her for thinking that. You'll never understand how I feel about her."

Cortes stared up at him, disbelieving. He said carefully, "You know what this means."

"Yes. Don't ask me what I'm going to do next because I don't know. First, I've got to finish thinking this out."

"I can't quit on my job. It's only fair to warn you."

Beck sighed. "Oh, hell, that's not what I'm talking about at all. Use your state's evidence offers on poor J. J. See what you can do for Marcy's father. That's a cruel little problem *you* have to face, isn't it? What I'm trying to prove is what I'm not."

He opened his hand and gazed at the flat disc of palmgun lying there. He teetered slightly on his feet. He said, "Damn mechanism," and let the gun fall into the water. It made a sucking gurgle as it hit and sank. He unpinned Marcy's belt buckle from his lapel and tossed it down next to Cortes. "You won't understand that, either. See, I'm being completely unselfish tonight. With all my worldly goods, I thee endow. I discovered responsibility today, Eddie, found it in a bar. But it was Marcy who pointed it out to me and I've got to prove to her I can see outside myself. I'm doing this for her and you reap the benefits.

"William Joseph Allison." Beck shook his head at Cortes and chuckled. "You can do me one favor, Eddie. Sometime—as soon as you're able—tell Marcy about this. I'd like her to know I did make a sacrifice, after all." His mouth quirked before he got it back in the shape he liked. "I guess I haven't given up vanity completely, at that. Oh, tell her lots of things for me. Tell her I gam-bled. Tell her I took a chance, that the coin landed on edge. I didn't steal her little mask to wear sometime. I only borrowed it for this once." He thought a moment. "I guess that's all."

Cortes said softly, "Steve—if you could kill me and still have Marcy, what would you choose?"

Beck allowed himself one swift glance out at Marcy. Then he said, "You're right, Eddie. You just can't know those things ahead of time."

He turned and walked away without looking back. He crossed the float, knowing that Cortes was gazing after him, and he made himself cross the boat dock without using the rail even if he did stagger a little. Behind him, he could hear Marcy calling to Cortes to join her in the water. Beck reached the dark sand. He could still hear her laughter tinkling through the night, chasing him. He stumbled once or twice in the sand because he couldn't see quite clearly but he kept his favorite smile fixed stiffly on his face. It seemed such a long way. But at last he could hear nothing except the march of his own feet across the ground as he walked away from her.

THE END

Made in the USA
Coppell, TX
05 December 2019